DEADLY REGRETS

Corran looked back toward his father and was set to whistle when he heard the scrape of metal on a rock. He glanced up and triggered one shot from the blaster carbine. The azure bolt streaked past Thyne as he leaped down from a large dolmen, then Thyne's right heel caught Corran in the shoulder and spun him to the ground. His blaster carbine bounced away, firing off two random shots. He felt Thyne's left arm tighten around his neck and then he was hauled to his feet as the alien straightened up, his body shielding Thyne from fire.

The muzzle of a blaster pistol ground in under the right corner of Corran's jaw. A glow rod lit up, bathing the right side of Corran's face with light. The muscles on the arm around his neck bulged, constricting his breathing and killing any thoughts of struggling.

Thyne growled loudly, sending angry echoes of his voice throughout the cavern. "Your partner is dead if you don't show yourself in five seconds."

Those five seconds took an eternity to pass for Corran, and he filled it with an unending series of *if-onlies*. *If only I had tucked the blaster pistol into my waistband when I took the carbine. If only I had the stiletto. If only I'd been more quiet in my advance.*

—From *Side Trip* by Timothy Zahn and
Michael A. Stackpole

The sensational *Star Wars* series published by
Bantam Books and available from all good bookshops

Children of the Jedi • Planet of Twilight
by Barbara Hambly

The *Empire* Trilogy by Timothy Zahn
Heir to the Empire • Dark Force Rising • The Last Command

The *Jedi Academy* Trilogy by Kevin J. Anderson
Jedi Search • Dark Apprentice • Champions of the Force

The Truce at Bakura
by Kathy Tyers

The Courtship of Princess Leia
by Dave Wolverton

The *Corellian* Trilogy by Roger MacBride Allen
Ambush at Corellia • Assault at Selonia • Showdown at Centerpoint

The *Cantina* Trilogy edited by Kevin J. Anderson
Tales from the Mos Eisley Cantina
Tales from Jabba's Palace • Tales of the Bounty Hunters

Tales from the Empire edited by Peter Schweighofer

The *Han Solo* Trilogy by A. C. Crispin
The Paradise Snare • The Hutt Gambit • Rebel Dawn

The Crystal Star
by Vonda McIntyre

X-Wing adventures by Michael A. Stackpole
Rogue Squadron • Wedge's Gamble
The Krytos Trap • The Bacta War • Isard's Revenge

More *X-Wing* adventures by Aaron Allston
Wraith Squadron • Iron Fist • Solo Command

The *Black Fleet Crisis* Trilogy by Michael P. Kube-McDowell
Before the Storm • Shield of Lies • Tyrant's Test

Specter of the Past
Timothy Zahn

The Magic of Myth
Mary Henderson

The *Bounty Hunter Wars* Trilogy by K. W. Jeter
The Mandalorian Armor • Slaveship • Hard Merchandise

Darksaber
by Kevin J. Anderson

Shadows of the Empire
by Steve Perry

The New Rebellion
by Kristine Kathryn Rusch

The Illustrated Star Wars Universe
by Kevin J. Anderson & Ralph McQuarrie

TALES FROM THE EMPIRE

Stories from STAR WARS®
Adventure Journal

edited by
Peter Schweighofer

BANTAM BOOKS
TORONTO · NEW YORK · LONDON · SYDNEY · AUCKLAND

This anthology contains stories previously published in
The Official Star Wars ® Adventure Journal from West End Games.

TALES FROM THE EMPIRE
A BANTAM BOOK : 0 553 50686 2

First publication in Great Britain

PRINTING HISTORY
Bantam edition published 1997
Bantam edition reprinted 1999

Bantam Books are published by Transworld Publishers Ltd,
61–63 Uxbridge Road, London W5 5SA,
in Australia by Transworld Publishers, c/o Random House Australia
(Pty) Ltd, 20 Alfred Street, Milsons Point, NSW 2061,
in New Zealand by Transworld Publishers, c/o Random House
New Zealand, 18 Poland Road, Glenfield, Auckland,
in South Africa by Transworld Publishers, c/o Random House (Pty) Ltd,
Endulini, 5a Jubilee Road, Parktown 2193.

Reproduced, printed and bound in Great Britain by
Cox & Wyman Ltd, Reading, Berkshire

For Mom, Dad, and David, who caught me when I stumbled, encouraged me when I struggled, and smiled when I succeeded.

Contents

Introduction: A Galaxy Filled with Stories ix
  Peter Schweighofer

First Contact 1
  Timothy Zahn

Tinian on Trial 26
  Kathy Tyers

The Final Exit 50
  Patricia A. Jackson

Missed Chance 83
  Michael A. Stackpole

Retreat from Coruscant 116
  Laurie Burns

A Certain Point of View 144
  Charlene Newcomb

Blaze of Glory 166
  Tony Russo

Slaying Dragons 198
  Angela Phillips

Do No Harm 214
  Erin Endom

Side Trip Part One 233
  Timothy Zahn

Side Trip Part Two 255
  Michael A. Stackpole

Side Trip Part Three 278
Michael A. Stackpole

Side Trip Part Four 299
Timothy Zahn

About the Authors 321

INTRODUCTION

A Galaxy Filled with Stories

by Peter Schweighofer

Behind every book there is a story—one contained not in the words on the pages but in the events that occurred as an imaginative spark grew to become a published work of fiction. The cast of characters includes writers, editors, original ideas, and a lot of work. This anthology is no exception, but the real story has much deeper origins.

Not so long ago, a blockbuster film brought a new generation back to the silver screen. George Lucas combined cutting-edge special effects with exciting characters and themes, capturing the collective mythic consciousness of moviegoers. Once again viewers were treated to the Saturday-matinee experience: swashbuckling characters, edge-of-your-seat cliffhangers, spaceship dogfights, the forces of good battling the minions of evil. The film was *Star Wars: A New Hope,* and nobody had seen anything quite like it before.

In homes across America, the *Star Wars* universe became real. Children of every age returned from movie theaters with dreams of becoming Han Solo, Luke Skywalker, or Princess Leia. They bought action figures that allowed them to invent their own stories, continuing the war against the evil Empire. Kids dreamed of what they would find in Mos Eisley and wondered what the spice mines of Kessel were like, or what creatures lurked in the Massassi temples on Yavin 4. They pretended to be brave Rebel pilots flying X-wing starfighters or dashing smugglers blasting through Imperial blockades in the *Millennium Falcon.*

The Empire Strikes Back and *Return of the Jedi* continued to fuel America's imagination. Novels and comic books explored events that occurred before and between the films. In their imaginations, kids turned their basements into the Death Star, where they battled with lightsabers like Ben Kenobi and Darth Vader. They built fortresses in the snow and refought the Battle of Hoth with snowballs. Children romped through the park with toy blasters, pretending they were fighting scout troopers on Endor.

Nobody was sure whether *Star Wars* was just another fad or something truly original. Despite their popularity, the films drifted off into the haze of American society's collective memory in the mid to late 1980s. The Kenner action figures of Luke Skywalker and Darth Vader were stored away in closets, basements, and attics. Sound tracks, scratched from numerous hours of play, were packed away with other old records. Novelizations were shelved with other science-fiction paperbacks and forgotten.

Other pursuits soon took the place of playing with action figures, reading comic books, and visiting the imaginary *Star Wars* galaxy. Fans grew up, went off to college, and entered the "real world" of career and family. The kids inside them were still there, but they were hidden in the deep closets, basements, and attics of the spirit. Sure, fans were glued to their television sets when the *Star Wars* films were broadcast on cable or the networks; for the most part, though, the wonder and excitement that had been *Star Wars* passed into little more than a fond recollection.

Then something amazing began.

New *Star Wars* stories appeared.

Timothy Zahn led the charge with *Heir to the Empire*. He enthralled fans in a tale packed with powerful villains, new worlds, mysterious aliens, massive starship battles, and, of course, everyone's favorite heroes from the movies. He brought back the magic that was *Star Wars*.

Timothy Zahn's popular books were followed by Dark Horse Comics series and more novels. Suddenly *Star Wars* was again on everyone's lips. Fans stormed book and comic stores looking for the latest releases.

There were rumors of new action figures. *Star Wars* trading cards returned with vivid original artwork. People realized there was even a role-playing game that would allow them to return to the days when they pretended to be Rebels battling stormtroopers and bounty hunters.

This new vision of *Star Wars* attracted new fans and reawakened that old *Star Wars* spirit—that kid who played with the action figures and wanted to become a Jedi Knight reemerged. Suddenly all the memorabilia was pulled out of storage, resurrecting the fond memories and dreams of a galaxy far, far away. Adults gazed longingly at the Magic Marker sketches of the Death Star battle they had drawn when they were children. They proudly displayed their collection of action figures. People reminisced about the first time they saw *Star Wars* and speculated about the fascinating territory a new trilogy would explore.

For twenty years, the fans kept the dream alive in their hearts—without a new trilogy or numerous reruns of television episodes. *Star Wars* is larger than the movies, greater than the fans. *Star Wars* is proof that spirited individuals can make a difference against seemingly insurmountable odds.

We are all part of this phenomenon.

The example of West End Games illustrates the nature of the *Star Wars* phenomenon. During the lull in *Star Wars* interest, this small game company decided that the ultimate space fantasy offered the perfect subject for a role-playing game. At the time West End Games—then based in New York City—had produced a fair share of war games and role-playing games. The company had only tested the waters of licensed properties with *Star Trek: The Adventure Game* and a *Ghostbusters* role-playing game. West End contacted Lucasfilm Ltd. and a licensing agreement was arranged.

Trying to create a successful game based on a ten-year-old film was a major risk. But the West End design team went to work, and soon produced a rule book and sourcebook packed with information on characters, starships, weapons, aliens, and droids. The *Star Wars Role-playing Game* was born.

At first, West End produced several game products, which the *Star Wars* role-playing market gobbled up. There were plenty of obstacles to overcome. Deadlines were missed and production schedules were lengthened by authors who delivered projects late and editors who were forced to rewrite manuscripts. Working with the Lucasfilm approvals staff, West End quickly learned what subjects were off-limits: for instance, the Old Republic, Clone Wars, and how the Emperor and Vader rose to power.

Since then, West End has helped expand the *Star Wars* galaxy and maintain continuity through the release of more than seventy-five sourcebooks, adventures, and supplements, including twelve Galaxy Guides, fourteen *Star Wars Adventure Journals,* and ten sourcebooks based on best-selling novels and comics.

The company's hard work and perseverance has paid off. Thanks to *Star Wars,* West End established itself as a leader in the role-playing-game industry, acquiring other popular media licenses; it has since produced role-playing games based on the *Indiana Jones* films, *Tank Girl, Tales from the Crypt,* and *Men in Black.* Today it continues to be the most successful licensing role-playing company in the world.

But West End's work with *Star Wars* hasn't been confined to the role-playing-game field. The company has coordinated its efforts with Lucasfilm and other *Star Wars* licensees to guarantee the continuity and retain the spirit of *Star Wars* in its products. West End editors have offered assistance to authors, answering questions, providing game books for reference, and even reading over rough drafts of novels. Game sourcebooks have provided technical data used in creating toys and other products based on starships and vehicles. West End staffers helped guide the creation of Decipher's Star Wars Customizi Card Game and Parker Brothers' *Star Wars* Monopoly. When the information contained in different products all fits together seamlessly, the *Star Wars* universe seems much more real.

Several West End designers have even moved into the greater *Star Wars* publishing universe. Bill Slavicsek updated Raymond Velasco's *Guide to the Star Wars Universe,* incorporating many new additions that maintain continuity with Timothy Zahn's novels, the new comic books, and West End Games sourcebooks. Bill Smith wrote the *Essential Guide to Vehicles and Vessels.* Other West End editors have contributed articles to Topps's *Star Wars Galaxy Magazine* and other periodicals. Like the movie heroes, these dedicated fans rose from humble beginnings to help shape the *Star Wars* galaxy.

Although the role-playing game might not be as popular or well-known as other *Star Wars* licensed products, a dedicated team of writers still works diligently to guide the role-playing adventures of fans as they explore the galaxy.

Some of you might be wondering exactly what a role-playing game is, and why *Star Wars* is so well suited to its purposes.

Simply, a role-playing game is just a more sophisticated version of the children's game "Let's Pretend." Most fans remember when they used to create their own *Star Wars* adventures, using action figures, a few vehicles, and the living-room furniture. Role-playing games are based on those same creative and imaginative processes.

Role-playing games involve interactive storytelling. A group of friends assumes the various roles of characters in the story, and their choices and actions affect the tale's outcome.

One of these players, the "gamemaster," tells the others what their characters see and hear, and portrays any "supporting cast members" the heroes encounter. Sometimes maps, game pieces, props, and miniature vehicles are used, but most of the action takes place in the participants' imaginations. The outcomes of blaster fights, speeder chases, and other conflicts are decided by simple rules involving the rolling of dice: the better the player rolls, the more successfully his character completes a particular task. Whether a character succeeds or fails at these challenges can dramatically change the story's outcome.

Since the participants are creating their own *Star Wars* stories, they don't play the actual characters from the films—instead, they create someone like them. Players might choose to be smugglers and Wookiees like Han Solo and Chewbacca. They can be starfighter pilots like Biggs or Dutch, or they can pretend to be aliens like Admiral Ackbar and Bib Fortuna. Since they're not using the movie characters, players may visit places and do things "offscreen." The *Star Wars Roleplaying Game* allows fans to explore fascinating areas only hinted at in the films: those other back alleys in Mos Eisley, the white corridors of Cloud City, the Forest Moon of Endor. It lets people create their own *Star Wars* adventures, complete with heroes and villains, planets, starships, and aliens.

The aim of the *Star Wars Adventure Journal* is the same: to explore the offscreen characters, planets, conflicts, and stories that fill the *Star Wars* universe.

When West End started publishing the *Journal* in 1994, the goal was to create a periodical to support the roleplaying game with exciting new stories, game adventures, and *Star Wars* source material. Under the careful supervision of Lucy Wilson, Sue Rostoni, and Allan Kausch in Lucasfilm's licensing department, the *Journal* quickly grew into a forum for both established and up-and-coming authors to continue visiting the fascinating *Star Wars* universe.

Before the *Journal*, *Star Wars* publishing was very exclusive. Only established authors were invited to contribute to a Bantam novel or anthology. Most had solid contacts in the publishing industry. Writers who had never published a science-fiction novel or two were not considered.

Novels focused on the major heroes, though the anthologies developed some of the background characters from the films more fully. Everyone wanted stories about Luke, Han, and Leia, but the concept of basing a novel on new characters without the main *Star Wars* heroes in the spotlight was risky. Would readers buy it?

Authors were permitted to introduce original characters to interact with the major heroes, but once their works were published, the events they narrated became a part of *Star Wars* continuity. Writers who created new characters had no other opportunities to develop them unless they were specifically assigned to write future novels. Some authors longed to return to play in the fascinating *Star Wars* universe.

The *Star Wars Adventure Journal* began to change all that.

Over time, the *Journal* became a place where qualified writers from all backgrounds could publish original *Star Wars* fiction. Every author's bibliography and fiction samples were scrutinized by West End and Lucasfilm—only those whose work was approved received invitations to contribute. Not every submission was accepted. Every article had to live up to West End's and Lucasfilm's high quality standards. The *Journal* was never a fanzine, although some of its authors had experience writing for such publications. It was a showcase for the best new *Star Wars* material available.

At first the *Journal* didn't emphasize short stories—they shared the 288 pages with game adventures and source material. Such regular features as "Galaxywide News-Nets," "Smuggler's Log," and "Wanted by Cracken" introduced new characters, starships, planets, aliens, and conflicts in the *Star Wars* universe, and offered ways to use them in the role-playing game. At the time of their publication in the *Journal,* all fiction pieces contained game information and sidebars offering tips for integrating elements from short stories into the game.

Subsequent issues unveiled the works of more polished authors and a rising level of excellence. At Lucasfilm's encouragement—and due to the increase in the quality of short-story submissions—the number of fiction articles grew.

The *Journal* became a source for *Star Wars* short stories inhabited by characters other than those familiar to fans of the movies. It was one of the few places where authors without a novel under their belt could officially write new *Star Wars* fiction. A generation of new writers created their own heroes: CorSec agents, cynical smugglers, rogue Dark Jedi, Rebel commando teams. Established authors returned to their favorite characters and created new ones. Everyone had a chance to roam around the universe they knew and loved.

The *Journal* created a whole series of *Star Wars* stories that set off into unexplored territory. It gave authors a special opportunity to write for their favorite film setting and expand the scope of the *Star Wars* galaxy.

I spent my childhood playing with *Star Wars* action figures, listening to the sound tracks, collecting trading cards, and reading novels and comic books. These kept the characters and myths of the movie alive in my imagination at a time when household VCRs were still rare. The *Star Wars* records—which appealed to my love for music—sparked images of the film in my mind. The trading cards brought movie scenes and characters back to life. Comic books developed plots and characters beyond the end of the film. The action figures helped me tell my own stories. My interest in *Star Wars* survived through the long years of waiting for *The Empire Strikes Back* and *Return of the Jedi*.

As I grew older, though, I soon found other pursuits to occupy my time. One of those was a strange new hobby called "role-playing games." Several kids in my neighborhood started playing something called Dungeons and Dragons. I watched them play once and it didn't seem too hard. Instead of wondering where I could buy a copy, I created my own fantasy role-playing game for my friends. It wasn't particularly ingenious, nor did it capture the complexities that were to appear in current role-playing games—but it was fun. Eventually I bought Dungeons and Dragons, the first of many role-playing games in practically every genre: fantasy, science fiction, historical. These provided an outlet for my creativity. I enjoyed running games for friends and creating my own adventures.

The *Star Wars* films fostered an interest in science fiction and fantasy literature that followed me into high school. All my spare money was used to purchase science-fiction novels in the local bookstore. I read Moorcock's *Elric* series, Tolkien's *Lord of the Rings,* and anything by Larry Niven. All this reading inspired me to dream up my own characters, worlds, and technologies, which eventually appeared in my own (admittedly mediocre) sci-fi stories.

I combined my role-playing-game and science-fiction hobbies by creating my own simple science-fiction board games, complete with intricate maps, counters, and cards. My friends and I played them often, though we didn't think they'd amount to much in the long term. How often does having fun develop into a lucrative career?

When I reached college age, I was determined to hone my writing skills and put them to use penning science-fiction epics of my own. Throughout my years at Hamilton College, I dabbled in science fiction—reading a lot of it and writing some of my own (better by now). I broadened my writing and publishing experience by reporting and typesetting for the college newspaper. My creative-writing professors encouraged me to explore other areas, such as poetry and historical fiction (which eventually became another hobby of mine). I even tested my organizational skills by coordinating the Hamilton College Writers Society.

During one summer vacation, I discovered treasure buried in the science-fiction shelves of the local bookstore: the *Star Wars Role-playing Game.* Two of my favorite hobbies—*Star Wars* and role-playing—had been merged. I bought the book on the spot.

Over the next few years, my friends and I occasionally explored the *Star Wars* role-playing universe during game sessions. We created our own legendary characters—heroes like the outlaw Dirk Harkness, and villains like the mysterious bounty hunter Beylyssa. Through our imaginations, we explored strange planets, escaped carefully laid Imperial traps, and blasted stormtroopers at every turn. For a few nights between semesters, *Star Wars* lived again in the minds of our gaming crew.

The *Star Wars Role-playing Game* was just that: a game, a pleasant pastime to fill college breaks, a hobby left over from childhood. Most childhood diversions, however, eventually crumble under the intimidating weight of the "real world," and with graduation from college, I was prepared to succumb to the inevitable nine-to-five drudgery of the workplace. No matter how much I loved *Star Wars* and role-playing, they could never provide me with a viable career. Not that I didn't try, mind you. I sent a few résumés out to game companies, including West End, but, as is often the case, most companies required a few years' experience in the industry. I had to start at one of the lower rungs on the publishing ladder.

As a recently graduated creative-writing major, I was well suited for a job in journalism: reporting for my hometown weekly newspaper was the only publishing job I could find. I spent two years reporting on town meetings, school events, and interesting people in the community. While this doesn't sound glamorous, I absorbed things every writer and editor should know. I learned how to meet deadlines, how to revise my writing to make it clear and exciting, and how to choose words and organize paragraphs to express my ideas clearly.

After two years, I was promoted to editor in chief when the previous editor stepped down. This new job quickly taught me how to be a team leader. Now I was critiquing reporters' stories, working with them to produce great articles. I got a crash course in public relations as I was forced to deal with the innumerable publicity seekers who plague small newspapers with their personal agendas, political crusades, and town-government conspiracy theories.

Although I was living at home, I was close to my *Star Wars* gaming friends. We continued our fantastic adventures through the Outer Rim Territories, freeing aliens from despotic slavers, infiltrating secret Imperial research bases, and escorting undercover Rebel agents on luxurious starliners.

We soon discovered we were not alone in our passion for *Star Wars*. A new novel called *Heir to the Empire* seemed to herald the dawn of a new *Star Wars* age. New comic books also began to appear. As soon as we heard that another Timothy Zahn *Star Wars* novel had been published, we ran to the bookstore. Our gaming crew scanned the new comic-book releases for *Star Wars* material. We were not alone in the universe—*Star Wars* fans everywhere were emerging from their slumber.

Change was in the air, and I began to think that if I could find the right job in the gaming industry, I'd be able to realize my dream of combining *Star Wars,* writing, and role-playing games.

With a year's worth of editing experience under my belt, I decided to try breaking into the gaming industry again. My first choice was West End for two reasons: the company was only three hours from my home in Connecticut, and it possessed the license for my favorite film-related role-playing game.

After I mailed my résumé and made a few phone calls, I was invited to meet West End's senior staffers and managers in their nondescript brown warehouse/office in rural northeastern Pennsylvania. I walked into the interview carrying a folder with my résumé and a few samples of my newspaper work. I also brought along a positive attitude and my love for *Star Wars* . . . and when I left the office, I was editor of the *Star Wars Adventure Journal*.

Since that day four years ago, I've worked with many authors. Some proved to be up-and-coming writers, others were *New York Times* best-selling *Star Wars* authors. Most suffered through my long, meticulous critique letters and rambling phone conversations. I hope some have learned to become better writers through our work.

Many of the new authors could have been viewed as risks. A beginning writer's work often needs more polishing than a story by an experienced author, but the end result is often well worth the effort. The *Journal* is proof that these risks have paid off. Those who made it through the months of writing, waiting, and revision have added their names to the growing list of published *Star Wars* authors.

In this anthology, you'll meet some of them.

My first mission in establishing the *Journal* was to find a *New York Times* best-selling author to create a story for the premiere issue. West End had developed a good rapport with Timothy Zahn, whose novels were already the inspiration for two game sourcebooks. I contacted Tim, who turned out to be extremely friendly and willing to help. At the time, he was not scheduled to write any more *Star Wars* novels—this story assignment would be a chance for him to return to some of his favorite characters.

Though he wanted to develop his archvillain, Grand Admiral Thrawn, Tim decided to write a background story for Talon Karrde. (Tim would investigate bits of Thrawn's past in subsequent *Journal* stories—"Mist Encounter" in *Journal* 7 and "Command Decision" in *Journal* 11.) "First Contact" revealed some of Talon Karrde's activities before the time covered by *Heir to the Empire,* confirming the smuggler's penchant for cleverly naming his starships along the way. The story is a brilliant display of Tim's ability to lead readers through a complex and devious tale packed with surprises.

After "First Contact," Tim contributed to other West End Games *Star Wars* products, including the *DarkStryder* campaign. Although he'd never worked on role-playing games before, Tim participated in several charity games where he has portrayed Talon Karrde and Grand Admiral Thrawn. He proved to be just as devious and scheming in role-playing games as he is in his fiction.

Convincing Timothy Zahn to write for the *Journal* was the first challenge. The next was to encourage other mainstream authors to contribute. Kathy Tyers was an obvious choice. After *The Truce at Bakura,* she had stayed active in *Star Wars* publishing through the various anthologies, just finishing a short story for the then-unpublished *Star Wars: Tales of the Bounty Hunters* anthology. She wanted to do more with a character she created for that story: Tinian I'att.

While "Tinian on Trial" was characteristic *Star Wars* fare, with its aliens and stormtroopers, Kathy's fiction treated many deeper emotional themes involving sacrifice, love, and freedom. Readers were also treated to a sneak peek at the story to come in *Tales of the Bounty Hunters,* which wasn't published until all three Tinian stories appeared in the *Journal.*

Michael A. Stackpole also offered the *Journal* a preview of his upcoming *Star Wars* fiction—"Missed Chance" appeared six months before *Rogue Squadron* went on sale. Mike's *X-Wing* books showed that characters other than the main heroes could support an entire novel. Mike has been combining game worlds and fiction for many years working in the role-playing-game industry since it began in the 1970s. Besides writing numerous game adventures, he's authored several novels based in role-playing settings for the Dark Conspiracy and BattleTech games. He's a good example of an author with promise making it in the major leagues of publishing.

While working with mainstream science-fiction writers was exciting, discovering talented new authors was truly rewarding. They were struggling to balance career and writing, hammering out short stories in their spare time. These people were the *Star Wars* fans who could be the notable science-fiction writers of the future.

I first met one of these, Patricia A. Jackson, at Sci-Con, a science-fiction convention in Virginia Beach, where she was rather outspoken during a panel discussion on freelance writing, and she later turned up when I ran a *Star Wars* role-playing-game adventure. Two weeks later, a manuscript turned up on my desk: a *Star Wars* story patched together from the characters and events of our game. I quickly learned that role-playing-game adventures—though they're fun while you're playing them—do not automatically make good short stories.

But Patty would not be discouraged. Her next story had a solid first draft, and was revised until it was fit for publication. It was the first of many fiction submissions. She was particularly proud of "The Final Exit," a story whose foreboding atmosphere closely matches the personality of Dark Jedi Adalric Brandl. Patty has become one of the *Journal*'s regular contributors. We still see each other at gaming and science-fiction conventions, and the two of us run a small writers workshop every year at Sci-Con.

Charlene Newcomb had contributed to every *Journal* when "A Certain Point of View" appeared. Up to then, all her stories had focused on a character she created called Alex Winger, the daughter of an Imperial Governor who was secretly working to free her planet from the Empire. Before "Point of View," Charlene finished the latest Alex Winger story and was wondering where to go from there. To help inspire her, I sent her a copy of a painting that had once adorned an old *Star Wars* game adventure. It showed a ship's officer and several aliens playing a hologame.

I told Charlene to write a story involving this scene so I could feature the color artwork in the *Journal*. She went to work and submitted "A Certain Point of View," in the plot of which she managed to highlight several elements of the painting. Framed by a large viewport, the picture reveals a greenish nebula swirling in the distance: a hazardous section of space called the Maelstrom. One of the aliens represented in it holds a large goblet—the helmet of an approaching stormtrooper is reflected in its glassy surface. In her story, Charlene even integrated source material about the Maelstrom and the starliner that originally appeared in the game adventure. The story provides a nice bridge between short fiction and previously published game material.

Most *Journal* authors concentrate on one area: source material, game adventures, or short stories. Tony Russo covered all the bases. His source articles have taken readers to Sevarcos, a world of Imperial prisons and swashbuckling spice lords, introduced them to an elite mercenary commando team, and explored the tyrannical holdings of the Pentastar Alignment. In his adventure, players had to try to free a frontier colony from the iron grasp of a crime lord. His story "Blaze of Glory" successfully combined the excitement and character interaction of a game adventure with source material about a commando team, all in the form of a short story.

Erin Endom, who practices and teaches pediatric emergency medicine, merged her medical knowledge and the drama of her job in a *Journal* story. "Do No Harm" is a good example of how new fiction can focus on and explore facets of the *Star Wars* universe otherwise glimpsed just offscreen. While many stories focus on Rebel commandos making desperate raids against Imperial forces, few contemplate the emotions of normally peaceful people who injure and kill others in battle. By demonstrating the conflict within a combat medic charged with saving lives, Erin brought a different perspective to the war between the Empire and the Rebel Alliance.

Angela Phillips also provided a new perspective on the *Star Wars* universe with her story "Slaying Dragons." Her young heroine, Shannon, has ambitions similar to characters in the *Star Wars* films—to rise from humble beginnings and make a difference in the galaxy. Her story is notable for its merging of the medieval theme of dragon slaying and the movie mystique of the noble Jedi Knights.

Laurie Burns started by using her experience as a newspaper reporter in her *Journal* story "Kella Rand Reporting." By the time she submitted "Retreat from Coruscant," she had moved on to integrating her characters into the more significant events in the *Star Wars* chronology. She chose to involve her independent courier in the New Republic's flight from Coruscant that occurred just before events in Dark Horse Comics' *Dark Empire* series. In writing, Laurie did her homework—while fitting her fiction into existing continuity, she included appearances by Garm Bel Iblis, Mara Jade, and Colonel Jak Bremen, characters Timothy Zahn created in his *Star Wars* trilogy.

That is perhaps one of the most exciting parts of working on the *Journal:* expanding the breadth of the *Star Wars* universe. Since it's a licensed publication, all the material becomes an official part of the continuity. Where else could a kid with a wild imagination and dreams of writing science fiction create stories based on the most popular films of all time? Stories that unfold in a galaxy where two bantering droids deliver plans for an Imperial superweapon, where a scoundrel smuggler becomes a selfless hero, and where a simple moisture farmer is transformed into the last Jedi Knight.

This anthology is the culmination of four years of adventure. Like the throne-room scene at the end of *Star Wars,* it is certainly not the end of the saga, only a momentary triumph before we return to work. As *Journal* editor, I do not stand alone; I've been blessed to work with some very talented individuals from across the *Star Wars* licensing universe. Like any epic adventure, we meet important people along the way who help us achieve our goals. The *Journal* owes a lot to those heroes working behind the scenes. West End's Richard Hawran, Jeff Kent, and Daniel Scott Palter have provided support and much-needed encouragement as the *Journal* grew from an idea to an illustrated, 288-page quarterly magazine. None of this would have been possible without the imaginative vision and perseverance of George Lucas. Lucasfilm's Sue Rostoni helped guide the *Journal*'s initial format and content, while Allan Kausch continued his meticulous patrol over continuity and quality. Timothy Zahn, Kathy Tyers, and Michael A. Stackpole have delighted readers (and editors) with stories in which they return to the characters and galaxy they love. Up-and-coming authors have contributed stories that expand the *Star Wars* galaxy's scope and still live up to Lucasfilm's standards of excellence.

The *Journal* has been a place where writers can realize their *Star Wars* dreams. These authors have risen from their humble beginnings to make a difference—however small in the grand scope of the *Star Wars* universe—in the galaxy far, far away they love so much. They all have stories to tell, tales that began as playful musings and imaginative romps through George Lucas's *Star Wars* playground.

You're about to read some.

First Contact
by Timothy Zahn

With a last sizzle of jittering repulsorlifts, the space yacht *Uwana Buyer* settled down into the landing field that had been hacked out of the Varonat jungle. "What a fine, civilized-looking place this is," Quelev Tapper commented, peering out the cockpit canopy. "You sure we didn't overshoot and land in someone's weed dump?"

Talon Karrde looked out at the pale yellow trees encircling the field and the thirty or so dilapidated buildings nestled in beneath them. "No, this is it," he assured his lieutenant. "The Great Jungle of Varonat. Home of a handful of third-rate trading depots and a few thousand colonists who haven't the brains to pick up and go elsewhere."

"And an ugly Krish named Gamgalon," Tapper said. "I don't know, Karrde. I still think we should have brought in the *Wild Karrde* and *Starry Ice* and had some decent firepower behind us. We're kind of like sitting mynocks here."

"We're here to observe, not make trouble," Karrde reminded him, popping his restraints and standing up. "Gamgalon wouldn't be bothering with these private Morodin-hunting safaris if there wasn't some big profit involved. I just want to know what he's up to, and whether we can carve a piece of it off for ourselves."

"All the more reason to have backup along," Tapper grumbled, checking the draw of his blaster as he followed Karrde to the hatchway aft. "But you're the boss."

"How very true. You ready?"

Tapper took a deep breath, exhaled it noisily. "Let's do it."

Karrde punched the control and the hatchway slid up into the hull. Sniffing at the exotic aromas, he and Tapper walked down the ramp and headed across the field toward a building with a faded *Port Facilities* sign hanging on it.

They were no more than halfway there when two men lounging beside another of the buildings peeled themselves away from their wall and moved casually to intercept the newcomers. "Howdy," one of them said as they got within earshot. "Welcome to Tropis-on-Varonat. Here for the sights?"

"That's very amusing," Karrde complimented him. "No, we're here for the hyperdrive mechanic we very much hope you have."

"Ah," the other said, glancing back at the *Uwana Buyer*.

"Yeah, I'm not surprised. The flashier the hull, the more crumbish the innards."

"Save the colorful language for the tourists," Tapper growled. "You have a hyperdrive mechanic here or don't you?"

The other eyed him a moment, then turned back to Karrde. "Your friend's a little short on manners," he said.

"He makes up for it in ability," Karrde said, pulling a handful of high-denomination coins from his pocket and sorting ostentatiously through them. "And in the understanding of schedules. We have some highly important business waiting for us on Svivren."

"Sure, I understand," the other said. "No offense, ah—?"

"Syndic Pandis Hart of the Sif-Uwana Council," Karrde identified himself. "This is my pilot, Captain Seoul." He chose one of the coins, held it up. "And we're rather in a hurry."

"Hey, no problem," the man grinned, jerking a thumb toward the port facilities building as he deftly took the coin from Karrde's hand. "Buzzy, go tell 'em they've got a customer. Rush job."

His companion nodded silently and loped off toward the building. "Name's Fleck, Syndic," the man continued. "Offhand, I'd say you're going to be stuck here for a few days. Got any plans?"

Karrde glanced pointedly around. "Would there be any plans worth having?"

"Matter of fact, there would," Fleck said. "Fellow here runs a pretty neat safari out into the jungle—got a trip heading out first thing tomorrow morning, in fact. Ever hear of Morodins?"

"I don't think so," Karrde said. "Big game?"

"The biggest," Fleck assured him. "Giant lizard-slug things, ten to twenty meters long. Make great wall or hallway trophies." His lip twitched sardonically. "They're not too fast or mean, either. Good way for a beginner to start."

"That's comforting to hear." Karrde looked at Tapper. "What do you think, Seoul?"

"Doesn't sound too dangerous, sir," Tapper said with just the right note of concern. "I trust you wouldn't be going alone?"

"Naw, there's four other hunters signed up," Fleck said. "And the boss always takes a couple of escorts along as guards. Safe as in a snuggy."

"I'd still recommend I accompany you, sir," Tapper persisted. "I used to be pretty good with a BlasTech A280."

"Let's find out first how much it costs to be as safe as in a snuggy," Karrde said dryly.

"Hardly anything," Fleck sniffed. "Not to a gentleman of your means. Only twelve thousand each."

Karrde smiled. "A man of means doesn't stay there by throwing money away. Fifteen thousand for the both of us."

Fleck grinned. "Hard bargainer, huh? Make it twenty."

"Experienced businessman," Karrde corrected. "Make it seventeen."

The other's forehead wrinkled, then cleared. "All right. Seventeen it is."

"Very good," Karrde said. "When do we leave?"

"Five-half tomorrow morning," Fleck said. "Just be here—I'll tell the boss you're coming. Don't forget to bring the seventeen." He pointed across the field. "You can get outfitted over at that building over there, and get a room for the night in the hotel next door. It's, uh, nicer inside than it looks."

"One would hope so," Karrde agreed. "I trust no one will be offended if we pass on the accommodations. The outfitters will know what equipment we'll need?"

"Sure," Fleck nodded. "Like I said, the boss runs these safaris all the time."

"Very good," Karrde said. "Come, Seoul, let's go see what they have to offer."

• • •

Varonat's sun was beginning to settle down behind the jungle by the time Karrde and Tapper finally made it back to the *Uwana Buyer* with their purchases. "I hope we gave them enough time," Tapper commented as they climbed up the ramp.

"I'm sure we did," Karrde said. "It doesn't take long for a professional to search a ship this size. And I'm not expecting Gamgalon to be employing amateurs."

Abruptly, Tapper touched Karrde's arm. "Maybe he is," he said, dropping his voice.

Karrde frowned. Then he heard it: a muffled clank from the aft section of the ship. "Should we take a look?" Tapper murmured.

"It would look suspicious if we didn't," Karrde said, grimacing. If this whole thing fell apart through the incompetence of Gamgalon's own people . . . "Nice and easy."

Moving quietly, they headed down the central corridor to the engine room, hearing another clank as they reached the door. Karrde caught Tapper's eye, nodded. The other nodded back, lowering his bundles to the deck and getting a grip on his blaster. Karrde touched the release, and the door slid open—

The woman sitting on the floor beside the open access panel was young and attractive, with a cascade of red-gold hair tied back out of the way behind her head. Her face was calm and controlled as she looked up at their abrupt entrance; beneath her jumpsuit, her figure was slim and athletic and nicely formed.

And in her hands were a hydrospanner and one of the power flux connectors from the *Uwana Buyer*'s hyperdrive. "Can I help you?" she asked coolly.

"I think you already are," Karrde said, the brief moment of surprise passing into relief. Gamgalon's searchers had not, in fact, fouled up. "I take it you're the hyperdrive mechanic."

"Cleverly deduced," she said. "Celina Marniss. You have any problems?"

"Only with the hyperdrive," Karrde said. "Why, were you expecting me to?"

Celina shrugged, returning her attention to the power flux connector. "I've known some men in my day who didn't think a woman could be decorative and competent at the same time."

"Personally, that's my favorite combination," Karrde told her.

She favored him with a look that was slightly amused, slightly strained-patient. "So you're Syndic Hart. Buzzy was most impressed with you."

"I'm ever so pleased," Karrde said. "I won't ask which way he was impressed." He nodded at the access opening. "Any idea yet what's wrong?"

"Well, for starters, your flux connectors are all about four degrees out of sync," Celina said, hefting the one in her hand. "They have to have been ignored for a long time to drift that far off."

"I see," Karrde said, his favorable first impression of this woman moving up another notch. Chin had assured him that the flux connector gimmicking would take an average hyperdrive mechanic at least a day to find. "I'll have to speak to my maintenance man."

"Personally, I'd fire him," Celina said. "I'll get these readjusted, then we can see what else is wrong."

"Good," Karrde said. "As Buzzy may have mentioned, we're in something of a hurry."

"Funny way to go about it," she said, nodding toward the packages in the corridor behind them. "Gamgalon's safaris usually take upwards of four days."

"It's been my experience that a failed hyperdrive normally takes at least six to ten days to fix," Karrde said.

"Possibly another reason to fire your mechanic," Celina grunted. "I'm guessing I can do it in two or three."

"What makes you think we're going on a safari?" Tapper asked suspiciously.

"The packages, for a start," Celina told him. "Besides, you're obviously well-off, and you talked to Fleck. He's Gamgalon's chief come-up flector—does his job pretty well." She shrugged, turning her attention back to the flux connector. "Besides, what else is there to do around here?"

"Cleverly deduced," Karrde said. "You're wrong about my personal wealth, though. I'm merely chief purchasing agent for the Sif-Uwana Council."

"I'd call that a marginal distinction," Celina commented. "Certainly given the casual way Sif-Uwanis approach management and money."

"Really," Karrde said, his estimation moving up yet another notch. He would have bet heavily that there wouldn't be a single person on Varonat who'd ever even heard of Sif-Uwana, let alone know anything about it. "Have you ever been there?"

"Once," Celina said. "It was a few years ago."

"Business or pleasure?"

"Business."

"What sort?"

She lifted an eyebrow at him. "I don't recall an invitation to play Questions Three with you, Syndic."

"No offense intended," Karrde said. "I merely find your presence here intriguing. You seem too skilled and well-traveled to be stuck out here in the backwater of the Ison Corridor. Not to mention your other obvious attributes."

He'd hoped to spark some reaction, to shake up that calm facade of hers a bit. But she refused to turn to the lure. "Maybe I just like the peace and quiet," she countered. "Maybe I'm trying to raise a stake to get out." She locked eyes with him. Green eyes, Karrde noted distantly. A very striking green, at that. "Or maybe I'm hiding from something."

Karrde forced himself to meet that gaze. There was a smoldering, almost bitter fire behind those eyes, driven by a turbulent swirl of emotion. He'd been right: she was no simple backwater hyperdrive mechanic. "You certainly instill me with confidence," he managed.

The corner of her lip twitched upward in a sardonic smile; and abruptly the fire vanished as if it had never been there. Or had been nothing but an act. "Good," she said briskly. "Maybe next time you'll stay out of your hyperdrive mechanic's way and leave well enough alone."

"I take your point," Karrde said, bowing slightly. "We'll be in the forward living areas if you need to know where anything is. Good evening."

He gestured to Tapper, and together they backed out of the engine room, gathering up their packages again as the door slid closed. "What do you think?" Karrde asked as they headed forward.

"You're right, she doesn't fit here," the other agreed. "One of Gamgalon's people?"

"Probably," Karrde said. "Backup for Fleck, perhaps, or else just a general snoop. Mechanics and other servicepeople tend to be invisible."

"Maybe." Tapper glanced down the corridor behind them. "If you ask me, though, someone of her talents would be wasted in straight surveillance."

"Agreed," Karrde said, pursing his lips. "Could be she doubles as saboteur."

"Or as ship thief," Tapper said grimly. "Gamgalon's covering up *something* with these safaris."

They'd reached the yacht's lounge now. "Well, he can't steal this one without considerable effort," Karrde reminded him as he dumped his packages on the lounge couch. "As to sabotage; well, we should be able to ungimmick the hyperdrive in twenty minutes if we have to. And the *Wild Karrde* can be here in four hours if we need it."

"I take it that means you're still planning to bring a comm-relay along?"

"Very definitely," Karrde assured him. "But I'm not expecting we'll have to use it. My guess is that we're going to find the safaris are just Gamgalon's way of setting up clandestine smuggler meetings, and that Fleck and company are here to screen out any Imperial officials who might object to the proceedings. Come on, let's get this gear organized. Five-half is going to come early enough as it is.''

The rest of the safari was already assembled by the time Karrde and Tapper emerged from the *Uwana Buyer* just before five-half the next morning. "Eclectic bunch," Tapper commented as they walked toward the group and the three Aratech Arrow-17 airspeeders waiting on the field beside them.

"Agreed," Karrde said, looking them over. A Thennqora, a Saffa, and two Duros, all resplendent in outfits and equipment as obviously fresh out of the box as the gear he and Tapper were wearing. Slightly off to one side, dressed in outfits that had just as obviously seen considerably more use, were a Krish, a Rodian, and Buzzy the laconic Human. "The group matches the escort," he added.

Tapper nodded toward the Krish. "That's not Gamgalon, is it?"

Karrde shook his head. "One of his lieutenants, I think. I doubt Gamgalon himself will be coming along."

"Ah," the Krish called, beaming about as cheerfully as it was physically possible for a Krish to manage as he beckoned toward Karrde and Tapper. "Welcome. You must be Syndic Hart. I am Falmal; I will lead your expedition."

"Pleased to meet you," Karrde nodded. "I trust we're not late?"

"Not at all," Falmal said. "The rest were merely early. May I present your fellow hunters: Tamish—" he gestured to the Thennqora "—Hav and Jivis—" the Duros "—and Cob-caree—" the Saffa. "Gentlebeings: Syndic Hart and Captain Seoul of Sif-Uwana."

"Pleased to meet you," Karrde said, eyeing each of the others. None of the names were familiar, but of course that didn't mean anything. He and Tapper weren't using their correct names, either.

"We waste time," Tamish growled. "Get on with the hunt, Falmal."

"Certainly," Falmal said. "If you will all find seats aboard?"

Karrde and Tapper chose one of the airspeeders and strapped in. A few minutes later Falmal climbed in beside their Krish pilot, and they were off.

"You run these safaris often?" Karrde asked as they flew low above the rippling yellow jungle.

"Only a few times per season." Falmal threw him a speculative look. "You were fortunate indeed to have arrived when you did."

Karrde gestured toward the rack of BlasTech rifles in the back of the airspeeder. "I'll consider it fortunate only if we catch something," he said. "I'm spending far too much money here for just a round-trip tour through a jungle."

"You will be successful," Falmal promised. "All are. Rest assured of that."

They flew for an hour before putting down in a hilltop clearing. A small, semi-permanent looking camp had been built there, four buildings grouped around a burned-off landing area. "You must use this place a lot," Karrde commented as they settled to the ground.

"It is the base camp for all safaris," Falmal said. "Here the pilots and airspeeders will wait while we continue on foot. Take your packs and weapons, please. We will move out immediately."

Ten minutes later they were all tromping along a barely discernible path through yellow trees, yellow-green bushes, and a pale violet ground cover that looked disturbingly like masses of fat worms. Falmal was in the lead, with Tamish, Karrde, and Tapper behind him. Buzzy was next, followed by Hav and Jivis and Cob-caree, with the Rodian bringing up the rear.

They traveled for nearly an hour before Falmal called a

break in a small clearing that opened off beside the path. "Bit out of shape for this kind of exercise," Karrde puffed as he got out of his pack and dropped it to the ground. "How far are we going today, Falmal?"

"Wearied so soon?" Falmal asked, throwing a sharp-toothed smile at him. "Not to worry, Syndic Hart. Three hours more, perhaps four, and we will be at the main hunting area."

"Morodins have been here," Tamish grunted from behind him.

Karrde turned to look. The Thennqora was crouched down at the edge of the clearing, prodding with a knife at a patch of dark discoloration cutting across the ground cover. "Morodin slime was here," he said. "Several weeks old."

"Well observed," Falmal said approvingly. "It was two months ago that one of our safaris hunted Morodins through this region. Unfortunately, their migration pattern has since taken them further away."

"Wonder why we didn't land closer to begin with, then," Tapper muttered.

"Perhaps airspeeders spook our intended prey," Karrde suggested, frowning. A meter behind Tamish, along one edge of the slime mark, a neat row of short pinkish shoots was coming up from beneath a group of yellow-green bushes.

And in the shadows behind them was a glint of metal. Stepping around behind Tapper, he started over for a closer look—

"Time to go," Falmal called, slapping his hands briskly. "Packs on, all. We must continue if we are to reach our destination with enough time to begin a hunt."

Karrde considered checking out the metal thing anyway, decided against it, and returned to where he'd left his pack. "You are a botanist, Syndic Hart?" Falmal asked.

"No," Karrde said as Tapper helped him into his pack. "Why?"

"I saw you looking at the Yagaran aleudrupe plants

there," he said, pointing a long finger at the pink shoots.
"You will see many such non-native plants in the jungle,
I'm afraid—leavings of previous visitors to the Varonat
jungle who were less than careful with their provisions."

"Provisions?" Tapper asked as he got his own pack on.

"Aleudrupe berries are considered a delicacy on many
worlds," Falmal said. "Some of those who join our safaris
insist on bringing their own provisions. A few carelessly
dropped seeds—" He gestured elaborately. "We can only
trust that the jungle itself will deal with such intrusions.
Come, we must depart."

They didn't spot any more slime remnants before they
reached Falmal's chosen camping spot, at least none that
Karrde could identify as such. There were no more
aleudrupe plants, either. Perhaps after that first time the
careless visitors had been warned.

"So," Tapper said, bringing two cups of steaming liq-
uid over to where Karrde had propped himself tiredly
against a tree beside their tents. "What do you think of
our fellow travelers?"

Karrde looked over at the others, still struggling with
the escorts' help to pitch their own shelters. "From the
level of complaining during this last hour, I'd say they're
exactly what they seem: bored, wealthy beings looking for
excitement and somewhat annoyed they're having to
work for it."

"Hardly your typical smuggler, in other words."

Karrde shrugged. "Maybe these are semi-legit businessmen Gamgalon wants to make deals with."

"There are a million places in the galaxy he could set
up private meetings without this much trouble," Tapper
pointed out, sipping at his cup.

"True. Incidentally, did you notice that piece of metal
stuck in the ground behind those aleudrupe plants at our
first rest stop?"

"Yes," Tapper nodded. "Looked to me like a transpond marker. Probably there either to mark the path or else to keep track of the Morodin migrations."

"Perhaps," Karrde said. "I can't help thinking, though, that Falmal reacted rather strongly when I started toward it."

"You think it's something less innocuous?"

"Could be," Karrde said. "Possibly part of a sensor array to—"

He broke off. Through the trees, from somewhere nearby, came a deep, rumbling growl. Across the encampment, Falmal straightened up as Buzzy and the Rodian unslung their blaster rifles. "This could be it," Karrde murmured, snagging his own weapon and levering himself to his feet. "Falmal?"

"Shh!" the Krish hissed. "You will frighten it. We will break into the same groups of three as in the airspeeders."

He hurried over to Karrde and Tapper as the others collected into their own groups and headed into the jungle. "Come. Quickly and quietly."

They headed out, blaster rifles at the ready. "How can the Morodins get through these trees?" Tapper asked. "I thought they were big."

"Morodins are long but slender," Falmal said, peering carefully through the trees. "They can move easily about the jungle. Ah—look!"

Karrde swung his blaster rifle around; but Falmal was only pointing at the ground. "Fresh slime trail," the Krish said. "You see?"

"Yes," Karrde said, eyeing the wide silvery line cutting across the ground cover and disappearing off into the trees. A remarkably straight line, too, veering only to get around an occasional tree.

"A large one, too," Falmal said. "Come. We will follow it."

"Doesn't seem very sporting," Tapper grunted as Falmal led the way through the trees.

"The trail will not last long," Falmal said over his shoulder. "It appears and disappears."

Karrde frowned off to his right. It was hard to tell through all the bushes, but—"Is that another slime trail over there?" he asked Falmal. "Paralleling ours about three meters away?"

"Yes, they usually move in pairs," the Krish said. "Quiet now. See, the trail is turning."

Ahead, the slime trail had turned sharply to the left. Karrde craned his neck; sure enough, the other trail was turning to remain parallel. "That's a pretty sharp angle," Tapper muttered. "You suppose something scared them?"

"Quiet," Falmal said again.

In silence they continued on along the trail. It changed direction twice more in the next few minutes, turns as sharp and precise as the first had been. And then, to Karrde's surprise, it split into two different directions. "How did it do that?" he asked.

"A third Morodin has joined," Falmal said. "Quiet. It could be just ahead."

"Maybe a third, fourth, and fifth," Tapper said, nodding to the right. The paralleling slime trail there had split into three lines, two of them angling off three meters farther along the ground ahead of it. Swallowing, Karrde lifted his blaster rifle and took another step—

And suddenly, there it was: fifteen meters long, rearing the front of its rounded body three meters up off the ground, a mottled yellow creature with spoonbill snout, stubby legs, and wide teeth.

A Morodin.

"Shoot it!" Falmal yelped. "Quickly!"

Karrde's rifle was already against his shoulder, the barrel tracking the huge creature in front of them. The Morodin reared another meter off the ground, giving out the same deep growl they'd heard back at the camp. Karrde squinted down the barrel . . . "Wait a minute," he told Tapper. "Hold your fire. It's just standing there."

"It is Morodin," Falmal snarled. "Shoot before it's too late."

But it was already too late. From their right came a sudden sputtering volley of blaster fire, catching the Morodin solidly across its flank. Tamish and Cob-caree, with the Rodian behind them, had arrived along one of the lines of the other slime trail. The Morodin growled once more, then toppled to the ground with a thunderous crash.

"Well shot," Falmal all but crowed. "We will summon the airspeeders, and the pilots will prepare your trophy. Let us return to camp now; the noise will have driven off the others." He looked speculatively at Karrde. "Perhaps tomorrow, Syndic Hart, will be your day for a kill."

"Perhaps," Karrde said, looking at the downed Morodin. So that was that. The big, dangerous Morodin safari . . . and it had turned out to be no more challenging than shooting a bruallki in a net. "I can hardly wait."

The pilots arrived within an hour, and for nearly two hours afterward the encampment was busy as they shuttled slabs of Morodin meat in from the kill and held interminable conversations with Tamish and Cob-caree as to which would get which part of the head and their preferences in trophy mount and framing. Karrde stayed out of the activity, retreating back to his seat by the tree with a portable melodium and leaving Tapper to handle their share of the work. He overheard one or two rather finely honed comments about poor sportsmanship directed his way, but he ignored them. Leaning back against the tree, eyes half shut, he let the music from the melodium envelop him.

And, surreptitiously, fiddled with the settings of the comm-relay concealed inside the device.

The sun was dipping low over the forest by the time the pilots finished their work and the airspeeders took off back toward base camp. "I trust you've been enjoying yourself," Tapper commented, sitting down beside Karrde and wiping his face with the sleeve of his no longer sleek hunter's outfit. "Some of the others think you've been sulking."

"I can't help what they think," Karrde said. "Don't get comfortable; we're going for a walk."

"Wonderful," Tapper groaned, hauling himself back to his feet. "What's the drill?"

"I've been playing a little with the comm-relay," Karrde said, standing up and slinging the melodium's strap over his shoulder. "If Falmal and company have been planting transpond markers in the vicinity, we should be able to pick them up with it. Nice and easy; let's not attract any attention."

They slipped out of camp and headed into the jungle. Karrde's hunch was right: almost immediately the rigged comm-relay found a signal, coming from the direction of the Morodin kill. Following the slime trail again, they soon reached what was left of the carcass, already busy with scavengers.

"There it is," Tapper said, pointing to a group of bushes a few meters away. "It's a transpond marker, all right. And right by one of the slime trails again."

"Yes," Karrde said, kneeling down for a closer look. The ground at the edge of the slime had been freshly turned, he saw. Almost as if something had been planted there . . .

He looked up sharply, catching Tapper's eye. The other nodded: he'd heard the faint crunching noise, too. "Coming from the camp," he murmured.

The sound came again. "Let's take the long way," Karrde murmured back, pointing to the section of slime trail Tamish and Cob-caree had arrived along earlier. Explaining to Falmal or his cohorts why he was carrying a melodium on a walk through the jungle could get awkward. Especially if they found the gimmicked comm-relay inside it.

They heard the crunching sound once more as they left

the site, but after that it seemed to fade behind them. Which was just as well. No more than fifteen meters into the jungle, the slime trail broke off; and when it reappeared three meters farther away, it had suddenly sprouted three more branches. "Uh-oh," Tapper muttered. "Which way?"

"I'm not sure," Karrde said, glancing behind them. The thought of a whole herd of Morodins prowling around was not an especially pleasant one. "Let's try this one," he said, pointing to the rightmost of the two trails. "We'll mark one of these trees first so we can backtrack if we have to."

Tapper was staring off into the jungle. "Let's try going a little farther in first," he suggested slowly. "We can always come back."

Karrde frowned at him. "Something?"

"A hunch," Tapper said. "Just a hunch."

Karrde pursed his lips. "How far in do you want to go?"

"About three hundred meters," Tapper said. "I remember a ridge in that direction on the map that overlooks a sort of wide depression in the ground."

Karrde grimaced. Three hundred meters in an unfamiliar jungle was nothing to be taken lightly. But on the other hand, Tapper's infrequent hunches were nearly always worth following up. "All right," he said. "But no farther than the ridge. And we head back sooner if our trail ends."

"Agreed. Let's go."

The slime trail split again a few meters along, and twice more made one of those short, three-meter breaks with new branches going off in different directions when it resumed. For a while Karrde tried to keep track of the number of lines, hoping to figure out how many animals they were dealing with here. But he soon gave up the effort. If the Morodins decided to get nasty, the difference between six and sixty of them would be largely academic.

"There's the ridge," Tapper said, pointing ahead at a

last line of trees that seemed to open onto blue sky. "Let's take a look."

They stepped forward and between the trees. There, stretched out perhaps 100 meters below them, was the wide valley-like depression Tapper had described.

And gathered together at one side of it were upwards of fifty Morodins.

"We've found the crowd, all right," Karrde muttered uneasily. The slope down from their ridge into the valley was mildly steep, but he doubted it would bother something with the size and musculature of a Morodin. In fact he knew it wouldn't; the slime trail they were following rounded the ridge and continued down without a break.

"Don't look at the Morodins," Tapper said. "Look at the slime trails."

"What about them?"

"Look at them," Tapper urged. "Tell me you see it, too."

Karrde frowned, wondering what he was getting at. The whole depression was full of the lines, that was for sure, clearly visible between the trees and over the trampled bushes. Lots of lines, showing the same bends and branches as the ones they'd encountered up here . . .

And then, abruptly, he got it. "I don't believe it," he breathed.

"I didn't either," Tapper said. "Look—one of them's trying it."

One of the Morodins had detached himself from the group and into the three-meter channel between two of the trails. Waddling quickly on those short legs, it moved to the first bend and turned to the left.

Into the first section of the elaborately constructed maze.

"Let's get back," Karrde said, shaking his head in disbelief. "I have a feeling we don't want Gamgalon's people finding us here."

"Too late," a soft voice said.

Carefully, Karrde looked over his shoulder. Two meters

behind him stood Falmal and two of the Krish pilots, all three with blaster rifles at the ready. Behind them stood a fourth Krish, gazing thoughtfully at him. "Indeed," Karrde said, lowering the muzzle of his own rifle and turning around to face them. "Well. At least we shouldn't have any trouble finding the way back to camp."

"Whether we return to camp directly has yet to be decided," the fourth Krish said in that same soft voice. "Put your weapons down, please. And tell me what you are doing here."

"We were looking for Morodins," Karrde said as he and Tapper lowered their blaster rifles to the ground. "In the process we stumbled on the fact that they're more than just simple animals." He cocked an eyebrow. "They're fully sentient beings, aren't they, Gamgalon?"

The Krish smiled. "Very good," he said. "On both counts. You know my name; what is yours?"

Under the circumstances, there didn't seem to be much point in continuing the masquerade. "Talon Karrde," Karrde identified himself. "This is my associate, Quelev Tapper."

Falmal hissed. "Was it not as I said, my liege?" he snarled. "Smugglers. And spies."

"So it would appear," Gamgalon said. "Why are you here, Talon Karrde?"

"Curiosity," Karrde said. "I've heard stories about these safaris of yours. I wanted to find out what was going on."

"And have you?"

"You're hunting sentient beings," Karrde said. "In violation of Imperial law. Even in these days, I imagine what's left of the Empire would deal rather harshly with you if they knew that."

Gamgalon smiled again. "You imagine wrongly. As it happens, the Imperial governor in charge of Varonat is fully aware of what is happening here. His portion of the earnings are quite adequate to insure that there are no such questions about the hunts."

Karrde frowned. "Surely you're not bribing an Imperial governor with scraps from safari tickets."

"Indeed not," Gamgalon said. "But as the safaris provide ideal cover for our planting and harvesting operations, it is in his best interests to allow them to continue."

"You're not bribing him with aleudrupe berries, either," Tapper put in. "You can buy those things on the open market for thirty or forty a packload."

"Ah—but not *these* aleudrupe berries," Gamgalon said smugly. "This particular crop is grown in soil saturated with Morodin slime . . . and during their growth, these berries undergo an extremely interesting chemical change."

"Such as?"

Falmal hissed again. "My liege—?"

"Do not worry," Gamgalon soothed him. "Consider, Talon Karrde, a merchant ship carrying three cargoes to a politically tense world: rethan-K, promhassic triaxli, and aleudrupe berries. All harmless, all legal, none worth so much as a raised voice from either Imperial customs or officials of the New Republic. The ship is sent on its way to the surface, where it is greeted enthusiastically by its customers.

"Who, a scant hour later, will be launching an attack on their political or military enemies. With weapons utilizing a blaster formulation fully as powerful as spinsealed Tibanna gas."

Karrde stared at him, a hard lump forming in his stomach. "The berries are a catalyst?"

"Excellent," Gamgalon said approvingly. "Falmal was right—you are indeed clever enough to be dangerous. To be precise, it is the pits of the berries that create this new gas from the rethan and promhassic. The fruit itself is perfectly normal, and can stand up to any chemical test."

"And the safaris mask both the planting and the harvesting," Karrde nodded. "With the transpond markers there to help you find the crops again after you've planted them. All the profits of weapons smuggling, with none of the risks."

"You understand," Gamgalon beamed. "And thus you must also understand why we can't allow any hint of this to leak out."

He gestured, and one of the Krish pilots stepped forward, bending awkwardly down to pick up the blaster rifles Karrde and Tapper had dropped. "Certainly I understand," Karrde said. "Perhaps we could discuss an arrangement? My organization—"

"There will be no discussion," Gamgalon said. "And my arrangements are my own. This way, please." The pilot straightened up, gestured to the side with Karrde's rifle—

And suddenly Tapper's hands snapped out, plucking the rifle from the pilot's hands and jabbing the muzzle hard into the Krish's torso. Diving into the cover of the nearest tree, he swung the rifle back toward Falmal and Gamgalon—

And dropped spinning to the ground as a pair of blaster bolts slashed through him from down the ridge to his right. A single shuddering gasp, and he lay still.

"I trust, Talon Karrde," Gamgalon said into the brittle silence, "that you will not be so foolish as to similarly resist."

Karrde lifted his eyes from Tapper's crumpled figure, to see the third Krish pilot step out of concealment along the ridge, his rifle steady on Karrde's chest. "Why shouldn't I?" he demanded, his voice sounding ugly in his ears. "You're going to kill me anyway, aren't you?"

"Do you choose to die here?" Gamgalon countered. "This way, please."

Karrde took a deep breath. Tapper dead; Karrde himself unarmed and alone. Completely alone—even the Morodins down below had vanished, apparently scattering at the sound of the blaster fire.

But, no, he didn't wish to die here. Not when there was any chance at all that he could live long enough to avenge

Tapper's death. "All right," he sighed. Two of the pilots stepped forward and took his arms, and together they all set off.

Karrde hadn't expected them to take him back to the encampment, and they didn't. From the direction Falmal was leading them, it looked like they were heading toward one of the other clearings they'd passed just before setting up camp. Undoubtedly where Gamgalon's airspeeder was waiting. "What sort of distribution setup do you have?" he asked.

"I have no need of assistance," Gamgalon said, looking back over his shoulder. "As I have said already."

"My organization could still be useful to you," Karrde pointed out. "We have contact people all over the—"

"You will be silent," Gamgalon cut him off.

"Gamgalon, listen—"

And from behind him came a deep, rumbling growl. A growl that was echoed an instant later from both sides.

The group came to a sudden halt. "Falmal?" Gamgalon snapped. "What is this? Why are there Morodins here?"

"I do not know," Falmal said, an uneasiness in his voice. "This is not at all like them."

The growls came again, from what seemed to be the same positions. "Maybe they've finally gotten tired of being the prey," Karrde said, looking around. "Maybe they've decided to hold a safari of their own."

"Nonsense," Falmal bit out. But he was looking around, too. And he was starting to tremble. "My liege, I suggest we move on. Quickly."

The roars came again. "Falmal, take the prisoner," Gamgalon ordered, his voice suddenly grim as he pulled a blaster from beneath his tunic. "You others: to the sides and rear. Shoot anything you see."

Warily, the three pilots spread out into the jungle, blaster rifles held high. Falmal stepped to Karrde's side, closed a tense hand around his arm. "Quickly," he hissed.

Gamgalon stepped to Karrde's other side, and together the three of them hurried forward. Ahead, through the trees, Karrde could see the glinting of sunlight from an airspeeder. Another chorus of Morodin roars came, all from behind them this time. They reached the last line of trees, stepping into the clearing—

And with a gasping sigh Falmal suddenly released Karrde's arm and stumbled to sprawl on the ground, a knife hilt protruding from his side. Gamgalon snarled and spun around, his blaster searching for a target.

He never made it. Even as Karrde reflexively ducked to the side, the Krish's tunic erupted in a brief burst of flame as a quiet blaster shot caught him neatly in the center of his torso. He fell backward to the ground and lay still.

Karrde turned; but it was not one of his fellow hunters whom he saw emerging from the cover of the tree they'd just passed. "Don't just stand there," Celina Marniss growled, lowering the tiny blaster in her hand as she passed him and headed toward the airspeeder. "My airspeeder's too far away—we'll take theirs. Unless you want to be here when those other Krish catch up."

"Nicely done," Karrde commented as the *Uwana Buyer* cut through Varonat's upper atmosphere toward deep space. "Nicely done indeed. Though I must confess a certain disappointment that it wasn't actually the Morodins finally taking their vengeance."

Beside him, Celina snorted under her breath. "Considering that they probably can't tell a Human from a Krish, let alone one Human from another, you should count yourself lucky it wasn't them. They'd have ground you into the dirt along with Gamgalon and his crew."

"Most likely," Karrde conceded. "Where did you get the recordings of Morodin growls?"

"Gamgalon took me along on one of his safaris once,"

Celina said. "Back when he still thought he might have a chance of recruiting me into his organization."

"So you weren't working for him. We'd wondered about that."

"I don't like Krish," she said flatly. "Even honest ones can't be trusted very far, and Gamgalon hardly qualifies as honest. Besides, all he wanted me to do was play spaceport spy for him. Not much future in that."

"Not anymore," Karrde agreed. "So as long as you were out in the jungle anyway, you went ahead and recorded some Morodin growls?"

She shrugged. "I thought it might be handy to have something like that on file. Turns out I was right." She threw him a look. "You owe me for those three recorders, by the way. Those things don't come cheap."

"I owe you for considerably more than that," Karrde reminded her soberly. "Why did you follow us out there, anyway?"

"Oh, come now," she scoffed. "Hart and Seoul? Not to mention a ship called the *Uwana Buyer*? It was all just a little too cute; and I remembered hearing about a smuggler chief who had a fondness for cute wordplay. So I took a chance."

"And it paid off," Karrde said. "You've earned a considerable reward. Just name it."

She turned to look at him with those green eyes of hers. "I want a job," she said.

Karrde frowned. It hadn't been the response he'd expected. "What kind of job?"

"Any kind," she said. "I can pilot, fight, play come-up flector—"

"Hyperdrive mechanic?"

"That, too," Celina said. "Anything you've got, I can learn it." She took a deep breath, let it out. "I just want to get back into mainstream society again."

Karrde cocked an eyebrow. "You have a strange view of smuggling if you consider it mainstream society."

"Trust me," she said grimly. "Compared with some of what I've done, it is."

"I don't doubt it," Karrde said, studying her face. A very striking face, with a striking body to go with it. Decorative and competent both; his favorite combination. "All right," he said. "You've got yourself a deal. Welcome aboard."

"Thank you," she said. "You won't regret hiring me."

"I'm sure I won't." He smiled slightly. "And since we're now officially working together—" he held out his hand. "You can call me Talon Karrde."

She smiled tightly as she took his hand. "Pleased to meet you, Talon Karrde," she said. "You can call me Mara Jade."

Tinian on Trial
by Kathy Tyers

Tinian I'att, the granddaughter and heiress of I'att Armament's founders, wrinkled her nose and tried not to breathe too deeply. The factory complex's demonstration room smelled like scorched meat and chemicals. She could identify five . . . no, seven formulas by their odors, a potentially catastrophic witch's brew. Occasionally, the demonstration explosives detonated harder, faster, or earlier than anyone anticipated, and even quadruple transparisteel didn't provide full protection.

Standing beside Grandfather Strephan, Daye Azur-Jamin rested his hand on a waist-high blast barricade. Daye's I'att Armament gray tunic accentuated his air of authority. So did the management comlink he wore on his belt. A prematurely gray streak marked the center of Daye's left eyebrow. "There's nothing patently wrong with stormtrooper armor, your excellency," he said, and Tinian admired his self-control. She knew how Daye felt about Grandfather's Imperial connections. "But a good marksman—or an idiot with a high-powered blaster—can pick out weak spots. Our field makes it invulnerable."

Imperial Moff Eisen Kerioth slapped a polished ebony swagger stick into one palm. Tall and lean, Moff Kerioth held his head thrust forward over an astonishing array of red and blue rank squares. Tinian, Daye, and her grandparents had expected tech advisors for this demonstration, and maybe a few army troopers, but never a Sector Moff with stormtrooper escort. Kerioth limped, favoring a stiff left leg and occasionally leaning on the swagger stick. "Sounds wonderful, boy. So why did your demonstration employee turn coward?"

Grandfather Strephan's old black Imperial service uniform set off his thick white hair. Grandmother Augusta fiddled with a side hem of her long green robe. She'd recently developed a rare degenerative syndrome, and Druckenwell's top bioimmunal specialist gave her only months to live unless she sought treatment. It wasn't available here in Il Avali, or at any other city on Druckenwell . . . and it was expensive. Behind Grandmother Augusta, the I'att family's Wookiee bodyguard Wrrlevgebev lounged against a pebbly gray duracrete wall. Wrrl rumbled a quick comment under his breath that only Tinian—who'd studied his language—could translate.

She didn't, but she shared Wrrl's disdain for cowardly employees. She fiddled with a collection of paraphernalia in her jumpsuit pocket: neka nut shells, droid adjustment tools, and her secret good-luck piece.

She would need all her good luck today. If I'att Armament sold its new armor-protective field, then her grand-parents could retire, and she and Daye would take over the factory.

Kerioth straightened his shoulders and neck, then poked Grandfather with his swagger stick. "Well, I'att? Who's going to get into that armor? We came a long way to see this." Evidently Grandfather had known the Moff years ago. Each man had chosen his own way to serve the New Order: Grandfather by protecting Imperial might, Kerioth by wielding it. Kerioth crooked a finger at Wrrl. "You. Wookiee. Come down here."

Wrrl curled back his lips from huge teeth and let out a punctuated howl. Kerioth had demanded that the I'atts disarm their Wookiee during his visitation, and Wrrl was already irritated. A red-blond stripe crossed Wrrl's face, fur almost the same shade as Tinian's shoulder-length hair. It was odd coloration for a Wookiee.

"What did he say, Tinian?" Grandfather's business acumen showed in the way he measured and accommodated the Moff. By comparison, Kerioth seemed . . .

Tinian tried to emulate her observant grandfather. Kerioth seemed blunt. And condescending.

She glanced at the shell pieces on the arming table. Eighteen white units lay beside the limp halves of a two-piece black body glove. Wrrl wouldn't fit inside the body glove, let alone the field. "Your excellency, he's too big," she translated. "The field nodes maximize at one point eight six meters of height and one meter of width."

Moff Kerioth lifted a narrow black eyebrow. "I'att, tell me again why your grandchild attends classified demonstrations."

Tinian bristled. She might be small and thin, but she was no child. Hadn't Kerioth noticed her company jump-suit?

Grandfather laid a warm hand on her arm. "Your excellency, Tinian is an invaluable team member. She has amazing instincts for explosives."

One stormtrooper stood at the center of the second

seating row up. "Sir," he said through his helmet filter, "if the Wookiee's too tall, what about her?"

Tinian blanched. Her . . . demonstrate? Stand in the wave trap and get shot at?

"From one extreme to the other," quipped Kerioth. "Invaluable team member, is she?"

Grandfather backed toward a code panel. From this wall, he could lower two quadruple-transparisteel blast walls between the wave trap and the four broad rows of retractable shielded seating. "Ah . . . yes, but Tinian is not our demonstration volunteer."

Kerioth shifted his weight. "She would fit. Are you totally confident that your armor is impervious to blaster fire?"

"Totally," murmured Grandfather.

"Then prove it."

"But . . . no. I shall call for a line droid."

"I perceive a certain lack of confidence." Moff Kerioth directed the taunt at his stormtroopers, but Tinian took it in the gut. Grandfather and Grandmother must reach that offworld health care facility. Love focused Tinian's courage, and so did her hopes. The field worked. She'd seen it tested.

"Grandfather?" She raised a hand. "I'll volunteer."

Grandfather, Grandmother, and Daye stepped forward, speaking simultaneously: "Wait—" "Tinian—" "No—"

Wrrl blinked huge blue eyes and suggested under his breath that Daye was built more like a stormtrooper than she was.

Tinian fixed Moff Kerioth with her stare. She was betting he'd act like a BlasTech Company bureaucrat she'd once met at a party—once he'd suggested something, no other idea would suit him.

Kerioth's smile spread slowly from his thin lips to cold, dark eyes. "Very good, ah, Tinian. A true trial of I'att Armament's excellence."

Before Tinian could change her mind, she dragged Wrrl to the arming table. "Help me," she ordered him.

Her jumpsuit would easily fit inside the black body glove. She also selected the upper-body corselet, the carapace and the breastplate, which armorers dubbed the Body Bucket when worn together. She shoved them at Wrrl. Rear-mounted on the carapace, in place of the usual instrument pack, I'att Armament droids had installed a heat dissipator and the field transmitter. A single new control stood out on the breastplate.

She slipped off her shoes and slid one leg into the body glove. She'd never heard so much silence. "Grandfather," she suggested, "explain how the body glove enhances the field."

"Tinian," Grandfather pleaded.

The glove's leggings sagged on her with wrinkles all down their length. She yanked her narrow jumpsuit belt out of its loops and secured the heavy black fabric. "I've memorized the speech," she insisted. "Should I deliver it?"

Moff Kerioth rested his swagger stick on one shoulder. "Please do," he purred.

Suddenly she disliked him. Daye had always insisted that he'd rather die in a noble cause than earn his living from an ignoble one, and she hoped this was only her nerves, whining out from the spot where she was stuffing them (to keep Daye from trying to stop her), that made Kerioth look suddenly sinister.

Daye was sensitive to an energy field he called the Force. He claimed that Force-sensitive was not a healthy way to be in Emperor Palpatine's New Order, and he'd cautioned Tinian and her grandparents that the Empire had stooped to violent repression in other parts of the galaxy . . . but Tinian didn't believe it. I'att Armament had supplied the New Order for years, profiting handsomely.

She shrugged into the body glove's top. As she smoothed loose black fabric over the floppy mess at her waist, she drew a deep breath. "The protective field produces anti-energy bursts just out of phase with blaster fire," she began. "Zersium flecks that we've bonded into the advanced body glove—" Tinian pushed up one slack sleeve and ran the back of her hand over the other forearm "—amplify the field. We see that as a key element of this new system—"

"The entire system has too often proved vulnerable." Kerioth's voice rose. "Eight years ago, I had a stormtrooper escort shot to pieces around me. I've dragged this ever since." He whacked his left leg with the swagger stick. "Are you comfortable in there, child?"

I'm not a child. "I'm fine." She squared her shoulders. "I'm sorry about your leg. May I finish?"

He swung the swagger stick. "By all means."

"We have thus eliminated weak spots," she said, "long known to insurrectionist elements. I'm ready, Wrrl."

Her Wookiee lifted the breastplate and carapace. Grandmother Augusta folded trembling hands in front of her long green robe. Daye took up a position behind Tinian. If she hesitated or even flinched, she guessed he'd demand to wear the armor.

She hefted the carapace. "There is insulation and a heat dissipator built into this piece," she explained, raising the back protector so Moff Kerioth and his escorts could see inside it. A black sleeve flopped down to cover her other palm. She pushed it up, bunching fabric back toward her elbow. "For the microsecond it takes for the field to reach full efficiency, the armor itself handles heat absorption. Insulation, plus this dissipator, almost eliminate thermal discomfort."

"Allegedly." Kerioth sounded sarcastic.

Tinian decided that she'd never please him except by demonstrating the product. Then he'd be impressed. Then he'd grant I'att Armament the most lucrative contract it'd ever earned. Thousands of stormtroopers would need this coverage. "Help me, Wrrl."

Wrrl fitted the corselet to Tinian's back and front, clamping it together at her shoulders. Tinian trusted Wrrl completely. Five years ago, she'd spotted him being beaten by a slave dealer. Bloody bunches of fur had littered the ground around the huge alien. Tinian—barely twelve—had dashed forward, disregarding Grandmother Augusta's protests (she could always move faster than either grandparent). She'd saved the creature's life. Little had she known that in rescuing Wrrl, she'd bought loyalty-to-the-death.

The shell pieces hung out over her shoulders. Tinian wriggled until they balanced.

Daye picked up the shoulder pauldrons, clasping them between long, sensitive hands. "Put these on, too," he murmured. The gray streak arched higher than the rest of either of his eyebrows. According to Druckenwell's strict population laws, she and Daye were too young to marry until they proved financial independence. Slender and bookish-looking with lively brown eyes, Daye had come to Il Avali to make a life for himself.

He was now officially Tinian's Second Undersupervisor and the very center of her life. She let him attach the pauldrons over her shoulders. They dangled to cover her elbows, enclosing her upper body with a loose, ill-fitting box. Field conduits clacked against each other when she turned toward Daye. If only she could reassure him—

"I know why you're doing this." He leaned close and stared down at her. "I don't like it, but I understand. No one ever calls you a coward and gets away with it." He squeezed her forearm. "Force be with you, love."

As he backed away, Tinian rotated a control on the breastplate. The first time she'd seen this field demonstrated, she'd worried at this point. The field didn't hum, buzz, sparkle, or even glimmer.

"Grandfather?"

As if awakening from the dead, he raised a small luma. Tinian held out her arm to one side. He switched on the luma. No bright spot appeared on her sleeve.

"As energy encounters the anti-energy field," Grandfather said, regaining his voice, "the field responds and cancels it. We're now certain the field is operating."

"Ready, Tinian?" the Moff asked. His voice was as bland as if he were inviting her to sit down for lunch instead of ordering her out in front of a firing squad.

Tinian stalked to the wave trap, feeling ridiculous inside the enormous bucket, pauldrons, and body glove. Built like a pocket at one end of the spacious demonstration room, the wave trap's baffled duracrete walls and floor angled together to absorb unthinkable bursts of energy. Tiny shadowed pits in its walls gave evidence of past demonstrations.

At least she couldn't smell the room anymore. Even without a helmet, the odor had stopped registering several minutes ago.

Daye stood close to the barricade, frowning. She drew up tall—for her height—and barely smiled across at him. Wrrl edged toward the code panel.

Kerioth swept his swagger stick toward three stormtroopers. "You three. Rifles," he snapped. They marched forward. Daye held both hands down at his sides. Usually, he kept one or both casually tucked in a pocket.

Tinian stared at the blast rifles. Those weren't the shiny new factory items she generally dealt with.

Daye glared at the nearest stormtrooper.

"Ready," snapped the Moff. Three rifles lifted. "Aim for weak spots."

Kerioth turned to eye Tinian. His lip curled. Evidently he enjoyed watching the I'att contingent sweat.

She knew that the armor worked. But staring down three rifle shafts, she momentarily lost control of her panic.

Instantly, Daye's face reflected her fear. He spun toward the trooper and tentatively reached for his rifle.

"Now," Kerioth ordered.

Three vermilion energy beams whizzed at Tinian's chest. She flinched, but she couldn't dodge quickly enough. Heat flashed over her back and shoulders despite the bucket's extra insulation. Daye froze and stared, stricken.

"Cease fire." Kerioth twirled his swagger stick.

Tinian straightened back up, let out her breath, then smiled weakly at Daye. The sale was as good as made. She'd done it, though she wished she hadn't tried to duck.

Daye thrust a hand into his pocket and frowned. Her momentary panic had probably jabbed him deeper than it'd frightened her.

Kerioth slipped a comlink out of his belt sheath. "Squads three, four, and five: seal entrances. No traffic or communication off grounds."

"Excuse me?" Grandfather stepped forward, obviously as confused as Tinian abruptly felt. "Sir, what is the meaning of this?"

Moff Kerioth tapped Grandfather's shoulder with his swagger stick. "Congratulations, I'att. I am buying your product."

"You sealed our entrances."

Kerioth clasped his hands at the small of his back. "It would be unfortunate if insurrectionist elements learned that we'd found a way to make stormtrooper armor invincible, would it not?"

We found a way? Tinian silently protested.

Grandmother Augusta glided forward, rustling her robes. "Our security has always been unparalleled, Moff Kerioth. You need have no fear concerning our—"

"*Naturally,* then," continued Moff Kerioth, "you understand that everyone who has worked above certain levels on this project must return with me to the Doldur system. This item must be manufactured under strictly regulated conditions. The New Order controls Doldur right down to food prices. It is the safest world for advanced military manufacturing."

It's your turf, Tinian realized. *You want this manufactured where you can watch.*

Grandfather's eyes narrowed. "I am sorry, but this family cannot travel. Augusta needs medical care."

Tinian fingered the black body glove's sleeve selvage.

"After all these years of hard work, they deserve peaceful retirement," she protested. "Daye and I are prepared to run the plant. We'll . . ." She hesitated, then plunged on. It was the only way. "We'll go to Doldur with you. But Grandfather and Grandmother are retiring to Geridard."

"No," said Kerioth. "You will return to Doldur with me. All of you."

"Sir," Augusta spoke up, "I apologize for making things difficult, but our application for the Geridard Convalescent Center has already been processed. We've advanced them 90,000 credits for life care."

Kerioth turned away. He tilted his chin as if rereading the I'atts' requests off the ceiling. When he pivoted back around, his condescending smile had returned. "You will not travel to Doldur? I cannot convince you?"

"Unfortunately, sir, it's impossible." Strephan folded his arms over his black uniform's decorated breast.

"Perhaps not so unfortunate. That enables me to dispose of your retirement and health worries simultaneously." Kerioth swung his swagger stick at the nearest stormtrooper. "Take them both."

Before Tinian understood, the stormtrooper whipped up his blast rifle and fired twice. Grandfather Strephan tumbled to the duracrete. Augusta gasped before she collapsed over Strephan.

They didn't move again. Too shocked to protest, Tinian covered her mouth with both hands. Daye bent his knees, ready to lunge. "Why did you do that?" he whispered.

Kerioth angled his swagger stick like a weapon at Daye's chest. "I'll let you youngsters in on a secret," he announced. "I have been sponsoring research into this type of anti-blaster energy field on Doldur. Emperor Palpatine will be most grateful when I present this invention as my own . . . with all the uncooperatives out of the way.

"You do wish to cooperate?" he asked blandly.

Grandfather! Grandmother! Stunned by her grief and horror, Tinian had to survive . . . to avenge them. She nodded. *Say yes!* she mentally begged Daye.

He straightened slowly, but he didn't speak.

Kerioth shrugged. "Binders for the boy," he ordered another trooper. "How long and how comfortably you live, boy, will depend on how well you *cooperate*." He stressed the word again.

Daye adjusted his stance, turning both feet out slightly. One trooper reached into a utility-belt compartment. Tinian glanced from the trooper to Daye. Daye eyed the trooper. Daye had learned some self-defense from Wrrl. He could move faster than anyone expected.

She must create a distraction.

"Wrrl!" she cried. "Help!" She spun around and dashed for the door.

Wrrl's roar frightened even Tinian. He slammed the code panel with one gigantic paw. A transparisteel blast wall plunged out of the ceiling, trapping Kerioth and two stormtroopers on the inside.

But four troopers remained. Wrrl rushed the pair blocking the exit, lifted each by a shoulder, and bashed their helmets together.

Tinian sprang through.

"Go left!" Daye shouted behind her. "Wrrl, stay with Tinian!"

Tinian whirled left and tried to run. One of her loose leggings tripped her. Blaster fire whizzed over her head. Wrrl tried to scoop her up with long shaggy arms. Fur shriveled where he touched her.

"Don't!" she cried. The field unpredictably damaged living flesh that touched it. Tinian scrambled to her feet. Wrrl sprinted past a bewildered-looking service droid. She caught a whiff of burned fur. "Daye?" she cried. "Wrrl, where's—"

Wrrl shrieked something about separating the stormtroopers.

They reached the lift tube. Tinian jumped onto its floor grid. It didn't activate to carry her upward. "They've shut it off!" she cried.

Wrrl stepped in front of her, clearly inviting her to climb onto his back.

There was no other way out of this bottleneck. Tinian switched off the armor field, vaulted up, and clenched her hands in front of Wrrl's throat, hoping nobody shot at them. Singed, matted fur brushed her face. The stormtrooper-sized breastplate dug into her stomach.

Wrrl leaped up the shaft wall, catching enormous claws—she hadn't even known that he had claws!—in its duracrete sides. Powerful muscles rippled under Tinian's hold. She clenched her knees around his sides, trying to keep her weight from choking him.

He dragged his weight and hers up to the main floor. A security droid rolled toward them, four claw-mounted blasters and scanners installed atop a perfectly balanced sphere. It endlessly repeated, "Halt! Drop all weapons! Halt—"

Tinian gulped a deep breath. "Recognition," she shouted over Wrrl's shoulder. Her voice ought to shut it off . . .

"Confirmed." The droid spun in place. It retreated, still broadcasting.

Daylight shone through the southeastern service door. Another pair of stormtroopers crouched beside it, obviously alerted over Kerioth's comlink. "Freeze," ordered one.

Tinian slid off Wrrl's back and slapped the field control back on. Then she dashed at them, too full of adrenaline to cower or even flinch this time.

While the troopers fired at Tinian, Wrrl sped past her on long, shaggy limbs. He reached them before she did and bodily flung them aside.

She'd never seen a Wookiee's full strength before. He terrified her.

Outside the service door, two energy-fenced conveyors connected the entry with I'att Armament's main receiving area. Wrrl howled encouragement at her.

Tinian leaped onto one conveyor and dashed toward

the open spaces and freedom. Fabric flapped around her feet, dangling but giving her feet some protection. She grabbed a fistful of loose fabric above each knee and pulled up. That helped a little, but she couldn't bend her elbows far enough to do any real good.

She jumped off the conveyor onto gray duracrete. A three-meter wall surrounded the complex, surmounted by a catwalk with heavy gun emplacements. When Tinian glanced up, her heart sank. Five stormtroopers dashed along the top of the wall, three from the north and two from the west, converging on the corner ahead of her and Wrrl.

Then she remembered her good-luck piece. "Wait!" she cried. She dug down through layers of clothing and extricated a small hunk of chepatite impact explosive. She'd picked it up the first day Grandfather (her mind spasmed in pure, illogical grief: *Grandfather!*) had let her work a full shift. A silly souvenir and dangerous, maybe, but she couldn't fling it hard enough to set it off.

Wrrl could. "Take this," she exclaimed. "Throw it— there." She pointed at the big corner gun. Two troopers aligned its sights on her and the Wookiee. "Then duck."

Wrrl bared his teeth, seized the explosive, and hurled it. Sweat trickled down Tinian's chest. She was roasting—

Dust, grit, and duracrete boulders blasted in all directions. A gap appeared beneath where the gun had been. Tinian sprinted toward it. Her shoulders and back flashed hot again. More troopers must have rushed in behind her.

The rubble pile was almost two meters high. Wrrl urged her to hurry.

Tinian yanked the bunched fabric and scrabbled upward. "How bad—are—you hurt?" she gasped.

He growled defiance.

"Wrrl—you need—a medic—"

He tossed his head and kept running.

Tinian scrambled over the top. A laser blast whizzed off

her right pauldron. That blast came from outside the wall! She flung herself backward into Wrrl's arms.

Wrrl yipped surprise. Had she singed him again?

He shoved her aside, grabbed a duracrete boulder, and heaved it down at the outside trooper. Then he woofed gently at Tinian, urging her out.

A blast from behind struck him. He howled.

"Are you all right?" Tinian cried.

He gurgled and pointed outside the wall.

"Not without you!"

Disregarding the armor field, he cuffed her with a huge paw. Tinian jumped down the rubble pile, spun around, and glanced up.

Wrrl stood framed by the gap. Another bolt caught him in his side. He screamed and turned full around, then lurched toward the stormtroopers inside the enormous guard wall.

Grief-stricken and stumbling with every other step, Tinian dashed across a weedy field that surrounded I'att Armament. This was a secure area, maintained in case of internal disaster . . . and to enable guard wall staff to watch incoming traffic.

Why weren't they chasing her? Had Wrrl stopped all of them?

Wearing heat dissipation armor, she'd shine like a beacon to IR sensors. It would be easy to tag her with heavy weaponry. Moff Kerioth was probably calling over to Il Avali Spaceport right now.

How could she have been so wrong about the Empire? When had it changed?

At the weed field's edge, dilapidated duracrete buildings formed a toothy perimeter. Tinian slapped off the field projector and stumbled toward an abandoned warehouse. Its door hung askew. Two maybe-Human derelicts scrambled deeper into shadows inside.

Tinian tried to imagine what they'd seen: the top half of an armless, unhelmeted stormtrooper? She pushed away from that warehouse and ran two more turns around bends in the alleys, but didn't find any better cover.

She shoved the flapping armor pieces up over her head, then shed the black glove like an old reptile skin. She was about to abandon it when a thought bigger than fear struck her: Moff Kerioth wanted this protection field badly enough to kill for it. She must use it to hurt Eisen Kerioth.

She dug her utility vibro-knife out of another jumpsuit pocket. Painstakingly she sliced vital components off the breastplate—three electronic c-boards, controls, conduits—then the carapace—insulation, plus the projector itself.

Overhead movement snagged her peripheral vision. A silent repulsorcraft sped over the warehouse row.

Tinian shrank into the nearest building's shadow. She stuffed everything small into her pocket along with her vibro-knife. Then she bundled the rest of the vital parts together. Dashing barefoot around the next corner, she stepped on something sharp and almost fell into a rubbish heap ready for droid pickup.

That gave her another idea. Limping, she hurried back to the debris she'd left. She scooped shell fragments into the body glove and flung them behind the rubbish, safer from detection. Then she limped deeper into Il Avali's bad quarter.

Happy's Landing must be nearby. She and Daye had visited the ale house several times, thinly disguised in working-class coveralls, looking for good music and flamingly spicy food. Luck and adrenaline got her there after only one wrong turn. She paused in the doorway, then plunged into its dark interior without giving her eyes time to adjust. It sounded nearly vacant. Late afternoon had never been Happy's busy hour.

She tripped over a bench. Nobody protested, so it must be vacant. She sank down, exhausted and ashamed. She had to get off Druckenwell, the only world she'd ever known.

But how? And . . . alone? Daye would meet her here, if he could.

She swallowed on a parched throat. Mustn't use her credit account. She dug into a third jumpsuit pocket and found a few credit tokens worth a cold glass of Elba water. She dropped them onto the table.

Then she pillowed her sweaty forehead on her arms and tried to think. She couldn't've gotten this far unless Kerioth had sent most of his troopers chasing Daye. Therefore, Daye must be a prisoner. (Her mind writhed again: *Daye! Wrrl, oh, Wrrl!*)

On second thought, she'd worn the invaluable armor. They'd've all chased her.

No, he'd codeveloped the anti-energy field. They needed Daye alive. Kerioth was undoubtedly tracking them both—

Daye Azur-Jamin flattened on the floor of a narrow service tunnel, scarcely breathing. During his first moments of flight, he'd been clipped by blaster fire halfway down his left thigh. It'd stopped throbbing several minutes ago. Now it simply felt dead.

Three pairs of white boots scurried past, outside the shaft's access panel.

They'd find him sooner or later.

Daye dragged himself past the panel, deeper toward the center of I'att Armament.

Using his tiny comlink, he'd monitored Eisen Kerioth's command frequency. Poor Wrrl had paid off his life debt in full, and enabled Tinian to elude pursuit, but Kerioth—who'd escaped his transparisteel cage by talking a trooper through code permutations—had ordered repulsorcraft. They'd catch Tinian quickly unless he could divert them.

Daye's comlink also let him follow stormtrooper teams as they hunted him. Kerioth had ordered all personnel off factory grounds—he meant to use IR scanning, and fewer warm footprints inside the factory would help.

It would be a race, then. I'att Armament's power grid lay under a force shield, open to the sky; the plant was built around it like a vast open square. In half an hour, Daye could crawl to the main power station. In two minutes more, he could backfeed the force shield into the power grid. That would take out the whole factory. Daye had hesitated to endanger innocent bystanders, but Kerioth was clearing bystanders away.

He probably wouldn't escape. But at least Eisen Kerioth wouldn't steal I'att Armament's anti-energy field—Daye and Strephan's own brainchild—and get away with it.

No one would ever know what Daye had done, either, except Tinian. She knew him too well.

The thought made him smile. He crawled on.

"Why, hello, Princess Tinian."

Momentarily terrified, Tinian flung herself upright. She breathed again when she saw two familiar people standing over her. Happy's Landing's current torch singer, Twilit Hearth, wore a scandalous, shimmering sapphire-blue gown. Twilit's mate, Sprig Cheever, sported a short, neat goatee and nondescript clothing. He set a glass of Elba water in front of her.

Tinian dashed tears away from her eyes and guzzled it.

Twilit touched her shoulder. "Hey. Hey, what's wrong?"

"I—" Tinian gulped. She needed allies, and Daye— deft reader of strangers' intentions—had liked these two. *(Where was he?)* "I've got to hide. I'm in big trouble."

"Hey, it couldn't be that ba—"

"Stormtroopers. They've shut down the factory."

"No," whispered Twilit. "Where's . . . you know, your prince?"

"I don't know," Tinian groaned.

Twilit seized Tinian's elbow. "Come with me. There's no time to lose."

Twilit pulled her through a dark, cluttered hallway behind the kitchen, then up one flight of stairs to a cramped little dressing-sleeping room.

"Twilit, thanks," Tinian objected, "but they'll search up here." She laid her valuables under an old boot rack, then startled. She'd sliced three c-boards off the control panel. Now she had only two.

"We'll hide you in plain sight." Twilit grabbed a shimmering red gown. "But we've got to move fast. Put this on."

She'd dropped one c-board! *Concentrate, Tinian. First you've got to survive.* Tinian eyed Twilit's curves, then glanced down her size-one jumpsuit. "Twilit, it won't—"

"You've only got minutes," said the singer. "Are you going to walk into their gunsights wearing that uniform?"

Tinian skinned out of her jumpsuit and yanked up the extravagant gown. To her shock, padding slid into position over all the right places. The singer was no more voluptuous than Tinian, not in the flesh. She glanced into the room's only mirror. Her face and someone else's body looked out.

"Not bad," said the singer, "but we can do better." She spun a pair of shoes across the floor toward Tinian and rummaged in a tattered duffel. "I assume you can sing."

"Not like you." Tinian gratefully pulled on one shoe. Too big, but it would protect her throbbing foot.

"Most Imperials wouldn't know a song sparrow from a cloud crupa. You know all my songs, I've watched your lips move." Twilit opened a jar and smeared something onto Tinian's face. Tinian submitted to several layers of paint and a rapid, hair-pulling fluff job before Twilit announced, "Break's over, Princess. Get down there and show your stuff."

Tinian eyed the mirror again. Only the stranger looked

out at her now. "Why are you doing this?" she asked. The stranger's lips moved when she spoke.

Twilit's face appeared beside the stranger's. Fire blazed in Twilit's blue eyes—the same shade as her own, Tinian realized. "The Empire and I had a disagreement four or five systems ago," Twilit answered. "Now get down there."

"But you—"

"I'm deathly ill. Couldn't sing another note for at least an hour. Go. Cheeve and Yccakic'll help."

Tinian tottered down the steps. Now that her eyes had adjusted, she could make out the ale house's interior. Two Human customers sat at one table, a lone Devaronian at the bar. On a clear, triangular stage raised above table level, Sprig Cheever crouched cracking his knuckles over the black, white, and green keys of a KeyBed that almost enclosed him. The other sentient band member, a Bith named Yccakic, plucked his Bottom Viol's five strings as he adjusted buttons along its tall upright neck. Redd Metalflake, the group's self-contained droid sound system, sat behind them audibly tweaking his circuitry.

"I'm . . . singing?" Tinian croaked. "Twilit feels poorly."

Cheever grinned down through the stage at her. "That'll work."

Tinian climbed up to stand beside him. He played two chords she recognized, and she launched into "All I Can Ever Do" with all the guts she could muster. Now that she'd slowed down, she could only think of Daye. How could she sing, with Daye in terrible danger . . . if he was alive?

Without warning, two stormtroopers sprang through Happy's front door. Tinian gulped. She covered the beat she'd missed by ad-libbing a lyric. One trooper glanced at her. Immediately he swiveled away. She felt relieved . . . and hurt, too. Was she that unattractive in real life?

The troopers bustled from table to table. Just as they

vanished into the kitchens, a seismic rumble rocked the ale house. Patrons slid under tables. Tinian flailed, trying to grab something, and connected with Yccakic's arm. "Off the stage!" Cheever commanded. Yccakic laid down his Viol and towed her down clear, narrow stairs, then out into the dusk-darkening street.

Three gargantuan fireballs lit the northern sky, rising under low clouds precisely where I'att Armament had stood.

Both stormtroopers dashed out of Happy's Landing. Passing without a backward glance, they sprinted up the street. A customer who'd followed Yccakic outdoors saluted the fireballs with a raised fist. "Down the rich!" he hooted. "Down the Empire! Up anarchy!"

"Hey," burbled Yccakic. "You okay, kid?"

Tinian's ears sang. Her vision blacked out from the edges inward.

She collapsed in a heap.

A beefy stranger stumbled into Happy's Landing near dawn. Tinian, still masquerading as Twilit, drooped on a bench close to Cheever. The stranger demanded a TrooperBreath, downed the chartreuse glassful, then looked around for company. Spotting Tinian and Cheever, he wobbled over. "That oughta help. I've been hunting and lifting all night," he declared.

"What's up?" Cheever set a hand casually on Tinian's shoulder.

"I just spent four hours slaving for the Empire. The head trooper rounded up all the muscle he could find out on the streets."

"What for?"

"He had us searching I'att Armament . . . or the crater that usedta be I'att Armament . . . for survivors."

The ale house spun around Tinian.

"Find any?" Cheever squeezed her shoulder.

The bulky newcomer shook his head. "The Big Moff's

speeder was the smallest wreckage we could identify. Other than that, nothing. Totality. Looked like an inside job to me." He burped, then grinned toothily. "Some brave, suicidal lunatic musta wanted to take it away from the Empire pret-ty badly." He raised a glass in wordless tribute.

Tinian stared. Daye, gone? All that promise . . . *broken?*

Not only Daye, but Grandfather, Grandmother, and Wrrl.

All her life.

She lost track of time after that. Some hours later, the band held council upstairs over the kitchens. "Time to leave Druckenwell." Cheever draped his long legs over a packing crate. "This place is too hot for me."

"Me, too," put in Twilit.

"We'll never get away," lamented a metallic monotone. Cheever had lugged Redd Metalflake upstairs and set the boxy sound droid on a stretch of floor. "Everyone picks on musicians."

Twilit folded her arms. "We'll go," she said firmly. "The last time we ignored Cheever, we nearly lost our instruments in an apartment fire. Is somebody onto us, Cheeve?"

"Not yet."

Tinian barely listened. She was in shock. *Nothing will ever touch me again. Nothing. No one. Ever.*

Yccakic flicked a series of folds around his tiny mouth. "Has anyone looked up outside? We've got a blanket of repulsorcraft sitting over Il Avali. Security will be double; at customs, triple. And we promised Tinian—"

"We'll make it," Cheever predicted.

Twilit cleared her throat. "Fix my ID for her. I'll lie low here for a few days."

Cheever raised an eyebrow.

Twilit shrugged. "If Comus can make my ID cover Tinian, he can run me a dupe, easy. I'll be okay."

Cheever stroked his short beard. "That'll work. But

Princess, about that . . . luggage of yours. I don't think we can risk taking it out through Imperial Customs."

That cracked Tinian's introspection. Even with a c-board missing, those pieces might help someone re-create the anti-energy field. "Wait," she begged. "The customs people will have no idea what your instruments are supposed to look like . . . right?"

Twilit shrugged. "They're musical morons," she agreed. "What are you driving at?"

"It's already in pieces," Tinian answered. "Attach them to your instruments."

Cheever stroked his goatee. "Ye-es," he drawled. "I can fit most of it to look like it's part of the KeyBed's insides."

"I'm good for a c-board or two," proclaimed Redd. A touch of reverb added confidence to his voice.

Tinian wondered if she were going crazy. She didn't care if she lived or died, but she must get that field trans-mitter out through customs. "Couldn't you get it off Druckenwell safer without me? If they catch me trying to pass Twilit's ID, it's the spice mines for all of us."

Affectionately, Twilit mussed Tinian's hair. "We know good people offworld," she said. "People who can use that stuff against the Empire. They'll want to talk to the I'att Princess. Guaranteed."

A door slammed. "She was there, all right," declared Woyiq.

Daye shuddered. The huge, beefy man's voice jabbed daggers through his injured head.

The other Human—or was he a Gotal? Daye's eyes wouldn't focus—turned to shush Woyiq. "Hey, keep it down!"

"Sorry." Woyiq slunk toward Daye's bedside. "Sorry." The huge Human had dragged Daye out from between jagged duracrete slabs, laboring in near-total darkness at the bottom of Il Avali's deep new crater. "Really, I'm sorry—"

Daye squeezed his attendant's hand. "Did you—"

"Wait," said the . . . yes, with horns like those it had to be a Gotal. "Get over here, you big battlewagon."

Woyiq shuffled even closer.

"You found her?" Daye whispered. "She's all right?"

The beefy man laid a hand on Daye's synthflesh-bandaged shoulder. Both of his legs had been crushed, too, and one hand . . . and they didn't dare carry him out to a medic. "She was at Happy's Landing, hanging out with the band. You guessed it right."

Daye swallowed. Even that small movement hurt. "Did you—"

"I told her we found no survivors. She—"

"Thanks. Thanks, both of you." Daye shut his eyes. He couldn't bear to hear how Tinian had taken the news of his alleged death, not yet. He half wished he could dissolve his body into nothingness and turn Woyiq's fatal pronouncement into fact.

But evidently the universe had spared him . . . most of him . . . for a while. He couldn't drag Tinian into the furtive existence he meant to lead now. Woyiq and his Gotal accomplice promised to sponsor him straight to the Rebellion as soon as Il Avali calmed down. The Rebellion needed his talents. They might be able to fix him up, too . . . somewhat.

In the meantime, he had decided it had to be kinder to let Tinian think him dead. She'd leave Druckenwell. Witty and capable, she'd make a new life.

He would never love anyone else, though. "Good-bye, Tinian," he murmured toward the wall. "May the Force be with you."

Customs bustled, quadruple anything Tinian had ever seen—but they passed, just as Cheever predicted. Tinian followed him up a stale passageway into the transport's fourth-class hold. They found seats close to Yccakic's.

Redd rode in the cargo hold, guarding the doctored instruments.

Tinian slumped down, glad this hold had no viewport. No last glimpse of Druckenwell would linger in her memory.

Alone in the galaxy except for two virtual strangers and an armload of illicit electronics, she'd find some way to help bring down the New Order. Every time she hurt Palpatine's Empire just a little bit, she'd dedicate that small victory to the memory of Daye Azur-Jamin and the life they could have had.

Force be with you, love. Leaning back, Tinian squeezed tears out of her eyes and braced for takeoff.

The Final Exit
by Patricia A. Jackson

A planet of interminable extremes, Najiba existed in a state of perpetual spring, delineating seasons in terms of electrical disruptions and torrential rainstorms. Ross stared into the maturing squall, intrigued by the erratic veins of lightning which arced across the obscure, night skies. Sheltered beneath his YT-1300 light freighter, the *Kierra,* the Corellian searched the turbulent atmosphere above the open flight pad, following several amorphous shapes that loomed above the heavy cloud cover.

Clipped with military precision, soft spikes of blond hair glistened with the rain as miniature drops accumulated in the longer length above his ears. Yawning, the smuggler leaned against one of the support struts. His sleepy, blue eyes stared from the shadows, regarding several natives who were huddled beneath the storm eaves of Reuther's Wetdock.

"194?"

Pressing the comlink against his cheek, Ross responded, "194."

Alluring, a feminine voice replied, "What's the deal, Ross? We've been sitting here for over an hour."

"Are you bored, darling?" he teased, grinning handsomely in the dim light.

"Do you want an honest answer or just my opinion? Come on, flyboy," she pleaded, "let's get moving."

"Don't get your circuits in a bunch." Affectionately he brushed a hand over the lower turret, wondering in what section of the onboard systems she was hiding. Fondly named after his ship, the feisty droid intelligence had a tendency to focus on the optical sensors, possessed by an unusually feminine curiosity.

"*Ol'val*, Ross," a voice greeted from nearby.

Despite the familiarity of the Old Corellian dialect, Ross tensed, casually thumbing the restraint from his blaster. Propping the heavy pistol against the holster, he stared into the closest shadows and focused on the stooped silhouette. "Reuther?"

The aging Najib bartender stepped into the rain, humbled beneath the onslaught of cold drops. Sheltered below the *Kierra*, he straightened, staring into the young Corellian's face.

Vivacious with old-world charm, his eyes were discerning and perceptive, contemplating Ross from head to toe. Meeting the smuggler's mischievous eyes, a proud smile played across his lips. "I see where you made the billboards in Mos Eisley last week. The Imperials are offering 5,000 credits for your head."

"Is that all?"

"Indeed," the old man chuckled. "Not nearly enough for a rogue with your credentials." Billowed red sleeves ballooned from Reuther's frail shoulders and arms, clashing with an oversized native tunic. Dampened by the rain, thinning gray hair was tightly braided against his freckled scalp. "It's good to see you, boy," Reuther whispered. Uncorking an intricately carved bottle, he poured a generous portion into a crystal goblet and handed it to the smuggler.

"Corellian whisky?" Ross questioned, sniffing the bitter aroma. "What's the occasion?"

"Growing old," Reuther croaked, nervously glancing over his shoulder, "and to having the strength to face tomorrow."

Suspicious, Ross followed the bartender's anxious eyes. "Quiet night, Reuther?" he asked, cautiously moving a hand to his blaster.

Sadly, the old man shook his head. "This is a desolate place when the Children of Najiba come home."

Familiar with the Children of Najiba, Ross scanned the night skies, well acquainted with the peculiar asteroid belt that had mysteriously claimed an orbit around the small planet. As ominous as the shattered rock moving above their heads, Ross discerned the somber tone of Reuther's voice. "Your message said it was urgent."

Muffled by the warm bodies crowded at the narrow blast door, a strangled scream suddenly erupted from the bar. The despondent cry fluctuated, a cacophony of sobs, which peaked above the violence of the storm.

"Just watch, my boy," Reuther cautioned. "I brought you here for a reason."

The crowd broke ranks, scattering away from the bulkhead frame. A Najib man, wearing the clumsy beige uniform of a port control steward, staggered from the bar, collapsing in the street. Cradled in his arms, he carried the slender, motionless body of a Twi'lek woman. Her pale, blue skin glistened with rain, faultless and smooth despite the cruelty of the shadows. With the delicate poise of a dancer, elegant arms swayed above her head, exaggerating the gentle arch of her neck and shoulders. Scantily clad in a faded tunic, her frail form convulsed in the steward's arms.

"That's Lathaam," Reuther began, "our port official, and that," he hesitated, "that used to be his woman, Arruna."

Ross shrugged the tension from his chest and shoulders, massaging a pinched nerve in his neck. "What happened?"

"Adalric Brandl happened," he replied evenly. "He blew in about 10 hours ago, demanding a ship with a pilot who could shoot as well as fly." Sighing, he added, "Well, you know the rule, Ross. When the Children of Najiba are home, no traffic on or off the planet. Lathaam, being the choob-head he is, made the mistake of informing Brandl of that fact." The anxious Najib rubbed the narrow ridge between his eyes. "Lathaam always did lack diplomacy skills."

"So Brandl killed the girl?"

"I ain't saying what he did." From the safety of the shadows, Reuther watched the lurid scene. Dubious, he averted his eyes, throwing his hands up with exasperation. "Truth is, Ross, Brandl never touched her. Never laid a hand on her," he puffed, "yet there she lies, dead. And there ain't nobody on the planet, not even you, who can tell me Brandl *didn't* do it."

"You've been living with the natives too long."

"I know what you're thinking, boy," Reuther scoffed. "Remember, I was once a bounty hunter, too. Brandl never pulled a blaster. Doesn't even have one." The bartender cleared his throat noisily, spitting into the wind. "His kind don't need blasters to kill." Shuddering visibly, he mumbled, "He's a 10–96 if I ever saw one."

"A 10–96?" Ross whispered.

"If you don't know, you better look it up," Reuther snorted. "Your life may depend on it."

Ignoring the patriarchal cynicism, Ross crossed his arms over his chest. "Where do I fit into all of this?"

"Brandl wants a pilot who can handle himself. I told him I knew a dozen or more suicide jocks who would come through the asteroids just to make an easy 1,000 credits . . . then I told him about you."

"Come on, Reuther," Ross snorted musically. "One man comes along and has the whole town running scared? Whatever happened to your militia?"

"Is that what it's called?" Reuther scoffed. Staring at the backs of the prying mob, he spat, "Farmers! All of them! Eager to bite every stranger, but afraid of stepping on their own tails. Look at them!" He stared into the small assembly gathered around the body. "It's easy to look into another man's misery and do nothing."

Grumbling among themselves, the crowd abruptly retreated into the street as a shadow moved from the back of the bar. Eclipsing the dim light radiating from the bulkhead, the stranger faltered in the doorway. "That'll be him," Reuther whispered. "I'll pay you 2,000 credits on top of whatever he offers you. Just get him off the planet!" Stepping back into the rain, he hesitated. "There's a bad noise about this one, Ross. Watch yourself."

Captivated by the peculiar events surrounding this outsider, Ross cautiously observed the reaction of the locals as Brandl swept past them, drawing the shadows in his wake. Struck by the unusual beauty of the stranger's face, the smuggler found it difficult to believe that such a man was capable of violence. Handsome, almost cavalier by appearance, Brandl's nose and chin were chiseled with stony nobility, polished by a quiet arrogance that aroused the smuggler's suspicions. Faded laugh lines framed a narrow mouth and thin lips.

Thick, dark waves of hair glistened with rain, interspersed with strands of white, which ran from his temples to the nape of his neck. As foreboding as the shadows of Brandl's face, the robe draped from his shoulders seemed to absorb the darkness about them, concealing any weapons and his hands from view. "Captain Thaddeus Ross?"

Wincing with mention of his first name, Ross brushed his duster aside, revealing his blaster and his hand poised over the heel. "Adalric Brandl?" he replied curtly.

Cordial, a genteel smile played across Brandl's pale lips, drawing a sharp angle over his prominent cheekbones. "I'll be brief, Captain. I need transport to the Trulalis system."

"Trulalis? You could catch the local skipper for half of what I'm likely to charge. Private transports don't come cheap."

"Integrity comes without price, Captain Ross. The bar owner assured me that you were a man of integrity." Squaring his shoulders, Brandl probed the smuggler's calculating eyes. "I'm offering 5,000 credits for transport to Trulalis, where you will accompany me to the Kovit Settlement."

"I don't leave port for less than 6,000," Ross countered, narrowing his eyes. "If you want company, it'll cost you extra: 1,500 credits."

"Agreed," Brandl whispered. Graceful, his long fingers retrieved a sealed credit chit. "Three thousand now and the rest on completion of my business."

Eyeing the sealed chit, Ross gushed, "Right this way." The smuggler extended his arm toward the freighter's lowered ramp. "Kierra, prepare to raise ship."

"Well it's about time!" she hissed. "I thought my docking struts were going to take root here."

Ross cast a final glance to the bar, saluting Reuther and the others who were watching from the sanctuary of the shadows. Confidently pocketing the credit chit, he flashed a reassuring smile and jogged up the ramp. Initializing the hatch seal, he moved along the familiar corridor toward the flight compartment. The Corellian grinned impishly, listening to Kierra's vindictive voice, as she engaged their peculiar passenger.

"Who the hell are you?" she demanded. "Never mind where I am. I'm where I belong, but you—"

"Kierra," Ross whispered, "meet our new client."

Seething with the brunt of Brandl's initial arrogance, Kierra vehemently blustered, *"Halle metes chun, petchuk!"*

"Koccic sulng!" Ross scolded, shocked by the scathing Old Corellian insult.

Pleasantly, Brandl returned his thanks for the rude statement and offered a challenge. *"Onna fulle guth."*

Before the droid intelligence could recoup for the invitation, Ross glared into one of her optical lenses. "That's enough!" he fired at her. "Open the power coupling and charge the main booster," he ordered. "Now, Kierra!"

Discharge static hissed over the internal comm, similar to the indignant gnashing of teeth. "Affirmative, boss," she replied.

Crossing his arms over his chest, Ross leaned against the interior hull wall, listening for the ignition of the ion engines. Focused on Brandl's insidious eyes, he whispered, "There aren't too many people who remember the Old Corellian dialect."

"In the course of my career, I've had to speak many languages." Cautiously, Brandl added, "I was . . . am . . . an actor."

"I don't usually transport passengers," Ross confessed. Stepping through the low bulkhead, he activated the interior corridor lamps. "You're welcome to use my quarters."

Brandl's gaze swept the length of the modest passenger cabin. Hesitant to enter, he paused in the bulkhead frame. "How long until we reach Trulalis?"

"An hour?" Ross shrugged dubiously. "I'll notify you when we arrive."

"Thank you, Captain, your hospitality is appreciated."

"Yeah, I bet it is," the Corellian mumbled under his breath. As the hatch automatically sealed behind him, he retraced his steps to the flight compartment. "Kierra, set the astrogation system for Trulalis."

"Check."

Sitting down in the acceleration chair, Ross quickly glanced over the flight console. "Okay, darling, bring up the emergency auto-pilot program we installed this morning."

"Not today, Ross," Kierra pouted. "I have a headache." Observing his reaction from several optical lenses, she dampened his fury, whining, "You forgot to cut the restraint servos, flyboy. So don't blame me for the glitch." A hushed snicker translated across the internal comm. "By the way, where'd you dig up the spook? He gives me the chills, Thadd."

"I told you not to call me that!" Ross hissed. Glaring into an optic sensor, he roughly booted the throttle, causing the freighter to shudder and slide on the pad.

"Gently, gently," Kierra cooed. Vexed by his dark mood, she added, "I hate it when you get this way. Your manners—"

"Never mind my manners!" Curbing his temper, he flipped a series of flight switches. The freighter shifted beneath him, resisting the planet's gravity as it rose from the external dock. "You just think about minding your manners," he scolded. Checking the data readouts for the latest asteroid activity, the Corellian grumbled, "Brandl's paying 8,000 creds for this trip, that's almost half a load of spice. You could at least try to humor him."

"Whatever you say, boss."

"And while I have your attention, run a code check on a 10–96."

"That's easy. It's listed by Imperial enforcement protocol as a mentally imbalanced person."

"No, there's got to be something more to it," he contemplated. "There must be something else. Research the dead files on all 10-codes with that designation."

"That could take some time."

"Good!" he snapped. "I want every description for a 10–96, everything from Imperial databases to Old Republic records."

Resistantly, Kierra replied, "Affirmative, boss."

Accompanied by a low hum, the hyperdrive cue flashed intermittently, recalculating the jump to hyperspace. Checking the onboard systems, Ross observed hyperactivity in the library programs, where Kierra was researching the peculiar 10-code. "Stand by, hyperdrive engaging," he announced, piping into the ship-wide intercom. Bracing himself against the acceleration chair, Ross activated the motivator, propelling himself, his passenger, and his ship into the multicolored explosion of hyperspace.

In the lower cradle of the ship, Ross sat in the swivel gunner's chair, swinging side to side, absently strumming his fingers against the turret firing controls. He closed his eyes and massaged a muscle spasm in his shoulder, wincing as the clenched tendon tightened then released. Oblivious to the spectacular display of light and color beyond the narrow viewscreen, he relaxed against the cool leather brace, drifting into the serenity of sleep.

"You know," Kierra whispered, "you make the cutest faces when you're asleep."

"I wasn't asleep," he lied, suppressing a yawn.

"Well heads up, flyboy! I have some intriguing data for you."

Ross sat up, rubbing the circulation back into his ears. "Let's hear it."

"Well, it seems that your mysterious 10–96 dates back long before the 10-code setup even existed. Now, according to the description, and I must admit I'm perplexed, the 10–96 came from an Old Corellian word, *ke'dem*."

Staring into the hyperspace vortex, Ross mentally mouthed the word. "Go on."

"Go on?" Kierra snorted. "That's it! Since before the Empire, a 10–96 has had two definitions, an imbalanced person and a *ke'dem*." Hesitant, she whispered, "Now without overinflating your ego . . . what's a *ke'dem*?"

"It's a variation of Old Corellian that means condemned or fallen."

"Well that would explain the modern terminology."

"Yeah," he whispered, "it would also explain what happened down there on the planet." The smuggler cupped his hands together, supporting his head and neck. "Kierra, darling, Adalric Brandl is a Jedi Knight."

"A Jedi? That *would* explain a lot of things." Momentarily, her optic sensor dimmed. "Stand by. Hyperdrive about to disengage. Three . . . two . . . one."

Leaning against the gunner's panic bar, Ross felt the vibration of the ion drives, set to ignite once the transition was complete. "Easy on the drive coils, Kierra."

"Aren't you coming to the bridge?" she asked.

"On my way," he replied, "but first I have to collect our unusual guest."

Blanketed by a protective cloud layer, the planet Trulalis was richly embellished with a spectacular landscape of verdant green. A mosaic of rolling grasslands, sprawling forests, and spacious oceans stood as an invitation to paradise for the space-weary traveler. Crisscrossed and separated at irregular intervals by feral wilderness, Trulalis offered innumerable flat fields for small transports to dock. Ross made a mental note to mark this planet as a potential checkpoint on his smuggling runs. A brief sensor scan pinpointed the closest suitable landing field. Compensating for the subtle shifts on the ground surface, he set down near a small hamlet.

On the surface, Ross shouldered his travel tote and secured an extra power pack to his holster. From the top of the ramp, he hesitated in the corridor, glimpsing Brandl from the corner of his eye. The eccentric Jedi was waiting for him outside on the trail, shadowed by the towering visage of the black trees. A seemingly invincible statue, the strange man stood with solemn conviction, staring into the hazy silhouette of the late afternoon sun. "Kierra, I'm still not sure what Brandl's up to. Keep your eyes open."

"Keep your comlink open," she replied. "You know how I worry."

"That's my girl," the Corellian chuckled.

Testing the soft earth beneath his boots, Ross strolled up to the familiar silhouette of his passenger. For the first time since leaving Najiba, he noted that both of Brandl's hands were visible, one of them swathed haphazardly in a black bandage. Through gaps in the makeshift dressing, he saw the tender pink of raw flesh and yellow seepage draining into the thick fabric.

Before Ross could question him, Brandl turned and started along the trail. "What did the Najib tell you about me?"

"He said you killed a Twi'lek girl," Ross blurted. After a moment he pressed, "Did you?"

The Jedi's reply was abrupt and forthright. "Yes." Brandl hesitated as the Corellian snorted reprovingly. "Please Captain, your contempt is small reward for a repentant pilgrim."

"You call murder a penance?" Ross spat.

"When it has become the least of one's crimes," the Jedi paused dramatically, "yes."

Brandl's apathy toward the woman's death was chilling, sending shudders throughout the Corellian's body. "How? You never touched her." Ross grasped Brandl's sleeve and pulled. "How did you do it!"

"I asphyxiated her."

"She suffocated? In an open room?"

"A sophisticated talent," Brandl sneered, "not meant for the faint of heart."

"You sound proud of yourself, Jedi!" Ross spat with contempt. "Makes you feel good to kill an innocent woman?"

"Evil springs from weakness and weakness from ambition; by this grand order every ambitious man is undone!" Deliberately, the Jedi challenged, "Tell me, Captain, you too are an ambitious man. Which of us is truly innocent?"

"Should I applaud now!" Ross taunted.

"If you wish!"

"Well before I hand over your accolades, tell me something. Was that a real line or just something you made up to ease your conscience?"

Petulant with the smuggler's indignation, Brandl turned on him. "If it's retribution you wish for me, Captain Ross, then I suggest you stay close at hand." Scowling furiously, he stared down his long nose. "You may yet have your satisfaction."

Provoked by the sinister edge in Brandl's voice, Ross drew his blaster. The Jedi apparently heard him, and spun around to face the blaster. Ross fired a three-round burst at the Jedi. Honed by several seasons as a bounty hunter, he centered the bolts to explode in the square of Brandl's broad shoulders. Before the deadly energy could land its mark, Brandl deftly snatched a cylindrical object from his belt. Momentarily, a narrow shaft of white brilliance ignited from the base, feinting and parrying with the precise motions of the Jedi's wrists. Deflected by the lightsaber, the blaster bolts were harmlessly shot off into the field.

Aghast, Ross could only watch as the destructive rounds dissipated into oblivion. Abruptly, he felt the crushing pinch of invisible fingers clenched against his throat, constricting his airway and lungs. Choking, the smuggler dropped to his knees as the serene landscape of Trulalis blurred before him. Gradually, the sensation faded, leaving the Corellian gasping to catch his breath.

"There is one rule of theater that applies to real life, Captain Ross," Brandl declared. "*Only heroes die.* Villains and cowards are left to suffer." Turning his back on the panting pilot, he snarled, "Now come along."

Ross shook the haze from his vision. "Is that another line?" he slurred lethargically.

Brandl trembled, visibly drained as he disengaged the lightsaber with required effort. "Not just a line, Captain, but an astute warning to the less-than-humble pilgrim."

Securing the lightsaber to his belt, the Jedi momentarily scanned the pale skies. "The settlement is less than a kilometer away. We had best move along. It will be dark soon."

Swearing off bruises, Ross bitterly wedged his pack against his shoulder and jammed his blaster into the holster. Quickly brushing past Brandl, he hissed, "Can't imagine why you'd be afraid of the dark."

Nestled within the dominant embrace of a mountain range, Kovit was well-protected from the harsh weather conditions of the northern highlands and the windswept plains of the coastal region. Staring down the mound into the modest farming community, Ross could vaguely discern movement in the dusty streets. Drawn by diminutive banthas, wagons creaked through the wide avenues. Dozens of people walked the streets, pausing to chat with a neighbor or to haggle over the local street merchant's wares. From a side alley, three boys grunted and sweated behind a battered landspeeder, coaxing the vehicle's engines to briefly ignite. Nearby, above the sporadic choke of the repulsorcraft, laughter betrayed a trio of children playing with an obsolete astromech droid.

Brandl hesitated at the crest of the mound, staring down into the settlement, as if reconsidering his options. Wilted, the Jedi's shoulders exposed a reluctance to continue. "Where are you from, Captain Ross?"

Startled by the abrupt question, Ross stammered, "Corellia originally."

"Do you find returning there difficult?"

"Homecomings are always hard." The Corellian shrugged, pursing his lips doubtfully. "At least for some of us."

Without further reply, Brandl continued down the trail, deliberately slowing his stride. Vacillating, he stepped through the settlement gates, as if expecting some invisible force field to bar his path. Nostalgically passing through the prudent rows of farm cottages, the Jedi admired the mastery of native architecture, as sculpted from the indigenous lumber. Herb gardens and prized flower beds adorned the private lawns, each tenderly manicured and maintained with fastidious care. As they approached the dry, dusty oval of the settlement common, Brandl covered his eyes, protecting them from the fading sun, as he stared into the rich, agricultural outback of the settlement, which extended far beyond the limits of the community to the base of the mountains themselves.

From the near center of Kovit, a macabre specter of architecture loomed above the rustic rooftops. Flyaway buttresses supported the main construction of the theater, unfurling like stony wings from the base. Packed with chalk-white limestone, the obelisk was unequivocally straight, seeming to elongate into the obscuring skies. Established intentionally in the heart of the settlement, the theater captured the waning rays of the sun, momentarily stealing the glory from the picturesque village. There was a somber sense of belonging that drew Brandl toward the structure, ignoring the startled glares of the settlement denizens.

As they passed through the outskirts of the community, Ross nervously observed a makeshift hangar and the crude snout of a Z-95 jutting from the narrow bay doors. The starfighter appeared operational, though crowded by its diminutive shelter, and eager for a skirmish. Distracted by the presence of strangers, several men gathered just beyond the shadows of the small livery, watching intently.

Thumbing the restraint from his blaster, Ross cautiously whispered, "Your adoring fans?"

"Neighbors, patrons, old friends." Brandl abruptly paused in the street, as if awakening from an illusion. "But that was another lifetime."

"Where do they stand in this lifetime?" the smuggler growled.

"Strangers."

Weaving through the haze of the fragrant gardens surrounding the theater courtyard, a woman and a young boy moved along the grainy, stone paths. The echo of their voices chimed with laughter as a private joke was shared between them. Brandl watched intently as they walked through the haze and into the dusty streets.

Fiery, auburn spirals cascaded from the woman's head, crowning her oval face. Unusually pale skin flushed in the faded brilliance, betraying an aversion to excessive sunlight. Tall but gangly, the boy was no older than 11 or 12 years. Broad shoulders framed his upper torso, seemingly too heavy for his slender form. Coordinated and rhythmic, his long legs showed nothing less than the promise of sharp, steady growth.

Startled by the dark apparition of Brandl, the woman hesitated and stood motionless in the street, meeting the Jedi's friendless eyes. The smile parting her full lips was quickly forgotten. Puzzled by her peculiar behavior, the child swept his gaze from her stony face to Brandl. Registering nothing more than a stranger, the boy leaned over his mother's arm and whispered something in her ear.

Obviously distraught, she pulled the child snugly against her and hurriedly continued their trek across the common. Brandl sighed remorsefully, then without explanation, resumed his walk toward the old theater. Beyond the archaic gate a decade or more of wild flowers had claimed the inner recesses of the theater yard, staggering the once straight path to the massive bulkhead doors. Residing over the darkened antechamber, bronze statues and sculpted metalwork lined the interior corridor.

Adalric Brandl moved gracefully into these familiar shadows, intuitively stalking the darkened corridors and spacious hallways beyond. The hollow shell of his memories traced the outlines and silhouettes of each molded tapestry, a display case of tarnished prop swords and shields, and finally the grand hall, where past audiences had come to experience the stage productions.

Ignoring the Corellian behind him, Brandl quickened his steps, moving into the immense auditorium. Deafening, the familiar resonating of applause and encouragement thundered and echoed inside his ears; but this illusion was short-lived. There was no audience to applaud, no actors to bow, no stage settings, nor props as he remembered them. The yawning mouth of the stage was disgracefully bare.

"Who is there?" a voice whispered from the darkness.

Brandl faltered, supporting himself in the elaborately carved doorway.

A thin, frail figure emerged from the darkness of the inner aisle. "Come closer," he gently commanded.

From the shadows along the back wall, Ross scanned the theater for other signs of movement. Thumbing the restraint from his blaster, he waited quietly in the musty wings of the chamber as Brandl continued into the hall toward the shadowy form.

"Adalric Brandl, is that you?" the old man croaked pleasantly.

"Master Otias," Brandl whispered, kneeling at his mentor's feet. "I am ashamed that you care to remember me."

Otias ignited a glow rod, casting a warm beam of light across his scaling face. He was dressed in a faded gray tunic, stained with lamp oil and sweat. The veins and muscles of his arms were pronounced and defined, built up from a lifetime of toil and lean with age. Clouded gray eyes were nearly imperceptible against a splash of dark spots and freckles. "Since when did shame ever come between an actor and his task director?" Brushing a trembling hand through his thinning silver mane, Otias whispered, "It's been 12 long years, Adalric. What brings you back to this stage?"

"Master O—" Brandl fell silent, cutting himself short.

"Come, come lad . . . there is nothing more obvious than an actor with a need to confess."

Abruptly, Brandl cowered beneath the glow rod. "I . . . I live my life . . . in a whirlwind!"

Dignified, Otias beamed proudly, recognizing the famous line. "Old Soveryn's final words of the fourth act. How closely you've come to rivalling his life." Resigned, the aging taskmaster sighed, a lifetime of exhaustion evident by his labored breathing. "Actors are granted license to live a thousand lives, Adalric; but you, you chose to live a thousand lies. If you have come to me as your advocate then speak from your heart, not from the void of a tragic character who has never been born."

Spittle flying from the corners of his mouth, Brandl raged, "I cannot!"

"Every tragic figure is tainted by a flaw, possessed by a need to save the world or himself from some unpardonable crime. No man can set himself before humanity and judge it, not without himself being judged." Otias gently unwrapped the makeshift bandage swathed about Brandl's left hand, wincing at the severity of the burn. The lightsaber's cauterizing bite was undeniable. "When we pursue shadows, we are destined to find the darkness." Staring into Brandl's face, Otias whispered, "And as you well know, the dark side has always had its price."

"What happened to me?" Brandl implored.

"You stared into the collective pith of all beings and judged it, without first looking into your own heart. Frustrated, you went looking for the tragic flaw without much success. When the Emperor came calling, you couldn't resist!" Otias whispered, "No one knows darkness better than a Jedi Knight, and no one was more suited to play such a role than you."

"I killed a woman!" Brandl gasped. "Suffocated her! I could feel her heart in my hand . . . in my mind! And I squeezed and squeezed—"

"You've killed many," Otias accused. "The Emperor has no blood on his hands; but he keeps an army of others who do."

"Otias, please, help me find the way."

"The way of the Force brings balance to the anarchy of life; but you Adalric," he shook his head reprovingly, "you didn't want balance. Your pride was so great and despite my warnings, you went in search of the unatoneable crime, which inevitably separates the hero from the indigent masses. And you found it, didn't you?"

Gasping for breath, Brandl croaked, "Yes! It was within me, within my black heart the whole time."

"It lies within all of us," Otias whispered, "if we dare to see." Exhausted, he sighed bitterly, again brushing a hand through his thinning hair. "I cannot vindicate you of the evil that you have brought upon yourself, an evil that you have wielded in the name of the Emperor for so long. I've spent the last decade watching, waiting for your return, rehearsing what I would say to you." Sadly, he whispered, "What you ask, I cannot give you. There can be no redemption for your crimes. The dead cannot forgive." Extinguishing the lamp, Otias turned his back on the distraught Jedi and moved away toward the stage.

Brandl slowly turned from the familiar silhouette, stung by the reality of Otias's words. Pressing the damp bandage against his wounded palm, he stepped into the outer arena, moving into the darkened wings in the rear of the theater. Without comment, he retraced his steps through the spacious corridors, past the archaic displays, and into the courtyard beyond the doors. Steeling himself against the violent images sparking through his mind, the Jedi surrendered to Trulalis's last waning sunlight, imagining that the impotent rays had the power to burn into his flesh.

Angrily, he fumbled beneath his robes, producing a large cylindrical object. Ross flinched momentarily, traumatized by his encounter with the Jedi's lightsaber. With recovering confidence, he noted that this object was much larger and was covered with minute control levers and data screens. As if wrenching the neck of an invisible foe, Brandl twisted the object before replacing it within his robes. Lightly, he heard the smuggler's footsteps behind him, moving with guarded discretion, as if to avoid disturbing his troubled thoughts. "I prefer your contempt, Captain," he whispered, his eyes flashing with violence. "Your pity disgusts me." Extending his long stride, he stormed out of the theater yard, unhindered by the thickened dust at his feet.

Framed by the dark cowl of the forest canopy, the *Kierra*'s ivory hull gleamed, a smooth, round tooth jutting from the heath. Guided by these moonlight reflections, Ross stumbled through the rutted trail, twisting his ankles against unseen rocks. "Kierra, lights!"

Squinting into the brilliant array of search beacons, the smuggler shivered, pulling the collar of his duster across his neck. A potent wind was descending from the high country, bringing with it the promise of rain. Inside the ramp corridor, Ross brushed a hand through his hair, reassured by the warmth flooding the freighter's interior. "Pump up the main boosters," he ordered with distraction, noting that Brandl had not followed him onto the ship.

Growing accustomed to the Jedi's erratic mood swings, Ross peered from the protection of the ramp door. Below him, standing at the foot of the ramp, Brandl stood motionless staring into the darkness as pale mists crawled over his shoulders and beneath his feet. "Brandl?" With his smuggler's sense aroused, Ross ordered, "Kierra, kill the exterior lamps."

"You can come out now," Brandl whispered, as the austere beacons were extinguished. "No one will harm you."

Ross pressed himself against the interior hull wall, propping his blaster and steadying his arm and shoulder to draw a clear shot. Hearing him, Brandl stared up into the darkened passage, disarming the Corellian with his sharp gaze. As the lanky figure of a boy emerged from the heath, Ross could feel the tension fade and stepped off the ramp, recognizing the child from their brief encounter in the settlement. Dressed in dark green clothes to match the forest at night, the child's face was flushed and sweated. Cautiously, he approached the two men and the freighter.

Awed by the sight of Brandl, enshrouded by darkness, yet haloed by the moon, the child moved gingerly toward the ship, compelled by an insatiable curiosity. He made no effort to shield his wonder, noting every measure of the figure before his eyes, as if committing his mere presence to memory. "It's true," the boy whispered. "You are a Jedi Knight."

"Who are you?" Brandl demanded, but there was no strength in his words. Even Ross could detect the half lie of denial trembling in his voice.

Handsome, the child grinned, turning his face up to meet his father's eyes. "Don't you know me?" he asked. Staring intently at the lightsaber swinging from the Jedi's belt, the boy angrily cried, "You named me! Jaalib, remember?" Recovering his manners, he rubbed the toe of his shoe into the yielding earth. "My last name is Brandl too."

Gently, Brandl caressed the boy's hair and cheeks, feeling the smooth skin beneath his fingertips. It was a peculiar sensation, which fired every nerve across his body. Despite the tenderness of that caress, Ross felt a sense of unease crawling into his belly.

"Is that a real lightsaber? I've never seen one." Chatty, the youngster added, "I've seen props for the stage, but . . ." His soft, tenor voice fluttered, prey to the silence as Brandl handed the weapon to him. Staring at it, Jaalib reached hesitantly for the lightsaber, then dropped his hand.

"Don't be afraid," Brandl urged.

"I'm not afraid," Jaalib said with confidence, taking his father's hand, rather than the lightsaber. A thin film of tears glistened in the corner of his eyes. Swallowing the emotion, Jaalib whispered, "I've come to warn you. I heard Menges and the others talking. They're angry that you came back to the settlement. Mother doesn't think they'll do anything; but I know that Menges has a ship."

Overhearing the boy, Ross snapped, "Kierra, check the sensors!"

Abruptly, the interior corridor lights went dark. "I suggest that you all duck!"

A tremendous explosion erupted near the aft of the ship and forest perimeter, accompanied by the afterburn blast of an outgoing starfighter. Dodging churned up roots, debris, and stone particles, Ross slid under the ramp, diving for cover beneath the freighter's hull. Sparks and molten debris scattered about his head and shoulders, singeing his clothing and hair. Thrashing wildly, he swiped the heated material from his skin. Nearby, Brandl was helping the frightened boy to his feet, whispering encouraging words to the traumatized child.

"Damage report."

"They got us, boss," Kierra pined. "Concussion missile." There was a brief pause as she analyzed the incoming data. "Shields are out. Engines are at 70 percent. There's a good chance the ion coils may seize if we push them too far."

"Can we lift off?"

"With you at the reins, flyboy," she chuckled, "anything's possible."

Protectively embracing the boy against him, Brandl whispered, "As long as we don't make ourselves known, he will pass."

"Look," Ross barked, "this is all very touching, but that last pass was just to get an approximate location. Next time—" he snorted anxiously, "forget it, I'm not waiting around for next time. Let's scratch gravel, now!"

Agitated by the sudden turn of events, Brandl cupped the boy's face in his hands. "Does your mother know you're here?"

"No."

"Then . . ." Brandl stammered, "how did you know?"

Playfully holding his father's hands, Jaalib smiled, "Otias told me the truth a long time ago. He let me watch the holos of your stage work. Mother didn't like it at first,

but she came with me and she cried the whole time."
Sadly, the boy glanced away, avoiding Brandl's eyes.
"When we saw you in the settlement common, as soon as
we got home she started to cry. So I knew it was you."
Staring at Ross, the boy frowned, knowing the inevitable
parting was soon at hand. "Will you ever come home?"

Brandl cradled Jaalib's smooth cheeks and gently kissed
the child's forehead. "I can make no promises."

Jaalib forced a smile. "I understand. Otias said that you
had other important roles to play, parts that a small world
like Trulalis could never offer." Clinging to his father's
presence, the boy whispered, "When I'm old enough, I'm
going to act offworld too. Otias said that he would help."
He hesitated. "I want to be as great as you are, Father."
The thin film of tears returned, threatening to spill over
his cheeks. "I won't ever forget you." Using the thick
canopy of the forest as a shield, Jaalib sprinted down the
trail and vanished into the night shadows.

"They never told him the truth," Brandl swallowed desperately, fighting back his emotions.

"Why didn't you tell him?" Ross snarled, sealing the
outer hatch.

"You give me credit for courage? A man of courage is a
man of conviction, Captain Ross." Brushing past the
Corellian, the Jedi whispered, "I lost mine the moment I
chose to believe in old legends."

Throwing himself into the acceleration seat, Ross fran-
tically began throwing the flight controls. His hands
moved diligently across the console with consummate
skill. Roused by the threat of a hostile starfighter swinging
in on the sensor scope, he initialized the booster ignition,
cradling the crippled ship in his hands. A low whine engulfed the flight cabin in static echoes and vibrations as
the ion drive labored to lift the freighter. The metallic
rattle of the deck plates reverberated through every corridor and in the spacious cargo bay.

"Oh," Kierra groaned, "that sounds bad."

"Never mind how it sounds, get started on bringing the

shield generators on line!" Struggling to maintain control of the freighter, Ross brawled with the partially ionized throttle, maximizing the power output through the damaged engine.

"The hard part will be getting through the atmosphere," Brandl whispered, glancing over the readout screens.

"We may never get off the ground!" Ross grumbled. "Kierra, where is he?"

"One Z-95 Headhunter, headed right for us and according to my readings, the ship exceeds the normal weight ratio for its class."

"Meaning?"

"Meaning more concussion missiles. He's fully loaded."

"Power up the main sentry turret," Ross mumbled, concentrating on the hampered freighter. "When will the shield generator come on line?"

"Give me five more minutes. Hydraulic pressure is building to functional levels."

"Well hurry it along. At this rate, we won't even get into space before he catches us." Ross stared into the underlying blanket of the lower atmosphere, shrouding his departure in the frenzy of night mist. "What can you do about fixing the ion drive?"

"Think happy thoughts," Kierra replied. "We have no cargo. We have no surplus material. And," she added with a hint of feminine pride, "this ship has always been under its weight ratio. We're lighter than a Gamorrean brain sack."

"How long before he intercepts us?"

"Let's just say I'm putting up the shields now."

Abruptly, the modified light freighter shook with the impact concussion of another direct hit. Bucking beneath the powerful blow, the *Kierra* drifted beneath the cloud cover as the destructive energy ricocheted over the aft shields, dissipating harmlessly against the hull.

"Damage?" Ross panted.

"The shields took it," Kierra replied wearily, still accessing the information from her multiple systems. "But the hydraulic level is already dropping. We won't survive much more of that."

Angling across the stratosphere, the Headhunter aggressively continued its pursuit. Hampered by the thickened atmosphere of Trulalis, it swayed from side to side, approaching for another strafing run.

Arming the lower turret, Kierra interfaced with the sentry gun, timing a sporadic burst across the forefront of the attacking ship. Not expecting retaliation from the crippled freighter, the fighter stuttered through the atmosphere, its left wing section erupting into flames. Avoiding the turret's deadly accuracy, the Z-95 dropped back, barrelling out of range. "That should keep his head down for a while."

"Not long enough," Ross argued. Eluding Brandl's cautious eye, he grumbled, "If there's something in your Jedi survival book, now's the time to spring it."

Brandl nodded, his face notably drained and haggard. Reaching inside the fold of his robe, he again produced the peculiar capsule. The cylindrical-shaped device was cleverly fitted for concealment as a hydrospanner or mechanic's tool. Staring at the object, Ross recognized it from their brief excursion at the theater. As he watched, fascinated, the control head flashed intermittently from a hidden power cell.

"What's that?" Kierra crooned. Intrigued by the odd unit, her optical orb brightened, extending the focus on the transmitter.

"It's a transponder," Brandl replied. "And it's been transmitting for nearly an hour." The Jedi sighed with effort, leaning against the broad back of the acceleration chair. In the harsh light of the flight cabin, his arrogance could not hide the gaunt cheeks and stress lines that had begun eroding the handsome visage of a once proud man. The morbid signs of resignation and surrender were easily read in his noble face.

Without warning, the Headhunter broke off the chase, banking sharply toward the planet. Its aft engines betrayed haste, glowing with the throttle thrown full open as the fighter vanished into the dense cloud cover above the planet. Suspicious, Ross glared at Brandl, feeling the constriction of fear in his throat. "What's the catch?"

"You had better prepare yourself," Brandl whispered.

The proximity alarms blared, sending a deafening echo into the freighter's corridor and accessways. Exploding with tactical data and imminent warnings of ship-to-ship collision, the sensors closed on the gigantic structure of the massive Imperial Star Destroyer, newly emerged from hyperspace.

As the Star Destroyer moved across the viewscreen only a scant 100 meters from him, Ross slumped against the back of his chair, defeated before one shot could be fired. Slowly, scores of turbolaser batteries turned on them, targeting his freighter. Still hampered by a faulty ion drive, the *Kierra* bucked and lurched toward the Star Destroyer.

"Have they got us?" Ross moaned, massaging his eyes and forehead.

Kierra snickered nervously. "Does Boba Fett enjoy his job?"

"Could we outrun them?"

"We couldn't even out-think them at this point, flyboy. They've got us locked in tight."

Resting his head and arms against the flight console, Ross sighed, accepting the inevitable. "You've managed to sign my death warrant!"

"On the contrary, I've guaranteed your reprieve." The Jedi's mouth hinted at a sly grin.

"I have a price on my head! An Imperial bounty!"

"You are about to discover that the Emperor is quite generous, especially when one of his citizens sees fit to return his property."

"You're one of the Emperor's freaks?" Ross argued. "What were you doing on Najiba . . . You were running!" Staring at the Imperial Star Destroyer, he gasped, "You were running from the Empire? Why?"

"It no longer matters," Brandl whispered. "The time has come to confront the darkness and forsake it for what it is . . . just so many shadows."

"Well some shadows can kill!"

As they passed into the outer docking field, the freighter was engulfed in darkness. "Then let all be perfected in death."

Prying the forward deck plate from the flight console, Ross quickly unbuckled his blaster, stashing the belt inside with a hidden cache of thermal detonators and other illegal weaponry. Motivated by Imperial penalties for unauthorized equipment and arms, he retreated to a general utility closet in the corridor beyond the command cabin. Retrieving a small stash of blaster power packs, the flustered Corellian returned to the bridge to find Brandl peering curiously into the hidden compartment. "Kierra, make certain the shield housing is intact. I don't want them finding your power cell."

"A girl's got to have her privacy," she quipped. "Good thinking, boss."

Closing the hidden panel, Ross tripped the contamination seal. If the Imperial sensors went over the ship, they would bypass this area for contaminated mechanic's tools. Abruptly, the interior lights fluctuated as the power levels dropped, shifting to auxiliary mode. "All clear," Ross hollered.

"I've switched over my power couplings to a subordinate cell. Even if they do find my main generator, they won't know what it is. But," she teased, "that means I can't eavesdrop over the comlink or scan the perimeter!"

"For your own safety," Brandl began, "I advise you not to mention Trulalis."

Remembering Brandl's wife and son back on the planet, Ross nodded pensively. "Kierra, sweep all records and logs since we left Najiba, input data from a previous job. Where does that put us?"

"We dropped that baby tris off on Tatooine, remember?"

"Don't remind me," Ross replied wistfully. "Just erase the reasons and submit an addendum about engine trouble above Trulalis."

"Right, boss."

"And Kierra? Lose yourself. They'll probably go over every centimeter of this ship."

"Is that a hint of concern in your voice, flyboy?"

"Yeah," he grumbled. Shrugging the tension menacing his shoulders, he walked through the corridor to the hatch and deactivated the seal.

Before the ramp could fully lower two Imperial stormtroopers charged aboard the ship, leveling their weapons at Ross, shoving him against the hull wall. The force of the blow knocked the wind from his lungs and the Corellian doubled over, coughing desperately to catch his breath. Twenty or more stormtroopers were staggered outside the freighter, their weapons pointing into the ramp lift, trained on the dark Jedi.

Undaunted by the show of Imperial might, Brandl scanned the parade of white-on-black armor, until he met the familiar face of an Imperial officer beyond the periphery of armed soldiers. Stepping aside, the Jedi allowed three stormtroopers to rush past him into the ship.

"I trust you will cooperate," the officer announced. Pompously, he adjusted the brim of his black cap. "If not for your own sake, then for the sake of your companion."

Disguising a hint of defeatism with dramatic poise, the Jedi proclaimed, "How can I cooperate?"

"Think nothing. Do nothing. Say nothing until you are told."

Offering a hand to the panting smuggler, Brandl grinned slyly, his back to the Imperial entourage. "Captain Grendahl, you'll find that I do nothing very well."

Grendahl's face was menacing. "We're scheduled to rendezvous with the *Interrogator* within the hour. Inquisitor Tremayne is eager to see you again, Lord Brandl . . .

very eager." Pointing to Ross, Grendahl demanded, "Take him to the isolation area for questioning." Changing his demeanor with obvious fraudulence, Grendahl tipped his hat with mocking respect, "Please, Lord Brandl, your quarters have been prepared."

Massaging the bruises swelling on his chest and arms, Ross leaned his head against the antiseptically clean wall of the holding cell. Several hours had slowly passed, marked with isolated sessions of routine questioning. Abruptly, the door opened, admitting two stormtroopers and Captain Grendahl, who he recognized from the hangar bay. Pleasantly, the Imperial officer sat down across from him, setting a large datapad on the table between them. "Do you recognize this gentleman?" he asked, keying up a picture on the small screen.

Ross laughed softly, recognizing the distinguished curves of his own face. "Would it help if I said I didn't?"

Grendahl smiled generously. "No." Folding his hands against the table top, he sneered, "Interfering with an Imperial investigation is a crime punishable with imprisonment."

"An Imperial investigation?" Ross jeered. "It was a fight, and not a fair one," he argued. "Two stormtroopers against a Jawa, come on!"

"Never mind the odds," Grendahl replied evenly. "You still interfered; however . . ."

"However?" the Corellian scoffed, mocking the insipid officer.

"However, I am authorized to extend a generous amnesty if you will cooperate and answer a few questions."

"Amnesty?" Ross chuckled. He scratched his head, agitated. "Imperial amnesty is about as valuable as a Wookiee dwarf with no hair."

Grendahl frowned, covering his dismay with shrewd professionalism. "You have the Emperor's guarantee,

Captain Ross. Help us with one short investigation and you will be cleared of all charges."

Stalling, Ross demanded, "He owes me money!"

"I can't promise you will get it," Grendahl countered, "but you are entitled to 10,000 credits." Grinning malevolently, he watched the smuggler's startled reaction. "That's 10 percent of the bounty offered for Brandl's safe return."

Intrigued, Ross leaned over the edge of the table. "You mean to say Brandl's worth 100,000 credits?"

Anxious to keep the smuggler's attention, Grendahl silently acknowledged the query. "You're lucky to even be alive, Captain Ross. Adalric Brandl is highly unstable, capable of inconceivable atrocities. However, his value to the Emperor makes him an essential resource. Where did you find him?"

"Najiba."

Grendahl's face darkened, perplexed. "Najiba has stringent ordinances restricting traffic through the asteroid belt."

"By the time I got there," Ross explained, "no one cared about port control penalties. They just wanted him off the planet."

"Was there trouble? Was anyone harmed?"

The Corellian shrugged casually. "I never left my ship," he lied, "so I can't really say."

"And where were you going?"

"Mos Eisley, but," Ross laughed, "considering my last visit, I only planned to take him as far as Anchorhead. After that, he was on his own."

"Did he ever mention his connection with the Emperor?"

"Not until you had us in the tractor beam."

"The damage to your ship?"

"We were attacked by pirates," Ross replied rhythmically. "My hyperdrive failed and we just barely managed to arrive here."

Grendahl hesitated. "You keep accurate ship records,

Captain Ross. Your flight log and manifests substantiate your story."

"Call it a throwback to my bounty hunting days," Ross offered. "If you wanted your expenses, exact documentation was a necessity."

Tentatively peering into the room, a junior-grade lieutenant saluted Grendahl, ignoring the prisoner with him. "Captain Grendahl, sir, Admiral Etnam requests your presence on the bridge immediately, sir. Lord Brandl has been given the task of escorting the civilian to his ship."

"What!"

Ross concealed a sly grin behind the collar of his duster. Feigning surprise, he rose from the chair and leaned against the glossy table, pondering how Brandl managed to arrange this escort.

"Captain Grendahl," the lieutenant whispered, appalled by the outburst. "Admiral Etnam's instructions were quite specific. He is anxious to rendezvous with High Inquisitor Tremayne." Being Etnam's personal aide and fearing no reprisals from Grendahl, he nodded to the nearest stormtrooper and whispered, "Retrieve the prisoner."

Grendahl struggled to retain his composure, chafed by Brandl's influence, which despite his moment of dishonor to the Emperor, still held weight, even with the intrepid character of Admiral Etnam. Nostrils flared, he hissed between grit teeth, "Very well." Then to reestablish his ego in the company of those under his command, he straightened his hunched shoulders, erasing the sour scowl from his face. "You're free to go, Captain Ross," he growled. "The Emperor's clemency can be bountiful and far-reaching; but the next time you meddle with an Imperial investigation," he paused, "you may find yourself at the wrong end of Imperial justice." Folding his hands behind his back, Grendahl started up the corridor. "Remember that the next time you consider beating the odds."

Over the polished shoulders of several stormtroopers,

Brandl watched Grendahl's retreating back. Sneering behind the Imperial officer, the Jedi sniffed disdainfully as he led the smuggler into the corridor. "Are you a superstitious man, Captain Ross?"

Preoccupied by the armed escort behind them, Ross whispered, "My grandfather used to say that superstition was the foundation of a weak mind."

"Then we are surely doomed, for the basis of our civilization lays in the hands of high priests, shamans, and monks." Brandl laughed with genuine good nature. There was a spark of emotion betrayed by the brilliance of his eyes and Ross noted the deepening of the laugh lines framing his mouth. Adalric Brandl was in good spirit. "Your grandfather was a wise man."

Ross shrugged off the compliment. "Just another smuggler who found himself on the wrong end of Imperial justice." He sniffed, recalling Grendahl's threat. "That's why I became a bounty hunter, hoping to avoid what happened to him."

"And then?"

"And then I got bored. Guess it wasn't meant to be."

"We spend nearly the whole of our lives searching for the appropriate role that will mark the end of our existence with some moment of glory, ignoring the fact that fame and reputation are but mere perfumes of virtue. They never last."

"Is that another line?" Ross teased.

"Acting is a profound education in human nature and that is why I became so obsessed; but as my intellect improved, my morals failed and I became the very thing I most despised."

"And what was that?"

"Human. I was not a king, not a hero, not a god. Just a man trapped in the passion of the play."

"So what happens now?" Ross probed.

"My life has been one continuous drama," Brandl whispered, "a tragic one, I'm afraid. And I have stumbled through it, scene by scene, act by act, like some terrified neophyte. Tonight, Fortune calls for the final exit. I can no longer live the lie."

"You're going back to the Emperor, aren't you? After what he's done to you?"

"He did nothing but point in a general direction. I chose to go and do his bidding."

"What about your family? Your boy? What if the Emperor ever found out?"

"I assure you; no harm will befall them." Euphorically, he sighed, "They will be safe."

Ross believed him. There was a certainty about the Jedi that went beyond the sinister shadows that had once kept the two men at odds with each other. But the smuggler's conscience demanded a bit more for security. "How can you be sure?"

"I've never been more certain in my life." Placing a credit chit in the smuggler's hand, he closed Ross's fingers over it. Ross noticed another object in Brandl's hand, one which the Jedi tried to conceal when he folded his hands together over it. "The chit is the remainder of what I owe you and the Emperor's compulsory fee for capturing a dangerous renegade." He grinned malevolently, amused by his own sarcasm.

Slipping the chit in his duster pocket, Ross noticed the spherical, metallic shape beneath Brandl's hands, and noted the raspy acid erase etched into the explosive where the serial trace markers had been removed. Eyes wild with the revelation, he stared into Brandl's tranquil face.

"Consider all debts paid," the Jedi whispered. Turning curtly on his heels, he retreated in the hangar corridor with the escort in tow.

Ross hurried up the ramp, rush sealing the corridor hatch. "Kierra!" he hissed, sprinting through the access tunnel into the flight cabin. "Kierra, wake up!"

"What do you mean wake up!" she snapped. "The engines have been on line and waiting for the last hour. I even managed to knock one of the ion coils in place by popping the shield housing." She snorted, causing an erratic hiccup over the comm. "What's the rush? The main databanks were clean and according to this little astromech they had on board—"

"Never mind!" Ross shouted, strapping himself into the acceleration chair. "Brandl has one of my thermal detonators and I think he plans to—"

A muffled explosion reverberated through the docking corridors, blowing smoke and debris into the auxiliary bay. Piercing, high-pitched alarms began to blare, alerting medics and technicians to the area. Amid the chaos of shouting voices, the klaxons, and the sound of armored feet rushing to secure the area, the *Kierra* momentarily hovered above the flight pad. Several smaller explosions echoed from the passage, rattling TIE fighters and shuttle craft in the nearby racks.

Bewildered, Kierra gasped, "What would ever possess him to pull such a stunt?"

"He had to protect his family," the smuggler replied wearily.

"But with him dead, there's no guarantee the Empire won't find them. Then again," she mused aloud, "there's no guarantee the Empire will even look for them." Flustered by the infinite innuendoes, she quipped, "I'm just glad it's over."

"But it's not," he whispered. Banking sharply over an array of TIE fighters and ejector racks, Ross guided the *Kierra* out of the launch bay, repeatedly throttling the labored engines. "Brandl might have made his final exit; but the play is far from over . . . for us . . . or his family." The Corellian grinned nostalgically. Mesmerized by the verdant face of Trulalis, he watched the planet rotate before him, physically unmarred, innocently unaware, momentarily unchanged. He sighed, his smuggler's sense oddly at peace. There were no more shadows.

Casually resetting the astrogation system for Najiba, he braced himself as the *Kierra* stuttered across the open void and then vanished into the translucent brilliance of hyperspace.

Missed Chance
by Michael A. Stackpole

Corran Horn smiled broadly as the R2 droid's muted warble came to him from back in the darkened interior of the temporary hangar. "Yes, Whistler, you have done a good job of disguising this place." In his absence the droid had busied himself by strewing all manner of debris inside the abandoned vehicle shed. Between that and the growth of the purple *djorra* vine across the front of the shed, no one would guess that the structure hid the only X-wing fighter on Garqi.

Corran swung under the ship's sleek nose and squat-walked back to where the little green and white droid stood. Things had been moved around since he'd last visited Whistler and Corran suspected he was only seeing the latest in a long line of decorating schemes. "I'm sorry I haven't visited sooner, but the whole city is going quite insane about Rebel activity. The way everyone is being watchful, you'd think some slicers grafting New Republic slogans and graphics onto computer screens and public data displays was the same as murder."

The droid extended his I/O jack and plugged it into the port on a small datapad resting atop a can oozing an oily gray substance. The screen flicked to life and displayed the blade assembly for an X-wing's centrifugal debris extractor. A chirp ran from low to high as the droid's head swung from the image around to Corran.

The pilot blushed, then shook his head. "No, I haven't figured out how to get the part out of the Imperial Guards' possession. With the Rebel activity around here they've not slackened their security the way they normally would. Finding the spare parts and those proton torpedoes on the *Star's Delight* was the biggest thing to happen to Imps on this backwater, and it got Prefect Barris all hot to root out the Rebels here. I don't know who he thinks that will impress—the Emperor is dead and there's enough infighting on Coruscant that we even get word of it out here."

The droid's whistle scolded Corran as the image of the debris extractor faded into the crest of the New Republic.

"No, it's not a question of joining the Republic or not—and we've gone over this before. There is *no* Rebel activity here. The 'Rebels' they think they have are kids—students at Garqi Ag University. They couldn't help me get those parts away from Imps if I gave them months of instruction. Moreover, they'd get killed in the attempt." Corran shook his head adamantly. "Look, this is my problem. Captain Nootka brought those torpedoes because he thought he could sell them to me, or move them to his

Rebel contacts elsewhere. They got him caught, got his crew arrested and his ship impounded. I *might* owe it to him to try to spring him, but doing that without having this ship up and flying is not going to work."

As he spoke, Corran reached up and ran a hand along the side of the X-wing. It shared the green and white color scheme of the droid, though both of them could have used a few paint touch-ups. The fighter had been Corran's during his time with the Corellian Security Force, and Whistler had been his co-pilot and partner in countless missions to stop smugglers and other trouble-makers from disrupting life in the Corellian system.

Whistler let the datapad's screen go dark, producing a mournful tone as he did so.

"I know, Whistler, I miss taking those night flights, too." When Imperial entanglements made remaining in CorSec impossible, he took off with the ship and the droid. His purpose in coming to Garqi had been to lie low and avoid drawing Imperial attention to himself. Despite the fact that flying the X-wing put his life in jeopardy, he could no more refrain from flying than he could refrain from breathing—though he did make all of his flights at night to make it more difficult to locate him and his ship.

And dodging the local troops was simplicity itself. If I'd not sucked a rdava-bird into the starboard engine on that last flight, I'd still be flying and no one would think Garqi was a hotbed of Rebel activity. He sighed. "Now I'm stuck here because rich kids who have decided they want to shock their parents have started playing Rebel. It's all a game to them."

Again the droid scolded him with a sharp whistle.

"You're right, Dynba Tesc probably doesn't think of it as a game, but it's her own fault that she got caught last night. The Imps around here are not exactly storm-trooper caliber, but she left a trail that even our old Cor-Sec Imperial Liaison officer could have followed." He reached out and patted the droid gently on the head. "She'll spend some time in the local jail, then get kicked loose. Yes, she'll be interrogated, but they'll see she knows nothing and let her go. I'm sure of it."

Whistler tooted another question.

"Yes, if she were in danger, I would do what I could— but not because she's a Rebel. I've got nothing to do with the New Republic and just because the Empire hates the both of us doesn't mean we're allies."

Corran frowned heavily. "The Rebels might have killed the Emperor, and they're saying they have the last living Jedi on their side, but they're still a far cry from having the Empire down and out. My priority is to lay low while they attract more attention than I do. The Rebellion, such as it is, has come to Garqi, and that means it's time we're out of here."

He held a hand up. "No, no more protests. In fact, I don't want to hear any more Rebellion squawk out of you, got it? I'll be spending all my time working to maintain my cover *and* to keep my eye on the extractor. I'll figure out a way to get it, then we're on our way."

Corran started to turn away, but the droid caught hold of his sleeve with his pincer attachment. "What is it, Whistler?"

The droid hooted derisively at him.

"Yeah, well maybe back on the job I wouldn't have been so blasé about Dynba Tesc's problem, but now we're running from the law, not working for the law." He pulled his arm free, but looked back at the droid and hung his head. "Okay, no promises, but I will see what I can do. I look to take care of us first, though, right?"

Whistler's head spun around as he crowed triumphantly.

"Yes, saving her and her friends would look good in my datafile." Corran nodded to the droid as he headed back out of the hangar. *Unless the Empire is the one to put the notation in it, but they'd have to catch me first. With that extractor, I can avoid them—and that is the notation in my datafile I most want to see.*

• • •

Prefect Mosh Barris sat back in the overstuffed chair that he decided was almost as deep and as black as the depression in which he found himself. He felt old and tired, as if he were at a point in the universe from which any other direction was *up*. The only thing Garqi had to recommend it as a post had been its utter isolation and insulation from the Empire, and even that shield had worn thin in his year's tenure as the military prefect under the current—and seemingly ever-absent—Imperial governor.

"You see, Eamon," he began, "I had not expected her to make it easy for us, but this Tesc woman's ability to resist narco-interrogation is incredible. She steadfastly claims she knows nothing of the Rebellion and claims no connection with Lai Nootka or his *Star's Delight*. Even so, she seems to have an encyclopedic understanding of the phantom X-wing's flights—which she claims is because studying it was a hobby for her—and full knowledge of her crime. Of this 'Xeno' she claims is the ringleader of her slicer circus we have no record, and her speculation that he is a member of the *Delight*'s crew that eluded capture is one more black mark against us."

Eamon Yzalli nodded slightly as he slid the silver tray with the refilled snifter of Cassandran choholl. "Regrettable, sir. On the whole, one could be led to believe by all this that she knows nothing beyond what she has already revealed."

Barris took the glass and warmed it in his hands for a moment. "Looks can be deceiving, Eamon. Looking at her I see a woman who is more a child than adult—but that is standard among the adults here. This damned world is so fertile that the great agri-combines need nothing more than droids to tend the crops and accountants to tend the profits. The people of Garqi are pampered and unrealistic, hardly fodder for the Rebellion."

He drank in just enough of the Cassandran liquor to fill the hollow of his tongue, and let it pool there for as long as it took for the fragrant, fruity vapors to fill his sinuses. "Of course, *that* is what she wants us to believe."

"What is, sir?"

"That she is too innocent to be part of the Rebellion." Barris looked up at his green-eyed aide. "I cannot and will not be tricked by her. A long time ago I did nothing in a situation that called for action. I was deceived and I have paid for it since. It was a long time ago . . . but I have told you of it before, yes?"

The blond man returned to the sideboard and replaced the tray before turning and nodding to his master. "I do recall having been told something of the *alien* incident, sir."

"Yes, the *alien* incident." Barris stared darkly into the depths of the amber liquor. An alien—both humanoid and intelligent—had run him and his men around in circles on a planet that was—if it were possible—even more of a backwater than Garqi. This alien had killed his men, had brought down a TIE fighter and had even slain two stormtroopers using technology he stole from the Imperials in combination with native plants and animals. *I advocated a planetary bombardment to rid us of this menace, but Captain Parck invited this murderous creature to join the Empire. The Emperor chose* that *time to forego his normal xenophobia. He advanced Parck's career,* gave *this Thrawn a career, and started me on the long road from one humiliating post to another.*

Barris had hoped the Emperor's hatred for him would die with the man, but the Imperial institutional memory seemed to cherish the idea of taking him lower and lower. The man who had ousted Barris from his last post had been disciplined for having allowed the last Jedi Knight to escape Tatooine and murder the Emperor. That man's punishment had pushed Barris even further from the Galactic Core to the mottled red and purple world that was Garqi.

"I swore, Eamon, I swore that I would never let an opportunity to act decisively and forcefully slip away without redeeming myself. Uncovering and smashing the Rebels here on Garqi would allow me to do that."

"If I may be permitted, sir, you have an abundance of time in which to learn from Dynba Tesc what you need to accomplish this end. You have only had her for two days. She will break."

Barris tossed back the choholl and gritted his teeth against the fiery feeling it ignited in his throat and gut. "Would that what you say was true. I just received a priority message via a courier droid that indicated Kirtan Loor, an Intelligence agent, is being sent here by Coruscant to investigate. He will brief me on his arrival as to what his mission is, but we both know he is coming here to investigate *me*. He will find me deficient in some way and I will be sent to some other world that is even more wretched than this."

"I understand your alarm, sir."

"I think you do, Eamon, for we are alike, aren't we?"

"How so, sir?"

"We are both unhomed. I am hounded from post to post, with no claim to any world. You, on the other hand, are an Alderaanian, and without a world to call your own."

Eamon stiffened a moment, then nodded. "As you say, sir, neither of us has a home."

Barris' eyes sharpened for a moment. "I have a question I have to ask you, and I intend no disrespect. I've often thought of it, but I have said nothing because you have been so valuable to me. Had my predecessor not left you behind, and had you not made my arrival here so easy, I should have despaired of making any headway. Now that I will probably be gone from here soon, I think I have little to risk in asking it."

"Sir?"

"The Empire destroyed your world. How is it that you are content laboring for the servants of the Empire?"

Eamon's head came up and his hands disappeared at the small of his back. "Sir, Alderaan was a peaceful world.

We were unarmed and our people believed in pacifism. Our leaders chose to rebel. I, and I was not alone, revered order as much as I revered peace and left the planet. As this Rebellion robbed my people of peace, it also robbed them of life. Even so, I am at peace *and* I still revere order. You, my lord, represent order on this world, therefore I am content and honored to be in your service.''

"Well said, Eamon. I understand your feelings completely.'' Barris sat forward and rested his hands on the edge of his black lacquered desk. "The time has come for me to take action. To the Empire, failure to do *something* is seen as inability to do *anything*. I cannot afford that, not with Loor on his way. Though reminiscent of what the Death Star did to your world, I find myself forced to make an example of Dynba Tesc and publicly execute her. Once I do that her companions will scatter in terror. They will know I would have only killed her if she was of no more use to me, which means she gave me their names. We will learn who they are when they flee.''

The military prefect smiled coldly. "Let Coruscant deny *that* is decisive action!''

"Indeed, sir, it is decisive, however . . .'' Standing over by the sideboard, Eamon looked somewhat perplexed.

Barris reined his smile back in. Eamon Yzalli's perspective on Garqi had often proven useful and, not a few times, had steered Barris away from various *faux pas* that would have made his tenure more difficult. "You have an idea?''

"I do, sir, but only because of the question you asked before. It strikes me that if the local Rebels do have a way to defeat narco-interrogation—as the lack of success with Miss Tesc indicates—they may be sophisticated enough to wait out your action. More importantly, sir, I think it would be preferential to draw her confederates together, instead of scattering them, as making a martyr out of her would certainly do.''

"Yes, I see that, but how, Eamon?''

"Make your declaration about her execution public,

my lord. Schedule it for a week from now. This will agitate the Rebels. I will visit her covertly and tell her that I cannot abide seeing her die. I will arrange for her escape."

Barris' black brows collided in the depths of his frown. "You work for me. She will not believe you."

"But she will, sir, for even the most cynical of the Rebels would believe that I, an Alderaanian, have had a change of heart and wish to make amends for not acting against the Empire sooner. In addition, as they say, sir, actions will speak louder than words. I will arrange for her escape and prepare the way for her and her confederates to free the crew of the *Star's Delight*. We will even return to them their cargo of X-wing parts and munitions. The Rebels will all get together in the ship and prepare to leave. Your four TIEs will go after them and end the Rebel threat to Garqi in one dramatic fireball."

The military prefect tipped his snifter up and let the last drop of the choholl drip into his tongue as he considered the plan. "Are you sure my pilots can bring the ship down?"

"They will be able to if we render the shield generator inoperable." The ghost of a smile drifted across Eamon's bearded face as he started to pour more liquor into the empty glass.

"We will disable their blaster cannon, too."

"No, sir."

"No?"

"They need to be operable to provide verisimilitude, sir." Eamon inserted the cut-crystal stopper in the decanter. "If one of your TIEs were shot down, its loss would prove the danger the fleeing Rebels represented to Garqi. Of course, the fact that the Rebels were running away *and* were destroyed will be a lesson here to any who would seek to emulate them."

"I see." Barris admired the way the light shifted and glowed within the choholl. "Then should we not keep the X-wing munitions to prove the *Star's Delight* was smuggling things in the first place, or is this more verisimilitude?"

"We have the initial scans to show the smuggling, sir, and piecing together debris from the destroyed freighter will give this Loor character a great deal to do, occupying his time fully." Eamon smiled weakly. "Finally, sir, I will use delivery of the contraband to secure my passage aboard the ship. This way I will know when it is to leave, so our fighters can be prepared to sweep it from the sky."

"But you will not be on it?"

"No, sir. You will plant a report in our computer system here for one of their codeslicers to ferret out. It will indicate you had me executed for crimes against the Empire—unspecified, of course, but they will take it to mean I was found out. They will leave the moment that message is accessed, so they will tell us when they are leaving."

"And I alert our fighters to go."

"Exactly, sir." Eamon's face darkened for a moment. "The only difficulty with all this is that we cannot have any trace of what we are doing entered into our computer system here."

"Yes." Barris nodded solemnly and sipped the choholl. "Since their slicers can put stuff into our databases, we know they can pull it out again. Were they to find any indication of our operation, all would be lost."

"Precisely, sir. I shall make the arrangements, sir, if you have no objections."

"Objections? No. I will want reports, however."

"Of course, my lord." Eamon smiled briefly. "For your ears only, until it is time to reveal what you have accomplished in service to the Empire."

Dynba Tesc felt cold and achy, or at least she thought she did. Curled up on the steel cot, with her back pressed against the rough stones of the cell wall, she knew she should feel uncomfortable. Her body definitely was giving her all the sensory input to tell her she was, in fact, not feeling very good at all.

The problem is that with all the stuff they've pumped into me to pump information out of me, I'm not certain what I know and what I don't know, what is real and unreal. She coiled a blond lock around her right index finger, then sucked on the ends of the hair. A sense of security washed over her briefly, then she angrily flicked the hair away. *I am not a child, I can't retreat into childhood things to find comfort.*

But retreat she really did want to do, because she had never been more scared in her whole entire life. There was no question in her mind about that—clear of drugs or dosed to the top of her cranium. The terror of being arrested and tossed into jail had been enough to make her tell the authorities everything she knew.

The problem was she didn't know anything.

To her the Rebellion had been a distant conflict, one full of romance and heroism. The last True Jedi fighting the monster that destroyed his predecessors and a rogue of a smuggler winning the heart of a princess from a dead world—these were the things she knew about the New Republic. They had destroyed the Death Stars and the Emperor, but other than a change of the military prefect, those events had no effect on her or her friends at the university.

Then the *Star's Delight* had come to Garqi and had been taken for smuggling supplies to Rebels. She and others she met on the computer comnets—in temporary areas they sliced open and let close after the conversations were done—had mentioned suspicions that the New Republic had agents on Garqi. Dynba had found that prospect thrilling and not a little scary. People speculated about all sorts of things concerning the *Delight,* and a natural linkage was made between it and the phantom X-wing that had been reported flying at night all over Garqi.

Then she met Xeno. He sliced his way into one of the covert conversations—marking him as being better at codeslicing than anyone in the Imperial Security outfit on Garqi. Though he never said it, from his name and the fact that he only showed up after the *Delight*'s capture,

Dynba concluded he was one of the *Delight*'s crew that the local authorities had failed to pick up.

Xeno organized her and her byte-friends, keeping them all anonymous. She never knew what she'd find on her datapad once she linked into the planetary network, but it was always an adventure. Xeno showed her and the others how to graft slogans and graphics into the system, so datapad screens everywhere in the comnet would get New Republic messages at random intervals.

The shock and the outrage, as voiced by her parents and their friends, was wonderful. Dynba had struggled numerous times to maintain a straight face when some *atrocity* was being described to her by her apoplectic father, all the while knowing she'd composed the slogan and aimed it to hit his computer first. Doing things like that marked the highest point in her personal rebellion against his authority, and she found planning and executing new code assaults rather cathartic.

Dynba had long held the opinion that Xeno was grooming her and the others for something bigger—possibly the liberation of the *Delight* even—but she wanted to do something more. Abandoning the virtual realm of computers, she went out and bought a can of paint. In big, sloppy red letters she wrote "The death of a Tyrant is the triumph of Justice!" on the side of the Imperial Court building in the heart of the capital, Pesktda.

It had not occurred to her until later—about the time the local constabulary was putting her in binders—that having the store mix up a precise shade of red and charging the purchase to her personal account was not exactly the way to maintain her anonymity. The constabulary seemed to think her boldness meant she was dangerous and the interrogation to which she was subjected had been ruthless and efficient. Her lack of substantive answers angered her questioners and she knew she was in very serious trouble.

The door to her cell hissed open and the lights came up slowly. A small man with blond hair and beard entered and descended the metal-lattice steps to the floor. He turned back and gestured toward an unseen guard. The door clanked down, leaving her alone with this man wearing the uniform of the prefect's personal staff. She thought she recognized him, but she could attach no name to his face.

Dynba drew her legs up and tried to wedge herself more deeply into the corner of the cell. "I don't know any more."

The man nodded. "I know, child." He sank down in a squat, bringing his eye level down to hers. "It is my sad duty to tell you that Prefect Barris has decided to have you executed for your crime."

"What?" Dynba gulped air. "He can't."

"Oh, but he can." The man's green-eyed gaze flicked down toward the floor, giving her a moment to recover herself, then he looked back up. "I, on the other hand, cannot stand by and let this happen."

"What are you saying?" She thought she heard sincerity in his voice, and read it in his eyes, but the clothes he wore and the fact that a guard had followed his direction argued against any compassion on his part. The fact that he was there and talking to her at all made her wary of a trick. "You work for him. You won't help me."

The man broke off his stare and color rose to his cheeks. "Please, this is difficult for me as it is."

"Were I not here I might be more considerate. You work for a monster."

"I know." His hands balled into fists. "I am his personal aide."

"You! You are Eamon Yzalli!"

"I am."

"Then you are here to trick me." Dynba let her anger flow fully into her voice. "You should be ashamed of yourself."

Eamon sighed loudly. "I am."

"What?"

"I am ashamed." He swallowed hard. "I should have

seen sooner that to which I have chosen to be blind—the Empire corrupts people. I denied this truth and my denial is a crime that makes me complicit in the death of my homeworld, Alderaan. I came here and served here in hopes of forgetting. Then, when Prefect Barris was installed, I made myself a buffer between his capriciousness and the people of Garqi. Even now I tried to get him to moderate your punishment, but to no avail. I cannot allow your death to be upon my head, so I have chosen to act against him and for you.''

Dynba shook her head to clear her brain of the buoyant hope bubbling up into it. ''What can you do?''

A broad smile split Eamon's beard and in that moment Dynba thought him just a little bit handsome. *Like a hero of the New Republic.*

''What I can do and will do is this: I will arrange for your liberation. You will have approximately two days in which to execute a rescue of the *Star's Delight* crew. You and your confederates will board the ship and leave with it. Garqi is no longer safe for you.''

His eyes narrowed. ''Captain Nootka will need things to trade if he is going to resupply the ship and get to the New Republic. I will arrange for the contraband he smuggled here to be placed aboard—I can tell the workers we want the evidence replaced in the compartments to show an Imperial Intelligence agent how we found it. They will believe that and it will save us having to move it ourselves.''

Dynba's blue eyes widened. ''You're coming with us?''

Eamon nodded solemnly. ''I can cover *your* escape, but once the ship gets away there would be no concealing my part in all of this. When you are set to go, have one of your slicers get into the Imperial comnet and leave me a message as to where and when I should meet you.''

''I'll do it myself.'' Dynba swung her legs over the edge of the cot and her toes touched the cold floor. ''What you're doing, the people you lost on Alderaan would be proud.''

Eamon closed his eyes and nodded. "It is my hope you are correct." He reached out and took her hand in his, gently stroking warmth back into her flesh. "You only have to endure this prison for a few hours more, then you shall be free."

She gripped his hand tightly. "And soon after that, *we* shall be free!"

Barris raised a nearly empty glass in Eamon's direction. "I salute you, Eamon. It seems as if everything is going perfectly."

"Yes, sir. Dynba Tesc is secreted away, bringing her confederates together to free the *Delight* and its crew. She is also altering her appearance so she can claim to be Kirtana Loor, Imperial Intelligence agent, and take the *Delight*'s crew from custody without having to notify you for authorization. Several landspeeders have been organized for transport."

"And the *Delight* is ready?"

The small man nodded solemnly. "Using TIE pilots as workers was difficult, but once I explained the necessity of limiting knowledge of the operation to them, they agreed they were the best people for doing the job. The X-wing munitions are on board the *Delight*, though the spare parts appear to have been pilfered. As a skilled technician can convert them to work in Incom's T-47 landspeeder, my assumption is that someone in property storage gave himself a bonus. I have a few leads in that regard."

"We will deal with him, later." Barris snorted, drank and set his glass down. "The shields on the ship are disabled?"

"Yes, sir. We replaced a duplex circuit with its triplex equivalent."

"But a codepatch will allow them to bring the shields up."

"Yes, sir, but an initial diagnostic run on the ship will report the circuits as complete. Only when they discover the failure will they begin to look for the triplex. At that point slicing the proper sequence out of it will take approximately an hour."

The Prefect tapped a finger against the empty rim of his snifter. "An hour they will not have."

"Precisely, sir." Eamon refilled the glass with choholl.

"While you have been busy, Eamon, so have I." Barris winked at his man. "I have composed the report about your execution."

"Not on the system, sir?"

Barris smiled in response to the urgency in Eamon's voice. "No, of course not." He tapped the fingers of his right hand against the side of his white-haired head. "I have it all up here. You were terminated for 'anti-Imperial activity.' "

"Very good, sir."

"I may modify it. I want it to be perfect."

"I am certain it will be more than suitable, sir."

"I thought I would enter it into the computer just around sunset tomorrow. Things should be ready by then?"

"Yes, sir. Agent Loor will be arriving then, so he should see the pursuit and how you handle it."

"Excellent." Barris hefted the glass and raised it again in a salute. "The destruction of the *Delight* should make for great entertainment. I think I will have some friends in to watch."

Eamon nodded solemnly. "Very good, sir. I had already requested the kitchen prepare suitable refreshments for a gathering of ten. Will that be sufficient, sir?"

"Quite, Eamon." Barris sipped his choholl and smiled. "You anticipate my desires as well as my needs. What would I do without you?"

"A hypothetical question, sir." Eamon's expression became placid. "One hopes there is never need to answer it."

·   ·   ·

Her now-brown hair pulled back into a tight bun at the back of her head, Dynba stepped from the first landspeeder and tugged at the hem of her uniform jacket. She marched crisply to the door of the local detention center and drew from the jacket's breast pocket what looked to be an ordinary rank cylinder. She touched it against the I/O port beside the door.

Somehow, above the thundering of her heart, she heard a click and the door withdrew upward. At the other end of the short corridor she saw a guard standing behind a transparisteel shield look at her, then at the image on the screen of his datapad and back again. As he did so the blood drained from the man's face.

His clear anxiety gave Dynba a chance to conquer her own fear. Eamon had assured her that the rank cylinder he had given her would identify her as an Imperial Intelligence agent sent out from Coruscant to inspect Garqi. It made her Kirtana Loor and made her answerable to no one on the planet. A word from her and anyone could be sent to Kessel to mine spice while awaiting interrogation. "You will be someone they fear as much as you fear them. Use it and you will dominate them," he had told her.

And use it I shall. Keeping her steps crisp, and relishing the click of leather on stone, she approached the guard. "Are the prisoners ready for transfer?" She let the lilt of the common Core-dweller accent enter her voice, and underscored her words with impatient indignation.

The man's lower lip started quivering. "Transfer? I know nothing of . . ."

"Of course you don't." She drew her black leather gloves off by tugging on each finger in succession, then slapped them against the palm of her left hand. "The inefficiency of Rim-world officials should not surprise me, should it?"

"Well, I . . ."

"*You* were not going to venture an *opinion,* were you? What is your name?"

The man smiled weakly. "Which prisoners were those, my lady?"

"The crew of the *Star's Delight*." Her eyes became slits and she forced her nostrils to flare. "Returning them to the scene of the crime—you *do* know about using that investigative technique, don't you?"

The man furiously punched keys on his datapad. "Well, I . . ."

"Of course you don't—the technique predates the Emperor's murder by a year, so it hasn't gotten out here yet. You probably think he is still alive."

"Yes, my lady, I mean, no . . ."

Dynba barked a harsh laugh. "You don't know what you mean. Why the Rebels would strike at this witspare compost heap, I do not know."

"No, my lady."

The door to her right buzzed and slid into the ceiling. Three bedraggled figures, a small female Sullustan, a morose giant of a Duros and a Devaronian with several missing teeth and a broken horn shuffled through the doorway. They wore binders on their wrists and had another pair hobbling them. Each individual looked away from the dying sunlight pouring through the open doorway to the street.

Dynba looked up at the Duros. "Captain Lai Nootka, you and your crew are charged with treason. I am a representative of Imperial Intelligence and the resolution of your case is in my hands. Come with me."

She led the prisoners from the detention center and waved the landspeeders forward. Each prisoner was secured in a different speeder, then they headed off toward the hangar where the *Star's Delight* had been kept in impound.

The vehicles followed one after the other all the way to the spaceport. Dynba regretted not being able to tell the crew they were safe and with friends, but doing so would have put the mission in jeopardy. If the crew did not look scared and defeated as they rode through the streets of

Pesktda, someone could note their happy demeanor and that would attract attention to them and the operation. Eamon had pointed out that people tended not to pay too much attention to those who appear to be doomed because they might attract attention in doing so. Even before he'd said anything, she'd known that was true.

In keeping with her role as Loor, she met the gazes of the curious and held them until the others turned away. *I don't like making people afraid, but it is the only way to save these people and Eamon. And myself and my friends, too.* She kept her stare hard and terrifying throughout the ride until the speeders slid into the shade of the hangar.

The second her landspeeder stopped, she loosened her hair and shook it out over her shoulders. "Open the binders." She pointed at Nootka. "The ship is ready to go, complete with your X-wing munitions. Start pre-flight. The only thing on this world that can stop us from getting out of here are four TIE starfighters. Is that a problem?"

The Duros rubbed at his wrists as his driver tinkered with the binders on the starpilot's ankles. "We are matched for speed. We have hyperdrive, they do not. We have a blaster cannon, they have lasers. We have shields, they do not. I think we are not far from freedom."

"Dynba, you did it!" A Twi'lek woman came running down the gangplank of the long CorelliSpace Gymsnor-3 Freighter. With her head tails twitching excitedly, she brandished her datapad. "No alarms, no traces. We're clear."

"Good." Dynba looked past Arali Dil's shoulder, then frowned. "Are Eamon or Xeno here?"

Arali shook her head. "No one has been here except Sihha and me."

Dynba frowned. Prior to departing for the prison, Dynba had left a message with Eamon telling him when they planned to leave, and another to Xeno inviting him to reunite with his crew and escape. She had expected both of them to be present when she returned and she had especially wanted to see the look on Eamon's face when he realized his plan had worked perfectly.

"Arali, link into the comnet and see if you have anything from Xeno or Eamon."

"Right."

The Twi'lek and a Bothan had turned out to be the only non-Humans in Xeno's circle. The circle itself only had seven members, not counting Xeno, and all of them had thought it funny that even being so few in number, they had caused enough trouble for the Empire to send an Intelligence agent out from the Core to Garqi to deal with them.

Dynba had briefed everyone on their role in the Great Evacuation. Because of the Empire's xenophobic bias, neither Arali nor Sihha, the Bothan, would pass for Imperial officers, so they had remained with the ship while the five Humans used the speeders to get the prisoners. Now back in the hangar, everyone hurried aboard the *Delight* and prepared for departure.

"Interesting."

Dynba glanced away from the hangar opening and toward Arali. "What is?"

"Message to all of us from Xeno. He says his work here isn't done. He'll catch up with us later and we will all laugh about this."

"I'd prefer it if he came with us. I hope they don't need him to run the ship."

"Sihha can fill in—he was an astrogation student here."

"Right." Dynba felt a heavy darkness begin to spread from her stomach out to her limbs and stab straight up into her heart. "Nothing from Eamon."

"By the foul hearts of the Sith!"

Dynba whirled at the sound of Arali's voice. "What?"

The Twi'lek held her datapad out and Dynba snatched it from her trembling hands. "By order of Prefect Mosh Barris, at the conclusion and in resolution of his personal investigation into the actions of Eamon Yzalli, ordered

and carried out the discreation of an enemy of the state."
Her voice dropped to a whisper as she read. "He's dead."

The datapad slipped from her hands, but the Twi'lek
deftly caught it, then started pulling on Dynba's arm.
"Come on, we have to go."

Dynba pointed back toward the doorway. "Maybe it's a
trick."

"The Empire doesn't play jokes, Dynba. Eamon's
dead." Arali pulled her friend up the gangplank. "Let's
get out of here. We'll mourn Eamon on the trip, then
when we get to the New Republic, we'll find a way to get
even with the Empire."

Barris felt the comlink clipped to his belt vibrate like the
warning scales on a Gorgarian buzzadder. He opened his
arms to take in the whole of the crowd in his reception
room, then pointed them toward the eastern balcony.
"My friends, I have just been informed that the Rebels
have taken the bait in the trap that had been set for them.
If you will join me outside, I think you will find their end
a spectacular disaster."

Pulling the comlink from his belt, he thumbed it on.
"Garqi Eagles, you are clear to intercept and destroy your
target."

Arali got Dynba into one of the jumpseats in the cockpit
and strapped her in. "Barris got our last passenger, Captain. You better move now."

The Duros nodded to his mouse-eared pilot. The Sullustan chittered her way through a checklist. The low
hum of the repulsorlift drives filled the ship, then a gentle
tremble ran through it as the sublight drives began to
push it forward, up and out of the hangar. The nose of
the ship came around to the east, facing the ship away
from the sun and on a course that meant they would be
moving away from the star's mass as they left the planet.

That would permit them to enter hyperspace faster, and everyone on the ship knew speed was a virtue when escape was the object of the exercise.

Through the forward viewport Dynba got a spectacular look at the lights of Pesktda. She found the city where she grew up quaint and even beautiful, with lights winking on and off as gentle breezes stirred the dark, leafy canopy that covered everything. Part of her felt the loss of leaving the place of her birth, but that regret was nothing compared to the pain she felt over Eamon's murder.

The *Star's Delight* picked up speed and shot out of the spaceport. The Sullustan pilot kept the ship at a steady angle of ascent. As they broke above the shadow of the world, sunlight lit the sky. It passed quickly as the atmosphere thinned, then the stars above stopped shimmering and just hung there like distant jeweled sparks on the inside of a vast black bowl.

Captain Nootka hunched forward over a screen. "We have four starfighters in our wake. Shields to full in the aft arc."

The Sullustan hit a button on the console, but it remained dark. She hit it again, then shrieked.

Nootka reached over and hit the button himself. "Saricia, we have no shields."

"Invert and give me a shot." The Devaronian's bass voice came from above the companionway that led into the cockpit. Dynba looked back and saw an open hatchway that allowed access beyond the passage's ceiling.

Arali tightened down her restraining straps. "The blaster cannon turret is up top. We have to invert for him to shoot at targets coming from behind and below, otherwise he'll hit the cargo pods."

"Not a good design, is it?"

Nootka turned around and gave Dynba a hard stare. "This is a freighter, not a warship. Saricia is good."

"How good? Good enough to stop them?"

"Yes."

"Are you sure?"

The Duros shook his head. "If I am wrong, I will not live long in regret." He hit some more switches on the console. "You said the ship was in working order."

"That's what I was told. Eamon said . . ." Dynba's jaw dropped open. "He's not here."

The tips of the Twi'lek's head tails shook with a start. "We were set up, Dynba, set up to die by Eamon Yzalli." She flashed sharp peg-teeth. "I hope part of Xeno's work on Garqi is killing him."

Nootka glanced at his screen, then shook his head. "I would have hoped the situation would not get worse. We have a fifth ship closing fast." The ship shook violently and sparks shot through the companionway, while the thrummed rumble of Saricia's return-fire filled the cockpit. "Our armor will hold them back for a little while, but not long."

"Can we make the jump to lightspeed?"

"In the time we have left?" Nootka asked. "Not even if I knew where we were going and had the course already plotted into the nav computer. It looks now that where we are going is to the grave."

Corran Horn eased the X-wing's throttle forward and his speed started to climb faster as he left Garqi's atmosphere. "You should have told me sooner, Whistler, that's all I'm saying. It doesn't matter now, though. We can talk about it later. Now we have to get those TIEs."

The droid replied in a muted whistle that Corran found almost as depressing as the four-to-one odds on the fight. *Not how I wanted to do this, but I have no choice.*

Corran hit the thumb-switch on the X-wing's stick. The proton torpedo targeting system came up and painted a big yellow box around the slowest of the TIE starfighters. "That's target one. Give me the next closest one and mark it as target two."

Whistler complied instantly, then keened a question.

"Yes, if they're in range, get me comlink contact." Corran heard the hiss of static from the speakers in his helmet, then a clear channel opened up. "*Star's Delight*, the key-code for your shields is 349XER34, repeat 349XER34."

"Who is this?"

"Someone who just gave you your shields back. Eamon Yzalli sold you out. He's dead. What he *knew*, I *know*."

In the background he heard a voice excitedly shout, "It's Xeno!" The deeper voice, the one he decided belonged to Lai Nootka, overrode the shout. "349XER34 is the code."

"Exactly." Corran smiled. "Tell your gunner not to shoot the X-wing and I'll make his life easier. X-wing out."

Whistler tooted triumphantly.

"Not yet, buddy, not yet. Give me target one and lighten my acceleration compensator. I want to feel it when I move around." Nudging the stick over and back, he settled the box around the lagging TIE. The droid beeped intermittently as he tried to get a target lock. The target box went from yellow to red at the same moment Whistler's tone went solid and Corran hit the trigger.

The proton torpedo shot away from the X-wing and curved only slightly to port before it slammed into the TIE's ball-cockpit. The explosion shattered the starfighter's hexagonal solar panels. It sent their shards spinning away from the roiling, red-gold plasma ball spreading out from where the cockpit had once been.

"Acquire two."

Brief beeps melded into an uninterrupted tone as Corran hit a pedal and the etheric rudder brought the X-wing's nose around to port. He hit the trigger again and saw a proton torpedo burn into and through the second TIE. The torpedo hit it solidly on one of the solar panels and blasted through. The projectile glanced down, crushing the fighter's ion engine exhaust port and clipped the far side solar panel before exploding. The

TIE whirled off on a wobbly course before exhaust pressure from the engines tore the ship apart from the inside.

"Two down." Corran flipped his weapons control over to laser fire and linked the lasers for dual-fire. "Whistler, even out the shields."

The droid complied with the order as Corran brought the X-wing up in a quarter snap-roll. The maneuver stood the fighter on its port stabilizer foils. Tugging back on the stick, he brought the nose up and cruised onto the tail of one of the two remaining TIEs. It had broken left while its wing man had gone right—a strategy that was usually discouraged and went a long way toward confirming Corran's opinion of the Garqi garrison.

Whistler's excited hooting made Corran look up at his rear sensor monitor. *Coming in behind me. Not as bad as I thought.* "I see him, Whistler. Now you know why I didn't want to fight them at all."

The TIE in front of him began a slow loop to starboard. The move was slow enough that Corran was tempted to follow and light the ship up, but he knew giving in to temptation would have a price. *In this case it will be the TIE back there shortening the loop and melting my ship's tail. Not for me.*

Corran chopped his thrust back and pulled the stick to his breastbone. He looped the X-wing, then punched the throttle full forward and rolled out to port. That dropped him in on an attack vector to the TIE that had been following him. Tightening up on the trigger, he tracked ruby laser bolts across one solar panel, through the cockpit and into the other solar panel.

The TIE didn't explode. It rolled slowly to port, little blue tendrils of energy playing over its myriad surfaces. The X-wing overshot the ship, so Corran rolled and dove down through a loop to keep an eye on it. The TIE did not react and just continued spiraling along on its previous course, bound for a fiery collision with Garqi's atmosphere.

Pilot's gone, ship's running on momentum. Corran shivered, imagining for one second what it was like to spend your last seconds of life in pain, in a breached cockpit with all the atmosphere leaking out while cold poured in. *Not the way I want to go.*

Whistler's indignant yowl and the hiss of laser fire splashing against his aft shields shocked Corran. He immediately hit the right rudder pedal, whipping the X-wing's tail to port and out of the line of fire. Pushing the stick hard left, he rolled out to port, then pulled back and brought the ship's nose up and around in a loop. Halfway through that he rolled right and dove, but his sensors showed the TIE was still with him.

Why are the best guys always the last? Corran smiled at his own question. "Because the pilots who are bad die first. They were all probably daydreaming just like you." He sideslipped the X-wing to the right and the TIE followed him.

"Whistler, get me the *Delight* again."

"Nootka here, X-wing."

"Captain, this guy on me is good. Kill your shields and tell your gunner to shoot high."

"We just got our shields back."

"I know. Kill your shields."

"I do not understand."

"You will."

Corran rolled the fighter out to port, then kept a light hand on the stick. Nudging it left and right, up and back, he made the X-wing dance almost unpredictably. After every third or fourth move, when the ship had drifted to port, he'd push the stick down, then up right and right again. He'd level out and fly straight for a couple of seconds, then after that the random pattern would begin again.

When he saw the TIE begin to anticipate his pattern, Corran pulled the X-wing back through a big loop and dove straight in on an intercept course for the *Delight*. "Full shields aft, Whistler." Corran dipped and jerked the fighter through its pattern. Laser fire came in from the *Delight,* passing over his ship, but only by a margin of decimeters.

The TIE kept to Corran's tail as the X-wing turned and swooped down into a run that took it from bow to stern on the *Delight.* The TIE came in tight and sank below the level of the ship's fire. *He's low enough to strike sparks! This Imp's very good.* Corran smiled. *I gotta hope I'm better.*

As Corran's pattern ended, the X-wing drifted into a gentle glide along the *Delight's* spine. The TIE dropped in behind him and lined up for a shot. The first laser blasts hit the X-wing's aft shield and rocked Corran in the cockpit. *Now or never!*

Corran killed his thrust and cut his repulsorlift drives in at full strength. Acceleration jammed him down in the cockpit couch as the X-wing bounced up and away from the freighter's mass. The TIE starfighter shot through beneath the X-wing, pulling up abruptly to miss the freighter's engine cowling.

Punching the throttle forward and killing the lift drives, Corran sailed in on the TIE's aft. His targeting box went green. He pulled the trigger and filled the last TIE with laser fire.

The scarlet energy darts shredded the ship, puncturing the cockpit and melting their way through the twin ion engines. The TIE exploded brilliantly. The glittering plasma sphere burned like a star going nova, then imploded, leaving the void in its wake.

"X-wing, this is *Delight.* May we put our shields back up?"

"Affirmative, *Delight.*" Corran smiled. "Captain Nootka, have you got a course plotted out of here?"

"We have a course, X-wing."

"If you don't mind, I'll slave my navigation to yours and tag along. After all, I still owe you for the debris extractor."

"Consider the debt paid, X-wing, but come on along." Corran heard gratitude in the Duros captain's voice.

"This adventure will be a tale to tell, and I would have you there when I first tell it."

Prefect Mosh Barris bowed graciously amid the applause from his guests. The series of bright explosions and the spectacular light show of debris streaking through the upper atmosphere had been far more than he expected. *If you arranged that on purpose, Eamon, I shall give you rewards in excess of what I had already planned.*

He held a hand up. "Thank you, thank you all. I am pleased you have enjoyed how we have eliminated the Rebel threat to Garqi." Barris smiled proudly. "I was the architect of this event, but another carried it out. My aide, Eamon Yzalli. Eamon, where are you?"

"Indeed, where is he?"

Barris' head came up as a sharp voice asked the question from the balcony doorway. "Who are you?"

A tall, hatchet-faced man stooped slightly to make it through the door, then fixed Barris with a harsh stare. "I am Kirtan Loor, Imperial Intelligence. You have been expecting me?"

"Of course." Barris gestured up at the sky, spraying choholl from the glass in his hand. "You came too late to see what happened to the Rebels."

"Oh, I think I already know what happened to them." The Imperial officer's lip curled in a sneer. "As I came into the system, I was sent a report by this Eamon Yzalli. It indicates you arranged for the escape of the local Rebel organization on the *Star's Delight*. The report indicates this action was the preliminary gambit in your bid to usurp Governor Tadrin and transfer Garqi to the Rebel Alliance."

Barris' stomach slowly wriggled into a knot. Kirtan Loor reminded him of a young Grand Moff Tarkin, and the resemblance did nothing to stop the fear flooding Barris' mind. "This is wrong. This cannot be. Eamon must have planned this. Ask him, the accusations are not true."

"I would ask him, but I cannot find him." Loor's blue eyes narrowed. "An appendix to his report said he feared for his life at your hands. When I arrived here I read that you had ordered and carried out his elimination. That message came from you, directly, I've checked."

"Yes, but it was all part of the plan, don't you see?"

Kirtan Loor shook his head solemnly. "I don't see what you want me to see. What I *do* see is a Rebel collaborator with much to tell me about the enemy."

"But I know nothing about them."

"I doubt that very sincerely, Barris." Loor smiled with a cold superiority that weakened Barris' knees and sent his glass crashing to the floor. "By the time your interrogation is barely started, you will wish you knew even more, so you could tell me everything. You will be surprised how much information there truly is in your *nothing*—and you will learn to dread your punishment whenever you seek to feign ignorance as a shield."

Corran had fully expected the look of surprise on Dynba Tesc's face when she first saw him. "Greetings, Dynba. I'm glad you made it. I apologize for the rough time the *Delight* had."

The war between horror and joy in her expression even proved entertaining, though the ultimate victor in the struggle proved to be a stunned look. "Y-you're dead . . . at least you said you were dead. You're Eamon Yzalli, but you can't be."

Corran winced as hurt entered her voice. He scratched at his beard for a second, then shrugged. "I'm sorry for the deception. I intended for you to assume Barris had killed me and take off. I knew the TIEs would head out after you. I wanted to use you as a diversion one more time, so I could get away while the TIEs were busy with you."

A Twi'lek walked up behind Dynba and draped a head tail over her shoulder protectively. "The TIEs almost did us in because you disabled the shields. You tried to have us killed."

"Not my intention at all." Corran sighed. "I meant to have a message sent to you that would give you the code to bring the shields back up. I wanted to blame the shield tampering on Barris and have you protected, but the old fool went and deactivated my message account when he entered his death declaration about Eamon."

Dynba dug a gentle elbow into the Twi'lek's midsection. "Arali, if he wanted us dead, he'd not have come after the TIEs and given us the code. He still could have gotten away."

"Right." Corran nodded. "Exactly."

"So what did you mean about using us as a diversion 'one more time'?"

"Setting up the *Star's Delight*'s escape allowed me to get the spare parts I needed for the X-wing. I told Barris they had been stolen from storage, but I really just had the guys who helped me load the things put them in the back of my speeder. They were the TIE pilots, so now we're the only ones who know where the parts ended up."

Dynba smiled. "The parts, of course. The phantom X-wing flights ended about a month before the *Delight* showed up and was taken."

"I needed a debris extractor."

"So, then, you're Xeno. You got us together to eventually steal those parts for you."

"No, I'm Corran Horn, late of the Corellian Security Force." He smiled as Whistler came rolling up and patted the droid affectionately on the dome. "The droid here was Xeno."

Arali's head tails twitched with surprise. "A droid organized our little group?"

Whistler chirped emphatically and Corran beamed. "He worked with me in CorSec. In addition to astrogation programming, he's a fairly good codeslicer and had a facility for putting together sting operations. He was grooming you to get the parts for me, but he didn't mention it because he knows I don't really want anything to do with the Rebellion and the New Republic."

"It is a little late for that." Captain Nootka came walking over with two Republic officers in tow. "Helping us escape will lead Barris to figure out who you were, and you will be branded a Rebel."

"I don't think so. Barris is in plenty of trouble himself." Corran smiled broadly. "I once worked with Kirtan Loor, the Imperial Intelligence agent heading in to Garqi. This beard and dye job wouldn't have fooled him, so I had to move. That's the reason this whole operation got put together and involved you and your friends, Dynba. I would have kept you out of it, but I couldn't."

She shook her head. "You may think that, Corran, and may even want to believe it, but I think you couldn't leave us behind to face Barris' wrath if you weren't around to moderate him."

Maybe you're right, Dynba, but there is no true way of knowing. He nodded slowly. "Loor isn't the brightest of Imperial agents, but he can solve a case when it's handed to him in a package, and the package I left behind neatly implicates Mosh Barris in treason and Eamon Yzalli's murder. I should be clear."

One of the New Republic officers pointed at the X-wing. "That fighter just burned down four TIEs?"

Nootka tapped Corran on the shoulder. "He had the kills, Captain Dromath."

The other Rebel whistled. "They never got through your shields."

Corran shrugged. "Recharging shields is easier than finding paint to match."

The first officer nodded. "Look, Horn, I heard you say you don't want anything to do with the Rebellion or New Republic, but we need fighters like you."

"I'm not a joiner, Captain." Corran shook his head, then frowned down at Whistler when the droid jeered. "All I want is to be left alone. Your fight isn't my fight."

Dromath shrugged. "Perhaps not, but you're smart

enough to know the Empire won't leave you alone. You will fight them, just as you did in getting these folks out of Garqi. If you have to fight them, doing so with allies is a lot better than doing it alone."

"He's right, Corran." Dynba reached out and gave Corran's left hand a squeeze. "The New Republic needs you."

"I don't know."

"Not an easy decision to make, true." Dromath smiled. "Think about this, though—orders came through letting us know Rogue Squadron is being reformed and brought back to active duty. Any pilots who think they're good enough to join are encouraged to apply. From what Nootka said, you're good enough to at least look into it."

Whistler squawked derisively.

Corran rapped a knuckle on the droid's dome. "I'm better than that, and you know it. I could be one of the hottest pilots they've got. Of course, I'd need a new R2 unit."

The droid's blatted reply prompted laughter from everyone. Corran suddenly realized, as he heard their voices all mix together, that he'd not heard good, honest laughter in all the time he'd been on the run and in service on Garqi. Among the Imperials and their citizenry there was always something held back, a hedge against self-betrayal. *People couldn't let themselves go for fear someone might think ill of them and report them to the authorities.*

He thought for a moment. He knew all he really wanted was to be left alone, but Dromath had been right—the Empire would never leave him alone. Even if they were not there directly, even if Loor wasn't hot on his tail, the Empire's shadow would touch him except in places where it could not survive.

Among the Rebels.

In the New Republic.

"As being left alone isn't an option, I guess I might as well choose the folks with whom I have to co-exist." Corran slowly smiled and extended his hand to Captain

Dromath. "If I heard you correctly, I think Whistler and I just might have an interest in joining Rogue Squadron."

"It won't be easy, Mister Horn."

"From what I've heard, Captain, it wouldn't be Rogue Squadron if joining was easy. But easy I don't want." Corran winked at Nootka and smiled at Dynba. "Remember, I've just left a backwater world where my droid led a Rebel cell and I helped evacuate enemies of the state, all the while plotting to bring down the military prefect. After that, the only place I'll find enough excitement to suit Whistler here is with the folks who have two Death Star kills to their credit. If I were willing to settle for anything less, I'd be joining the Imperial Navy and thinking it was a good career move."

It occurred to Barris, as guards dragged him toward the interrogation chamber, that his ears had been as deaf to Dynba Tesc's protests of ignorance as Loor's would be to his. It struck him as ironic that his descent had begun when he had done nothing on a world far away, and it would end because he *knew* nothing on a world far away. He sought to share this insight with the men beside him, but it would only leave his throat disguised as hesitant laughter, punctuated by sobs.

And, somehow, he knew they understood.

Retreat from Coruscant

by Laurie Burns

Taryn Clancy idly watched a comm clerk notarize accep-
tance of the datacards piled on the repulsorlift cart
beside her. Suddenly, the background murmur of the old
Imperial Palace's message center disappeared under the
hooting of alarms.

The clerk looked up, face draining of color as she identified the warning tones. "Oh my skies," she said, sounding stunned. "Coruscant's under attack."

Taryn's eyes widened too, but she moved fast. "If you'll

sign that off, I'll be on my way," she said, swiveling to push the cart closer to the clerk's counter. "There's your mail," she added, pointedly holding out her hand.

The clerk blinked, looked at her datapad, punched a few keys, and mutely handed it over. Taryn swiftly inspected her authorization, keyed in her own code, then jerked the clerk's copy out and tossed it on the counter. "Thanks," she said over her shoulder, already three steps toward the door.

Out in the corridor the alarms continued at an urgent pitch, but as she squeezed aboard a turbolift, Taryn was relieved no one seemed panicked. Though the New Republic had made the transition from military force to galactic government, the former Rebels obviously hadn't forgotten how to react to an Imperial attack. She bit her lip, knowing her hopes of leaving were optimistic at best. If Coruscant really was under attack, the planetary shield had probably been raised, and she and Del were stuck for the duration.

But she had to try. After all, who wanted to be stuck on the palace's landing pads like a clipped mynock while the Empire tried to reclaim its former capital?

Not me, she thought, emerging onto the bright, windswept platform and blinking at the brilliance of the midday sun. Reverberations from half-a-dozen ships' engines thrummed around her, and ahead, the *Messenger* added its throaty roar to the mechanical chorus. Del had the ramp down and waiting, and as she dropped into the pilot's seat, a quick scan of the displays showed they were nearly ready to lift.

"Heard the alarms," Del said, already strapped in at the co-pilot's station. "What's up?"

"Us, I hope," Taryn said shortly. Another look at the displays, and she flipped on the comm and hailed palace flight control. Her heart sank as her request for liftoff was curtly denied.

Too late—the planetary shield had been raised. The

Empire was up there, the New Republic was down here, and she and the *Messenger* were stuck in between.

Taryn slumped back in her seat. It wasn't just that she had a schedule to keep. The Core Courier Service promised prompt service among the Core Worlds, and with crates full of communications still filling half her hold, she didn't want to get too far behind. But late deliveries were nothing compared to what Taryn feared was about to happen—an all-out war for possession of Coruscant. Port gossip had predicted that the Empire, despite the recent loss of Grand Admiral Thrawn, was gearing up to strike at the heart of the New Republic.

It looked like they'd been right.

"Well, heck," Del said, staring out at the platform where a transport—apparently in defiance of the controller's orders—was lifting off. "What're we gonna do now?"

Taryn watched the transport fade to a pinprick in the sky. If the *Messenger* belonged to her, she'd be tempted to do the same. But a smart captain didn't take chances with company property. "We wait," she said, reluctantly keying off the engines. "At least until help arrives."

If it ever did, she added silently. The Imperials would've knocked out the comm relays first thing, cutting off the New Republic's ability to call for help from its fleets scattered through the galaxy. They had orbital defenses, of course, but—A tiny flash caught her eye, and she leaned forward to squint out the cockpit's transparisteel viewport. "Blast," she whispered.

Del followed her gaze and saw the almost indiscernible flashes of turbolaser fire high in the sky. "We're stuck now," he said.

They watched in grim silence for a while before Taryn abruptly wondered, "How long can the planetary shield hold up?"

"I dunno," Del said. "Depends on what they throw at it, prob'ly. Couple of days, maybe . . . or a couple hours."

She glanced at him. Under his gray mustache, her first

mate's mouth was tight. And no wonder—after three decades with the courier service, he was just days away from retirement. Studying the lines on his face, Taryn mentally contrasted his years of experience to her own, and suddenly felt overwhelmed with her fledgling status as captain. It *was* only her fourth run at the helm of the *Messenger*.

And it was up to her to get them out of this.

For a second she felt a niggling of the old fear; the one with her father's voice that said she flew for the courier service because she didn't have the guts to do anything else. All through her childhood, Kal Clancy boasted of his own bravado at the helm of his freighter, then he'd spent her teen years trying to mold her in his image. He hadn't bothered concealing his disappointment when she hadn't lived up to his expectations.

She looked at Del again. He'd been delivering mail longer than she'd been alive, and hadn't ever made captain. That said something for her, didn't it? *Didn't it?*

Stop it, Taryn ordered herself. *So being captain of a courier isn't very challenging. That doesn't mean I'm not competent.*

Shaking off her father's image, she tried to think what to do next.

Does it?

After a few hours passed with no sign of Imperial ships slipping down from the sky, Taryn's nerves began to ease. Seven hours after the alarms first sounded, full night had fallen, and she was starting to get annoyed.

"Well, that's it," she declared after another request for information from flight control was politely sidestepped. "We can't leave, they won't let us move, and they won't tell us anything. I'm going in there to find out what's going on."

"Who you gonna ask?" Del asked.

"Mon Mothma herself, if I have to," Taryn said.

Del snorted, but getting into the palace proved unexpectedly easy. After an initial hassle with two New Republic security officers, once they discovered she captained the freighter on the platform, Taryn found herself ushered into a turbolift. One of the guards poked his head in after her and punched a button on the call panel. "Good luck," he said, giving her a mock salute as the doors slid shut.

That was easy—too easy, she thought, wondering what that salute thing meant. She was still puzzling over it when the doors opened on a corridor clearly far removed from the service section of the palace where she'd made her delivery earlier. Same basic decor, but this section had an unmistakably brisk military air.

As did the two armed troopers standing against the wall across from the turbolift. They eyed her alertly as she stepped out, then she saw the other two, standing on each side of the lift. Trying to ignore the four pairs of eyes trained on her, she glanced down the corridor. At one end, a blast door slid open and a frowning officer stalked toward her. Halting a meter away, he gave her a quick once-over.

"I'm Colonel Bremen," he identified himself. "And you're—?"

"Taryn Clancy, captain of the *Messenger.*"

He nodded curtly. "If you're armed, you'll have to leave your weapons outside," he said, producing a hand-held weapons scanner.

"I'm not," Taryn said, but Bremen ran the device over her anyway.

"All right," he said, apparently satisfied. "Follow me."

A guard fell in line behind her as Taryn followed Bremen through the blast doors into another corridor. She glanced curiously into open rooms as they passed, feet faltering as a face she thought she recognized from the holovid flashed into view. Was that *really* Mon Mothma? And if it *were* the New Republic's Chief of State, just where was this Bremen taking her?

There was no time to speculate, as he stopped beside a

door and gestured for her to enter. Taryn stepped into the small office and looked at the man seated behind the desk. Good-looking and about the same age as Del, he looked vaguely familiar but she couldn't place him.

That is, until Bremen shut the door and brushed past her. "Got another one for you, General Bel Iblis. Captain Clancy of the *Messenger*," he said, and Taryn tried not to stare. She'd expected to be pawned off on some palace flunky, not brought to the man in charge of Coruscant's defense!

"Captain Clancy." Bel Iblis nodded to her courteously as Bremen folded his arms and took up a position against the office wall. "I understand you'd like an update on the situation."

"Yes, sir, I would," she said, making a conscious effort to relax and not stand at attention. "What's going on? And when will I be able to leave?"

Bel Iblis studied her silently. Just as Taryn began to fear she'd been too brash, he grimly answered. "Coruscant is surrounded. Our defenses have been forced to retreat, and we estimate the planetary shield will fail by morning."

Taryn forgot not to stare. "What'll happen then?"

"We're not waiting to find out," he said. "We'll be pulling out tonight."

"You're leaving?"

"We have no choice," Bel Iblis said heavily. "There's no way to get word to our fleets in other sectors, and even if we did, they couldn't get here before the shield fails."

"But, what about the New Republic?" she persisted. Was the fledgling government really going to crumble that easily?

"The New Republic will survive," he said. "Only its headquarters will move." Something like old pain briefly shadowed his eyes. "We don't want Coruscant destroyed too, when all the Empire wants is to destroy us. Once we're off the planet, the populace ought to be safe enough."

Bremen abruptly unfolded from the wall and opened his mouth, but subsided at a look from Bel Iblis. Taryn glanced from one to the other, suddenly aware of the tension between them, then looked back at Bel Iblis. "Where will you go?"

"Good question," he said. "That's where you come in."

"Me?" she said, warily.

"We need all the lifting capacity we can beg, borrow, or steal for the evacuation," he said, watching her intently.

Taryn got it, right away.

"The *Messenger*'s not that big," she protested. "Not that fast, either. Besides, I work for the Core Courier Service, not for you. The New Republic can't just hijack my ship!"

"Actually, we can," Bel Iblis said. "And will. But not for what you think." He leaned forward, looking grave. "We've got to get word to the sector fleets that the New Republic has evacuated Coruscant and will regroup at a new base. Secrecy is absolutely vital—we can't take the chance of the Empire tapping into any transmissions and overhearing the location of our rendezvous point. So," he spread his hands suggestively, "we send out couriers."

Taryn remained silent. She suspected he hadn't said "courier" by chance.

"Usually, we'd send out a messenger in an unmarked Intelligence ship," Bel Iblis said. Bremen opened his mouth, and again, the general shot him a warning glance. "But we need everything we've got for the evacuation."

"What if I refuse?"

"You're welcome to remain here on Coruscant," Bel Iblis said. "Or leave on one of our transports. We'll recompense the courier service for use of the ship, of course."

Some choice, Taryn thought sourly. *Stuck here waiting for the stormtroopers, or on the run with the New Republic.*

She sighed. "So, when do we leave?"

. . .

Once she'd thought about it, Taryn had to agree using the *Messenger* for cover was actually pretty clever.

For one, the datacard—with its report on the retreat from Coruscant and the rendezvous location—was nicely anonymous, tucked in a crate with thousands of other datacards; communications bound for other Core Worlds. And that crate was just one among dozens exactly like it, stacked one on top of the other in the *Messenger*'s hold.

For another, the prospect of trying to sneak past an armada of Star Destroyers was almost made bearable by the sight the bulky Colonel Bremen made, stuffed into a spare uniform they'd scrounged up that was at least two sizes too small. Tugging at the too-tight collar, he stood in the cockpit doorway with the slight frown that never seemed to leave his face. Taryn didn't have to look away from her engine displays to know the uniform's pant legs ended somewhere above his ankles. Her mouth quirked slightly before she remembered Bremen was here to keep an eye on her and Del, and there was nothing funny about the situation they were in.

Her hands tightened on the controls. "Go strap in," she ordered Bremen. "We're almost ready to lift." When he didn't move, she glanced over her shoulder questioningly. "What?"

"I'll stay here," he said.

She shrugged.

"Do what you want." Del snorted. He and Bremen hadn't exchanged half a dozen words since the New Republic officer had come on board, but they clearly hadn't hit it off.

"You should let me pilot," Bremen said, again. "This isn't some simple mail drop, you know."

"No," Taryn said adamantly, as if this hadn't already been covered in Bel Iblis' office. "We made a deal. The New Republic can use my ship, but no one's flying it but me." Considering they were basically being shanghaied, she'd been surprised Bel Iblis had agreed. As it was, she half suspected the general had assigned Bremen to this mission just to get rid of him. The two clearly didn't get along. She glanced at Del. "Ready?"

"Ready," he confirmed.

She eased in the repulsors. Below, the comforting lights of Imperial City dwindled to pinpricks as they gained altitude. Bel Iblis had said the gaps between the surrounding Star Destroyers were guarded by smaller capital ships, so each pilot would have to pick their own escape route and make a run for it. "We got a course yet?" she asked Del.

"Nav computer's working on it," he said. She threw a quick look at Bremen, balancing himself in the cockpit's doorway, then checked the sensors. Nothing close enough to worry about, but she'd have to stay sharp. Bel Iblis wanted as many ships as possible in the air and moving when he dropped the shield. With the whole swarm fleeing at once, they hoped to at least create a little confusion as they tried to sneak past the waiting Imperials.

Flashes of light danced where the planetary shield was still getting blasted, the opalescent haze shifting and rippling as it was hit. Taryn changed course slightly, aiming for a clear spot, then checked her chronometer. Almost time.

Del flipped on the comm, already tuned to the escape frequency, and as Taryn stared at the shield, she wondered what the people left below would face. Would the Empire be content to simply retake Coruscant and leave its citizens in relative peace? Or would it feel the need to punish them for not repulsing the New Republic in the first place?

Either way, she was out of it now.

"Ought to be down any time," Bremen said from behind her, where he too was watching the shield flash under the Imperial assault. "Too bad this thing doesn't have much in the way of weaponry."

Taryn's mouth tightened at the slur to her ship. As she'd already pointed out, mail freighters weren't prime targets for anyone, even pirates. There was no need to go around bristling with armament—usually. At the moment, she conceded a little more firepower might come in handy.

Several large masses started to register on the scopes, indicating the gauntlet ahead. Taryn had never seen so many Star Destroyers in one place, and another wave of self-doubt assailed her. She'd never done anything like this before, except in her imagination. Maybe she *should* let Bremen take the controls—

And then, it was too late.

"It's down," Bel Iblis' voice rang out over the comm. "Clear skies, people, and may the Force be with you!"

The planetary shield was down, and the scramble was on.

Far to port, Taryn was aware of a planet defender ion cannon being used from the surface to clear a path for some of the fleeing ships, but she kept to her own vector as they cleared the atmosphere and the waiting Imperial ships came into sight.

There it was—her path to freedom—straight between two Star Destroyers flanked by five smaller Dreadnaughts. They looked like two ferocious Dorax dogs surrounded by feisty puppies, and she swallowed, edging the drive up to full. Even at top speed, the *Messenger* couldn't be called fast, and she could only hope they'd be overlooked in the swarm fleeing from the surface.

And for a while, her hopes seemed answered. Aiming for a gap between the two Dreadnaughts furthest away from the Star Destroyers, the *Messenger* pelted along in the wake of another freighter, a transport, and a sleek starfighter. Alongside and slightly behind were two heavy transports. The Dreadnaughts fired, but with so many small targets, the shots were erratic and for the most part simply sizzled into space.

Their shield indicators were still green, they were nearly past the Dreadnaughts, and Taryn was beginning to think they just might make it unscathed when a sudden sharp lurch of the ship threw her and Del against their restraints, and sent Bremen tumbling forward to sprawl unceremoniously over the sensor scopes.

"Get off!" she gritted, then clenched her teeth as another hard *thunk* spilled him to the deck. With a jolt, she saw a lot more ships around them than had been there a moment ago. Identification was easy as a TIE fighter roared past, firing at the transport ahead of them driving for deep space.

"Del?" she said. The grizzled first mate needed no further urging, loosing a volley of laser fire at the TIE fighter harassing the transport up ahead. Behind them, a dull *clunk* indicated another hit, but Taryn kept going. Their course was calculated and set; if she could just get the *Messenger* a little further away from the planet, they could make the jump to lightspeed, and safety.

One of the transports off to their side suddenly exploded in a fiery flash. Wincing, Taryn changed course slightly to steer clear of the twisted metal and spared a quick glance at the shield indicators.

Only to wish she hadn't. The indicators had gone from green to red, and they flashed with each hit. A diagnostic message was forming on the panel, the sensors showed another of those blasted TIE fighters swooping up behind them, and Taryn didn't think the *Messenger* could take too many more hits.

"Hang on," she warned Bremen, still on the deck, and threw the freighter into a dive. The TIE fighter shot past overhead, and as she brought the ship's nose back up, Taryn saw the starfighter ahead had circled back to help.

The X-wing's laser cannon flashed as it screamed toward them, and on the scopes, one of the dots behind them disappeared. The X-wing turned its attention to the TIE fighter she'd shaken while Taryn swiped at the sweat on her face and put the drive to full again. Up ahead, the freighter and transport were nowhere to be seen. Either they'd already made it to safety—or they'd been destroyed.

Del cursed as the *Messenger* shuddered from another series of hits to the rear. The shield indicators flashed red, then went black, and the diagnostic message began to blink. "We've lost the deflectors," Taryn shouted. Swallowing back the metallic taste of fear, she was poised to plunge the ship into another dive when the console pinged, indicating they'd reached their hyperspace point.

Wrapping a hand around the levers and acutely aware of the TIE fighter closing in on them, she gently pulled back, and was rewarded by the sight of stars streaking to starlines, then fading into the mottled sky of hyperspace.

Hurtling through hyperspace toward Coriallis, Del and Colonel Bremen had plenty of time to firmly establish their mutual dislike.

Bremen didn't hide the fact that, as civilians, he didn't trust Taryn and Del to be competent. He made it clear he thought Bel Iblis should have commandeered the *Messenger*, kicked off her regular crew, and used an all-military crew to complete the mission.

Taryn tried to shrug it off, but Del retaliated by offering up barely concealed barbs concerning the New Republic's ignominious retreat from Coruscant, while Bremen grew tighter-lipped with each crack. She thought the game childish, but as long as Bremen was busy with Del, he wasn't breathing down her back, so she didn't say anything about it.

The two had disappeared into the hold more than an hour ago, and she stood in the wardroom, wiping grease off her hands. They would be changing course at Coriallis in a few hours, and she wanted to try out the newly repaired deflector system before it was actually put to the test.

She never got the chance.

As she strode toward the cockpit, the *Messenger* seemed to hesitate underfoot, then gave an awful shudder as stressed hull metal squealed in protest. Caught mid-step,

Taryn grabbed at the bulkhead for balance, then got thrown into the cockpit as the ship seemed to slam into some immovable force. Clattering crates and a yelp sounded from the hold, while in front of her, the mottled sky of hyperspace unexpectedly became starlines, and then, with a final sickening lurch, coalesced into the starfield of realspace.

They'd been forcefully yanked out of lightspeed, and Taryn didn't even have to check the scopes to know why. Straight ahead, filling the transparisteel viewport, was an Imperial Interdictor cruiser.

Nor were they its first catch. A transport with New Republic markings drifted nearby, linked with an Imperial shuttle. Taryn wondered if it were one of the many that had so recently fled Coruscant.

"What happened?" Bremen demanded, pounding up the corridor as she got to her feet. On his heels, Del sported a fresh gash on his forehead. No answer was necessary as the comm crackled to life and a brisk voice from the cruiser *Requital* ordered them to prepare to be boarded.

Taryn sank down in the pilot's seat, mind racing. The datacard was well-hidden, and unless the Imperials were determined to read each and every missive in the hold, she didn't think they'd find it. The thoroughness of their search would probably depend on how suspicious they were. Her and Del's identification was in order; Bremen might be harder to explain, but she'd think of something. Should she admit that they'd just come from Coruscant, or—?

"I'll do the talking," Bremen announced, interrupting her thoughts. "You two keep quiet and let me handle it." He held out a hand, apparently expecting Taryn to hand over the captain's bars pinned to the front of her uniform. She stiffened.

"No, *I'll* do the talking," she corrected him with some asperity. "You looked in a mirror lately?" Clad in that ill-fitting uniform, the Imperials would never believe he was

captain of the *Messenger*. Ignoring Bremen's flush of outrage, she told Del, "Go back to the airlock and wait to
assist the boarding party."

"Yes, ma'am," he said crisply, backing out of the cockpit.

"Cooperate with them, *fully*," she called after him
warningly. Outside, a shuttle from the *Requital* was approaching, but they still had a few minutes. Looking at
Bremen, she raised an eyebrow. "Now. You were saying—?"

"Do you have any idea how serious this is?" he snapped
back. "What do you think they're going to do once
they're on board? Take a look at your permits, tell you to
have a good day, and just leave?"

"I certainly hope so," Taryn said. "That seemed to be
General Bel Iblis' idea behind using us as the courier.
Look, *I'm* the captain here, and *I* have the proper ID to
back it up. You have any better ideas?"

His resistance was plain, but she did have a point.
"Okay, then," Taryn said. "You don't talk unless you're
spoken to, you do everything the Imperials ask, promptly
and courteously, and if you're carrying any weapons, you
lose them now, before they come on board. Understand?"

Bremen's face looked as stiff as a droid's and his eyes
glittered, but he managed a short nod. "Good," Taryn
said, releasing a breath she hadn't realized she'd been
holding. "Let's go back and meet our guests."

While the Imperial shuttle pulled alongside, she dug
out the *Messenger*'s permits datapad. She just had time to
get back to the airlock and straighten up authoritatively
before it slid open and five Imperials strode in.

The lead, a middle-aged man balding under his naval
officer's cap, halted just inside while the other four troopers, all armed, fanned out in the corridor. "Commander
Voldt," he briskly identified himself. "Who's in charge
here?"

"I am." Taryn stepped forward. "Captain Taryn Clancy, of the Core Courier Service. This is my crew."

Voldt eyed her, gaze lingering on the curves of her uniform, then slid a glance over Del and Bremen. He noted Bremen's exposed ankles, then flicked pale eyes back to her. "Courier service? This a mail ship?"

"Yes, sir," Taryn said. "En route to Coriallis."

"Where from?"

She'd already decided there was no sense lying. The vector on which they'd been yanked out of hyperspace pretty well spelled it out. "Our last scheduled stop was Coruscant," she told him. "But we dropped into the system, saw what looked like the entire Imperial fleet around the planet, and decided to give the place a pass. Didn't want to get mixed up in anything, you know?"

He nodded slowly, not looking entirely convinced. "You didn't deliver your shipment?" he asked. "Don't your employers promise prompt delivery?"

Taryn allowed herself to look slightly taken aback. "Well, yes," she said. "But they frown on dropping in on a war zone even more."

Voldt stared at her, then snorted. In amusement, or disbelief, she couldn't tell. At his casual hand gesture, two of the troopers disappeared to search the ship. "Let's see some identification," he suggested.

"Certainly." Taryn passed him the permits datapad. He transmitted the ship's license and registry information to the *Requital* to be checked out, then inspected their identification, raising an eyebrow when Bremen failed to produce an ID. Bremen managed to look both embarrassed and earnest as he muttered, "Sorry, sir. Got robbed in port."

Voldt flicked that speculative glance over his uniform again. "Looks like that's not all they took," he commented. "How inconvenient for you."

Bremen nodded. Voldt stared at him a moment longer, then glanced at the two troopers returning from searching the ship. "No one else aboard, sir," one reported, while the other stepped up holding two blasters.

"Who do these belong to?" Voldt asked.

"That one's mine," Taryn said, indicating the blaster she kept hidden under the sleep pad in her cabin. She looked at Bremen and Del. "Whose is this?"

"Mine, Capt'n." Del stepped forward. "I know you don't like us carryin' on board, so I had it stashed in my bunk. Sorry," he added, looking sheepish.

"We'll discuss it later," she said repressively, wondering where Bremen had "lost" his weapon so it wouldn't be found.

Voldt gave her an unfathomable look, then nodded to the trooper, who stepped back, still holding both blasters. He handed the datapad back to Taryn. "Captain, I'd like to see the contents of your hold, if I may."

Despite the phrasing, it wasn't a request.

Taryn led the way, trying to gauge how suspicious the Imperials were, and how complete they might insist on making this search. So far, Voldt's manner hadn't given anything away. Casually, she looked over her shoulder. "If you don't mind me asking, sir, why were we stopped? Is this some sort of checkpoint?"

There was no mistaking the amused snort this time. "You could call it that," Voldt said dryly. His eyes were fixed on the sway of her dark hair against her back. "It could be considered a checkpoint for traitors."

"Traitors?" she echoed, carefully.

"Traitors to the Empire," he said, finally looking up as they reached the hold. "Rebels, fleeing from Coruscant. We've driven them off and rescued the populace from their terrorist ways, but now, like the cowards they are, they're scurrying off to wherever they think they'll find safety." His thin lips turned up in an unpleasant smile. "We don't intend to let them run too far."

Taryn wondered if Interdictor cruisers were sitting along all of the most well-traveled hyperspace lanes leading from Coruscant. If so, a good many fleeing ships had undoubtedly fallen right into the Imperials' trap, including that transport she'd spotted earlier. Perhaps even themselves.

She shook off the thought. *No, so far we're doing fine.* The only thing to worry about was the datacard, and that was well hidden somewhere inside the crates that filled the hold. Reassured, she keyed open the door and gestured for Voldt to step in.

He did, glancing around the room and then stepping over to peer at the stacks of sealed crates. "These are bound for Coriallis," he noted, studying the labels on the outermost crates.

"Yes, sir, that's our next stop," Taryn confirmed.

"But where's the shipment you *didn't* leave on Coruscant?" He swung to face her, one eyebrow raised in query.

Where was it, indeed? Taryn's stomach clenched as she considered the question. Not only had they delivered the mail bound for the Imperial Palace, but they'd off-loaded the regular Coruscant mail, too. There was nothing here to back up her assertion that they hadn't landed on the planet.

Excuses vied for space on the tip of her tongue, but before she could blurt any of them out, Del stepped forward.

"I moved 'em out of the way, Capt'n," he said, and indicated three crates piled haphazardly in the far corner. Each was labeled bound for Coruscant, and she held her breath as Voldt insisted on opening up all three. But randomly picking out datacards to inspect, he found them all properly labeled with Coruscant destinations. Relieved, Taryn slanted a glance at her first mate, wondering whose mail had been borrowed to pull off this masquerade. Clearly, Del and Bremen hadn't spent *all* their time back here bickering.

"Hmmph," Voldt grunted as he replaced the last crate's lid, and looked around the hold as if hoping to find Mon Mothma herself hiding among the load lifters.

Pointing at two of the troopers, he ordered all the crates examined. But the search was cursory, with the troopers merely opening them up and confirming there was mail inside.

Brusquely ordering the crates resealed, Voldt motioned for Taryn and crew to follow him, and strode back down the corridor to the airlock. Calling the *Requital,* he confirmed that the *Messenger*'s permits were in order and then, looking somewhat disappointed, told Taryn they were free to go.

Trying not to let her relief show, she had to work harder to keep from shooting a told-you-so look at Bremen. The four troopers rejoined them, and after an unexpected handshake from Voldt, during which he held on a tad too long for Taryn's liking, the Imperials headed back to their ship.

She got the nav computer busy recalculating their course, then turned the freighter around and drove for the stars, trying to grab enough distance to jump to lightspeed. Glancing again at the captured New Republic transport, Taryn wondered what fate awaited its occupants.

When the console finally pinged, she cupped her hand around the hyperdrive levers, gently pulled them back, and gratefully left that particular problem behind.

Not that she didn't still have problems, she thought in exasperation nearly a week later, staring out at the empty expanse of space before them and acutely aware of Bremen looking over her shoulder, as usual.

The rest of the trip to Coriallis had been uneventful, and once there, Bremen had programmed the nav computer with a new course. Since then, they'd dropped in and out of hyperspace a dozen times on their way to intercept one of the New Republic's battle fleets, somewhere in the Borderlands.

At least, Taryn thought it was the Borderlands. She

didn't recognize the majority of the places they popped in on, and Bremen saw no reason to enlighten her—about their location, or anything else. He curtly informed her she'd get control of the *Messenger* back once they intercepted the fleet and delivered the message.

Well, here they were at the intercept point. So where was the fleet?

"They might be a little late," Bremen said, and Taryn glanced over her shoulder to see a furrow creasing his brow. "They *are* scheduled to be here," he added at the expression on her face.

"If they don't know we're coming, what are they scheduled to meet?" she asked. Bremen ignored the question; clearly, this was yet another bit of information that mere civilians couldn't be trusted with. Since they'd dropped into the outer edges of a system and were skulking around like thieves instead of getting closer to one of the planets, Taryn figured the New Republic had an outpost here that its fleet was checking up on. Bremen just didn't want to get close enough for her and Del to take a look.

She sighed. Despite a week of close quarters living, or perhaps because of it, Bremen wasn't any easier to get along with. She'd finally had to order Del to stop his needling—if only she could order Bremen to knock off his condescending manner, as well. His attitude reminded her far too strongly of her father.

Because it was possible the fleet had been delayed, and because they really had nowhere else to go, the *Messenger* simply drifted for the next several hours. Taryn was sitting in the cockpit staring out at the stars and trying to recall astrogation charts of the Borderlands region when Bremen came in and dropped into the co-pilot's seat.

Mildly surprised, she glanced over as he studied the long-range sensors. He'd finally stopped hovering over her, apparently reassured she wasn't going to break into the nav computer to find out where they were if he didn't keep an eye on her every minute. Naturally, she had, only to find that all records of their past several jumps had been erased.

So it wasn't so much a matter of trust, as that it simply didn't matter.

"You don't think much of us, do you?" she said.

He took his time looking up. "Pardon?"

"It's not just you and your New Republic on the line here, you know. It's me and Del, too," she said. "If you're caught, we're caught. You think we're going to do anything to mess this thing up?"

"Not deliberately, no," he conceded. "But accidents happen. What about when Voldt wanted to see the Coruscant mail—you hadn't thought of that, had you? What if there hadn't been anything to show him?"

"That cloak and dagger stuff is *your* department," she retorted, but the comment stung. He was right; and instead of getting defensive, she should admit it and learn from the experience. "That doesn't justify treating us like dimglows, and keeping me in the dark about where we're going. I have a right to know."

He folded his arms and gave her a level stare. "Captain Clancy, it's no secret I don't think you or Del Sato should have been allowed on this mission. You're civilians, and more of a hindrance than a help. You can't be expected to make the kind of split-second decisions needed to keep us out of trouble."

Taryn flushed, and concentrated on keeping her temper as he continued. "But you're here anyway, so consider being 'kept in the dark' as your protection. If you don't know anything, you can't give it away."

"What do you take me for?" she asked, affronted. "If I wanted to give you up, I would've done it when Voldt was aboard. You'll notice I didn't."

"No, you didn't," he agreed. "But it's better to be prepared than be sorry."

Taryn was debating whether it was even worth discussing any further when she was saved from a decision by a sudden blip on the sensors.

A ship, emerging from hyperspace about 30 kilometers away.

She reacted before Bremen did, flipping switches to start bringing the engines on line. "Del!" she yelled down the corridor, trying to maneuver the sluggish *Messenger* around to face the oncoming ship. As it came into view, Taryn identified it as a slightly battered-looking Skipray blastboat, with no markings indicating who it might belong to. But it clearly wasn't the fleet.

Great, she thought grimly even as the comm light flashed, indicating the starfighter was hailing them. She flipped it on as Del arrived, noting the engines were only up to point three-five power. They wouldn't be able to run, just yet.

A cool female voice came over the comm speaker. "Unidentified freighter, do you need assistance?" it asked, as the Skipray slanted to the side a bit, putting it just out of line with the *Messenger*'s laser cannon. Taryn kept the freighter turning to face the potential threat as she answered.

"This is Captain Clancy of the *Messenger,* and thanks, but no, we're fine," she said quickly, before Bremen could jump in. He got out of Del's seat and stood in the small space between them, frowning out at the blastboat.

"Captain Clancy? You're just who I'm looking for," the voice said as Taryn took another look at her displays. Up to point six-five power; at least they could start moving. She started the ship sidling away as the Skipray's pilot asked, "I wonder if I might speak with your guest?"

An unexpected request, and there was a slight inflection on the last word that made Taryn glance up at Bremen. To her surprise, he appeared to be gritting his teeth. "This is Bremen," he said shortly.

"Ah, Colonel. This is Mara Jade," the pilot identified herself. "I see you made it off Coruscant in one piece." She sounded vaguely amused.

"Get to the point," Bremen snapped. Taryn and Del

looked at him in astonishment. Even at his most supercilious with them, he'd never been downright rude.

"The *point* is that your rendezvous with the Borderlands fleet is off," she said, clearly unruffled. "They took a detour, and won't be through here for days. High Command's already sent a new courier out to their location, so you're off the hook."

"I wasn't notified of any change," Bremen said.

"You're *being* notified."

"Why'd they send you?" he shot back.

"Because word of the fleet's location came through one of my contacts in the smuggler's coalition," she said. "Information *is* what we're getting paid for."

Now Taryn thought she understood Bremen's animosity. If this Mara Jade were a smuggler, Bremen's law-and-order stance wouldn't allow him much in the way of tolerance. "Do you have any confirmation of that?" he was asking.

"Just the fleet's new location," she answered coolly. "If you're ready, I'll transmit it to you." A data feed light on the panel lit up, and a series of numbers scrolled past on the display. "Not that you need it," she added. "High Command said you could go on home."

"Thanks, but maybe we'll just stick around here a while longer," Bremen said, clearly still suspicious.

There was a pause from the Skipray. "Suit yourself," Mara finally said. The comm light winked out as the ship swung around and started heading away. Before Taryn could ask Bremen how long he planned to wait, another ship suddenly dropped into space ahead of them.

Bremen swore viciously even as Taryn recognized the distinctive shape of a *Carrack*-class cruiser. "Go, *go!*" he barked at her as the comm light lit up again and a harsh voice ordered them to stop or be destroyed. Taryn turned the freighter away from the cruiser's ominous bulk and slapped at the thrust. She and Del were slammed back in their seats as the *Messenger* leapt forward, Bremen somehow managing to hang on as they drove for deep space.

Out of the corner of her eye, Taryn saw the Skipray had turned and was coming back to their position, and a moment later, the sensors told her why.

The cruiser had launched TIE fighters.

"Oh blast it, not again," she muttered. Luck had seen the *Messenger* through its first encounter with TIE fighters; she doubted it would be any match for them this time. "Del, get us a course out of here," she snapped, trying to gauge how soon the two fighters would overtake them.

"I can't—I don't even know where we are!" he snapped back.

"What about those?" Taryn indicated the coordinates Mara Jade had transmitted, still displayed on the console.

"No!" Bremen objected. "She could have set a trap. That cruiser didn't just show up by chance." He lurched as a thump to the *Messenger*'s rear indicated that the TIE fighters had caught up. "Now she's back to finish the job," he added bitterly, glaring at the Skipray as it headed towards them.

Lasers flashed as it neared, and Taryn wondered if he were right. But the Skipray zipped past overhead, and a moment later one of the dots on the sensor scopes blinked out. "I wouldn't hang around, if I were you," Mara Jade advised, and Taryn decided it was time for one of those split-second command decisions Bremen thought beyond her.

"Use 'em," she ordered Del, who was already busy with the nav computer. Bremen protested, but before he could intervene another hit rocked the ship, sending him stumbling. By the time he'd clawed his way back up to position behind Taryn, the *Messenger*'s shield indicator flickered an ominous red again.

Hands tense on the controls, Taryn tried to avoid the laser fire which peppered their aft end. But the old freighter simply wasn't a match for the faster starfighter. If it weren't for the Skipray harassing the TIE and forcing it to split its attention between two targets, the *Messenger* would've already been blown to bits.

They still might be.

Another hard lurch threw Bremen against the back of Taryn's chair. Clinging to the seat, he looked over her shoulder at the sensors and shouted something. Just as she glanced down at the displays and realized with a jolt that the cruiser's remaining two TIE fighters were on their way to join the attack, the nav computer finally pinged.

She pulled back the levers, and they escaped into the blessed emptiness of hyperspace.

It turned out to be a rather short hop.

Barely an hour after their escape from the cruiser, the proximity alarm clanged, indicating a minute to breakout. Bremen had spent most of the trip threatening to abort the jump, but even he was unwilling to risk stressing the *Messenger* with a second unexpected emergence.

Despite Taryn pointing out that the Skipray had aided in their getaway, he remained convinced that Mara Jade had sold them out to the Imperials. He saw no other explanation for the cruiser's appearance. "A panthac doesn't change its stripes," he said darkly, but declined to explain the comment.

The console pinged again, and Taryn eased back the hyperdrive levers. Mottled sky became starlines, which became stars. They'd arrived.

There was nothing nearby, but the long-range sensors showed a number of ships some distance off their port side. Within moments, they were close enough to identify. It was, indeed, the New Republic fleet.

She let Bremen do the talking when the Mon Calamari cruiser *Hope* hailed them. Its captain confirmed a messenger from the New Republic had already arrived. "But we're still glad to see you," Captain Arboga added in his gravelly voice. "The datacard he brought us appears damaged, and we'd like to compare it with yours to fill in the blanks."

The only thing left to do was drop Bremen and his datacard off. Greatly relieved at the prospect, Taryn headed for the *Hope*. They were still several kilometers out when Bremen stepped into the cockpit holding a small circular object.

Her eyes widened in horror when she saw it. "Where did *that* come from?"

"The hold," Bremen told her grimly. "Ironically, in the same crate the datacard was hidden. The Imperials must have planted it when they restacked the crates." The card in his other hand indicated that it, at least, had escaped Imperial treachery. "That must've been how they found us," he added grudgingly, a half-hearted concession that the cruiser's appearance hadn't been Mara Jade's fault, after all. Leaning past Taryn, he flipped on the comm. "Captain," he reported, "we've found a homing beacon—"

"And we've found who's tracking it," Arboga cut him off. "Take a look aft."

Taryn glanced at the scopes and stifled a groan. The cruiser they'd so recently escaped had appeared behind them. Jabbing the drive up to full, she mentally cursed as the sudden thrust shoved her back in her seat. She and Del had been so close to going home. Now here they were, stuck in the middle of another battle between the Empire and the New Republic.

"It's no match for the entire fleet," Del said, sounding surprised the cruiser continued to follow them.

"But it's more than a match for this scow, if we don't get out of range," Bremen added tightly. He glared at Taryn. "Can't you get a little more speed out of this thing?"

She clenched her teeth. Enough was enough. "Just shut up," she gritted. "If you'd done *your* job and found that damn beacon when they planted it, we wouldn't be in this mess."

Bremen opened his mouth, but a *thunk* to the rear cut off whatever he'd been about to say. The deflector indicator flickered weakly, and Taryn glanced down to see a diagnostic message scroll across the display. She looked at Del. His face was tense as he, too, summed up the shields' sorry state. The *Messenger* shuddered with another hit, and the diagnostic message turned red and began to flash. Del looked grimly resigned.

Leaning forward, Taryn tapped a button and a previously dark section of the board lit up. "The backup shield generator," she said shortly at Del's astonished expression. "I finished it while fixing the main after we got away from Coruscant."

"But, we didn't have all the parts," he said.

"You just have to know where to look," Taryn said, thinking of how she'd cannibalized the main generator to jury-rig the backup. Redundant shields were a precaution she'd learned from her father, and she'd installed a backup generator in every ship she'd worked on. Seldom needed, she hadn't hurried to get the *Messenger*'s up and running. But the retreat from Coruscant had changed her mind. "It won't hold up for long," she added, as another hit rocked the ship. "But maybe it'll last long enough."

Nursing all the speed out of the freighter she could, but still painfully aware it wasn't enough, Taryn drove for the distant safety of the *Hope*'s bulbous bulk. Lured into finishing off the tempting target, the cruiser followed.

It followed too far.

Just when the shields' diagnostic message was scrolling past in red again and Taryn despaired of lasting much longer, suddenly, they were there.

The *Hope*'s turbolaser punch was joined by two other Mon Cal cruisers, and the Carrack cruiser abruptly gave up the chase as its commander realized they'd strayed within firing range of the New Republic fleet. Flames danced along scorched sections of its port side, and a small explosion briefly illuminated the hull above one of its dorsal exhaust ports. Apparently deciding retreat was the prudent course of action, the cruiser banked away, its powerful sublight engines driving for deep space.

But it wasn't fast enough.

The brilliant flare from the exploding cruiser lit up the *Messenger*'s canopy. Out her port window, Taryn caught a glimpse of fast-moving specks—X-wings, returning to escort formation around the fleet after pumping deadly proton torpedoes into the ship's damaged areas. The fireball began to fade as she approached the *Hope*'s hangar bay.

Behind her, Bremen was silent. Cycling back the repulsors and gently setting the ship down on the deck, Taryn waited expectantly for a critique.

"You didn't tell me we had extra shields," he said instead.

"You didn't ask."

"Yes, well—" He hesitated so long that Taryn half-turned to look up at him. The habitual frown was still there, but his eyes were direct as he admitted, "When the main generator went, I figured we were done for."

"We almost were," she said. "Credit my father—he's the one who taught me how to get things up and running on practically nothing but hope and air. After Coruscant, I thought we could use an extra set of shields."

"They certainly came in handy," Bremen agreed. He paused again, even longer this time. "Look," he finally said, "I know I objected to you two being on this mission, but . . . all in all, it's worked out okay."

Okay? Taryn stared at him, disconcerted. They'd been shot at, yanked out of hyperspace and boarded, and had eluded an Imperial cruiser to successfully deliver the datacard. Was this his idea of a compliment?

Bremen flushed slightly at her expression, but added, "We're always looking for good pilots, and if you've a mind for a career change, the New Republic could use someone like you."

She didn't know what to say.

"Think about it," he said. "I'll leave you some contacts

to get in touch with, if you're interested. You, too," he told Del.

"Not me," Del said. "I'm retirin'."

Taryn glanced at him in surprise. That's right; after 30 years of hauling mail to the same old ports along the same old route, once they finished this run his piloting days were done.

Was that really what she wanted to look forward to?

"Thanks for the offer," she told Bremen. "I'll think about it. But right now, I've got a route to finish. Not to mention, figure a course back to Coriallis."

Bremen leaned over Del's shoulder. "This ought to help," he said, punching up a chart on the nav computer. Before leaving, he handed her a datacard and urged again, "Think about it."

As Taryn cleared the *Hope*'s hangar bay and headed toward the first of a short series of hyperspace hops that would take them back to the Core, she tried to imagine what her father would say if she gave up delivering mail and started flying for the New Republic instead.

Would he say something patronizing—or would he be pleased? She considered it a minute, then shrugged. Gazing out at the stars, she realized she no longer cared what he said.

Taryn smiled as she pulled back the levers and the stars streaked, then faded to the swirling sky of hyperspace. She was back on course.

A Certain Point of View

by Charlene Newcomb

Heh, heh, Lieutenant, I think he's got you this time!''
engineer Dap Nechel chuckled.

Lieutenant Celia Durasha ran her hand along the barrel of her blaster and glanced at Nechel. She knew how much the short, bearded alien enjoyed these ritual matchups between the *Kuari Princess'* navigator and Detien Kaileel, the security chief. Their banter enlivened the luxury liner's routine passage along the Relgim Run between Endoraan and Mantooine.

"Just wait a minute now, Dap," she said, holstering the blaster and leaning across the holo gameboard to study her farangs and waroots. Celia frowned, her emerald-green eyes narrowed. The chief's last move had indeed given him the advantage.

Seated across from her, Security Chief Kaileel wore a grin—at least Celia thought she detected a grin. The Kabieroun's long snout hid most of his mouth.

"Come now, my dear crimson-haired friend," Kaileel said, his Basic heavily accented, "shall we try another game?" Dark intelligent eyes twinkled, reflecting the yellowish-green light of the gameboard. He sat back, his giant frame obscuring the overstuffed pillows that decorated the sofas on the *Kuari Princess'* observation deck.

Shaking her head, Celia rolled her eyes. "Why is it, Dap," she kidded the engineer, "that I seem to lose every time you're around?"

Dap smiled at her mischievously, then winked at Kaileel. "I bring the Chief good luck!"

"I don't think I'm going to invite you to any more games!" Celia laughed, falling back onto the sofa. Sighing, she stared out the viewport at the mottled lights of stars rushing past them as the ship travelled through hyperspace. "Wish I had time for another game, Chief. We'll be coming up on Mantooine soon, and I'm supposed to be on the bridge."

Chief Kaileel nodded, muscles rippling along his elongated neck. "I imagine the captain would appreciate the presence of his best officers at their respective duty stations."

"Indeed," Dap agreed.

"I'll have some free time after we make orbit. Shall we get together, say, at 1930?" Celia asked.

"No good," the Chief replied. "I have some things to take care of on Mantooine. I won't be back until much later."

"Things to take care of, eh?" Celia kidded him, picking up her nav-aid datapad from the seat. "All right, Chief, when do I get to meet this new girlfriend you've been harboring on Mantooine?''

"And what about the ones on Aris and Vykos?" Dap added.

Kaileel blushed a darker shade of green than normal and straightened in his seat. "No girlfriends," he told them, tugging at the earhoop hanging from his left lobe. "Just . . . friends."

"Okay, if you say so," Celia replied, a sly smile tugging at the corner of her lip. Standing up, she brushed a stray red hair off the silky white sleeve of her uniform and carefully adjusted the blaster holstered around her hips. "Well, time for work, gentlebeings."

Dap took one last gulp of his drink and bounced down from the sofa. "Ah, yes," he said, "an engineer's work is never done. *Vetoosh,* friends."

"*Vetoosh,*" Celia replied as Dap headed down the corridor. "Chief K?"

"Yes, Lieutenant?"

"Any progress on finding those missing blasters?"

Kaileel swung his massive head. "No," he said. "I'm afraid the captain will be unhappy with my report. I've been over this a dozen times with my security people. It's hard to believe one of them might be lying. But this is the third incident. All those blasters were in secure lockers in our offices. I just don't see how anyone else could have taken them."

"And they haven't turned up anywhere on the ship?"

"I've had scanning teams searching every centimeter of the *Princess,* though I don't expect to find them here," he said. "No, I'm afraid this last batch may have been smuggled off the ship at one of our port stops and will turn up in Rebel hands like those the Imperials discovered on Mantooine."

"You sound worried, Chief," Celia observed.

"This will not look good on my record, Lieutenant," Kaileel reminded her.

"Chief, your record is impeccable!" she told him. "You've got the best security team this side of the Rim!"

"With a dozen weapons missing?" he grimaced. "Thank you for your vote of confidence, little Crimson."

Nodding, Celia watched him rise, his huge form towering far above hers. "I'll talk with you when you return from Mantooine." She started to walk away, then turned back to face him. "I want my rematch!" she called. "You're not going to win again!"

The decks were crowded with passengers boarding the *Kuari Princess* in Mantooine for the return trip through the Maelstrom Nebula to Endoraan. Celia nodded politely to a group of Ithorians and three Corellian businessmen. She smiled at a young couple, still dressed in their wedding finery. Obviously on their honeymoon, they didn't seem to notice anything around them, only each other.

"Ticket, please," hostess Kelsa Vilrein asked a very wealthy-looking female passenger.

"Miss," the woman asked, "can you tell me where the observation deck is? I don't want to miss our entry into the Maelstrom. I've heard so much about it."

"That's on the Lido Deck," Kelsa told her. "The captain will announce our approach. Of course, you realize we won't enter the Maelstrom for 15 hours."

"Yes, thank you, my dear."

Kelsa tipped her head toward Celia. "Good evening, Lieutenant."

"How are you, Kelsa?" Celia asked the dark-haired woman.

"Ticket, please," she replied, glancing down to check another passenger's accommodations. "Homthor Deck. That's up two levels." She winked at Celia. "I'm fine, Lieutenant."

"Has Chief Kaileel come back on board?" Celia asked.

"He returned about a half hour ago. Ticket, please."

"Thanks, Kelsa."

"Celia?"

The voice was familiar, but one she hadn't heard in a long time. Looking around, Celia stared wide-eyed. Her heart skipped a beat.

"Adion? How in the worlds—"

"I'd recognize that red mane anywhere!" he exclaimed, reaching out to take her hand. "Celia Durasha. Good skies! What are you doing so far from Lankashiir?"

"I'm the *Kuari Princess'* navigator. And look at you—"

"What do you think?" he asked, tugging at his tunic to straighten any part of the uniform that might dare to be out of place.

"Lieutenant . . . hm," she said, eyeing his tall muscular frame. Adion Lang looked more handsome than she remembered. Maybe it's the uniform, she thought. "I like it."

"Celia, you look absolutely ravishing," he told her.

"Shh!" she replied, turning her head as the heat rose in her cheeks. "You're not allowed to embarrass the ship's navigator."

"All right, I'll try not to."

"I'm good friends with the Security Chief, Lieutenant Lang. Any misbehavior and I'll have him throw you in the brig!"

"Yes, ma'am," he grinned. "You haven't changed at all, Celia."

"Not one little bit!" she laughed. "Now, c'mon. Let's get out of the line of traffic." Leading him through the ship's corridors toward the observation deck, Celia couldn't help but notice the two white-armored shadows that followed them at a discreet distance. "Friends of yours?" she asked.

Adion glanced back. "Oh, them? Don't worry about them. Just a couple of guards who were lucky enough to accompany me," he replied nonchalantly. "Tell me, Celia, how long has it been?"

She thought for a moment. "Seven years, I guess."

"A long time," he said. "Tell me about you, your family. I'm afraid I've lost touch with your brothers."

"Well, Jak is still in the Navy, stationed on board the *Relentless*. Bern is a lieutenant with an armored battalion in the Generis Sector, and I just spoke with Raine last week. His unit was preparing to ship out to Ralltiir—some kind of local trouble, I suppose. I miss them all terribly, but especially Raine."

"I guess that's natural—he is your twin brother, after all," Adion said. "But what happened to all your grand plans? I thought you would attend the Academy like your brothers."

Celia frowned, unable to ignore the incoming tide of emotions that were attached to that subject.

Adion stopped in the middle of the corridor, obviously aware that he'd touched on a sore spot. "I'm sorry," he told her, taking her hand into his. "I can tell something's wrong."

"It's okay," Celia said as old feelings of anger flooded her senses. "My application was never forwarded past Sector."

"What! Who would do such a thing?"

Staring past Adion, her voice trembled, full of bitterness. "Commander Reise Durasha."

"Your father?"

Nodding, Celia walked away from Adion. She ran her hand along the gold handrail that lined the ornately decorated corridor.

"But why?" Adion asked, taking two giant strides to catch up with her.

She stopped, planting her arms across her chest, and looked him straight in the eye. "I believe his words were, 'No daughter of mine is going to attend the Academy. It's no place for women,' or something to that effect."

Adion lowered his eyes, shuffling his feet on the ship's polished marble flooring. His silence stung louder than a thunderclap.

"You, too? You agree with him?" she asked, trying to temper her anger and hurt.

"Celia, you would have been remarkable at the Academy. But do you know where most women end up after graduation?"

She glared at him. She knew all right. Backwater worlds, crummy assignments, with little chance to prove yourself, or to ever see a promotion. But it never mattered to her. She had longed to wear the uniform, to proudly serve as others in her family had done for generations.

"Your father was only thinking of your well-being," Adion said.

"My well-being? Excuse me, why would he be so concerned about a daughter he barely knew."

"And yet you wanted to follow in his footsteps! See your family every three or four years, if it was convenient? Celia," he admonished her gently, "how can you still be upset with him after all these years?"

"He interfered with my life, Adion. He had no right to make that decision for me."

"Perhaps you're right."

"Can we drop this subject?" she asked. "You haven't told me what you're doing on the *Kuari Princess.*"

Adion looped his arm through hers. "Show me your ship," he said, "and I'll tell you about my assignment to Aris."

"Aris? Sector HQ, eh?" she smiled, leading him up the grand staircase to the Lido observation deck. "I'm impressed. A plush job, no doubt."

"You are looking at the new assistant to the Moff," he told her.

"Congratulations, Adion! That's wonderful." She stopped, turning to look out one of the viewports. Mantooine loomed ahead of them, the glare of sunlight illuminating the horizon as the ship's orbit took them across the terminator into day. "It's so beautiful up here," she sighed. "But just wait until we enter the Maelstrom Nebula."

"I've heard about it," he said, his voice softening. "But it can't be as spectacular as the lovely red hair I used to tug on from my seat in physics classes." He pushed a loose curl away from her face then touched her lightly on the cheek. "I've missed you, Celia."

Celia blushed and looked away from him. Adion reached out to turn her face back toward his. Putting his arm around her waist, he pulled her close. Slowly, his lips met hers. For a brief moment neither one noticed the curious on-lookers who passed by.

Trembling, Celia pulled away from him. Old memories rushed in upon her senses. There may have been a time, years ago, when she would have followed him to the ends of the galaxy. But then he'd left their homeworld to attend Raithal Academy and she hadn't seen or heard from him in all these years. Did he expect to pick up right where they'd left off?

Her eyes fixed on his. There was something different about him, something in those piercing blue eyes that she couldn't quite put her finger on. "I've got to go, Adion. We'll be leaving orbit soon and I'm supposed to be on duty now."

"May I see you later?" he asked.

"I—I'll check with you in the morning," she said, turning to leave.

Confused by emotions he'd stirred deep within her, emotions she thought she'd left behind in the past, Celia hurried away. She needed time to think. Some safe harbor. And she knew exactly where to find it.

The door slid open into a modestly decorated office. A hologram on one wall displayed a cross section of the *Kuari Princess*. A dozen monitors occupied another wall to the right of a desk that was littered with a half dozen datacards.

Chief Kaileel was hunched over his computer terminal.

He glanced up at Celia, a momentary look of annoyance vanished quickly, replaced by a gentler expression.

"Good evening, dear Crimson. May I help you with something?"

"I, uh, thought I'd get a brief update on those missing blasters, Chief," she said unconvincingly.

Kaileel's large dark eyes frowned at her over the top of the monitor. "I have nothing new to report, Lieutenant," he replied, eyeing her suspiciously. "Was there something else I might help you with?"

Celia's eyes wandered around the room. "I've got the bridge watch for another hour, then I'll be ready for our rematch."

Kaileel drummed his long green fingers on the desk. "It is rather late, you realize."

"You're not trying to get out of this game, are you?"

"Of course not, Lieutenant. I shall be off duty in two hours."

"Good," Celia replied, glad she'd have the game to keep her mind off a certain handsome Imperial lieutenant. "Then I'll expect you to meet me on the observation deck."

The edges of Kaileel's mouth curled upward behind his snout. "Oh, my dear little crimson-haired friend, I would not miss the chance to beat you again for all the spice on Kessel!"

"Beat me?" she smiled, her mood suddenly lighter. "Don't count on it, Chief!"

"Get to your bridge, little one. Drive your ship! Steer us a straight course!"

Leaning over the desk, Celia's face grew serious. "You look tired, Chief," she said. "Is everything all right?"

Kaileel leaned back into his chair. "Yes—well, no," he admitted when he saw the frown on her face. "I had some disturbing news on my visit to Mantooine."

"Chief?" another voice called from the doorway. "Sorry to interrupt, Lieutenant."

"What is it, Raban?" Kaileel asked the security officer as Celia walked behind the desk to stare out the viewport.

"We've got a report of a fight between two passengers at the Galleria Shop."

"Who's on it?"

"Brankton. And we've sent in a backup."

"Keep me posted," Kaileel told the man, then turned to smile at Celia. "This may turn out to be an exciting cruise."

"We haven't even left orbit yet!" Celia marvelled.

"And you thought your job was interesting."

"Chief, what were you about to tell me—the news you got on Mantooine?"

"Later, my dear. I'll tell you later."

Celia eyed her old friend. There was something bothering him. But before she could probe for more information the captain's voice sounded over the intercom. "Chief Kaileel, is Lieutenant Durasha with you?"

"Yes, Captain," Kaileel said.

"I was just on my way to the bridge, sir," Celia added.

"Lieutenant, I need to speak with you privately. Will you meet me in my office right away?"

"Of course, sir. On my way. I wonder what that's all about," she said as Kaileel clicked off the intercom. "I'll see you in a couple of hours, Chief."

"Captain Glidrick, you wanted to see me?"

"Please, Lieutenant, sit down," he said. Stenn Glidrick was a middle-aged man with brownish hair that was just beginning to streak with gray. Like Celia, he was dressed in blue trousers with a gold stripe down each leg. Medals decorated his white tunic—a reminder to everyone of his service in the Imperial Navy.

"What is it, sir? What's happened?"

"I received a message from your father—"

Celia stood up abruptly, her face reddening. "My father sent you a message?'' she asked, the anger in her voice unmistakable.

"Please, Lieutenant—"

"I want nothing to do with him—"

"Lieutenant Durasha, sit down!" the captain ordered. He took a deep breath. "Your father sent word through me, because he knew what your reaction would be. It's about your brother—"

Celia paled. "What?" Her hands trembled as she grasped the edge of Glidrick's desk and collapsed into the chair.

"He's been killed," the captain told her. "I'm sorry."

Closing her eyes, Celia chewed on the inside of her lip, trying to force back the tears. "Captain, I have three brothers. Which one—"

Glidrick glanced down at the datapad. "It's Raine," he said. "Your father said there are more details on this holo that accompanied the message I received. Take all the time you need, Celia. I'm truly sorry."

"Thank you, sir," Celia replied numbly, taking the holo from him. She rose slowly from the chair and somehow managed to find her way to her quarters. Alone, Celia listened to the message. When it ended, she paused it, staring at her father's frozen holo image. The small room seemed to close in around her.

Unconsciously, Celia ran her hand back and forth across her holster, then downward, brushing against her soft leather boot. She unsheathed the knife hidden there. It had been a special gift from Raine, one he had given to her the night before he'd left for his last term of service. Sitting beneath Lankashiir's star-filled skies, they had reminisced about the good times they'd had exploring the forests of their homeworld.

She turned the knife over several times. Light from the holo image touched the steel gray blade and cascaded across the desk. Her small hand melded perfectly around its handle which was carved from rare ebon. She studied the flaming red jewel embedded just above the blade, watched it sparkle brilliantly even in the dimly lit cabin.

Good memories seemed no more than a distant echo now. Celia set the knife down, rubbed her hand wearily across her brow and clicked on her father's message again.

"Your brother Raine has been killed by Rebel forces on the planet Ralltiir," the figure in the holo said. Reise Durasha looked much older, and much thinner than when she'd seen him last. His gray-green Imperial Army uniform seemed to hang loosely on his bent frame. Dark shadows ringed his eyes. "I know how close you and Raine were . . ."

Celia buried her face in her hands and burst into tears. Emotionally exhausted, numb with grief, sleep finally ended her pain. When the cabin intercom buzzed more than an hour later, she awoke suddenly. Slowly, she reached over and clicked it on.

"Durasha here," she said wearily.

"Celia, I thought we had a game this evening."

She stared blankly at the comm panel.

"Celia?" the Chief called again, more insistently.

"Oh, Chief," she finally said, "I forgot."

"Is everything all right?" he asked. "We don't have to play tonight—"

"No, just give me a few minutes."

When Celia arrived on the observation deck, the holo gameboard was darkened. A tall glass of some exotic beverage sat on the edge of the playing table.

"What's this?" Celia asked, pointing toward the drink.

"Zadarian brandy. You sounded like you could use a good stiff drink," Kaileel told her.

Celia blinked a tear from her eye. She picked up the brandy, swirled it around the glass thoughtfully, and finally took a long sip. The brew trickled down her throat, but its warmth did nothing to diminish the chill she felt. She could feel the Chief's eyes upon her.

"What has happened?" he asked.

Staring out at the stars blurring past them in hyperspace, Celia didn't seem to hear him.

"Celia?" He stood up, placing his hand lightly on her shoulder.

Trembling, Celia turned toward Kaileel and looked up into his eyes. "My brother—" she cried, burying her face in his chest.

Kaileel wrapped his long scaly arms around her. He held her tightly. "I'm so sorry, my dear little Crimson," he said.

When her tears dried, Celia told her old friend how Raine's unit had been ambushed by Rebels at the spaceport on Ralltiir.

Kaileel shook his head sadly. "So many will die," he said quietly. "On both sides."

Celia's eyes grew wide. "You don't support the Rebel cause, do you?"

"Let's just say I disagree with the Empire's methods of resolving this conflict," he told her.

"What do you mean, Chief?"

Kaileel gazed out the viewport. "Think of the Maelstrom Nebula, Celia," he said.

"What about it?"

"From Mantooine—how does it appear?"

"It's barely a speck," she replied.

"True," he nodded. "What happens when we enter the Nebula?"

She threw him a puzzled look. "Is this a class in astrophysics, Chief?"

"Please, follow along with me," he said.

"All right. When we enter the Nebula our communications don't work well. And our sensors are blinded. But what does that have to do with—"

Kaileel held up one long green finger. "From a great distance we can only surmise the hazards the Nebula may present to us. Why is it that until we're close, until it touches us, we don't recognize the danger?

"The Empire is like that, little Crimson. From a distance, we may not feel the danger—we're too far removed from its touch. But once it is upon us, we will hear and see only what the Empire desires.''

''My family serves that Empire, Chief. My brother died fighting for it, too,'' she reminded him. ''You'd better not let others hear you speak like this. They might suspect you were the one who stole those—'' She stopped mid-sentence, sitting up abruptly, and leaned over the holo gameboard.

Kaileel eyed her, then thoughtfully swirled the reddish liqueur in his own glass.

''You gave those blasters to Rebels on Mantooine?'' she asked quietly. ''Was *that* the business you had to attend to?''

Before the Chief could answer, Dap Nechel bounded into the room.

''Why didn't you tell me you were playing?'' he asked, his voice filled with an exaggerated anguish.

Celia fell back onto the overstuffed pillows. She looked from Kaileel to Dap, then turned away. Kaileel straightened in his seat and took a long slow sip from his drink.

''I'm sorry,'' Dap said. ''I seem to have interrupted a private conversation. I'll go now.''

''No, it's okay, Dap,'' Celia said. ''Stay. We were just setting up the board.'' She pressed a button on the side of the game table. A greenish glow lit their faces and a dozen warriors appeared, standing at attention, weapons held at right-shoulder arms, on each side of the holo board.

''Celia, we don't have to play—'' Kaileel began.

''It's all right, Chief,'' she said. ''Your move.''

As Dap climbed onto the sofa next to Celia, Kaileel positioned his waroot. Celia moved one of her farangs. Chief countered by advancing another one of his warriors.

Celia studied the gameboard. Sitting up, she pulled her blaster from its holster and rubbed her hand along the barrel contemplatively. "Hmm, Chief," she said, "that was not a wise move."

"Really? I believe it all depends on your point of view," he replied.

"My point of view?" she frowned.

"Open your eyes, dear Crimson. Look at what is happening all around you."

Dap eyed his two friends. "What are you two talking about?" he asked. "Will one of you please tell me?"

Celia looked away.

"Celia's brother was killed by Rebels on Ralltiir."

"Oh, dear. That's terrible, Lieutenant. I had heard about the insurrection there on the holo newsvid. But the Empire is dealing with those Rebels," he said. "And the ones on Alderaan. Yes, indeed. They won't be giving the Empire any more trouble."

"Alderaan?" the Chief asked.

"Good skies, have you not heard the news—well, no, I guess not if you've been sitting here the last hour."

"What has happened on Alderaan?" Celia repeated.

"The Emperor's servants discovered that several of the leaders of the Rebellion were from Alderaan—Bail Organa himself, and his daughter, the Princess Leia. Our forces have made an example of that world."

"What do you mean?"

"Alderaan has been destroyed."

"What!" Celia exclaimed.

Kaileel shook his head sadly. "Did I not tell you this?"

"The whole planet?"

"It's nothing but billions of particles of dust now," Dap said.

"Millions of people, like pawns," Kaileel said, pointing at the characters on their gameboard, "for the Emperor to do with what he will."

"But, Chief—"

"I fear the game is up," Kaileel said softly.

Frowning, Celia leaned over the gameboard to check their warriors' positions. "You're not giving up that easily," she said, suddenly catching Dap's startled expression out of the corner of her eye.

Chief Kaileel exhaled deeply, letting out a big sigh. Celia looked up. Two stormtroopers had blaster rifles aimed at her friend.

"Indeed, Rebel spy," Adion Lang's voice rang out menacingly. He stepped out from behind the stormtroopers. "The game is up."

"Adion!" Celia exclaimed, carefully holstering her blaster. "What's the meaning of this?" She made a point of standing slowly, not wanting to alarm the stormtroopers. "Chief Kaileel is no spy."

"Please, Celia, don't try to defend this traitor. We know all about this," he paused, searching for the right description, "creature's activities. We have proof that he has supplied weapons to Rebel agents on Mantooine. And considering the conversation I've just overheard—"

"You've been spying on us!" Dap exclaimed.

"That is my job. I'm sorry, Celia, that this . . . thing . . . has cultivated your friendship. Just remember what *his* friends have done to your brother," Adion said. "Raine would still be alive if it weren't for traitors like him."

His cold words cut into Celia's heart like a vibroblade. She'd lost her brother to the Rebels. And now she was losing her best friend to the Empire. She looked at Kaileel—she would never blame him for Raine's death. She hoped he could see that in her eyes.

"It's all right, dear Crimson," Kaileel told her. "I am only one. But the Empire will soon learn that the ones will multiply by the hundreds of thousands. And one day, we shall not be put down."

"Take him away," Adion ordered the stormtroopers.

"Excuse me, Lieutenant," Dap said. "If you'll not be needing me, may I go?"

"Yes, Chief Nechel," Adion told him, "though I may ask for a statement from you later."

"I see," Dap replied. "Yes, indeed, whatever you require. You know where I'll be."

Celia watched them put binders on Kaileel's wrists. His strong muscular arms twitched nervously as he stood up. Towering above them, he would have been an intimidating sight if it weren't for the blaster rifles they had trained on him.

"Move it," one stormtrooper ordered Kaileel, shoving his rifle into the chief's chest.

"Take him to ship's security and keep a close eye on him, Sergeant," Adion ordered. "Remember, he knows that place better than anyone on this ship."

"Yes, sir."

As they led Kaileel away, Celia stared after them. "What will happen to him, Adion?"

"Dear Celia, don't concern yourself with these details," he replied, reaching out to take her hand.

"I don't understand this, Adion. I thought you were an administrative aide."

He shook his head. "I'm sorry I had to lie to you, Celia. I'm with the Imperial Security Bureau. We've been watching your security chief for several months now."

"I thought I knew him so well. I never suspected—" she said, covering her face with her hands.

Adion took Celia into his arms. "There, now," he said, "everything will be all right. Come, sit down with me."

"Gentlebeings," a voice rang out over the ship's intercom. "This is Captain Glidrick. In approximately 30 minutes, the *Kuari Princess* will emerge from hyperspace to enter the Maelstrom Nebula. You won't want to miss the spectacular view from the Lido Deck's observation ports. It will be a sight you will never forget."

"The Nebula—" Celia sighed. Kaileel's comparison of the Empire and the nebula filled her mind . . . *until it touches you, you may not realize the danger it presents.*

"Forget what that old creature said to you, Celia. His thoughts are dangerous."

Celia looked up into Adion's blue eyes. They seemed

cold and vacant. Who was right? Empire? Rebel? She'd
been hurt by both of them. Could she ever embrace one
or the other? She didn't know what to think anymore.
"I've got to talk to him, Adion."

"That's not a good idea, Celia."

"Please—just for a few minutes."

"I will have to question him first, but before we reach
Aris I'll let you see him."

Nodding weakly, she rested her head on Adion's shoulder.

The cell door slid shut behind her. Celia stood rigidly,
staring at Kaileel. After more than 10 hours, she was finally able to talk to him, just as Adion Lang had promised.

Shaking her head, she placed her nav-aid datapads on
the chest just inside the door and began pacing back and
forth across Kaileel's cell. Her hand nervously fingered
her empty holster.

"You admitted it!" she finally shouted at Kaileel.

"What else was I to do, Lieutenant?" he asked her.

Stopping dead in her tracks in front of him, Celia
rolled her eyes in disgust. "Lie!"

Kaileel stared past her as if looking out some nonexis-
tent viewport. "To what end? My dear little Crimson," he
said, turning to look into her eyes, "I know you are not
that naive."

Celia clenched her fists and pounded Kaileel's muscular chest. "I just don't understand, Chief!" she cried.
"What has the Empire done to you?"

"Nothing."

"Then why did you get yourself mixed up with these
Rebels?"

"What the Empire is doing is wrong," he told her, "it's
immoral. Remember what I told you—that certain point
of view—stop looking at the Empire from a distance. Take
a look up close, Celia. You will see. All freedom-loving

beings know this is true." He took her hand into his, pressing it closely to his chest. "And I know, deep in my heart, that one day you will understand."

Staring up into his huge black eyes, Celia pushed down the lump in her throat. "I just don't know, Chief—"

The door into the cell slid open.

"Time's up, Lieutenant. I'm afraid you'll have to leave."

"But it's only been a couple of minutes. Can't I stay a little while longer, Sergeant?"

"I've got my orders, Lieutenant."

The stormtrooper motioned her toward the door. Celia frowned at Kaileel. She finally walked away from him, stopping to glance back one last time.

"I still want my rematch with you, Chief!" she told him, reaching for the datapads on the chest. "I won't let them take you off this ship until I get a rematch!"

The datapads slipped from Celia's hands, clattering to the floor. She bent down to retrieve them, inconspicuously withdrawing the knife from her boot. Standing abruptly, she drove the knife under the stormtrooper's helmet and into his neck. He screamed in pain as she forcefully pulled him out of the doorway, bashing his head against the wall. Her hands shaking, she twisted the blade one last time as the trooper collapsed to the floor.

"C'mon, Chief," she said, re-sheathing the knife in her boot, "we've got to get out of here!"

A second stormtrooper appeared in the doorway. Diving to the floor, Celia recovered the fallen trooper's blaster rifle and opened fire. Her shot nicked the wall as the stormtrooper backed away from the door. Jumping to her feet, Celia scrambled to the doorway and blasted him as he ran down the corridor.

"Let's go, Chief!" she shouted, throwing the blaster rifle back to him.

Following her, Kaileel stepped over the two dead stormtroopers. "Tell me, dear Crimson, do you really expect us to get out of here alive?" he asked. "Where's the rest of our security people?"

"Dap arranged for a little problem on the Bazaar Deck," she said, retrieving the second blaster rifle.

"Good old Dap. You think the turbolift's the best way down to the hangar bay?"

"Should be all clear, Chief."

"Amazing."

"You've got a lot of friends on board the *Princess,* old man!"

"Is there a barge—"

"Already prepped. I disconnected the robot pilot and did a little rewire job so I could fly it out of here."

"And into the Maelstrom," the Chief added.

"We'll be safe there."

Thirty seconds later the turbolift doors opened onto the luxury liner's dimly lit hangar. Two barges which were used for piloting passengers to and from the ship occupied the high-ceilinged room. Peering into the bay, Celia motioned for Kaileel to follow her.

They were halfway across the bay when Adion Lang walked down the ramp of the nearest barge. His blaster was pointed toward Chief Kaileel, but his eyes were transfixed on Celia.

"Put your blasters down," he ordered them.

Celia stared at the blaster in her hand. "Adion, please," she said, her voice trembling, "let Kaileel go."

"I was afraid you'd try something like this, Celia. You always were rather impetuous. But I think you know I can't let him go," he told her. "Now, please, put your blaster down. You don't want to kill me."

Celia searched Adion's eyes. There was no emotion there, no spark of life. It can't end like this, she thought. *There's got to be something I can do.*

Chief Kaileel moved slowly to lower his blaster. "I'm sorry, little Crimson," he said, suddenly jerking the rifle up to fire at Adion. His first shot went wide. Half a heartbeat later, a blast from Adion's rifle caught him across the chest. Kaileel managed to get off a second shot, but it ricocheted wildly, bouncing off the hull of the barge. Kaileel collapsed, mortally wounded, onto the cold metallic floor of the hangar bay.

Celia dropped her blaster rifle and rushed toward her fallen friend. "You didn't have to kill him!" she screamed at Adion. Tears threatened to blur her vision. But she forced them away as she knelt beside Kaileel's body.

Adion approached her cautiously, kicking both blaster rifles across the hangar floor. "Why, Celia? Why were you helping him escape?" he asked her. "You're no Rebel."

"He was my friend," she said quietly, ignoring the contempt she heard in Adion's voice. She wondered what had happened to the young man she'd once admired, the man she had loved.

"You'll have to come with me, Celia," Adion said.

"Don't make me, Adion," she told him, her eyes still fixed on Kaileel's body for fear they might betray her true feelings. "Won't you let me leave?"

"It's my duty, Celia," he said coldly, his blaster trained on the back of her head. "You're under arrest for treasonous acts against the Empire."

Celia picked up Kaileel's limp hand, tenderly running her fingers across it. "Looks like this game's going nowhere, Chief," she told him. "How will I ever get my rematch?"

Adion moved a step closer, his tall frame casting a dark shadow across Kaileel's face. His leg brushed up against Celia's back and she cringed at his touch.

"Get up, Celia."

A tear trickled down her cheek. Slowly, she turned and looked back at Adion. Her hand slipped unnoticeably toward her boot. Her fingers clamped around the handle of the knife.

"Get up," Adion repeated, grabbing her left arm, dragging her up so that their faces were barely centimeters apart. He shook his head, and for one brief moment Celia thought she detected a hint of regret. Then his blue eyes narrowed. Blinded by his own hatred, Adion never noticed the flash of steel until Celia slashed him across the arm.

His eyes grew wild as he cried out in pain. The blaster slipped from his hand and skittered across the floor as Celia lashed out again. Trying to protect himself from the attack, Adion lost his grip on her. She fled across the hangar and up the ramp of the barge.

As the hatch slid shut she could hear Adion shouting her name. "Celia, don't do this!"

Seconds later, the barge lifted off the floor of the hangar bay. The small transport slipped quietly outside into the swirling Maelstrom Nebula.

From the viewport, Celia watched the *Kuari Princess* fade as the barge moved away from the luxury liner and deeper into the nebula.

"Stalemate, Chief," she nodded to herself. A bitterness crept into her voice. "Nobody wins this round."

Blaze of Glory
by Tony Russo

"Every mercenary wants to be remembered." Lex "Mad Vornskr" Kempo paused a moment as the jungle browns and greens of Gabredor III rose up toward their diving freighter. With a sardonic smirk, the spacer twisted around in the pilot's seat and gazed at Brixie.

"A mercenary doesn't retire gracefully. There's no such thing as an Old Mercs Home either. What a real mercenary wants is to go out . . . in a blaze of glory."

"Really?" Brixie Ergo shifted around nervously in one

of the acceleration chairs situated behind the co-pilot's station. Space was tight in the modified Corellian light freighter, especially up front. The craft rattled and shook as the vessel plunged deeper into the planet's atmosphere. Kempo smiled a toothy, wicked grin.

"Absolutely."

What sounded like a cross between an order and snarl came from the fur-covered being currently occupying the co-pilot's seat beside Kempo.

"Leave the rook alone." Sully Tigereye was a Trunsk, a stout alien species well known for their fighting ability and equally legendary short temper. Bristly brown hairs covered the length of Tigereye's body except for his face and the palms of his hands. As if emphasizing his displeasure with Kempo, two shiny, sharpened tusks protruded from his lower lip. Brixie recalled stories her parents had told her as a child, about Trunsks being the showpieces of many a carnival show as gladiators and ring fighters.

If Sully Tigereye had ever been part of such a show in the past, he never let on. What she did know was that he had once been a highly decorated member of an elite New Republic infiltrator unit. No longer with the New Republic military, he continued to serve with his former colonel in a band of mercenaries called the Red Moons. It was Tigereye who had been appointed as team leader for this mission, and it was Tigereye who had chosen Brixie to come along as combat medic, although it was for a mission that Brixie still did not quite understand. Just sitting close by Lex Kempo and Sully Tigereye made the former medical student uncomfortable, as if she was part of a group she did not truly belong to.

The mercenaries' target was a Karazak Slavers Guild operation lurking in the jungle swamps and dense foliage on Gabredor III. Like the few Red Moon operation files she had a chance to study during her training period, any further information on the exact target and their reason for assaulting it would not be explained in detail until they landed. That protected not only the Red Moons, but those who hired them. All of this secrecy just didn't make any sense to Brixie. What could they hope to accomplish against an entire camp of slavers? Who thought up this brilliant strategy, anyway? Then again, she chided herself—joining a mercenary force like the Red Moons so she could find her parents was not exactly a brilliant strategy either.

Tigereye continued to berate Lex Kempo. "I didn't ask her to be part of this team to keep you entertained. Just fly this junk pile, if you don't mind."

Unlike Sully Tigereye, who looked naturally forceful yet showed a surprising concern for others, "Mad Vornskr" Kempo easily looked like he had just fallen out of a grim entertainment holo. He claimed to have served with over a dozen different private armies and militias, even a brief stint in the Imperial Army as a scout, as evident from the customized suit of scout trooper armor he wore. The normally eggshell-white armor pieces had been carefully dulled and therma-painted with a camouflage scheme that matched Gabredor's jungle environment. Extra holsters and pockets hid a variety of throwing blades, holdout blasters, power packs, grenades, medpacs, glow rods and other necessities. With his closely-cropped hair, thin blaster scar on his right cheek and gray eyes, Kempo acted a lot like the intimidating walking arsenal he appeared to be. Still, Tigereye had touched a nerve. Kempo turned defensive as the ship shook again.

"I'm just trying to let our combat medic in on the mysteries of the merc psyche, oh fearless leader."

Brixie sensed almost immediately that Tigereye simply hated that expression. The Trunsk settled for turning his baleful face on Kempo. Trunsks were not known for their cordiality, especially under stressful conditions.

"Can we have a little less talking please?" The fourth member of their group spoke up in a whiny voice. Of all who called themselves members of the Red Moons, Hugo Cutter was the last person Brixie would probably think of as a mercenary. An escapee from a psychotrauma ward maybe, but never a soldier. Cutter's hair was as wild and unpredictable as the stares that came from his eyes. Before the start of the mission, Lex Kempo had remarked to her that Hugo Cutter had once been enrolled in the prestigious Imperial Engineers Academy, only to be disbarred after he found it more interesting to blow things apart than put them together. Then again, Kempo always did have a knack for exaggeration. Especially when he talked about himself.

The ship dipped again. Cutter, sitting beside her, inhaled sharply. She reached out a hand to calm him. Cutter reacted by clutching the satchel bag in his lap even tighter.

"Don't touch me!"

"I'm sorry," she faltered out an apology. "I just thought . . ."

"Thought what?" He began to laugh hysterically. "That I would need help from the likes of you?"

"Don't knock it," Kempo murmured quietly with a twisted smile.

"Quiet. All of you." Tigereye warned as he checked the pocket navigator he carried in a special pouch as part of his weapons harness. Huge yellow eyes glanced up and caught the reflection of the Human with the unkempt hair in the forward cockpit screen. They locked on Cutter like targeters. "Especially you. Stop fidgeting. We're almost down." Cutter's nervousness was wearing even his own patience thin. Their craft shook again. He closed his eyes tightly.

"You know how much I hate insertions!"

"Relax. You clutch those shaped charges any harder and you're likely to set them off."

"Doubtful." The freighter dipped sharply in the thickening atmosphere of Gabredor III. He gulped. "It takes a detonator firing at triple frequency intervals to properly set off a Mesonics focalized explosive."

"I'll make a note," the fur-covered Trunsk growled as

he glanced over at Kempo. "How much longer till we reach the landing point?"

Kempo checked the navigational readings as they flashed by almost too quickly for Brixie to keep up. "A few more minutes. Sensor masking is holding up so far. A Z-95 patrol upstairs didn't even bother to sniff our contrail."

"I'll feel better when we're down. Brixie, get your gear ready to go."

"Right" she tried to keep her voice steady as she unfastened her restraint harness. The freighter suddenly lost power and began a steep dive. Brixie was immediately thrown into a wailing Cutter, who was positively revolted by her close proximity. Kempo wrestled the controls back. Regaining her footing, Brixie tried to ignore Cutter's expression and his tightly closed eyes.

"What was that?" Tigereye asked.

Kempo shook his head. All business now, he was fighting to bring the ship back under control. Red lights broke out all over the engineering panels. Alarms hooted noisily. The freighter abruptly rolled right and pitched down hard. Tigereye began flipping switches—the ship's starboard maneuvering thrusters were not responding.

Kempo quietly cursed between clenched teeth. "Where did procurement pick up this piece of Corellian crud anyway? I've seen better hulks from Socorro!"

"Can you land?"

Kemp looked directly at Tigereye. "You want an honest opinion?"

Brixie could tell that, this time, Kempo was no longer joking. Systems were failing all over the vessel. Beside her, she overheard Cutter whimpering. Some mercenary he made.

Tigereye unsnapped his own seat belts. "All hands to the lifepod now! This is no drill!"

The others spilled out of their chairs, rapidly grabbing equipment and supplies in emergency order and tossing them into the lifepod. For only a moment during the chaos, Brixie found herself watching Lex Kempo almost curiously. The Corellian pathfinder was still standing before the controls of the battered, falling freighter, gesturing with his hands locked together in an odd sort of way. Perhaps it was a ritual known only to spacers and their ships, she thought. The last thing she saw before the interior lights failed was him grinning at her as he usually did. Their fates and the ship's were about to part ways in a most violent fashion.

"Hope you signed up for the duration, Lady Brix. From now on, it gets nothing but interesting!"

Ten thousand meters later. Straight down.

"You know," said Hugo Cutter. "If you were Han Solo or Wedge Antilles or any one of a hundred other pilots I know, we wouldn't be here right now."

"Shut up," Lex Kempo snapped back. "I didn't see you help land the pod." Of course, it was difficult for the pathfinder to make an argument considering that the Red Moon assault team was dangling inside an escape pod caught in the thick canopy of Gabredor's jungle.

"Would it help if I did this?" Brixie's voice called from deeper inside the pod. A secondary hatch blew off, slicing vines and branches. Without means of further support, the pod fell the remaining 40 meters until it landed in the thick bough of an ancient swamp tree. Tigereye scratched his bruised head as he and the others spilled out of the pod and hit the dirt.

"No."

Kempo was the first to pick himself up off the jungle floor. He quickly checked the small arsenal of weapons he carried. Content, he turned and mock-saluted Sully Tigereye.

"The Red Moons have landed."

"Thanks for the update. Brixie?"

"Yes?" The rookie pulled herself over. She had joined the Red Moons only two months ago, training at a distant base with other recruits who were either disgruntled or disappointed with the New Republic's efforts to liberate the remainder of the galaxy. Her parents, both dedicated to the medical sciences and the saving of lives, had been conscripted into military service with an Imperial faction which called itself the Pentastar Alignment. Brixie had signed on with the Red Moons as a medical technician, hoping to somehow put an end to her parents' servitude. She was still struggling with the ill-fitting armored hat that had been issued to her earlier by the Red Moons' procurement detail.

"Did you pull that hatch lever?"

She bit her lower lip. There were worse things one could do than to get a Trunsk angry. Uncomfortable, she resigned herself to her fate. "Yes sir, I did."

"And what did I tell you before?"

She rolled her eyes a bit. "Don't do *anything* unless you tell me to do it."

"Exactly." Figuring that he really shouldn't be angry with her, he snatched the helmet off her head and made several adjustments to the inner web straps. After a moment, the helmet fit her perfectly. "Now pay attention and stay close."

"Yes, sir!"

"And can that *sir* nonsense."

"Yes . . ." Catching herself, she shrunk back to help collect equipment from the lifepod.

"Excuse me," Kempo stretched his aching frame. "You know how I hate to interrupt your instruction of the troops but . . ."

At long last, Tigereye was finally irritated with his unamusing tirade.

"What is it, Kempo?"

"Can you please direct me to the bad guys so we can fry them and find a way off this lovely vacation spot?"

"Wrong attitude. This is not some search and destroy job like the last one you botched on Dantooine. This is a search and rescue. Here are the particulars that need rescuing.''

He handed Kempo a datapad. Images of two young faces appeared in full portrait and side view modes. A distinct frown formed on the pathfinder's face as Brixie also looked at the datapad screen over his shoulder.

"Kiddies. We bailed out on to this mudball just to save a couple of pups?'' Kempo tossed the datapad back at Tigereye. "The colonel must have gone nuts.''

"Hey!'' Cutter spoke up. "Colonel Stormcaller is the last sane person left in the galaxy. I can personally vouch for that.''

"All bow. The Pirate King of Corellia has spoken,'' Kempo spat sarcastically as he affixed a grenade launcher underneath the muzzle of the "procured'' stormtrooper blaster rifle he carried. "So the four of us are going up against a slaver camp to yank two kids out with no ship. I'd say we're off to a famous running Red Moon start, Tigereye.''

"Who are they? Why are they so important?'' Brixie started to say "sir,'' but managed to clip it off in time.

"Don't bother,'' Kempo answered as he spun a DL-18 blaster pistol around on his index finger. "Our job is not to question why. That's what diplomats and tax collectors are for. We're soldiers. We get paid to solve the problems their kind create. And I want you to know, Trunsk, that I intend to get paid very well for this little field trip.''

Tigereye eyed him coldly as he handed the datapad to Brixie. "Study their faces and descriptions carefully. We need them alive. And intact.''

"But we don't have a ship. Shouldn't we wait for a rescue pickup?'' Brixie started to say.

"You're the team medtech,'' Tigereye's gaze hardened to dynaglass. "Is anyone here injured?''

She glanced at Kempo and the expressionless Hugo Cutter. So this was the life of the mercenary, she thought sullenly. Blindly taking orders. Crawling around on an unforgiving world, enemies all around them. No relief forces. No help. No remorse. She shook her head slowly.

The shriek of a snubfighter engine high over the tree canopy suddenly broke the silence. After a tense moment, it finally passed. Creatures and other tree dwellers began to slowly hoot and call again through the dense foliage. Kempo's expression turned grim.

"They found the crash. We better start moving."

Tigereye immediately agreed.

"I can re-triangulate the coordinates of the slaver camp from our position here. I'll take the point. Kempo, you take the rear. Make sure you have your survival kits and critter repellents. The slavers chose this moss rock for a reason, and that's probably because these jungle worlds can be downright hostile. All right. Move out!"

The slave master Greezim Trentacal relaxed in his chair aboard the transport freighter *Atron's Mistress,* fanning his face with the elaborately decorated hide of a lexiaus beast. His darkened quarters aboard the large freighter were filled with decorations and trinkets from a hundred different worlds. Trentacal sighed, letting his jowled complexion rest on his palm as he propped his head up with an elbow. A lithe, sparsely dressed Human girl moved around him, her gestures as light as the spice-laced air. She offered him a cup of wine. Annoyed, he brushed her offering away as he looked to the shadow hiding there in the darkness.

"Just how long is this going to take, Vex? You know how I hate sitting here in this humid jungle."

In reply, a voice slithered back. "We await another shipment of slaves from the last expedition near the Rim. By dawn tomorrow, the ship should be completely filled."

"Good," Trentacal yawned. Details. Minor little details. The slaves down in the cargo holds of his ship were just tiny portions of merchandise compared to the credits he could be making. It was one of the problems of doing business with the Pentastar Alignment.

To suggest that the Pentastar Alignment was just another Imperial warlord faction, just another pale pretender to the mighty former Empire, was a foolish assumption. The Alignment perceived itself as the Empire reborn. Led by a Grand Moff named Ardus Kaine, the Alignment had ignored Grand Admiral Thrawn's attempt to consolidate Imperial forces, carefully waiting until it could mount its own campaign against the New Republic.

Unlike other warlords, the Alignment was extremely organized and well-equipped thanks to the corporates, powerful companies formerly allied with the Empire. Now that one of these corporates, specifically the PowerOn Conglomerate from Cantras Gola, was secretly threatening to bolt and join the New Republic, the Pentastar Alignment was doing everything it could to prevent it. So the Alignment had turned to the Karazak Slavers Guild to solve its New Republic problem.

How completely ironic, Trentacal mused, that the children of the Cantras Gola ambassador had been kidnapped by his slavers. The note left in their place made the ambassador's situation quite clear. As long as the ambassador held off any further talks with the New Republic, the children would remain alive. The delay would be long enough for agents from the Alignment to completely sever the ties between Cantras Gola and the New Republic. In the end, Cantras Gola would remain loyal to the Pentastar Alignment and, in turn, the Karazak Slavers Guild would continue to conduct its operations on Gabredor III unhindered.

There were some benefits to this type of business arrangement—Trentacal had decided to keep the children as payment for his work. The Alignment had no opinion on the matter; the ambassador himself would be experiencing a most unfortunate accident and be quietly replaced . . . with a more reliable Alignment official.

The slave master glanced sideways at the ambassador's

children chained to the cabin's far wall and admitted that they would make fine additions to his household. Still, everything had its price. What, he wondered, would be the price for keeping these two?

Trentacal motioned to the slave girl at his side and took the cup of wine from her delicate hands. His thick palms caressed her expressionless cheek. The girl had been mute since a child. She had been among the first of the slaves he had kept for his own. He cupped his fingers under her chin and turned her head so that she could see the frightened children.

"Soon you will have others to instruct in the fine art of caring for me."

The shadow stepped forward, barely discernible in the darkness of Trentacal's private cabin. Trentacal watched his bodyguard and confidant, a Defel, as he stood before the stateroom's viewports. Vex's thick body was completely covered in layers of rippling black fur that absorbed all surrounding light. In his right hand he held a comlink close to an attentive ear, his head bobbing slightly as he listened to what sounded like little more than static. Outside the viewports lurked the tangled jungle growth of Gabredor III and the surrounding clearing that comprised the staging camp. Lookout towers armed with heavy repeating blasters rose from the jungle floor. On either side of the bulbous freighter, slaves were being led into the ship under the scrutiny of Karazak thugs. It was a fabulously efficient operation, Trentacal assured himself. After all, it was his.

"What is it, Vex?" The Defel was responsible for not only his master's security, but for the entire slaver operation on Gabredor. When summoned to the defense of his master, very few survived to tell about his rage. Trentacal did not mind the fear surrounding his kind's fearsome reputation either.

Vex thumbed the comlink off and turned slightly, not liking to stare too long at the pool of light that bathed his master. "One of the Z-95 patrols has spotted the wreckage of a light freighter some distance from here. The ship had come in low and fast, using some type of countermeasures to elude long-range sensors and our patrols. Whoever they were, it appears they did not want any attention.''

"Was it a ship from the New Republic?" Trentacal asked cautiously, suddenly alert.

The wraith's eye slits narrowed as he explained. "I do not think so. They would not risk coming so deep into Alignment territory. Doing so could mean an all-out war between them. That is something the New Republic is not willing to risk. The only way to know is to interrogate the survivors. But the main lifepod from the ship was not found in the wreckage. My trackers are still searching for it."

Trentacal slammed a meaty fist down on the armrest of his sumptuous chair. The serving girl sprang back in terror.

"Then it must be the Alignment. They've crossed us!"

The black head shook slowly. "I do not think it is the Pentastar Alignment either, Master Trentacal. Their resources are vast. They have no need for small strike teams. If they wanted to, they could attack with an *Enforcer*-class picket cruiser or something similar."

"Then who?"

Vex's eyes slid toward the far wall and the two figures chained silently there. The slovenly slave master sharply inhaled, understanding immediately. Whoever these intruders were, they were coming for *them*.

"Vex, I think you should activate the security perimeter."

"It has already been done, master."

"Ged it ob of me!" Lex Kempo, the mercenary's mercenary, whined like a bantha calf as he pulled at the slimy, multi-folded creature that had fallen on his head. Brixie was trying her best to pry it off with her vibro-knife. Sully

Tigereye just watched them. If the situation had been different, he might have been amused.

"Get it off of him, Brixie," the Trunsk unsheathed a combat vibro-axe from his weapons harness.

"I'm trying!"

"Can we go home now?" Hugo muttered as he sat on a dead log, tired and agitated.

"I'm sorry we're boring you!" Kempo snapped. He had the creature by both hands and was forcibly pulling it off when the little beast whipped out a tail appendage and squirted a powdery jet in his face. Coughing and sneezing uncontrollably, Kempo knocked Brixie into the brush. Cutter laughed.

Tigereye swore, his patience exhausted.

"That does it. Exobiology class is now over!"

Tigereye grabbed the thing by its now-extended tail and swung. The vibro-axe removed the flailing appendage. A greenish fluid squirted over everyone. The creature flopped off Kempo's head and expired at their feet.

Humiliation forgotten, Brixie immediately snapped open her medkit and examined the grumbling pathfinder's head for puncture marks or other lacerations that would indicate a bite. She used a water jet to clear off his face. A quick spot test of the creature's blood revealed that it was not inherently dangerous. Unfortunately, there was little she could do for their wallowing morale. They had been trudging through the jungle for almost a day now. Tempers were as short as grenade timers.

"I feel like a droid with a bunch of haywire receptors and a bad servo creak. Thanks kid," Kempo wiped at his face with the moisture cloth Brixie had given him. "What was that thing?"

Tigereye considered for a moment. "I don't know, but you're lucky it wasn't poisonous. I suggest the next time you hear a noise, you might want to look up as well as around." Kempo fell quiet as he poked sympathetically at the growing welt on his forehead. Cutter continued to chuckle.

Tigereye turned his ire on the squatting demolitions expert.

"I don't recall giving any order for a rest break, Hugo."

"Well, you guys looked so busy fooling around with that thing that I didn't want to disturb you."

"Time's short. You're on point. I want you to scout ahead and make sure there aren't any more surprises waiting for us."

The frazzled-haired engineer pointed at his own chest, startled. "You want me to . . . scout? Sully, you know I don't scout. I blow things up into itty-bitty pieces. Everyone in the unit says I make a poor scout."

"Consider it a valuable life lesson. Brixie's gotta finish checking out Kempo, and someone has to watch over her."

Hugo rose angrily to his feet, the charges still rattling around in his camo bag. He drew a blaster pistol from a holster.

"Fine, but who's going to watch over me?"

"Enough complaining. Scoot!"

Hugo vanished over the dead log he had been sitting on, still complaining loudly as he walked off. Tigereye shook his tired, grizzled head. Removing the map pad, he checked their current coordinates with the expected slaver encampment. They should be reaching their security perimeter soon. He looked up momentarily to watch Brixie dab a medicated ointment on Kempo's head. She was also looking at him.

"Problem?"

"No, I was just wondering," she stumbled over her words. "I mean, everyone spends so much time arguing and insulting. You don't act exactly like what I've seen. You know . . . like professionals."

She stopped, believing she had somehow completely insulted them. Now it was Kempo's turn to laugh. Even Tigereye, surprisingly, was not offended.

"You've been watching too many entertainment holos,

Brixie. Not all of us pretend to be the master merc like Kempo."

"Who's pretending?" Kempo interrupted, still rinsing his eyes. "Don't let our sparring fool you any, kid. We go back a long way. Far enough back to hate each other's guts and still be the best of chums."

"Hugo's your best friend?" Brixie looked confused. "But you don't act like best friends."

Tigereye pursed his lips. "Everyone in this company, everyone in the Red Moons that is, comes with a story. Your parents for instance. You don't like the way the Alignment is treating them, do you?"

"My parents were both taken from their clinic and forced to work for the Alignment military as combat surgeons. It's almost as if they've been locked up. I just want them back."

"Hugo's parents were Imperial nobility. He lived on a corporate world during the reign of the Emperor. His parents tried everything to keep him under control, including locking him up. I was treated like an animal once. I know what it's like to be caged. When you go through life like that, sometimes you need someone to keep you in check. Hugo minds over me like I mind him."

Kempo pulled himself to his feet and handed the salve back to her.

"Remember kid, the first rule of soldiering is to not let appearances fool you. Tigereye didn't choose us for this team just because of our singing voices. Tigereye's got more combat experience in his little right toe claw than most Imperial generals. Hugo can make an AT-ST dance a jig and explode with just a spanner and a thermal detonator. My job is to make sure we survive to brag about this little tale. And in case we do fall apart, Lady Brix, your job is to put the little pieces back together so I can collect my finish fee."

Brixie felt completely embarrassed. What she had mistaken for open hostility among the three veterans was actually their way of dealing with yet another impossible situation.

Hugo Cutter's head suddenly appeared over the log.

"Excuse me. I don't want to interrupt your talking about me, but I think I found something."

From a distance, the sensor mast appeared like a metal chrome ball mounted on a pole slightly taller than the surrounding vegetation. Others just like it rose approximately 20 meters to either side. They positioned themselves almost 30 meters away from the distinct-looking sensor fence.

"Looks like we found their perimeter," Kempo muttered quietly to Tigereye, not anxious to trip any possible acoustical pickups. Behind them, Cutter and Brixie waited anxiously.

"Or we tripped over a buried, outer perimeter line already." Tigereye checked his own detection instruments. Despite his concern, the possibility of an outer barrier was unlikely here. The everpresent moisture and local lifeforms would make short work of almost anything made of metal or complex circuitry buried in the humus. He glanced back. "All right Hugo, you're on."

Cutter took off his service jacket and dumped the contents of his bag of tricks on to it. Shaped charges, broken datapads, anti-vehicle grenades, droid parts and bits of c-board and chips spilled everywhere. Kempo eyed the strange assortment with some disdain.

"You're carrying enough junk to supply Industrial Automaton."

"Spare me," Cutter snapped back as he set to work. Brixie watched the entire process with interest as Kempo and Tigereye took up sentry positions close by. Not even realizing she had been recruited to assist him, Cutter was asking her for tools from the tech kit and bits from the scrap pile. In minutes, a truly strange conglomeration of sensor boards, probe droid chips, scanners and communication jammers was taking shape.

"Is this going to work?" she asked.

Cutter took a moment to sit back and admire his creation with a small sense of satisfaction. "They banned me from the Imperial Engineering Academy. They laughed at me. Well, does this look like the work of a madman to you?"

Brixie stared hard at the device. Cutter looked up at her, perhaps sensing the thoughts crossing her mind. A crooked little smile formed across his lips.

"Don't bother answering that."

A crashing sound from the nearby bushes startled all of them into silence. Kempo growled over to them, "Keep down. Someone just set off one of my door bells."

Tigereye pulled out a set of macrobinoculars. Keeping his view on the trail they had just come from, he waited for several long moments. He saw a brief movement and focused. Through the viewfinder, he saw a scaly head sniffing the ground. Moving the binocs slowly, he finally caught the rider wearing a camosuit to blend against the jungle backdrop. The rider was clenching a long force pike in his free hand as he examined Kempo's "door bell," a tree limb tied across the trail with thin cord.

"What is it?" Kempo whispered.

"Looks like a tracker. Riding some kind of two-legged reptoid."

Kempo used the targeting sight on his stormtrooper rifle to watch the newcomer.

"I see him now. Another might be close by," he whispered.

"Another won't make any difference. All it takes is one report to bring the whole slaver camp down on our heads."

"Those odds are good enough for me." Kempo unsnapped the scabbard on his back and handed Brixie a very sharp vibrocutlass, its blade and edges blackened for military duty. She dubiously took the weapon in her hands.

"What's this for?"

"You get to watch my back for a change. I've had enough of this mud crawl." Kempo started running toward the trees. "The rest of you take down the fence. I'll handle the bad guys!"

"Kempo! I didn't . . ." Tigereye snarled at him just as the pathfinder took off. Brixie and Cutter looked to him for guidance. "Don't just sit there! Hugo, disarm the fence. Brixie, you cover him!" No sooner had he said that when he too had disappeared through the thick growth.

Kempo dropped to one knee as he sprang through the trees, startling the tracker and his mount. He fired the blaster rifle at short range, but missed the rider.

The rider spurred the trained reptoid and charged. The creature snapped at the open air just by his head, then tried to cleave him open with serrated feet claws. Kempo fired back, his stolen set of Imperial scout armor taking the brunt of the beast's charge as it sent him sprawling. The impact knocked the blaster rifle out of his hands.

Poised above him, the tracker raised his force pike to strike. A howling, fur-covered missile burst from the trees, turning the tracker's attention away. Sully Tigereye crashed against both tracker and beast, his vibro-ax swinging and connecting against the creature's thick hide. The reptoid screamed from the terrible injury and bolted away, carrying its rider reluctantly along with it. With the tracker's back turned to them now, Kempo picked up his fallen weapon and fired. A screaming burst of energy struck the tracker square in the back, killing him before he struck the ground. The injured reptoid, now riderless, kept on crashing loudly away through the foliage.

Tigereye brandished his vibro-ax at Kempo.

"I should have let that thing take a bite out of you, if only to teach you a lesson."

"I was doing just fine before you showed up."

"Let me guess—you had him exactly where you wanted him," the Trunsk snorted as he caught his breath. "Check the body. If we're lucky, he didn't have a chance to report in."

"We're never that lucky," Kempo retorted as he headed over to the body of the dead tracker.

Hugo got to his feet, holding up the contraption. Brixie looked on, eyeing him and his spontaneous invention dubiously. He began to move slowly toward the sensor mast, fumbling for the power switches that would activate the united parts. He suddenly stopped in his tracks.

"What's wrong?" Brixie half-whispered to him, trying to watch him and their surroundings at the same time.

"Something about this type of sensor mast."

He took another step. A whine came from the datapad's power coupling. The device was not used to handling the power requirements of the other components. The two and a half meter tall mast loomed over his head as he slowly approached. An expression of recognition came over Cutter. He stopped in his tracks, making quick adjustments to the components in his hands.

"Now I remember!"

"Remember what?" Brixie sputtered.

An intense beeping came from Hugo's contraption. Before Brixie's eyes, an alternating pattern of light began to phase from the sensor mast. She gasped as the solid-looking ground before their feet suddenly evaporated, exposing a cargo speeder-sized ditch trap. Explosives and mines lay at the bottom of the excavated pit. Hugo smirked.

"A holographic trap. Very sneaky. Very expensive. These slavers have better security than I thought. Did you see how I set the multiphase emitter to turn off the hologram?''

Brixie had been watching Hugo so intently that she almost did not hear the sound of dead leaves and underbrush being crushed behind her. She spun around, Kempo's vibrocutlass in her hands. A second tracker and his reptoid leered at her like predators about to pounce. A threatening rumble echoed in the sharp-toothed beast's throat as the tracker leveled the point of his force pike at Brixie's throat.

"Ah, Hugo?" she gulped.

The sound of a female scream cut through the jungle air like the edge of Sully Tigereye's polished vibro-ax. The Trunsk plunged through the jungle, back toward the sensor perimeter.

Tigereye stumbled into a clearing in time to see Lex Kempo drop from the trees and fall on the tracker. The reptoid bucked underneath them as the pathfinder slapped a now familiar-looking organism on the tracker's head. The tracker, his eyes completely covered by the filmy creature, knocked Kempo off as he swung the force pike wildly.

The whole scene looked completely ridiculous until the blinded tracker spurred the reptoid forward. A shot from Tigereye's own heavy blaster brought the tracker down, but the creature still charged into and over a shrieking Brixie.

"Brixie!" Tigereye bellowed, leaping forward.

The beast suddenly became quiet and rolled away from the startled girl in a heap—Kempo's vibrocutlass buried up to its hilt in its scaly chest. She looked more terrified than hurt as Tigereye ran up to her.

"Are you okay?"

She gulped once and fought to bring her fear under control.

"Yes . . . yes I'm fine."

Even Cutter was stunned as he looked up at the tree branch where Kempo had jumped from.

"And I thought I was crazy," he muttered.

Kempo had gotten to his feet. Brixie watched him for some time, trying to think of some way to thank him without sounding petty. Shrugging the incident away, the pathfinder turned his back to her and retrieved his vibrocutlass. He then moved to the body of the fallen tracker, switching off his comlink. Exhaling hard, Brixie collected her medkit and gear, not desiring to look on the scene anymore.

In the meantime, Cutter and Tigereye had turned their attention to the disarmed sensor mast and the exposed pit trap.

"Can we go around it?" Tigereye had exchanged his vibro-ax for the map locator. Cutter triumphantly held up his device.

"No problem. Those slavers are probably scratching their heads, wondering how we did it."

"If the slavers stick around long enough to wonder." Tigereye interjected. "We have only one shot at this. Karazak slavers aren't stupid. Once they figure out we bypassed their perimeter, they will probably leave their paid guns behind to pick us off while they jump planet with their valuables—including the children."

"Sully," Brixie slung a medical pack over her shoulder. "Before we go any further with this, I have to know who these children are. The least you can do is tell us why their lives are more important than ours."

"The kid's right," Kempo added as he sheathed the vibrocutlass in its carrier. "I'm deliberately jumping out of perfectly good trees for these pups. You owe us that much."

Tigereye sighed. "They're the children of the ambassador to Cantras Gola."

"Cantras Gola is a corporate world." Brixie found herself getting angry. "An Alignment world. What's so important about that?"

"Everything," Tigereye silenced her. "Kempo is right, Brixie. We're soldiers. We don't ask questions. We supply answers. With an entire corporate world about to sway over to the New Republic, and the New Republic unable to openly confront the Pentastar Alignment, you need someone else to fight the battle. We are that someone else."

"But I thought the reason why the Red Moons broke away from the New Republic was because the New Republic wasn't doing enough. Now we're fighting their battles for them!"

"Helping the New Republic win Cantras Gola helps everyone. Like it or not, returning these kids alive to the Cantras Gola ambassador is crucial. We need to take that slaver ship before it gets away. It's the only way to save those kids and for us to get off this planet. Now are there more questions from the ranks?"

The four of them looked at each other, the faint odor of ozone from blaster fire still in the air around them.

"I suppose it's too late to request a transfer?" Kempo remarked.

The longer he waited, the more Greezim Trentacal nervously paced about the deluxe stateroom aboard *Atron's Mistress*. The trackers sent out to investigate the crashed freighter's missing escape pod had not reported in for several hours. There was more to the mysterious, downed vessel than even Vex had anticipated.

"They must be soldiers. Or worse. Mercenaries." He shuddered at the thought. The incentive of credits and personal fortune that drove beings to enslave other beings also drove them to fight for foolish causes.

"Well?" He looked to Vex, still poised like a dark statue beside the stateroom's viewports. He dropped the comlink from his ear.

"The tracker team is still not responding. In addition,

one of the perimeter sensors seems to have malfunctioned, although I do not know why yet."

"They're here!" Trentacal put a hand over his mouth, completely alarmed now. "Lords of Atron! They're here already! Give the order to debark. Immediately!"

"As I pointed out earlier," the Defel spoke quietly but firmly, "we have not loaded the latest shipment of slaves." He gestured at the large prefabricated building that served as a temporary clearing-house for the newest arrivals. "They have to be tagged and medically scanned. Many slaves from this shipment are to be sold to the Hutts. You know how displeased the Hutts become when they are sent inferior wares."

"You can medically scan them after they have been loaded. Do as I command!"

Vex's expression did not change. He bowed slightly.

"I will give the order personally, master. We shall depart immediately."

Trentacal rushed out of the stateroom to his own sleeping quarters. The Defel wraith looked upon the ambassador's children, still chained to the cabin wall. Expressions laden with fear and loathing gazed back up at him. The girl, several years older than her brother, tried to protectively shield him from Vex's penetrating, awful stare.

Suddenly, the wraith was gone. The girl blinked, uncertain whether or not to believe her eyes. She had not imagined the disappearance. Abruptly, the cabin door bolts clanged solidly shut, locking them in darkness again. Her brother whimpered. She held him a little tighter, silently wondering what would become of them.

Something touched her shoulder. The girl gasped loudly, if only long enough for a hand to clamp down over her mouth. She recognized the pained expression of Trentacal's favorite slave girl. How long had she been hiding here, waiting for Vex to leave? The slave pressed a key into her hand and made a gesture with her finger to her lips.

Before she could say a word of thanks, the door to

Trentacal's private chamber was suddenly shoved aside, the slave master's bulky outline filling the doorway. His face was masked in shadow.

"What's going on in here?"

Lying prone in the foliage ahead of the assault team, Lex Kempo aimed the macrobinoculars at the clearing in the jungle growth before him.

"What do you see?" Brixie whispered beside him.

The slaver camp consisted of several watchtowers, a few prefabricated buildings and a currently vacant landing pad for a snubfighter-sized craft. In the middle of the camp, the jungle's heavy humus had been pressure-formed flat to provide room for the large cargo transport situated there. Beings of all origins were being rushed into the ship, which was not a good sign.

Kempo chewed slowly on a bit of protein survival wafer as he continued to sight the camp through the binocs. "Looks like we're outgunned maybe seven to one. There are four watchtowers armed with blaster cannons: two close to us, two past the freighter. The camp is crawling with thugs. See that bunker right beside the ship? Looks like their command center. All sensors, communications and defensive controls are probably housed in there."

"Are those hatches on the side?"

Kempo frowned as he zoomed the binoculars. "You've got laser eyes, kid. Those are definitely gun ports. It doesn't matter, that bunker might as well be half a light year away. We'll get cut down before we even reach the freighter."

"Not if I can keep them occupied," Cutter's voice murmured behind them.

Kempo and Brixie looked around in unison at Cutter and his bag of magic tricks. In his hands he had one of the oddly concave Mesonics focalized explosives, the kind used to demolish structures. Squatting beside Hugo, Sully Tigereye made a hand gesture, fingers spread open wide which he turned into a fist. Kempo snorted derisively, but still nodded in agreement. Confused, Brixie poked at Kempo.

"I'm not familiar with that hand signal," she whispered to him. "What does it mean?"

The pathfinder smiled grimly as he switched the safety off on the grenade launcher mounted to his storm-trooper blaster rifle.

"It means hang on to your pretty head. We're about to make some noise."

The slave girl lunged at Trentacal, a slender metal object in her hands. Despite his size, the slave master could move quickly if he wanted to. In seconds, he had the girl's arms pinned. She strained silently against his grip, trying to bite his hands. Trentacal held her long enough for him to press the emergency call. The wraith and several armed guards appeared in moments, just as Trentacal pushed the slave girl roughly to the cabin floor.

"Fools! All of you! You're supposed to protect me!" He held up the knife he had taken and pointed it at the slave girl. "I want you to vaporize this insolent thing and get us out of here! And pray that my next wish is not all of your heads on a serving platter!" The guards drew their energy weapons, aiming them at the slave. The ambassador's daughter cried aloud, trying to shield her brother from the cruel scene.

A muffled explosion rattled the huge transport. Trentacal's eyes bulged in mute surprise as he watched two of the guard towers tip over and collapse in perfect unison.

Kempo and Brixie had made it only as far as the make-shift landing pad for the camp's snubfighter when the snouts of several huge blaster cannons appeared from slits in the command bunker. The heavy weapons were laying down a withering curtain of fire, pinning them there.

"Hold still!" Brixie was still trying to apply a medical wrap to Kempo's singed right leg. The pathfinder had unexpectedly been the first target of the heavy blaster attack.

"Look at the size of those guns!" Kempo clucked his tongue in a tisking manner. "They probably ripped them out from some capital ship."

"Who cares! Can you see Hugo and Sully?"

Kempo poked his head slightly around the corner and shot a slaver guard in the torso, dropping him instantly. He spotted Cutter's familiar tousled mane of hair as he hid from the energy fire coming from the command bunker. The prefabricated structures he hid behind would not last for long.

"Hugo's trapped over by those buildings." He tapped his comlink switch twice, but there was no reply. He shook his head. "I can't raise Sully, but I think he made it to the freighter."

When Kempo looked around the corner again, the bunker's weapons were aiming once again for Cutter. Energy beams rained down all over the demolitions expert, burning away huge chunks of the prefabricated structures. Kempo shouted over the din back to Brixie.

"Hugo's gonna be a little smoking pile of nothing unless we do something to shut those guns up!"

Surprised by his words, she looked over at the impregnable command bunker. "But shouldn't we be going for the freighter? That's our way out of here!"

"Leaving teammates behind is *not* in my employment description."

Kempo took a step back and jostled something. The niche where they were hiding served as a storage shed for the landing pad. He disappeared for a moment inside and returned with a grav-cart and a half dozen large cylinders with prominent warning labels plastered over them.

"I think it's time we extended a warm Red Moon greeting to our slaver friends."

* * *

Two guards armed with stun prods stood by a secondary
boarding ramp of the cargo transport, shoving as many of
the enslaved beings as they could into the ship. Many of
the slaves, panicked by the explosions and screaming
beams of energy fire, had taken this opportunity to run.
The guards were in no place to argue. One by one, the
other loading ramps were closing as the ship began its
final preparations for takeoff. A message crackled over
the guards' secure comlinks. Relieved to be as far away
from the shooting as possible, they began to climb the
ramp. As one of the guards turned to follow the slaves in,
he noticed a slave without a restraint collar. He growled
to his partner as he seized the Trunsk by the arm.

"Hey! They forgot to put a pain collar on this one."

Sully Tigereye turned around. Sharpened fighting
claws seized the startled guard by his chin. In his other
hand, he aimed a heavy blaster pistol at the second guard
and shot the stun prod right out of his hands. The guard
spun and ran.

"There will be no more pain collars. Not as long as I
live." He clenched the first guard by the jowls of his neck
and swung his face close. "Now that I have your undi-
vided attention—where's your boss?"

Working quickly, Kempo and Brixie stacked the cart with
the fuel cylinders they had found as well as the explosives
and grenades they were carrying. The cannon fire around
them was getting closer and closer.

"Come to think of it, there's one small problem with
this plan," Kempo muttered half-aloud.

"We don't have time for problems!" Brixie replied,
wincing slightly as a piece of the nearby landing pad was
blasted apart by a bunker weapon.

"One of us is going to have to pilot this thing up to
their doorstep."

They both looked at each other, eyes frozen. A tight little grin began to form across Kempo's face. He took Brixie's hand and kissed the back of it.

"Don't worry kid, I just volunteered." The pathfinder climbed aboard and took up a position by the cart's steering controls, trying to hunker down low. He handed her the stormtrooper rifle.

"Keep them occupied long enough for me to get up close." He activated the cart's repulsorlift controls. The cart surged slowly forward as he smirked back at her.

"Just don't let people forget about me, right?"

She shook her head. There was something about his expression that she had never seen before. There was so much she wanted to learn about him and no time left.

As the grav-cart emerged, Brixie took up a position to the side of the landing pad. She fired the rifle's grenade launcher, spitting concussion explosives at the hardened outer shell of the command bunker—for what little good it would do.

The grav-cart zigzagged across the clearing. For what felt like an eternity, the bunker's blaster weapons clumsily tried to follow him, just barely missing. Just as the grav-cart reached the bunker, Brixie could see the pathfinder time his leap—only to stumble on the cart's side railing. His foot caught, he was dragged relentlessly along until . . .

The next second, she was looking up at the failing light of the evening sky. The shock wave had knocked Brixie flat on her back. She staggered to her feet. Where there had been a command bunker, there was now only the jagged remains of a permacrete foundation. Even the sides of the cargo transport had been scorched by the blast. Slavers were running wildly in all directions. She moved to the edge of the heart of the fire, shielding her face as she looked for a familiar form to stagger out.

Kempo had to come out. That's the way the holos always ended. The hero always walked out.

Nobody did.

Hugo grabbed her by the arm and began pulling her over to the ship.

"No!" she screamed at him. "We won't leave a team-mate behind! We can't!"

He had to drag her away from the inferno.

The explosion was so huge it shook the cargo transport violently on its landing legs.

The transport bridge's accessway popped open. Tiger-eye shoved the guard into a few of the crewers standing there. Several reached for weapons, but they were not fast enough. Energy beams ricocheted across the bridge. When it was over, Tigereye waved the blaster pistol at the survivors.

"Everybody in the escape pod! Now!"

They filed into the bridge's lifeboat pod. Tigereye sealed the hatchway behind them, locking them inside. After securing the bridge, he then tapped his comlink.

There was no need. Brixie and Hugo Cutter appeared at the bridge's accessway. The demolitions expert's shoulders were sagging. Brixie was crestfallen, tears streaming down her cheeks.

Tigereye understood immediately. Kempo. The explosion.

His hands balled into fists, Tigereye wanted to scream. He wanted to tear the bridge apart. He grabbed the guard he had taken prisoner and slammed him against one of the control consoles so hard the impact dented the panels. He shoved the datapad before the guard's eyes, pictures of the ambassador's children flashing on the tiny screen.

"They're not among the slaves held down below. So *where* are they?"

The guard gestured at another doorway on the bridge.

"They're in the master's quarters! In there!"

Tigereye tossed the heavy blaster pistol to Cutter as he unsheathed his vibro-ax.

"Set weapons to stun. We need those children alive."

"I'm coming too," Brixie stepped forward, shaking, still clenching Lex Kempo's stormtrooper rifle with whitened knuckles. Tigereye gestured at the guard.

"No. You have to watch him."

Brixie pivoted and shot the guard using the blaster rifle's stun setting at point-blank range. The guard slumped over into unconsciousness.

"He's going nowhere," she replied tersely as she inserted two stun grenades into the rifle launcher.

Tigereye and Cutter regarded each other, surprised.

Muffled blaster fire erupted from somewhere behind the door, followed by a painful scream. Tigereye gestured to Cutter at the door controls.

"Open it. Now!"

The well-appointed domain of the slave master was almost completely dark. The slave master himself was dead, slumped over in his lounger. Brixie immediately took a step toward the young girl and her brother still chained to the wall, but Tigereye held her back. From the way they were cowering in silence, he could tell something was not right.

"Someone else is in here," Tigereye whispered.

"That is correct," a voice from the dark declared.

Crouching low, the mercenaries separated as they made their way into the cabin. As she moved past the lounger, Brixie's foot grazed something soft. She inhaled sharply as she saw the torn throat of a dead slave girl lying on the floor, a hold-out blaster still clutched in her tiny hands. The slave master's guards lay dead close by.

"She saw an opportunity to escape," the voice explained matter-of-factly. "I had to convince her otherwise. Take a good look, mercenaries. Your fate will be the same as hers."

A shape lunged at Cutter, sending him sprawling across the floor. In just moments, the shape appeared again, claws burying deep inside Brixie's protective vest. The thing shoved her into the wall, knocking her senseless. The stormtrooper rifle clattered to the floor.

Holding her injured head and side, she heard more fighting. Trying to focus, she saw their attacker stand against the dim light of the cabin's viewports for only a moment. She immediately recognized the shaggy, black-furred creature from her medical training at the university. No wonder the lights were out!

"It's a Defel! A wraith!"

Tigereye found the cabin's lighting controls and flipped them to their maximum setting. Glowspheres filled the room with brightness. The terrifying creature screamed in agony, trying to shield its eyes from the powerful lights.

Surrounded and blinded, the Defel spun around wildly. Brixie had picked up the stormtrooper blaster rifle. Hugo Cutter was back up on his feet, blaster pistol in hand, his face badly bruised. Sully Tigereye's gaze narrowed to a chilled yellow as he took a step forward, vibro-ax in hand.

"The only fate you should be worrying about . . . is your own."

The cargo ship, almost fully laden with freed slaves, climbed slowly into the sky above Gabredor III. Below on the night-eclipsed surface of the planet, the destroyed slaver camp burned with a vengeance. Tigereye had made it a point that they should leave plenty of Red Moon marks for all to find there. Knowing they had been targeted, the Karazak Slavers Guild would have to look long and hard for another place to conduct its business. And with the children of the Gola ambassador safely aboard the ship, the Pentastar Alignment had lost as well.

In Brixie's heart, it was a hollow victory. They had tried to search the wreckage of the command bunker, but the fire was simply too hot. She sat in a chair on the transport's bridge, keeping to herself as Tigereye and Cutter familiarized themselves with the ship's astrogation controls. She finally thought about taking the helmet off her head. With a tired sigh, she undid the straps and let the helmet fall to the deck beside her feet.

Tigereye looked over at the sound. During her training, it had been difficult for her to judge the Trunsk—to separate reputation from reality. The same clawed hands which had so eagerly torn the Defel to pieces were the same hands which gladly unlocked the pain collars of dozens of slaves.

She finally realized why he had chosen her for this mission. There were some things that cannot come with training or preparation, they must be experienced and felt. Brixie had experienced the camaraderie and the fear, seen the violence and death that was all part of the life of the blaster-for-hire. For a brief moment, Tigereye's expression softened. He and Hugo would mourn the loss of their lifetime friend in their own ways.

Her gaze fell upon the bridge's visual screens. Gabredor III was falling slowly away. She found herself wishing Lex was here, wondering what his reaction would have been to her realization. He probably would have just winked at her.

Then she saw the remains of the slaver camp on the screens. A chill ran down her spine—there was something familiar about the shape of fires down there. Kempo's voice echoed in her mind. In his own words, the pathfinder had indeed gone out in a blaze of glory.

From hundreds of kilometers above, the explosion that had flattened the command bunker appeared like a fiercely glowing crescent . . .

A red moon.

Slaying Dragons

by Angela Phillips

Improper Passcode—Access Denied . . .
Improper Passcode—Access Denied . . .
Improper Passcode—Access Denied . . .

"A plume of smoke from the end of the canyon heralded the approach of the dragon. Veni drew closer to his elder sister as Vici activated her light-saber."

Improper Passcode—Access Denied . . .
Improper Passcode—Access Denied . . .

"Veni trembled at the sound of 20 powerful reptilian legs plunging toward him in deadly synchronization. But Vici was not afraid. Though only 16 years old, she held the mighty power of the Force tightly in her hands. The dragon drew closer."

Vweep! Access Granted . . .

Shannon Voorson set her story platform aside and turned back to the monitor. "Finally," she muttered. This code had taken longer to slice than usual. Still, she reflected, any code one computer can generate, another can imitate. First Law of Slicing. Now, she thought, let's see if we've found anything interesting . . .

"Oh, yuck," she sighed when she saw the contents of the file she'd entered: a register of six new Star Destroyers nearing completion at the nearby Kuat Drive Yards. What stupid names they have, she thought—the *Impervious*, the *Penetrator*, the *Inflexible*, the *Indomitable*, the *Inexorable*, and the *Exterminator*. If I were naming Star Destroyers, she thought, I'd give them names like the *Iron Hand*, the *Raptor*, or the *Titania*. Still, what do you expect from people with so little imagination they let computers come up with their access codes?

Shannon heard voices through the thin pre-fab walls of her room; someone had entered the apartment, and her parents were greeting the visitor. Deciding to investigate, she saved the Star Destroyer files under the password "dumbnames" and shut down her computer's code program.

The Voorson family had been techs at Kuat Freight Port for generations. Most of them had spent their entire lives aboard the station—they were born in the company Wellness Center, educated in the company school, apprenticed to and then hired by Kuat Port Support Services.

They married co-workers, raised their families in company housing, and rarely left the station, even to go so far as the planet Kuat itself. There was no reason to leave— the company stores on the station provided everything they needed, the pay and benefits for KFP workers were among the best in the system, and they had the pride and satisfaction of knowing that, as members of the Kuat Engineering conglomerate, they were helping build the finest starships in the galaxy. Still, every so often a Voorson would look beyond the comfortable walls of a station apartment to see what the rest of the thousand-thousand worlds had to offer. Shannon's cousin, Deen, was one of these wandering Voorsons.

"Deen!" she squealed excitedly at the sight of the young man embracing her father. "Oh, Deen, it's you! You're finally here! Where have you been? What have you been doing?" Shannon leapt at the guest.

Her cousin turned to catch her. "Hey, Little Bit, I've missed you! Oof!" He grunted, as he tried to lift her off the floor. "You've grown, Little Bit—let me look at you! You're so tall now, and your hair is so long—when I left, you were a baby, with braids only to your ears, and Aunt Nell had you sleep with a scarf on to keep them from standing straight up in the morning!"

Nell Voorson nodded, and smiled wryly. "Now I have to keep her from chewing the ends."

"Oh, Deen," said Shannon, "I've missed you so—come and see my room! It's all different now, and I have my own computer and everything!" She tugged on his hand.

Deen smiled indulgently at the child. "I've missed you, too, Little Bit, but don't you think your parents want to talk to me too?"

"Oh, go with her, Deen," said Nell. "You can talk while Johan and I get supper on."

.   .   .

"I can't believe you're really here," said Shannon, hopping up and down in the center of her room. "It's been four whole years! What have you been doing?"

"Slaying dragons."

Shannon laughed. "No, Deen, really!"

"Really! Well, sort of. Helping to slay artificial dragons—I've been working as a tech." He took a seat next to Shannon's computer.

"Where?"

"Oh, different places," he said. His dark eyes wandered over the room. "Are you still reading those old stories grandmother gave you?" he asked as he spotted the story platform on her computer.

"Yep," said Shannon, "even though Mother says I should outgrow them, like dolls."

"I don't see many dolls here," said Deen.

"Yep. I like computers now. I'm a slicer. I can slice into anything."

"Anything?" Deen asked, chuckling.

"Anything. So who do you work for? What kind of work do you do? Do you get paid a lot? Do you fix droids, or ships, or what?"

"Hey," said Deen, "one question at a time! I work for some friends I made, right after I left here. They're good friends. I don't get paid a lot, but I like what I'm doing. Mostly I work on ships . . ."

"What kind?"

"Small starcraft, mostly, but some larger ones, and anything else that my friends need fixed. I have to be flexible."

"What's the hardest thing you've ever had to fix?"

Deen paused. "Well," he said, glancing at the closed bedroom door, "a few months ago, I had to adapt some airspeeders to operate at 20 degrees below freezing . . ."

"And did they work?"

"Well enough . . . That's *Vici of Alderaan,* isn't it?" he asked, pointing to the story platform on the computer.

"Yup, it's still my favorite. Vici is so brave."

"One who has the Force need have no fear," Deen murmured.

"That's what Vici's grandfather tells her. Say," Shannon asked, "did you get a chance to visit Alderaan? Before . . ."

Deen shook his head. "No. I never did. I wish I could have. But I never had the chance."

"It's not fair," said Shannon, settling on the floor.

"That I never got to Alderaan?" asked her cousin.

"That they blew it up. Stupid Empire. Why'd they do it? Grandmother always said Alderaan was a planet of peace and beauty. There weren't any weapons there. Why'd they do it?"

"Because of that," said Deen, pointing.

"Because of my story platform?"

"Because of that story," said Deen. "That story, and others like it. The stories of Alderaan were more dangerous to the Emperor than any weapon."

"How can a story be more dangerous than a weapon?" asked Shannon.

"Because of the ideas in it. On Alderaan, people still believed in the Force. On Alderaan, people remembered the Jedi Knights and the Old Republic. The people of Alderaan remembered the way things were in the galaxy before the coming of the Empire, before the days of hate and fear. And their stories, libraries and universities held all of the ideas that can destroy the Emperor—that love is stronger than hate, that people are stronger than weapons, that combined together the people in this galaxy have a strength the Emperor can never oppose." Deen's eyes were shining.

"So the Emperor," said Shannon, "destroyed Alderaan to destroy all these ideas?"

"He tried," said Deen, "but he didn't succeed. He can never succeed. The only way for him to control all the ideas in the galaxy would be for him to kill or enslave everyone in the galaxy, and that's impossible. He can't win. The more crimes he commits, the more people will stand up to fight him . . ."

"Deen," asked Shannon, "are you a Rebel?"

Deen put a hand to his mouth.

"It's all right," Shannon added, "I won't tell anybody. Not even Mom and Dad. Here," she said, switching to the computer, "look what I found today. Just before you got here. I'll give you a copy if you want . . ."

"How did you access this?" Deen asked, staring at the list of Star Destroyers. "Do you have any idea . . ."

"It's easy to slice into Imperial files; they have computer-rigged pass-names. I make up my own codes myself. Usually animal names, like 'nerf,' or 'bhillen,' or even 'dog.' "

"I can't believe this," Deen said, still reading the data-screen. "Do you know what this is worth—do you know what will happen to you if someone catches you at this?"

"No one's ever gotten past my codes," said Shannon proudly.

"Maybe no one's ever considered investigating the files of a nine-year-old girl," said Deen. "You've got to stop this—you'll get yourself killed!"

Shannon bit her lip. "Does that mean you don't want copies of the files?"

Mistress Voorson called them to dinner, cutting off Deen's answer.

Gathered around a pot of stewed bhillen, the family discussed the last four years: Shannon's schooling, Nell's promotion to senior docking supervisor of Kuat Freight Port, Johan and Deen's work as techs. Johan complained about impatient starship captains expecting miracles. Deen told horror stories of combatting heat, cold, humidity, dust, ice, offensive flora, fauna, microbes, and every other threat to machinery on backwater worlds he neglected to name.

"You actually found moss growing in the ships' coolant coils?" asked Johan.

"Yep," said Deen. "Two hours before launch."

"Did you get 'em cleaned up in time?"

Deen grinned. "Skin of our teeth."

"The Force was with you," his uncle said.

Nell frowned slightly. "It's good to have you home, Deen, after so long. I was beginning to think you'd left us for good. And now," she said, "here you are. Are you in trouble, Deen? Do you need anything?"

"Nell," her husband protested, "can't a boy fly in without an ulterior motive?"

Deen stared at his plate. "Actually," he said, poking his custard with a spoon, "I was wondering . . ."

"Ah, here it comes," said Nell.

"My friends," Deen continued, "the ones I work with . . . They've had some problems lately, lost a lot of equipment . . ."

"Lost?" asked Nell.

"Uh, yeah, damaged. Beyond repair."

"How?" asked Johan.

"Well . . . there were a lot of asteroids, and—it's a long story, but the point is, we need a Colony Class 23669 power generator, and . . ."

"Why don't you contact the factory, then?" asked Nell. "If you put your order in now, you could have the generator in six months or less, barring rush orders from Imperial Procurement."

"We need it sooner than that, and we've heard a generator's being shipped out of here to an Imperial outpost within two weeks."

"I don't see what that has to do with you," said Johan.

"Well, see, Aunt Nell, you control the docking stations, and we figured if we could arrange docking clearance, you could slip in our barge driver in place of the Imperials' . . ."

"I cannot believe," Nell said, "that you are sitting at my dining table talking about hijacking 25 million credits worth of power generator as if you were asking to borrow a speeder.''

"But Aunt Nell . . ."

"You're talking about stealing that generator, aren't you?"

"But . . . we could pay you . . ."

Nell's mouth fell open. Johan found his voice. "Deen, do you hear what you're saying? This isn't just another prank, like the time you sliced into the school comm-system with phony evacuation drills . . ."

"This is treason," Nell finished. "Deen, I don't want to hear another word about these so-called friends of yours. Now, because you're my nephew, I'm not going to turn you in and we're all going to pretend this conversation never happened. Is that perfectly clear?"

The meal ended in silence.

Shannon couldn't sleep that night. Hearing voices from her parents' room, she crept to their door to listen.

"The Alliance is desperate for equipment, Nell!"

"Do you think I care? Johan, that Alliance will never feed my family or give Shannon an education that'll get her off this station!"

"But the Empire . . ."

". . . Owns this system, and everything in it. Including us. And they have ways of disposing of traitors. Accidents. Johan, do you honestly believe it was a coincidence your brother died in that reactor malfunction less than a week after he'd repaired those Rebels' ship? Nothing is worth the safety of my family, Johan, nothing. Not the Alliance, not Alderaan . . ."

"Not even Deen?"

Shannon didn't stay to hear her mother's answer.

Deen left the next morning after a tense, silent breakfast.

"If you change your minds," he began.

"We won't," his aunt said. "Now drop the subject."

"But if you do," Deen persisted, "I'll be in-system for a few days. Here's a signaller you can use to contact me," he said, dropping the hand-held electronic device on a table near the door. "May the Force be with you."

"Destroy that signaller," said Nell after the door had closed.

"I'll do it, Mom," said Shannon, snatching up the device and darting to the reclamator. The appliance disposed of the morning's trash with a satisfying "crunch"— but the signaller remained hidden in Shannon's pocket.

The elder Voorsons behaved as if Deen had never come; if Shannon mentioned his "friends" or his request for aid, she was sent to her room without discussion.

"I can't understand it!" she said to herself on one such occasion. It's not as if the station doesn't mix stuff up all the time, she thought. Mother's always complaining about this-or-that going missing. Bugs in the station net—that's what she always says. If she gave Deen that generator, everyone would just think it was another computer mistake . . .

Rolling out of her bed, Shannon flipped on her computer. A few minutes and slices later, she had the list of upcoming exports scrolling across her screen. There it is, she thought, a CC-23669 generator, to be picked up at loading dock 42, at 1430 hours, five days from now. All right, she thought, if I change the pickup date, Mother will surely notice and stop us. Can't change the dock number either, that would make a huge fuss. But if I changed the time . . . How long does it take to link a driver to a barge? Daddy says he can do it in less than an hour—would two hours be enough?

She changed the pickup time to 1230 and hoped her mother wouldn't notice. Then she pulled Deen's signaller from under her pillow.

• • •

"Who are you?" asked the security guard.

Shannon gulped and tried to look cute and harmless.

"Shannon Voorson, ma'am," she said.

"Oh, Shannon," the woman said, recognizing the child, "why aren't you at school yet? What're you doing here?"

Shannon knew that "I'm running away to join the Rebellion," would not be a popular answer to that question. Fortunately, she had come prepared with a lie.

"My daddy forgot his lunch, so's I'm bringing it to him before I go. A bhillen sandwich—see?" She set her portable computer down and opened the thermabag to thrust it into the guard's face so that she was sure to catch the aroma of Bestinnian tang-root.

"Oh, ah, yeah, sure," said the guard, pulling back and blinking. "Go find your daddy. I'm sure he'll love it."

"Thanks," said Shannon. She bolted off, thinking that raw tang-root was pretty stinky, but there was no way that guard was going to dig past it and find Deen's signaller.

She continued down the corridor toward her father's work area for a few more steps, ducked into an alcove, peeked out to see that the guard was gone, and then doubled back toward dock 42.

The techs hadn't arrived at the dock yet that morning, so Shannon had no trouble slicing her way into the cargo container with a few connecting cables from her portable computer. After a surprisingly long crawl over, under, and around the generator to the front of the container, she settled down with her book-chips to wait for Deen.

"You sure this'll work, Deen?" said Boo Rawl, captain of the Rebel barge driver *Long Run*.

"For the thousandth time Boo, yes! My aunt is the docking supervisor at this port. She wouldn't have signalled for us to come if she didn't have everything at this end arranged. I didn't live through the evacuation of Echo Base just to get blown out of the sky by my own family."

"I'm not nearly as worried about your family as I am about what you've done to my sublight engines," said Boo.

"I didn't do a thing to your precious engines, Boo," said Deen, "all I did was add an ST box so the port will read our transponder signal as the Imperial driver's. Standard Operating Procedure, straight out of Cracken's Field Guide—I do it all the time."

"Yeah, well, you seemed to be getting pretty close to my cobulators with that hydrospanner . . ."

"Oh, quit griping and hail the port—we're practically on top of them."

Boo Rawl shrugged and opened a channel. "Kuat Freight Port, this is Drive Craft 36DD, requesting permission to link with the barge in . . ." Boo paused to check a datapad. "Loading dock 42."

"Drive craft, your transponder signal is unclear," said a cold voice from the station, *"Please transmit clearance code to confirm your identity."*

Boo gave Deen a pointed stare as he sent out the code. "Uh, sorry about the transponder, Kuat," he said, "new tech on board was tweaking the sublights, obviously got a little carried away."

"Identity confirmed," answered the controller, uninterested in Boo's explanations. *"Driver DeeDee, you are early. Link techs will be at dock 42 at 1430."*

Boo turned again to Deen, who gestured innocence but said nothing.

"Ah, are you sure about that, Kuat?" asked Boo. "My orders say pickup at 1230."

"I will check, DeeDee," said the controller.

Boo shut off the comm. "Isn't that one of your aunt's people?"

Deen nodded.

"Then what's the problem?"

"I dunno . . ."

Kuat hailed the driver: *"It seems you are right, driver DeeDee,"* said the controller. *"You are listed for 1230 . . ."*

Deen smirked at Boo.

"However, there will be a slight delay—the techs' orders say 1430. They will be back on duty within the hour."

"No problem, Kuat, I'll wait," said Boo. He shut down the comm again. "Now what?" he asked Deen.

"We wait for the techs to finish lunch, like you said."

Boo rolled his eyes. "What if Security decides to visit us while we're waiting?"

"Boo, you worry as much as my friend Voren," said Deen. "Security'll be on break too."

"Yeah, off playing Whack-a-Bothan, or Bobbing for Calamari." Boo sighed. "I hate waiting," he said.

"Finally! I thought they'd take forever!" said Boo as they received the signal that the last of the linking clamps had secured the cargo container to the barge driver. "Kuat, this is driver *DeeDee*," he said, cutting off the latest scarlet-rated offering of *Billi B and the Paradise Gang* and hailing the station. "I've linked up to the barge here, and I'd like to check the cargo before I leave."

"Go ahead, DeeDee."

"All right, Deen," Boo said as he cut the comm. "She's all ours. Let's take a quick peek and vanish before the real barge driver *DeeDee* shows up."

Deen entered the airlock connecting the access hatch on the cargo container.

"Is the generator all right?" asked Boo as Deen entered the hold.

"The generator is huge—you don't really want me to spend two days inspecting . . . Wait a . . ."

"What?"

"I saw something move . . ."

"Hi, Deen!" said Shannon, popping into view. "Is this the generator you wanted?"

"Shannon!"

"Who's the kid?" Boo asked.

"My cousin . . . Shannon, does your mother know you're in here?"

"Of course not. We'd better get moving."

"We?" said Deen. "What do you mean, we?"

"I'm joining the Rebellion," she answered, hauling out her portable computer. "Now come on, we've got to go."

"Absolutely not," said Deen. "You are going straight back home."

"How?" said Boo. "The dock's been depressurized, and I'm not too thrilled with the idea of calling the techs back, having them unlink us and re-pressurize the dock, explaining the kid to Security, and then waiting to get linked up again. I'm not crazy about dragging some poor kid into danger, but we have no choice. She's on for the haul."

"He's right," said Shannon, climbing into the driver cab. "Close those hatches and let's go!"

"But . . ." Deen began.

"The Imperial driver will be here in . . . less than 30 minutes," said Shannon, checking her chrono. "Set our coordinates for hyperspace, comrade," she told Boo.

"Name's Boo. Now keep quiet, kid, I gotta talk to your mom's folks."

Shannon nodded. Deen stood in shock.

"Kuat, this is barge driver *DeeDee*. My cargo is secure and I'm ready to go."

"*Affirmative, Driver DeeDee*," said the controller. "*You may leave port when ready; thank you for choosing Kuat Engineering, and please be careful of repair drones on your way out.*"

"No problem, Kuat," said Boo, "and thanks for everything." He began piloting the barge away from the dock. "This is almost too easy," he said. "Deen, your aunt is the best . . ."

"What did she have to do with it?" asked Shannon. "I set the whole thing up!"

"What do you mean, you set it up?" asked Deen.

"Mom was too scared to help you—you knew that, Deen," Shannon said. "So I changed the pickup time."

"And Aunt Nell . . ."

"Doesn't know a thing."

Boo was astonished. "The kid set this up? I'm impressed. Great cousin you got here, Deen. Though it would've been nice if she'd gotten the techs here sooner."

"Sorry, Boo, I, uh, sort of forgot to change their orders," said Shannon. "How long 'till we can jump?"

"We've just cleared tractor beam range—let me get past that one drive craft . . . Aw, no, I don't believe it!"

"What?" asked Shannon.

"See ahead? That's the real barge driver *36DD,* come to pick up the generator."

"You sure?" asked Deen.

The comm light flashed. *"Unknown Driver,"* said the controller, *"return to dock immediately."*

The three Rebels looked at each other.

"Keep going," said Deen.

"Repeat," said the controller, *"unknown Driver, return your barge to dock and you will not be harmed."*

"Yeah, right," muttered Boo.

The Imperial drive craft positioned itself between the Rebels and the spacelane.

"Get around it!" said Shannon.

"How?" said Boo. "The *Long Run* ain't no snub-fighter—linked to a loaded barge, it moves like a drunken Hutt . . ."

"What's its shield tolerance like?" asked Deen, pointing out the viewport, where at least a dozen TIE fighters were converging on them.

"Oh, beautiful," said Boo, "I knew this was too easy."

The comm light blinked again. *"Unidentified Driver,"* said a familiar female voice, *"this is Senior Controller Voorson with your final warning. Reverse your heading and return to dock 42, or our security forces will open fire."*

"Lovely," Boo muttered. "Deen, take the guns. Blast anything between us and freedom."

"Wait," said Deen, "I have an idea—Shannon, follow my lead," he said, slapping the comm panel.

"Controller Voorson," he said, "call off your attack. We have your daughter." He nudged Shannon.

"Mom, Mom, it's me! Don't shoot!" she said.

The comm panel was silent.

"You think that'll stop 'em?" Shannon asked.

Laser blasts bounced off the driver's shields.

"There's your answer," said Boo. "Take the guns, Deen!"

Deen hit the firing buttons. The small turbolasers managed to hit two oncoming TIEs, and three more were disabled by flying debris. Deen kept firing.

"Rebel Driver," said Nell Voorson, her voice touched with panic, "turn back now. Security will not permit you to escape."

"We ain't askin' for permission!" shouted Boo, continuing to plow forward. A TIE's solar panel clipped their shields; the TIE flew apart, colliding with one of its fellows.

"Boo, the shields are gonna go any second," said Deen, still blasting at their attackers.

"Rebel barge driver," said Nell Voorson, "this is pointless. Stop now or be destroyed . . ."

"Sorry, Auntie, there's no going back now!" said Boo.

"Rebel . . . Deen!" Nell pleaded. "Deen, think of what you're doing—think of Shannon—Security won't listen to me!" she shouted, "they won't let you go!"

"I'm sorry, Aunt Nell," Deen began.

"Watch the TIEs!" Boo warned; the stream of tiny fighters continued to pour at them.

"We're gonna hit that driver!" Shannon cried as the Imperial barge *36DD* loomed before them.

"Not if they're smarter than we are," said Boo.

Deen bit his lip and Shannon covered her eyes as the drivers converged. Nell Voorson's voice continued to beg for sanity over the comm panel. A bead of sweat rolled down Boo's face. "I don't think they're gonna . . ."

At the last moment, the Imperial driver ducked beneath the *Long Run*. Their shields brushed, buckled, and collapsed as they zoomed past the other ship and into clear space. Four laser bolts from four different TIEs burst past the *Long Run* just as Boo pulled the jump levers; all three Rebels held their breath as the starlines merged into the blur of hyperspace.

"Are we safe now, Boo, are we safe?" asked Shannon.

"Depends on two things," said Boo. "First, whether or not your mother called ahead to Venir or Renegg for Interdictors . . ."

"And whether or not we hit somebody," Deen finished.

Shannon crept into her cousin's lap and laid her head on his shoulder. All three Rebels remained tense, silent, waiting for either a fatal crash or a jerk out of hyperspace into Imperial custody.

The minutes dragged on. Shannon realized that, whether she lived or died, she would never see her parents again; she began to cry. Deen held her close, wiping her tears and rocking her.

"Hey," said Boo softly, "it's been 30 minutes. We're clear."

"We're away?" said Shannon.

Boo nodded. "Free and clear, kid—welcome to the Alliance."

"Little Bit," said Deen, "I'm sorry I got you into this . . ."

"I'm not," said Shannon, putting on a smile. "Come on, now, Deen—let's go slay some dragons."

Do No Harm
by Erin Endom

It all seemed pretty straightforward the day I was called into Commander Briessen's office. "Temporary detached duty," he called it. Naturally I wondered what kind of detached duty a hospital-ship medic warranted, but I didn't have to wonder very long—only until Lieutenant Haslam showed up.

I have to say he didn't look like a topnotch commando. A couple of centimeters taller than I, light brown hair thinning on top, pale blue eyes, roundish face, slender build; he looked like an accountant. But everyone in the Rebellion knew his reputation by then. What could he possibly want with me?

I found out in short order. Gebnerret Vibrion, the political head of another Rebel cell, had been captured by the Imps and was undergoing interrogation on Selnesh, a notorious prison planet in the Irishi Sector. He knew too much to be left in custody; he had to be either broken out or killed quickly. Okay, I could understand that. I hadn't been with the Rebellion very long, but even I knew that given enough time, anyone could and would break under interrogation: physical torture, drugs, threats to loved ones—everyone has a breaking point. So where did a medic come into the picture? It turned out Vibrion was a rather elderly human male with Zithrom's syndrome, a kidney problem requiring him to take continuous doses of Clondex in order to stay alive. It was a pretty sure bet the Imps wouldn't be taking tender care of his medical problems. Even worse, before he died he'd go into delirium. And who knew what secrets he'd give away then?

So I reported to the mission briefing with no small amount of apprehension. I hadn't joined the Rebellion for a life of adventure; I'd signed on to save lives. (Skies, that sounds pompous. It's more accurate to say I'd signed on for a steady job doing what I'm good at, for the benefit of the Good Guys.) I felt even more out of place when I met the other team members, commandos all: Melenna, a tiny, cheerful, exquisitely beautiful woman with a cap of loose golden curls and the coldest blue eyes I've ever seen; Gowan, a big dark guy, definitely the strong silent type; Enkhet, a tall, skinny, pale kid whose appearance fairly screamed "slicer"; Liak, a (relatively) small Wookiee with long golden-brown fur and an almost palpable aura of calm about him; and Haslam, regarding us all with his coolly analytical gaze.

"The plan," he said after a long moment, "is to get in, get Vibrion, and get out as quietly as possible. We're not going to take down the Interrogation Center; we're not going to slaughter Imps; we're not out for glory. We're gonna get Vibrion. Period.''

His tone of voice was making me uneasy. ''Get him in what sense?'' I asked.

''In whatever sense we have to,'' Haslam replied calmly. ''If we can evacuate him, fine. If we can't, we can give him a quicker and easier death than the Imps will, and we can keep him from talking. Have you got a problem with that, *Doctor* Leith?'' He stressed the title just a little.

Actually, I did. I could see his point: burdened with a nonambulatory rescuee, there was almost no chance the team would make it out intact. On the other hand, I was a doctor, and my job was to do everything I could to save my patient. I kept my mouth shut for the moment, but the twisting sensation in the pit of my stomach was picking up considerably.

''So,'' he addressed the others. ''Basic very-dumb-orphan scoop-and-run—you've done it a hundred times. We infiltrate the center incognito—Melenna, Liak, you're the prisoners; standard smugglers-suspected-of-Rebel-sympathies scenario. Gowan and Enkhet are storm-trooper guards, I'm the officer in charge. Aurin—'' he turned to me, ''you'll have to be another prisoner. You're taking passage with Melenna and Liak to Sestooine, you've been picked up by mistake, and you don't know anything about anything. Just keep your mouth shut and you'll do fine. How much equipment will you need to bring?''

Luckily I'd had the foresight to think this out ahead of time. ''I can manage with one medpac,'' I replied a little shortly. ''I'll need to pack it with extra Clondex and some special equipment.''

''Good. We'll get to the prison sector, find out where he is, then get rid of the guards and break into his cell. Once we get in, your job is to get him alert and moving quickly if at all possible. If you can't, we'll have to . . . break out without him.'' The others nodded casually; I had the feeling his hesitation was entirely for my benefit.

"Once he's up, we get back to the shuttle. For this part, we'll take the repair access tunnels." He touched a button on the tabletop console, and a holographic schematic of an Imperial-style installation leaped out of the center of the table; another adjustment, and a series of passages were outlined in red. The route from the prison cells to the docking bays was long, tortuous, and confusing.

Melenna chuckled. "This is where Liak comes in. His people are tree-dwellers; he can find his way through any strange maze of branches with never a wrong turn. For some reason it works on space stations as well. We don't understand it, but we don't argue with it."

"The tractor beam's just a single," Haslam continued. "Weak design—says they don't think anyone can escape. Gowan, you'll break into the main computer and disengage it while our medic here is fixing Vibrion. At full power and with some of Enkhet's fancy shiphandling, we should be able to break free long enough to make the jump to hyperspace. Questions?"

If anyone else had any, they weren't admitting it; the only response was a series of crisp nods from the other team members. I had one, and it was bothering me enough that I didn't even react to the interesting fact that Gowan and not Enkhet was the computer jock. Haslam looked at me sharply, but only said, "Okay, dismissed. We'll meet outside the shuttle at 0600 tomorrow, bay 36. Get some sleep, everyone. Aurin, stay a moment, please."

Once we were alone, I said, "You left something out of the briefing. What if I can't get him moving? I don't think you mean for us to just go off and leave him alive. Who gets to do the dirty deed?"

"Frankly, I'd rather have a medical droid along," Haslam said coolly. "Put a glitch in its programming, and it does exactly what the mission calls for and it doesn't develop any moral scruples at the last minute. Unfortunately, Emdees are expensive. Human medics are a lot cheaper and easier to replace."

"Nice to know I'm expendable," I murmured under

my breath. Haslam ignored the comment, but after a moment some of the coldness faded from his face, leaving a look of—almost—helplessness.

"Aurin, I don't get any thrill out of killing. I've got a job to do here, just like you. The fact is, we can't leave him to die at the hands of the Imperials, or of his disease. And it's not just because of the information he'll spill. Interrogation is . . . well, not a pleasant way to die. I want to get him out as much as you do, but it may not be possible. The question is, if it comes to that—can you give him something to make it quick and easy for him?"

"You're asking me to kill him. I can't do that." If I was sure of nothing else in this confusion, I was sure of that much. Apart from any other considerations, I'd sworn an oath before they let me out of the Byblos Academy of Medicine: boiled down, it consisted of *"First, do no harm."*

Haslam wasn't surprised. "Okay," he sighed, "it's my responsibility. I'll take care of it." Then, in a whisper, "Blast it, I wish they wouldn't do this to me."

I hesitated. I didn't like the train of thought developing in my mind: *Look, if the guy's gonna die anyway, isn't it your job as a physician to make sure it's as easy as possible? If we can't get him out, Haslam is gonna shoot him. If you can't square your conscience enough to overdose him with potassium and make it fast and painless, can you at least sedate him enough so he sleeps through it?*

But that means I'm helping Haslam kill him. I'm being dragged along on this mission to save his life if it's at all possible, not to help end it.

You're on this mission to serve your patient as best you can, whether it means saving his life or helping him die as easily as possible.

Skies, I hate this!

"I can give him some conergin," I heard myself saying abruptly. I was dimly surprised to hear that my voice was flat, steady; my insides certainly weren't. "It won't kill him, but it'll put him down deep enough to let you do what you have to."

Haslam looked up sharply. "You'll help me?"

"I'll help you. But only after I've tried everything I can to get him moving and out of there. And this is a medical problem, not a military one. It has to be my decision. Not yours." I held his eyes with my own, feeling sick. "If that's not acceptable, you and the Rebellion can find yourselves another medic. Or a droid."

"Done," Haslam replied, grasping my wrist as if closing a business deal. Which, of course, we were.

The flight to Selnesh was relatively short, only four days in hyperspace. Of course, four days with the dilemma I had hanging over my head is an eternity and then some. I spent them packing and repacking my medpac for greatest efficiency, mentally reviewing the resuscitation plan, and getting used to the weight of the hold-out blaster up my left sleeve. Melenna had handed it to me just after boarding as a matter of course.

"Wait!" I'd blurted. "I don't want this. I don't even know how to use it."

"Real simple." Melenna shrugged. "Point and shoot."

"But I don't want it! I'm a doctor! I don't shoot people!"

"This go-around, you may have to." Disgustedly, Melenna pushed up my tunic sleeve, fastened the little holster around my forearm, and snapped it down with a final-sounding click. "If you can't, don't. Just try not to shoot any of us, okay?"

We popped back into normal space over Selnesh about the mid-afternoon of the fourth day. If I'd set out to build a prison planet from the core outward, this would have been it: a gray rocky ball in the middle of nowhere, its sun no more than a bright bluish star. "Bleak" did not even begin to describe it. The surface was totally bare of color or vegetation. The sterile white plasteel dome of the prison sat like a fungus directly below us as we descended. There was literally nowhere else to go on this world that would support life for more than a few hours. I could see why nobody escaped from here.

While Enkhet, already in his stormtrooper armor, exchanged code strings and pleasantries with the docking bay, the rest of us lined up in preparation for deception. Melenna wore free-trader's gear, Liak only his fur, and I a plain civilian tunic and trousers; the precious medpac was fastened around my waist under the loose, long tunic. All three of us wore wrist binders. Gowan, also in armor, held a blaster rifle carefully pointed at the floor. Haslam was in a gray officer's uniform and looked, at least to me, thoroughly official and intimidating.

The jar of landing in the bay was slight; evidently Enkhet was as good a pilot as everyone said he was. I clenched my fists tightly, the cut of the binders into my wrists announcing, *I don't like this. I want to go home. Right now. I'm not cut out for a life of adventure.* Somehow sensing my nervousness, Liak turned around and growled something incomprehensible but reassuring-sounding.

"Pretend you're in a holovid," Melenna suggested brightly. "Playing the part of a prisoner. That's what I do. Just don't say anything. Let the Lieutenant do the talking—it's what he's here for."

"Thanks," I muttered. Nerves always take me in the stomach, and mine was turning somersaults just then. Better the stomach than the hands, anyway—a doctor had better have steady hands, whether she's nervous or not.

Enkhet joined us from the cockpit. "All clear," he announced casually. "No challenge. They sound bored."

"Good enough," observed Haslam. "Let's move out."

Getting past the docking bay was a lot easier than I'd expected. Haslam, doing a perfect imitation of an Imperial officer—clipped speech, formal stance and all—identified himself as one Lieutenant Grallant, operating number 13398247, and us as smugglers and possible Rebel sympathizers. The base commander, who looked as if he'd heard it all one too many times before, waved us tiredly back toward the passage I figured had to lead to the holding area.

We filed down the gray hallway, ending up in a large bay with cell-lined hallways branching off at regular intervals. The central computer bank was inhabited by four stormtroopers holding blaster rifles at least as big as the ones Enkhet and Gowan wielded, and a crisply pressed officer type wearing captain's insignia who looked a whole lot more alert than his commander. The officer glanced up as we came in, and the troopers all shifted slightly to aim their rifles not precisely at us but definitely in our direction. I suddenly found it harder to breathe. Part of my brain was seriously considering saying "Count me out, thanks, I don't want to play anymore," turning around and walking back to the ship. Since this would have ruined Haslam's pretty scenario, and I was too frozen to move anyway, I kept still and silent.

Haslam repeated the name-rank-and-operating number business for the officer, who (thank the skies) didn't seem inclined to be challenging. Instead, he helpfully fired up the computer and assigned the three of us cell numbers. Prisoner processing apparently took place inside the cells, rather than in the open area—to reduce the incidence of breaks, I guessed. Since a break was precisely what we had planned, I didn't find this information encouraging.

Enkhet pressed the muzzle of his blaster into my back, pushing me forward. Captain Whoever stepped forward to help get us hardened criminals into cells for processing. Haslam stopped him with an upraised hand.

"I'm going to have to ask you and your men to leave for a few minutes."

"What?" the captain asked blankly.

"I need you and your men to leave the area temporarily." Haslam spoke even more quietly, with an air of complicity. "I'm with Intelligence. We suspect these prisoners have had access to top-secret information about the movements of various Rebel cells. It's not that we don't trust a loyal Imperial officer, but the presence of these prisoners here has to be kept absolutely top secret until interrogation is complete. I'm sure you understand.''

''Does Commander Caton know about this?''

''No, and it's important to the war effort that no one knows just now. I can't tell you any more. I shouldn't even have said this much. The reason I brought them here is because I know the reputation of this base's officers and men. There's no more secure place in the galaxy.''

''I understand,'' the captain said gravely, and motioned the troopers to follow him out the door. Evidently flattery went a long way.

''I'll also have to disable the security cameras temporarily. Just until they're processed, you understand. No one must know of their presence here.''

''Understood.'' And it was as easy as that. The Imps simply walked out and closed the doors behind them. Gowan, helmet off, was already slicing into the computer; after a moment, the cameras mounted around the ceiling went dark.

Haslam moved lightly around the room checking for I didn't know what, while Enkhet removed our binders. Melenna stretched her arms and hands forward to remove the stiffness. ''You didn't have to tighten them quite so much,'' she complained mildly. ''My hands are asleep.''

''You're the one wanted to be convincing.''

Liak growled an admonishment, and the squabble— probably the latest chapter in an ongoing saga—ceased. Meanwhile, I was digging into my medpac again, assuring myself one more time that none of the precious equipment or drug vials was damaged. The ticklish clenching of my muscles, the usual prelude to a full-bore resuscitation, was beginning to push through my fear. ''Where is he?'' I demanded.

''I'm looking,'' Gowan replied absently, his attention entirely occupied by the flashing images on the screen. ''Okay, here it is. Cell 2826.''

"Well, come on, let's go!"

"Aurin," Haslam spoke quietly. "I'm in command of this mission. We go when I say."

"Haslam," I said in the same tone, "you got us past the Imps. Now it's a medical mission. That's my department, remember? There's a man dying in one of these cells. I've got work to do. Let me do it." The words "or else" hung in the air. I didn't know quite what "or else" would involve, but Haslam realized I was serious anyway. He half-laughed, half-sighed, and gave the move-out signal.

The cell was at the far end of the center hallway. While Enkhet stood guard near the hall entrance—Gowan had stayed behind to compute some more—Haslam entered a complex code into the keypad at the side of the door. It slid open to reveal a thin, gray-haired human male lying on the pallet at the far end of the small room. He rose half up on one elbow, eyes widening at the sight of us. I absorbed details as I moved quickly to his side, unstrapping the medpac from around my waist: he was very pale, his eyes sunken and his lips dry, indicating dehydration, but he was awake, alert and aware. I'd been prepared for a patient at death's door, and was surprised at how relatively good he looked.

"Is this the rescue party?" His voice was soft and hoarse, but held a hint of wry humor.

"That's us." Melenna had followed close behind me, and gave him a dazzling smile I suspected would get any man off a deathbed in short order. She'd probably intended it that way. "Anything to make the mission a success," she'd commented briefly during the ride in. If flirting with the rescuee would help, she'd do it.

"I wasn't . . . expecting you." He had to breathe in the middle of the short sentence; yes, he needed some help. During the exchange I had been rapidly unpacking my equipment; now I placed the IAU—Intravenous Access Unit—on his upper chest and pressed the activation switch. While the catheter burrowed through his skin in search of the large subclavian vein leading directly to his heart, I opened two ampules of Clondex, one of endogenous steroid, a cordine patch, and a liter of serum-replacement solution, and laid them down ready to hand. Liak crouched beside me, ready to help if needed; Haslam stayed alert at the door.

"Hey," Melenna remarked, "never underestimate the power of a woman."

"You're in better shape than I thought you'd be," I commented as I worked.

"I had three vials of . . . Clondex when I got here . . . been underdosing myself. I only . . . ran out two days ago."

"How'd you get them past the body search?" Melenna demanded.

"Swallowed them." Weak as he was, Vibrion winked at her. Melenna followed this statement to its logical conclusion and grimaced; funny, I wouldn't have thought her the squeamish type. I ran the scanner over his body, noting the small heart—another sign of dehydration—and the shrunken kidneys and adrenals, which went along with the Zithrom's. Blood pressure was a little low, heart rate a little fast, but otherwise everything looked pretty normal. I allowed myself a sigh of relief. *This isn't going to be as bad as I thought, thank the skies. And remember, the next time Briessen wants to send you out on one of these things, say no.*

The IAU clicked, and a backflow of darkish venous blood appeared in its access chamber, indicating the catheter was in the vein. I injected the first unit of Clondex and the steroid rapidly, then started feeding in the serum solution as fast as I could. I had to be careful here; giving a large volume of fluid too fast could tip him over the other way into lung and kidney failure.

"How're we doing?" Haslam asked. "We've gotta move out soon."

"I need a few more minutes. Have they caught on to us?"

"No sign yet," he said, "but let's not push our luck.

Liak, go open the access tunnel entrance and stand by."
Liak lumbered up from my side and out the door, ruffling my hair with his big paw as he passed.

The fluid bag was nearly empty; I squeezed it to get the last few drops into my patient, then disconnected it. Already Vibrion was looking better, his eyes less sunken and color coming back into his face. I gave him the second round of Clondex, then slapped the cordine patch onto his neck. He flushed red, a hand going shakily to his forehead as the stimulant took hold.

"The headache will pass in a minute," I said. "This'll help you keep up. We need to get out of here. Can you sit up?"

Vibrion nodded, wincing as I helped him to a sitting position and rechecked his blood pressure; it was holding steady. So far, so good.

"Liak's got the tunnel open," Haslam said, calmly but with a note of underlying urgency in his voice. I hauled Vibrion to a standing position, Melenna stepping in to get a shoulder under his arm for support, and rechecked the scanner's readings; his pulse had gone up 10 beats per minute to compensate for the change in body position, but blood pressure remained stable.

"Okay?" I asked him.

"Okay." He smiled wanly. "Let's go."

The access tunnel ran parallel along the hallway, a brightly lit, dusty passage just tall enough to stand up in (Liak and Enkhet had to slouch) and just wide enough for one. Melenna, Vibrion and I, linked in the tail position, shuffled sideways. Liak led, followed by Enkhet and Gowan; Haslam was in the middle, where he could monitor everyone at once. It was slow going, with a couple of back-up-and-start-over maneuvers at first. I hadn't the slightest idea where we were going, and wasn't sure if I cared. I'd done what I came to do, and the post-code ebb of unused adrenaline had left me drained, flat, and hungry. Melenna, on the other hand, was looking keyed-up and nervous.

"This is taking too long," she hissed at Haslam, just ahead of her. "How long do you think it'll be before the Imps figure out something's up? They're not all idiots, you know."

"I'm aware of that, Melenna," Haslam said with careful calm. "It's only been eleven minutes. We have time." Eleven minutes? How could it only have been eleven minutes? It felt like hours since I'd walked into that cell.

Liak grunted something from the head of the line, and we kept shuffling along. I glanced repeatedly up at Vibrion, reassessing his condition; after a few minutes he was dripping sweat—it was hot in the tunnel—and noticeably paler as the cordine flush wore off, but he gently squeezed my shoulders and kept moving. It occurred to me that fragile as the old man appeared, anyone who—at his age, and burdened by chronic illness—could found and run an entire cell of the Rebellion had to be tougher than tempered titanium. He was certainly proving it now.

After a long few minutes more of this business, we all stopped at a signal from Liak: we were nearing the docking bay. The plan was to throw a concussion grenade into the bay while we remained under cover in the tunnel; with the guards incapacitated and the tractor beam hopefully deactivated, we would scurry to our stolen shuttle, take off, and evade pursuit long enough to complete the run-to-jump for hyperspace.

At least, that was the theory.

We all crouched down on the dusty floor of the tunnel, except Vibrion, who sat down rather suddenly, as if his legs would no longer hold him. Melenna propped him up against the wall while I scrabbled in the medpac for another cordine patch. I wasn't sure of the wisdom of giving him another round—it might send him into heart failure—but I wanted it handy if he did need it. A flash of white caught the corner of my eye at the far curve of the corridor, and I glanced up.

A stormtrooper, flattened against the curving wall, was just edging around the corner, blaster up and pointed directly at me.

Ambush, I thought, very coldly and clearly, as time slowed to a halt around me. I couldn't seem to get in a breath—the nauseated stunned emptiness was almost exactly what I'd felt at age six, after falling off a balcony flat onto my stomach. But my mind, trained to function logically in a crisis, kept clicking right along: *There isn't time to warn Haslam. You're blocking the others—they can't shoot around you. If you fall, Vibrion's next in line.*

You've got a blaster.

My right hand pulled the little hold-out blaster from its holster under my left sleeve, leveled it at the trooper, and fired. The shot angled upward just enough to pass between the breastplate and the bottom of the helmet; it took him square in the throat, and he let out a choked gurgle and dropped to his knees. His helmet flew off as he went down, allowing me a brief glimpse of a very young man, light brown hair damp with sweat and clinging to his skull, clear gray eyes wide in amazement, before he toppled flat onto his face.

I had just time to be amazed that I'd actually hit him before I was surrounded by blaster shots: Haslam and the others had caught on to the fact that something was going on behind us, and were shooting over my head in a perfectly choreographed blast-and-duck pattern that said they'd been in situations like this before. The rest of the troopers, their cover blown, had moved around the corner into the open and were blasting away at us. I started to turn back, with some confused idea of shielding Vibrion with my body, but Melenna hissed at me, *"Stay down!"*

Her statement was punctuated by a dull, but extremely loud, explosion from the direction of the docking bay that shook the walls around us. I swallowed to equalize the pressure in my ears and got off a couple of random shots toward the troopers, at the same time groping behind me with my left hand for Vibrion's wrist. His pulse was rapid and slightly irregular, but strong; he squeezed my hand in weak reassurance.

During all this, I'd forgotten to try to breathe again. I gasped, and air rushed into my lungs, making me suddenly dizzy. I dropped my forehead onto my wrist; curled awkwardly in a semi-fetal position on the floor, there wasn't much else I was capable of. I stayed there, clutching Vibrion's hand, until someone sharply wrenched at my shoulder.

"Come on!" a voice shouted roughly. "We're going!"

I looked up to see Gowan bending over me, helmet off and a charred crease of blaster burn slanting across his forehead where a bolt had winged him. He grasped my wrist, hauled me to my feet, and slung me forward toward the docking bay. Behind us lay only a heap of white armor, the gray-eyed boy hidden beneath his comrades. The floor of the bay was similarly littered with the limp bodies of troopers and officers, all knocked unconscious simultaneously by the blast of Liak's concussion grenade. Haslam, at the entrance waiting for us, grabbed my arm and dragged me up the shuttle ramp just behind Melenna and Vibrion; he was leaning heavily on her shoulder, knees buckling and plainly on the verge of collapse. Gowan, following us in, hit the door latch and headed for the cockpit at a dead run; the engines were already roaring in startup sequence. Haslam dumped Vibrion and me onto the passenger seat, rapidly strapped us in, then turned to follow Melenna aft.

"Where are you going?" I gasped.

"To man the guns," he flung back over his shoulder, not missing a step.

"Guns? I thought shuttles didn't have guns!"

No answer but the jolting rise of the craft; then we were flung backwards by the steep drag of acceleration as the shuttle shot forward. The next few minutes were a rough approximation of a whirling repulsorlift ride I'd gone on once during a Coruscant Fete Week: moving straight up, down, sideways, in a corkscrew, and several less-conceivable directions, all at breakneck speed, in pitch darkness (the cabin lights had gone out during the second high-speed maneuver), and this time with the added thrill of people shooting at us. I could dimly hear Haslam and Melenna's casual crosstalk as they shot back; evidently this shuttle did have guns. Vibrion was too far away for me to reach, but sat crumpled in his restraints, his eyes sunken again into his head but sparkling. People say emergency medics are excitement junkies, but this was getting ridiculous. Haslam was right about Enkhet's piloting, though; even I could tell he was doing a superb job of keeping us in one piece. Finally the ride turned into a high-gravity Aurin sandwich, pressing the breath out of my lungs as the shuttle made the star-stretching jump to hyperspace.

The next few minutes were a blur, as I got Vibrion settled more comfortably and gave him some more fluid and another half-dose of Clondex. Haslam had taken a blaster shot to the left shoulder, which had managed to miss the great vessels and nerve plexus; I cleaned and dressed his and Gowan's wounds. Melenna, who'd been in plain view of the troopers and without armor or any other form of protection, didn't have a scratch on her.

"That's why we keep her around," Enkhet quipped cheerfully, strolling into the common room from the cockpit. "She's our luck." Melenna thumped him lightly on the top of the head with a derisive chuckle, and Enkhet tugged teasingly on a curling golden strand.

I finished Haslam's dressing and was halfway through repacking the medpac, thinking a hot drink sounded like a good idea, when the shakes hit. I always get a little trembly after a code; usually it passes off after a few seconds, but this time it got steadily worse. I knelt on the deckplates in the corner of the common room, face turned to the wall, while the ugly, jeering thoughts crawled around in my brain.

You shot that trooper. You killed him. I thought you were sup-posed to be a doctor, remember?

I had to! It was him or us.

Yeah, right. All that pious moralizing about your oaths, and do no harm, and the sanctity of sentient life—and none of it really meant anything, did it?

It wasn't just me, not just my own life. I had a patient to protect. I had the whole group to protect.

Oh, come off it! You had to protect them? Who appointed you Hero of the Universe? Face it—you can mouth off all you want to about morality, but when it comes right down to it, you took a life. You're not a healer, you're a killer.

"Aurin?"

A hand touched my shoulder, and I turned. Gowan knelt next to me, looking tired and battered and absurdly young, open concern in his dark eyes. I just looked at him, unable to get any words around the hessa-ball that had suddenly taken up residence in my throat.

"You know," he said slowly, "you did a good job in there."

"I killed him." A deep breath let me speak, but couldn't keep the tremor out of my voice.

"I know. And I'm sorry you had to . . . but I can't say I'm sorry you did." His voice was even, quiet. "Listen to me. Aurin . . . this is a war. The point of war is that if you can kill enough of the people on the other side, they'll quit. That's a hard thing to live with. What's even harder is, sometimes people get caught up in the killing who don't really belong there. And I think you're one of those people."

"You can say that again." A shaky half-laugh, half-sob escaped me. "I'm supposed to keep people alive, not . . . this."

"Exactly. And that's what makes what you did today so valuable. The Rebellion doesn't have anything like as many troops as the Empire does. If we can't stay alive long enough to win this war, we've thrown our lives away. Look at it this way: you helped keep all of us alive a little longer to fight this thing. And you kept Vibrion alive, and that's even more important, just because of who he is. Because he can bring in others who believe what we're doing is right.''

I hadn't expected such gentleness, such eloquence out of this dark man who had barely spoken during the entire mission. The hard knot in my throat promptly dissolved into tears. Gowan put an awkward arm around my shoulders as I cried, hot tears of shame, of self-recrimination, of grief, and of sheer reaction to the events of the day.

The tensions and pain gradually drained out of my body along with the tears. After a few minutes I simply stopped crying and slumped exhausted against the wall, dashed my sleeve across my eyes and smiled shakily up at Gowan.

"I'm okay now. Really," I added at his doubtful look. "Sorry I cried all over you. I'd just . . . like to be alone for a while.''

He nodded and stood up. "Do you want anything? A drink?''

"Not now, thank you.''

He nodded and moved forward toward the cockpit.

"Gowan?''

He turned.

"Thanks.''

He nodded again and walked away. I just sat there for a while, eyes closed, mind drifting. For the most part, I'd done what I came to do. I'd gotten Vibrion out of the prison alive; I'd made it out myself, and so had the rest of the team. And if all that was partly due to my having violated my oath to do no harm . . . well, maybe allowances could be made for having done a wrong thing for a right reason. Maybe the pretty rules of medicine don't hold up as well in war. Either way, there was nothing I could do about it now . . . except to wish that gray-eyed boy oneness with the Force that binds us all, and to go on with my life and my job as best I could. I sighed, got up—

aching like the aftermath of a stun blast—and went in search of that hot drink.

They gave me a medal when we got back—the Field Achievement Award, the one they give all the field operatives who make it back from their first mission. I still have it. I threw it in a drawer and haven't looked at it since. But like a half-healed wound, I always know it's there.

Side Trip Part One
by Timothy Zahn

The hazy edge of the planet was just disappearing from beneath the *Hopskip*'s control room viewport, and Haber Trell was trying to nurse a little more power from the ship's as-always finicky engines, when his partner finally reappeared from her tour aft. "Took you long enough," Trell commented as she dropped into the copilot seat beside him. "Any trouble?"

"No more than usual," Maranne Darmic told him, digging a hand underneath the silvered clasp tying her dark-blond hair back out of the way and scratching vigorously at her scalp. "The cargo straps managed to hold through that classic signature liftoff of yours. I'd say we didn't get rid of all the itch mites in the hold, though."

"Never mind the vermin," Trell growled. Next time they had a twenty-grade unbalanced cargo, he promised himself darkly, he'd make *her* do the liftoff. See how smoothly *she* managed it. "How about our passengers?"

Maranne sniffed. "I thought you didn't want to hear about vermin."

"Watch it, kiddo," Trell warned. "They're paying good money for us to smuggle these blasters out to Derra IV."

"And obviously don't trust us ten centimeters with them," Maranne countered. "They wouldn't be babysitting them like this if they did."

Trell shrugged. "Can't say I really blame them for being cautious. Ever since that big defeat or whatever it was out in the Yavin system, the Empire's been spitting fire in fifteen directions at once. I've heard that some of the independents hauling Rebellion stuff decided it was safer to take the advance money, dump the cargo, and burn space for better havens."

"Yeah, well, I don't like hauling for desperate people," Maranne said, shifting the focal point of her scratching to a spot farther down the back of her neck. "They make me nervous."

"If they weren't desperate, they wouldn't be paying so well," Trell pointed out reasonably. "Don't worry, this'll be the last time we have to deal with them."

"I've heard *that* before," Maranne said, sniffing again. The proximity-sensor alert began to warble, and she leaned forward to key for a readout. "Sure, this'll pay for the engine upgrades you want; but then you'll want sensor upgrades, and—"

She broke off. "What?" Trell demanded.

"Star Destroyer," she said grimly, activating the weapons section of her board and keying in the power boosters. "Coming up fast behind us."

"Terrific," Trell growled, checking the nav computer. If they could escape to lightspeed . . . but no, the ship was still too close to the planet. "What's their vector?"

"Straight toward us," Maranne told him. "I suppose it's too late to dump the cargo and try to look innocent."

"Freighter *Hopskip,* this is Captain Niriz of the Imperial Star Destroyer *Admonitor,*" a gruff voice boomed from the speaker. "I'd like a word with you aboard my ship, if I may."

The last word was punctuated by a single gentle shiver running through the deck beneath them as a tractor beam locked on. "Yeah, I'd say it's definitely too late to dump the cargo," Trell sighed. "Let's hope they're just on a fishing expedition."

He keyed for transmission. "This is Haber Trell aboard the *Hopskip,*" he said. "We'd be honored to speak with you, Captain."

"Well," Captain Niriz said, his voice echoing across the vast emptiness of the hangar deck as he eyed the four beings standing in front of him. "Most interesting. Our records show the *Hopskip* as having two crew members, not four." His gaze paused on Riij Winward. "Newly hired, are you?"

"Our previous ship had to leave Tramanos in something of a hurry," Riij told him, striving to keep his voice casual. The fake ID the Rebellion had provided him was a good one, but if the Imperials decided to dig past it they would undoubtedly come up with his recent connection with the Mos Eisley police on Tatooine. That wasn't a connection he was anxious for them to find. "We needed a ride to Shibric," he continued, "and since Captain Trell was going that way, he was kind enough to offer us passage."

"For a hefty fee, I imagine," Niriz said, his eyes shifting to the muscular Tunroth standing at Riij's right. "Rare to see a Tunroth in these parts. You're a certified Hunter, I presume?"

"*Shturlan,*" Rathe Palror rumbled, his voice almost subsonic.

"That's a twelfth-class Hunter," Riij translated, trying to draw Niriz's attention back to him. Palror's distinguished service with Churhee's Riflemen would raise even more eyebrows than Riij's own record if the Imperials found it.

"Excellent," Niriz said. "A Hunter's talents may prove useful on this mission."

At Riij's left, Trell cleared his throat. "Mission?" he asked carefully.

"Yes." Niriz gestured, and a lieutenant standing beside him stepped forward and offered Trell a datapad. "I want you to take a cargo to Corellia for me."

"Excuse me?" Trell asked carefully as he took the datapad. "*You* want *me* to—?"

"I need a civilian freighter for this job," Niriz said. His voice was gruff, but Riij could hear a distinct undertone of distaste. "I don't have one. You do. I also don't have time to locate someone else to do the job. You're here. You're it."

Riij craned his neck to look over Trell's shoulder at the datapad, his earlier trepidation about their IDs and cargo giving way to cautious excitement. For a Star Destroyer captain to ask for help of any sort—especially from a scruffy civilian freighter pilot—was practically unheard of. It implied urgency and desperation; and anything that bothered a senior Imperial officer that much was definitely something a good Rebel agent ought to look into. "What do you think?" he prompted.

Trell shook his head. "I don't know," he said. "It'll throw our schedule all to blazes and back."

Riij ran a series of highly vulgar words through his mind, making sure the frustration didn't show on his face. Trell, unfortunately, was *not* a Rebel agent, good or otherwise, and he clearly wanted nothing to do with any of this. "It wouldn't take all that long," he cajoled carefully. "And all good citizens have a duty to help out."

"No," Trell said firmly, offering the datapad back to the lieutenant. "I'm sorry, Captain, but we just don't have time. Our cargo's due on Shibric—"

"Your cargo consists of six hundred cases of Pashkin sausages," Niriz interrupted coldly. "I presume you're aware that the governor has recently decreed that all foodstuff exports now require an Imperial license."

Trell's mouth dropped open a couple of millimeters. "That's impossible," he said. "I mean, the inspectors didn't say anything about that."

"Just how recent was this decree?" Maranne asked suspiciously.

Niriz gave her a thin smile. "Approximately ten minutes ago."

Riij felt his stomach tighten. Urgency and desperation, indeed. "Off-hand, I'd say we've been set up," he murmured to Trell.

Niriz's eyes flicked to Riij, returned to Trell. "I am, however, prepared to waive that requirement this one time," he continued. "Provided you're prepared in turn to deliver your sausages a little late."

"As opposed to not delivering them at all?" Trell countered.

Niriz shrugged. "Something like that."

Trell looked at Maranne, who shrugged. "It's a two-day round trip to Corellia from here," she said. "Add in delivery time, and we're talking three days, tops. It'll be a scramble, but our schedule can probably absorb that."

"Not that we have much choice in the matter." Trell looked back at Niriz. "I guess we'd be delighted to help you out, Captain. What's the cargo, and when do we leave?"

"The cargo is two hundred small boxes," Niriz said. "That's all you need to know about it. As for departure, you'll leave as soon as your sausages are offloaded and the new cargo put aboard."

At Riij's side, Palror rumbled again, and Riij had to fight to keep his own face expressionless. If some bored Imperial took it into his head to poke around beneath the top three layers of sausages in each box . . .

"Don't worry, we'll keep them cool," Niriz promised. "There won't be any spoilage."

"I'm sure they'll be safe," Trell said. "Where does this cargo of your's go?"

"Your guide will fill you in on those details," Niriz said, gesturing behind them. Riij turned to look—

And felt the breath catch in his throat. Stepping around the stern of the *Hopskip* toward them, his stained Mandalorian armor glittering in the overhead light—

Trell swore under his breath. "Boba Fett."

"It's not Fett," Niriz corrected. "Merely, shall we say, an admirer of his."

"A former admirer," the armored figure corrected, his voice dark and muffled. "The name is Jodo Kast. And I'm better than Fett."

"Not that that means much," Niriz said, his lip twisting. "I've always found that a competent stormtrooper could handle any three bounty hunters without working up a sweat."

"Don't push it, Niriz," Kast warned. "Right now you need me more than I need this job."

"I need you less than you might think," Niriz retorted. "Certainly less than *you* need an Imperial pardon for that mess you left on Borkyne—"

"Gentlemen, please," Trell jumped in hastily. "I'm a businessman, with a schedule to keep. Whatever your differences, I'm sure you can lay them aside until this job is finished."

Niriz was still glowering, but he gave a reluctant nod. "You're right, Merchant. Fine. You and your crew can rest in the ready room over there until the cargo's been transferred. As for you—"

He leveled a finger at Kast. "I'd like to see you in the

bay control office. There are a few things I want to make sure you understand."

Kast nodded gravely. "Of course. Lead the way."

Niriz stepped into the bay control office, the armored figure striding in right behind him. The door slid closed; and at long last Niriz could let the unnatural stiffness drain out of his posture. "I'm afraid I'm not very good at this, sir," he apologized. "I hope I did all right."

"You did just fine, Captain," the other assured him, reaching up to twist his helmet free and pull it off. "Between this armor and your performance all four of them are completely convinced that I'm Jodo Kast."

"I hope so, sir," Niriz said, his stomach tight with concern as he gazed at those glowing red eyes. "Admiral . . . I have to say one last time that I don't think you should do this. At least not personally."

"Your concern is noted," Grand Admiral Thrawn said, running a gauntleted hand through his blue-black hair. "And appreciated, as well. But this is something I can't delegate to anyone else."

Niriz shook his head. "I wish I could say I understood."

"You will," Thrawn promised. "Assuming this plays out as anticipated, you'll have the entire story when I return."

Niriz smiled, thinking about all the campaigns he and the Grand Admiral had been through together out in the Unknown Regions. "When *hasn't* something you planned gone as anticipated?" he asked dryly.

Thrawn smiled faintly in return. "Any number of times, Captain," he said. "Fortunately, I've usually been able to improvise an alternate approach."

"That you have, sir." Niriz sighed. "I still wish you'd reconsider. We could put one of my stormtroopers in the Mandalorian armor, and you could direct him by comlink from somewhere nearby."

Thrawn shook his head. "Too slow and awkward. Besides, Thyne's fortress will certainly have a full-spectrum surveillance set up. They'd pick up any such transmission and either tap in or jam it."

Niriz took a deep breath. "Yes, sir."

Thrawn smiled again. "Don't worry, Captain, I'll be fine. Don't forget, there's an Imperial garrison nearby. If necessary, I can always call on them for help."

He slid the helmet back over his head and fastened it in place. "I'd better go supervise the cargo transfer—we wouldn't want Merchant Trell's precious sausages to be damaged. I'll see you in a few days."

"Yes, sir," Niriz said. "Good luck, Admiral."

It was called Treasure Ship Row, and it was billed as the most exotic and eclectic trading bazaar anywhere in the Empire. Dozens of booths and shops of every size and description ran its length, with hundreds more nestled up against its edges, weaving in and out of Coronet City proper. Humans and aliens sat at open-air counters or stood beside doorways, hawking their wares to the thousands of beings jostling their way through the narrow streets.

A vibrant, exciting place; but for Trell, a bit intimidating as well. The merchant part of him was intrigued by the range of merchandise available, as well as by the variety of potential customers an enterprising dealer could sell those goods to. But at the same time the part of him that had driven him into the isolation of space in the first place felt distinctly ill at ease in the middle of such crowds.

Maranne, walking beside him, didn't seem to feel any such discomfort. Neither did the two Rebel agents, striding along behind him. As for Kast, in the lead, he doubted any of them could tell what he was feeling. Or cared, for that matter.

"Where exactly are we going?" Maranne asked, taking an extra long step to get in close behind Kast.

"This way," Kast said, veering through the crowd toward the side.

The others followed, and a moment later all five were standing in the narrow walkway between two shuttered booths. "Here?" Trell demanded.

"The booth you want is five ahead on the left," Kast told them. "Curio shop—owner's named Sajsh. You—" he pointed a gloved finger at Trell "—will tell him you have a cargo for Borbor Crisk and ask for delivery instructions."

"What about the rest of us?" Riij asked.

"You'll go out first," Kast said. "Stay out of the conversation, but watch and listen."

Trell looked out into the flow of the crowd, a shiver running down his neck. Something about this didn't feel right, but it was too late to back out now. "Maranne, make sure you're where you can cover me," he told her.

"There will be no shooting," Kast assured him.

"Glad to hear it," Maranne said. "You don't mind if I cover him anyway?"

Kast's invisible eyes seemed to bore into hers through the helmet visor. "As you wish," he said. "All of you: move."

Wordlessly, the others filed out into the crowd, Kast bringing up the rear. Trell gave them a count of fifty to find their positions, then followed.

The curio shop was easy to find: a small, somewhat dilapidated open-air booth with an enclosed back room that had been inexpertly added on long enough ago to look almost as moldering as the booth itself. A lizardine creature of an unfamiliar species was leaning on the counter, watching the crowds passing by. Taking a deep breath, Trell stepped over to him.

The lizard looked up as Trell approached, his alien expression unreadable. "Good day, good sir," he said in adequate Basic. "I am Sajsh, proprietor of this humble establishment. May I be of assistance?"

"I hope so," Trell said. "I have a cargo for someone named Borbor Crisk. I was told you could give me delivery instructions."

A three-forked tongue darted briefly from the scaled mouth. "You have been misinformed," he said. "I know no one by that name."

"Oh?" Trell said, taken aback. "Are you sure?"

The tongue flicked again. "Do you doubt my word?" the alien spat. "Or merely my memory or intelligence?"

"No, no," Trell said hastily. "Not at all. I just . . . my source seemed so sure this was the place."

Sajsh opened his mouth wide. "Perhaps he was only slightly incorrect. Perhaps he meant the shop to my kill-hand." He pointed to his right, to an equally dilapidated booth that was currently closed up. "The proprietor will return at the seven-hour. You can return then and ask him."

"I'll do that," Trell promised. "Thank you."

The lizard snapped his jaws together twice. Nodding, Trell turned and pushed his way back into the stream of pedestrians, face hot with embarrassment and annoyance. "Well?" Maranne demanded, sidling up beside him.

"Kast had the wrong place," Trell growled, glancing around. But the bounty hunter was nowhere to be seen. "Where are the others?"

"We're right here," Riij said, coming up through the crowd behind him. "Kast said to head back down the street and he'd meet us."

"Good," Trell said tartly. "I've got a few things to say to our esteemed bounty hunter. Let's go."

Sajsh and the unknown man finished their conversation, and the latter moved away back into the mass of browsers and shoppers. Two booths over, Corran Horn set down the melon he'd been examining and eased into the flow behind him.

The stranger didn't seem to be trying to lose himself in

the crowd. Though any such effort would have been quickly negated by the company he linked up with: a hard-eyed, competent-looking woman, a young man about Corran's own age, and a yellow-skinned alien with several short horns protruding from his chin. For a moment the four of them conversed; then, with the contact man leading the way, they continued on down the street.

At the edge of Corran's vision, a heavyset figure stepped to his side. "Trouble?"

"I don't know, Dad," Corran said. "You see that foursome up there? Tooled brown jacket, blondish woman, white-spiked collar, yellow-skinned alien?"

"Yes," Hal Horn nodded. "The alien's a Tunroth, by the way. Fairly rare outside their home system; most of the ones you run into these days work with high-stakes safaris, mercenaries, or bounty hunters."

"Interesting," Corran said. "Possibly significant, too. Brown Jacket just waltzed up to Sajsh's booth and tried to make a delivery to Borbor Crisk."

"Did he, now," Hal said thoughtfully. "Have Crisk and Zekka Thyne patched up their differences while I wasn't looking?"

"If they did, I wasn't looking either," Corran told him. "Either Brown Jacket and his pals are incredibly stupid, or else something very odd is going on."

"Either way, I doubt Thyne will simply pass on it," Hal said. "Did Brown Jacket happen to mention where they could be contacted?"

"No, but Sajsh has that covered," Corran said. "He said they might want the owner of the booth next to his and suggested they come back about seven."

"Where they'll be asked to have a quiet conversation with a group of Black Sun heavies." Hal stretched his neck to peer over the crowd. "Well, well—the plot thickens. Look who our innocents have hooked up with."

Corran rose up on tiptoes. There was Brown Jacket and his friends; and with them—

"I'll be shragged," he breathed. "Is that Boba Fett?"

"No, I don't think so," Hal said. "Possibly Jodo Kast, though I'd have to get a closer look at the armor to be sure."

"Well, whoever it is, we've definitely moved into the big time," Corran pointed out. "Mandalorian armor doesn't come cheap."

"When you can find it at all," the elder Horn agreed. "This is getting odder by the minute. I take it you've had some thoughts already?"

"Only one, really," Corran said. The group was moving off again, and he and his father set off to follow. "Thyne wouldn't be stupid enough to kill them out of hand, certainly not until he knows who they are and what their connection is to Crisk. That probably means bringing them to the fortress."

"And you think you might be able to invite yourself along?"

"I know it's risky—"

" 'Risky' isn't exactly the word I had in mind," Hal interrupted. "Getting into the fortress is only the first step, you know. You think you'll be able to simply march up to Thyne, slap the restraints on him in the name of Corellian Security, and march him out?"

"We do have the legal authority to do that, you know," Corran reminded him.

"Which means nothing at all inside his stronghold," Hal countered. "You have any idea how many CorSec agents have gone after top Black Sun lieutenants like Thyne and simply vanished?"

Corran grimaced. "I know," he said. "But that's not going to happen this time. And if getting into the fortress is only the first step, it still *is* the first step."

The elder Horn shook his head. " 'Risky' still doesn't begin to cover it. For starters, we don't even know what game Brown Jacket and his Mandalorian friend are playing."

"Then it's time we found out," Corran said. "Let's stay close and see if we can find an opportunity to introduce ourselves."

They had gone perhaps two blocks—though where Kast was leading them Trell hadn't the faintest idea—when they heard the shout.

"What was that?" Riij demanded, looking around.

"There," Palror rumbled, pointing his thick central finger to the left. "Argument starting."

Trell craned his neck. There was an open-air tapcafe that direction, with a long serving bar at the rear and perhaps twenty small tables spread out in the open space in front of it beneath a wide, Karvrish-style woven-leaf canopy. A slightly built man wearing a proprietor's apron was standing in the middle of the dining area, a half dozen large and rough-looking men wearing mercenary shoulder patches looming in a threatening circle around him. The chairs from a nearby table were scattered back or lying on the ground, indicating a quick and unruly departure from them. "I think the argument's over," he said. "It's gone straight to trouble now."

"Come on," Riij said, angling that direction. "Let's check it out."

"Leave it alone," Kast ordered. "It's none of our business."

But Riij and Palror were already heading off through the crowd. "Blast," Trell growled. Stupid idealistic gornt-brained Rebels—"Come on, Maranne."

A line of onlookers had started to form at the edge of the tapcafe by the time he and Maranne broke through the stream of pedestrians. Riij and Palror were already to the mercenaries, who had opened their circle around the tapcafe proprietor in order to face this new distraction.

And now Trell could see something he hadn't been able to before. Standing beside the proprietor, clinging tightly to his waist in terror, was a young girl. Probably his daughter; certainly no more than seven years old.

Trell hissed a curse between his teeth. It took a particularly vile form of low-life to threaten a child. But that didn't mean he was going to follow Riij's lead and charge in blindly like a mad Jedi Knight on Cracian thumperback. "Backup left," he murmured to Maranne. "I'll take right."

"Right," she murmured back. Dropping his hand casually onto the grip of his blaster, Trell started drifting behind the ring of onlookers to the right—

And with a suddenness that startled him, the fight started.

Not with blasters, which had been his main fear, but with hands and feet as the two closest mercenaries lashed out at Riij and Palror. With three-to-one odds on their side, the mercs must have felt weapons to be unnecessary.

They got a shock. Riij had clearly had some good training in unarmed combat, and Palror was a lot faster than Trell would have guessed from the alien's bulk. Riij's counterattack sent his opponent reeling back; Palror's threw his merc slamming back with a horrendous crash into one of the other tables, sending it spinning and scattering its chairs across the floor.

Someone swore viciously. The downed merc scrambled to his feet and rejoined his comrades, their former casual semicircle now reformed into a deadly, no-nonsense combat line facing their attackers. The proprietor had taken advantage of the distraction to hustle his daughter back across to the bar; heaving her up and over to the relative safety behind it, he turned back to watch.

For a long moment the combatants stood motionless facing each other. Trell kept drifting toward his chosen backup position, his eyes on the mercs, his hand tightening on his blaster. Would they draw now, in which case Riij and Palror were probably dead? Or would sheer pride dictate they beat such insolent opponents bloody with their bare hands?

The watching crowd was obviously wondering the same thing. Trell could feel their tension, their excitement, their bloodlust . . .

And then, out of the corner of his eye, he spotted movement to his left. The mercs caught it, too, anger-filled eyes shifting that direction—

Their expressions changed, just slightly. Frowning, Trell risked a look of his own.

Jodo Kast had stepped forward out of the ring of on-lookers.

For a moment the bounty hunter just stood there, gazing silently at the scene. Then, stepping to one of the tables at the edge of the tapcafe, he pulled out a chair and sat down. Crossing his legs casually beneath the table, he folded his arms across his chest and cocked his head slightly to one side. "Well?" he asked mildly.

And with that one word the decision was made. No mercenary with a speck's worth of professional pride was going to use weapons against outnumbered opponents who hadn't themselves drawn. Not with a bounty hunter like Jodo Kast watching.

Roaring obscure and probably obscene battle cries, the mercs waded in.

At that first exchange Riij and Palror had had the element of surprise. This time they didn't. They did their best, certainly—and still better than Trell would have expected given the odds—but in the end they really had no chance. Less than ninety seconds after that battle roar, both Riij and Palror were on the floor, along with two of the mercs. The remaining four, not all of them looking all that steady on their feet, were grouped around them. One of them looked around, jabbed a finger toward the proprietor cowering at the bar. "Them first," he snarled, breathing heavily. "You next."

"No," Kast said.

The merc spun around to face him, almost losing his balance in the process as a damaged knee tried to buckle under him. "No what?" he demanded.

"I said no," Kast told him. His hands were in his lap now, concealed under the table, but his legs were still casually crossed. "You've had your fun; but I need them alive."

"Yeah?" the merc snarled. "What, you got a bounty to collect on them?"

"You've had your fun," Kast repeated, but this time there was frosty metal glittering in his voice. "Leave it and go. Now."

"You think so, huh?" the merc spat. "And who do you think's gonna stop—?"

And abruptly, right in the middle of his sentence, he dropped his hand to his blaster and yanked it from its holster.

It was an old trick, and one that had probably given the merc the desired edge in many a facedown. Unfortunately for him, it was a trick Trell had seen used countless times before; and even before the other's hand had reached his blaster grip Trell was hauling out his own weapon. At the other side of the ring of bystanders he spotted Maranne also drawing—

The merc had good reflexes, all right. In that split second he froze, his weapon not quite cleared of its holster, staring from beneath thick eyebrows at the four blasters suddenly pointed at him from the circle of people around the tapcafe.

Trell blinked as it suddenly registered. *Four* blasters?

Four. Two people down from Maranne, a bulky middle-aged man also had a blaster trained steadily on the mercs . . . and out of the corner of his eye, Trell could see the fourth blaster sticking out from his side of the crowd. Held with equal steadiness.

The merc spat. "So that's how you want to play it, huh?"

"We're not playing," Kast said icily. "As I said: leave it and go. If you don't—"

Trell never saw the warning twitch he was watching for.

But Kast obviously did. Even as the merc started to haul his blaster the rest of the way free of its holster there was the brilliant flash of a blaster bolt from the direction of the bounty hunter's table, and a roar of rage from the merc as his holster and the blaster muzzle behind it shattered.

"—I promise you will regret it," Kast finished calmly. "This is your final chance."

The merc looked like he was about two seconds short of a complete berserk rage. But even furious and with a burned gun hand, he was in control enough to know when the odds were stacked too high against him. "I'll be watching for you, bounty hunter," he breathed, straightening up from his combat crouch. "We'll finish this some other time."

Kast bowed his head slightly. "Whenever you're tired of life, mercenary."

The merc gave a hand signal. The others helped their two casualties to their feet—one groggily starting to come to, the other still in need of basic portage—and the group straggled their way through the onlookers and out into the crowd.

Kast waited until they were out of sight. Then, pushing back his chair, he stood up, the blaster he'd used on the merc's weapon already secreted back in whatever hidden holster it had been drawn from. "The show's over," he announced, looking around at the bystanders. "Stay and buy a drink, or get moving."

The proprietor was already beside Riij and Palror, helping the former to a sitting position, when Trell and Maranne reached them. "You all right?" Maranne asked, offering Palror a hand.

The Tunroth waved it away. "I am not hurt," he said, rolling to his feet and flexing an elbow experimentally. "I was merely temporarily disabled."

"You're lucky the condition wasn't permanent," Trell reminded him. "You should have left it alone like Kast told you to."

"Yeah," Riij said, holding his stomach as he got to his feet with the proprietor's assistance. "Thanks, Kast. Though I wouldn't have minded if you'd stepped in a little earlier. Say, before they started pounding on us?"

"Six mercenaries wouldn't have backed down in front of three blasters," Kast told him. "I needed you to take some of them out first."

He half turned. "If I'd known it would be five blasters instead of three, I might have moved sooner."

Trell turned to look. The two men who'd drawn with them were standing there watching. "Thanks," he said. "I wouldn't have counted on getting that kind of help in a place like this."

"No problem," the older man shrugged. "The Brommstaad Mercenaries have always had a tendency to consider themselves above the bounds of normal civilized behavior. And I've never liked it when children get threatened."

"Besides which," the younger man added, "we were starting to get thirsty anyway."

"Drinks?" the proprietor asked eagerly. "Of course; drinks for all of you. And meals, too, if you are hungry— the finest I have to offer."

"We'll take the long table in the back," Kast said. "And some privacy."

"Yes, good sir, immediately," the proprietor said. Giving them a quick bow, he scurried off toward the table Kast had indicated.

"My name's Hal, by the way," the older man said. "This is my partner Corran."

Trell exchanged nods with them. "Pleased to meet you. I'm Trell; this is Maranne, Riij, Palror, and—"

"Call me Kast," Kast cut him off. "Son or nephew?"

Hal blinked. "What?"

"Is Corran your son or nephew?" Kast amplified. "There's a family resemblance about the eyes."

"People have mentioned that before," Corran spoke

up. "Actually, it's just coincidence. As far as we know, we're not related."

Kast nodded once, slowly. "Ah."

"The table seems ready," Hal said, pointing in that direction. "Shall we go sit down?"

"Oh, sure," Hal said, taking a sip from his second drink. "Everyone around here has heard of Borbor Crisk. Fairly small-time criminal, though, as criminals go—strictly local to the Corellian system. Of course, if you're looking for impressive intersystem criminals, we've got some of those, too."

"We're not interested in impressiveness," Trell pointed out. "Criminal or otherwise. We've got a cargo to deliver to this Crisk character, and then we're out of here."

"Yes, you mentioned that," Corran agreed, eyeing the other and trying to read him. It was hard to believe these people were really the simple errand boys they appeared, especially after the incident with the mercenaries. But if this was some kind of deeply clever plan, he was blamed if he could figure it out.

At least, not from the outside. It was about time he made his pitch to get a little closer to the middle. "The thing is this," he went on, looking around the table. "Two things, actually. Number one: considering who Crisk is, your cargo is probably illegal and certainly valuable. That means that you not only have to worry about Corellian Security coming down on you, but also other criminals who might try to take it off your hands. And number two—" he hesitated, just slightly "—the reason Hal and I came to Corellia in the first place was hoping to find jobs with Crisk's organization."

"You're kidding," Riij said. "Doing what?"

"Anything, really," Hal said. "Our last job went really sour, and we need to recoup our losses."

"That's why we were following you, see," Corran said, trying for the proper balance of assertiveness and embarrassment. "I overheard Trell talking about Crisk, and thought—well—"

"We thought maybe we could go with you when you went back to see him tonight," Hal took the plunge.

Trell and Maranne exchanged glances. "Well—"

"We don't actually *know* we're seeing him tonight," Riij pointed out. "That other booth owner may not know anything more about Crisk than Sajsh did."

"That's a good point," Trell agreed, throwing an odd look at Kast. "This could be nothing but a blind alley."

"Well, in that case, you'll need help finding him," Hal said with a wonderfully genuine-sounding eagerness. "Corran and I are locals—we have all sorts of contacts around the area. We can help you find him."

"One of you can go," Kast said.

Corran looked at the bounty hunter, blinking in mild surprise. It was the first time he'd spoken since they'd sat down at the table. "Ah—good," he said. "Just one of us?"

"Just him," Kast said, nodding toward Hal. "Trell and the Tunroth will go with him. I'll be behind as rearguard."

"What about Riij and me?" Maranne asked.

"You two and Corran will go back to the ship," Kast told her. "You'll transfer the cargo onto the ship's landspeeder so it'll be ready for delivery."

Trell and Maranne eyed each other again, and Corran could see neither was particularly happy with the arrangement. It was equally clear, though, that neither was all that eager to argue the point with the bounty hunter. "All right," Trell said with a grimace. "Fine. What happens if no one at that other booth knows where Crisk is either?"

"That won't be a problem," Kast said. "Trust me."

"Interesting person, Jodo Kast," Hal commented as the three of them headed back toward Sajsh's booth. "Have you worked with him long?"

"This is the first time," Trell told him, looking around

uneasily. There were far fewer shoppers at this hour than there had been earlier, and despite his innate dislike of crowds he found himself feeling unpleasantly exposed right now. "Actually, we're not working with him so much as we are working for him. Palror, can you see where he's gotten to?"

"No, don't turn around," Hal said quickly. "We might be under observation, and we don't want to tip them off that we've got a rearguard."

Trell threw him a sideways look. There was something in his voice right then that emphatically did not belong in a down-luck drifter. A tone of authority, spoken by a person who was used to having his orders obeyed . . .

Palror rumbled. "Trouble," he said.

Trell craned his neck. He could see Sajsh's booth ahead now, closed up for the night.

The booth beside it, the booth they were headed for, was also closed.

"Great," he growled, stopping. "Still no one there."

"No, don't stop," a soft voice came from behind him. Trell felt his heart seize up. "What?"

"You heard the man," a different voice said, this one coming from behind Hal. "Keep walking."

With an effort, Trell got his feet moving again. "Are you with Borbor Crisk?"

There was a snort. "Hardly," the first voice said with obvious contempt. "Keep it casual, and don't try to be clever. We'd prefer to deliver you in fully working condition."

Trell swallowed hard. "Where are we going?"

"For now, behind Sajsh's booth," the other said. "After that . . . you'll see."

"I'm sure," Trell murmured, heart pounding in his ears. Still, there was one thing the kidnappers didn't know. Jodo Kast, one of the finest bounty hunters in the galaxy, was somewhere behind them. Any minute now he would jump out from wherever he was hiding, blasters blazing with micron accuracy, and flip the tables completely on them. Any minute now, and they'd hear the roar of blasters. Any minute now . . .

He was still waiting for that minute as the kidnappers herded the three of them aboard a speeder truck, sealed the doors, and drove off into the gathering dusk.

Side Trip Part Two
by Michael A. Stackpole

Corran Horn's feeling that something was wrong got a big boost from his first glimpse of the *Hopskip*. The freighter looked as if someone had taken a stock Corellian YT-1300, split the disk along a line running from bow to stern, flopped one half on top of the other, then patched it together with whatever scrap metal was conveniently at hand. Corran had seen uglier ships, but none that were supposed to be operational.

He waited for Riij to close the gateway to the hangar

bay before he made a comment. "I guess smuggling doesn't pay what it once used to?"

Maranne's hard eyes flashed angrily. "We're traders, not smugglers."

Corran raised his hands. "Call it what you want. With Imp rules and regs out there, what starts as a trading trip could end up as a smuggling run."

Surprise played through Maranne's dark blue eyes, then she turned away and scratched at the back of her neck. "I'll get the landspeeder." Her surprise at his comment made her statement come a bit too fast, and Corran thought perhaps he caught a hint of fear in her words.

Definitely more here than meets the eye. The second he saw the ship, Corran abandoned any suspicion that these people were hard-edged smugglers coming to deliver supplies to Borbor Crisk. The things Crisk needed to wage his little war with Zekka Thyne and Black Sun for supremacy in the Corellian underworld weren't the sorts of things that would be entrusted to the crew of the *Hopskip*. *Actually, for Crisk to depose Thyne would require a Star Destroyer, which this ship isn't, and a legion of stormtroopers, which isn't hidden here.*

Corran saw Maranne disappear through a hatch in the freighter, so he turned his attention to Riij. "Shipping with her can't be too rough. She's pretty easy on the eyes. Known her long?"

The slender man shook his head, then ran a hand across his short, spiky white hair. "Just along for the ride. If I do some work, I get some pay by the time we reach our destination." Riij smiled carefully. "You been working with your partner long?"

"Off and on." Corran shrugged. Riij's quick questioning of Corran about his background played to most people's tendency to want to talk about themselves. *It's a technique you learn to exploit when fishing for information from suspects. Either Riij has had training, is very private, or both.* "Known him for a long time, but started running together recently. Bonded through bad times, you know? Like you and the Tunroth."

"You recognize him as a Tunroth?"

"Hal and me, we might be locals, but that doesn't mean we've not been around." Corran took a step back as Maranne lowered the rear loading ramp on the *Hopskip*. "He got a life debt toward you or something?"

"Life debt is a Wookiee thing." Riij frowned, then started up the ramp to the freighter's hold. "Rathe and I are just traveling on the same ship. No connection beyond that."

"Got it." Corran kept an easy smile on his face while cataloguing the information Riij had just supplied him. Corran knew life debts were a matter of Wookiee honor, but he only knew of them because of the Imperial warrants and advisories about Han Solo and the Wookiee working with him. *Most folks don't know Wookiees exist or, at best, know Imps use them for slave labor. Folks who know more about Wookiees are usually Rebel sympathizers.*

He followed Riij up the ramp and started looking around for clues to what the *Hopskip*'s crew was doing in Coronet City. As a member of the Corellian Security Force, Corran had access to most information about the Rebellion and its connections to Corellia. *At least I have it when that worthless Imp Intelligence liaison officer isn't around.* While it was true that two of the Alliance's heroes were from Corellia, the Emperor's tightening of his grip on Corellia and the placement of forces on the world had kept the Rebel presence down. Corran knew there were Rebel cells in residence, and he'd gladly have run any of them in, but he didn't see them being so bold or so desperate as to try to hook up with Crisk.

Corran slid past the battered nose of the old landspeeder—like the ship, it looked as if it had been cobbled together from parts. It only had two seats, like a fancy speeder, but had a flat bed grafted on to the back. Except where dents let silvery metal show through, an even, dirt-brown coat of primer covered the vehicle. *Not fast, not strong, but beats hauling this stuff on my back.*

The bank of boxes that Maranne and Riij were freeing

from cargo-net tie-downs immediately attracted his attention. They were uniform in size and non-descript, but that struck Corran as odd. All of them had exteriors formed out of green duraplast that was a couple shades darker than his eyes, yet none of the rectangular boxes bore the streaking and scarring common on duraplast boxes. None had holographic tags, scuff marks or other signs of use, yet all had been bound with duraplast cables and fixed with a holographic seal.

As he lifted the first one from the top of the pile he felt nothing shift inside the boxes, nor was there a need for him to locate the box's balance point. He shook his head. "Where did you guys get *sleight* boxes?"

Maranne and Riij both stopped as Corran set his box down on the landspeeder's bed. The woman frowned. "What's a *sleight* box?"

"If you don't know what a *sleight* box is, maybe you aren't smugglers." Corran tapped a finger on the top of his box. "It looks ordinary, but it has a low-power repulsorlift coil matrix and power-supply built into the casing. It neutralizes the weight of whatever is inside. These boxes could be full of thermal detonators or air, and we'd never know. Smugglers developed them to trick customs officials, but most customs-droids know what to scan for now."

Maranne set her box down next to his. "Interesting story. Seems you've done more smuggling than we have."

"Maybe, or maybe I just know more about smuggling than you do." Corran gave her a sly smile. "For example, I know no one smuggles a cargo that's made up of unknown items. What's in these things?"

The woman shook her head, her dark blond queue lashing her from shoulder to shoulder. "Don't know. Don't want to know."

"I find that hard to believe." Corran frowned at her. "I don't know what kind of game you're running here, but these *sleight* boxes won't fool CorSec's droids. If this is stuff being hauled for the Rebels, they'll find it and you'll be in serious trouble."

Riij slid his box onto the flat bed. "If we were Rebels and we knew what was in these boxes *and* it was meant for the Rebels, we'd be a lot more worried about the Empire than we would their puppets here on Corellia."

"You think CorSec's people are Imperial puppets?" Corran flicked that suggestion away with a wave of his hand. "CorSec's concerned with the integrity of the Corellian system, nothing more. If they tolerate Rebels here, the Imperial presence increases. Who wants that?"

Riij's brown eyes flashed dangerously. "What you're telling me is that CorSec's people are willing to repress the enemies of a vicious regime so they don't get Vader's boot across their own necks. If I was a Rebel, I'd find it very difficult to tell the difference between CorSec agents and the Imps."

Corran forced himself to go over and pick up another box so he wouldn't immediately snap back at Riij. The smuggler's arguments had been heard often—and loudly—on Corellia. Corran, whose father and grandfather had both preceded him into CorSec, had long believed that CorSec could do the most good by keeping the Imps out of its solar system security problems. If Corellia could take care of itself and set itself up as a neutral party in this civil war, the citizens of Corellia would benefit.

While that position made perfect sense, and was defensible, it was also a position made at the top of a very slick slope. CorSec's directors had already forced the local divisions to accept Imperial Intelligence Liaison officers to monitor and coordinate operations with Imperial Garrisons. Kirtan Loor, the liaison officer his division had been saddled with, had proved thoroughly arrogant and barely functional. He and Corran did not get along at all.

Corran hefted another box. "I think, from CorSec's view, they have a hard time telling the Rebels apart from honest criminals like me. I don't, but that's because I've got the right perspective. The Rebs aren't honest criminals at all.''

Maranne smiled. " 'Honest' criminals?''

"Yeah, honest. I know that what I'm doing violates the law, but I do it because that's what I do. I take the risks, I make some money, or I get sent to Kessel. It's all very straightforward.'' Corran placed his box on top of the first one he'd set down. "The Rebels, they do everything I would do, but they say they are entitled to do it because the law is wrong and the Empire is wrong. They're really just making excuses for their actions so they can feel they're noble when they're really no better than I am.''

"What an interesting perspective.''

Corran spun at the sound of the faintly echoed voice. Jodo Kast stood in the cargo hatchway, blocking most of the view of the docking bay. Corran ducked and dodged his head to try and see past the bounty hunter, but with no success. "Where's Hal?''

"I would expect, right now, he is very nearly at Zekka Thyne's fortress.''

"What?'' Riij's shout of surprise filled the cargo hold. "You were there to protect them. What happened?''

Kast stepped into the cargo hold, then leaned rather casually against the bay's internal bulkhead. "Thyne's people were waiting for Trell and the other two. There were seven of them—including the Brommstaad Mercenaries. I waited until they'd headed off east, then I returned here.''

Corran slammed a fist down on top of a *sleight* box. "East is where Thyne has his little palace.''

Kast nodded. "Hence my assumption about their destination.''

"And you did nothing to stop them?'' Corran jabbed a finger in Kast's direction. "You're some hot bounty hunter in this Mandalorian armor who can shoot the blaster from a man's hand while sitting down, and you didn't stop them?''

"There were seven of them and only one of me. I already did the math for you on that match-up—I might have gotten them, but they would have killed your people.''

Riij shook his head. ''Rathe could have taken his share of them.''

Maranne nodded. ''Trell would have been good for at least one.''

''And Hal could have popped a couple . . .''

''A couple wouldn't have done it.''

''. . . Or more, *if* he'd been given a chance.'' Corran looked from Riij and Maranne to the bounty hunter. ''Are all three of you so naive you don't know what's going to happen to our people? Thyne's going to ask them about their connection to Crisk and, if they know as little as you do, he's going to have to work real hard to get answers he trusts. I'm not too wild about him going at Hal like that.''

Kast shrugged his shoulders. ''You can always find yourself another partner.''

''If you think I'm going to abandon Hal, I'm going to have to shuck you out of that armor and beat some sense into you.''

Kast's head came up as he moved away from the wall, silently emphasizing just how much bigger than Corran he truly was. ''Hardly the reaction I'd expect from two criminal associates. Out of proportion, really. You're acting as if there is a closer bond between you.''

Corran gave Kast as cold a glare as he could. He did resemble his father a bit, around the eyes and through the face, but otherwise he was a compromise between his mother and father. She'd been tiny and had the bluest eyes Corran could ever remember having seen. His green eyes were a midpoint between her eyes and his father's hazel eyes, as his brown hair was a match between her blond and his father's once black hair. Even his height formed a bridge between that of his mother and father.

''It wouldn't matter if Hal was my clone—he's my *partner*, which means I'm responsible for him.'' Corran jabbed a thumb back against his breastbone. "I actually understand what that sort of responsibility means, Kast, and what it means is that I'm not going to leave Hal to Thyne's untender mercies."

Kast folded his arms across his armored chest. "You'd dare take on a Black Sun crime lord?"

Maranne paled. "Thyne is Black Sun?"

"Claw-picked by Prince Xizor, if the rumors are true." Corran leaned on one of the green boxes. "He's crazy-cruel and wholly nasty, but he does operate with a profit motive in mind. This cargo may have been for Crisk, but we could offer it to Thyne and ransom our people."

"I don't think so." Kast produced a datacard from a pouch on his belt and flipped it over to Maranne. "That card has the location and time for a new meeting with Crisk. Deliver the cargo there, then come back here and prepare to take off."

Maranne caught the card. "We're not going anywhere if Haber isn't here."

"I know." Kast gave her a quick nod. "It's my intention to head out to Thyne's fortress and secure the release of your friends."

Corran barked out a sharp laugh. "You balk at taking on seven guttersharks, but you'll free our friends from Thyne's fortress all by yourself? Better check that math, Kast."

"The odds are substantial, but I anticipate success."

"Yeah, well, this is Corellia, and Corellians have no use for odds. I think I'd trust in your success if I was along to enhance it."

"I work alone."

"Ha!" Corran jerked his head toward Riij and Maranne. "You work with them, you can work with me." Corran shook his fists out. "Save us both some trouble and just say yes now."

Kast hesitated and silence stole over the cargo bay. The mercenary studied Corran and even though he could not see Kast's eyes, he could feel the man's hard stare raking him up and down. Corran forced himself to look at the helmet's black slit, inviting a challenge and ready to react to Kast's next move.

The bounty hunter's arms slowly unfolded. "I will go find us a landspeeder."

"Good." Corran realized, as he replied, that he'd been holding his breath. *Hal's going to go crazy when he hears what I did. Facing down a bounty hunter like Kast. It had to be done, but it could have been done better. I'd never run away from a fight with a guy like that, but there's no virtue in picking one, either.*

Darkness swallowed Kast's form, then Corran turned and looked at the other two. "You're in way over your heads, aren't you?"

Riij shrugged. "I'm not sure what's going on, but I don't like Rathe being captured by a Black Sun crime lord."

"Well, Borbor Crisk isn't much better. We're caught in the arena between two Cyborrean battledogs. Neither of these guys plays well with others, as you've seen."

Maranne brandished the datacard. "What are we going to do? We're supposed to meet with Crisk and give him this stuff."

"The first thing we do is find out what this stuff is." Corran looked at the seals on the boxes already loaded on the landspeeder's bed. "Good, here's one that's junked. See if you can find another."

Riij started looking at new boxes while Corran fished in his pocket for a small hydrospanner. "This ought to do the trick."

Maranne came over and frowned. "What do you mean the box is junked?"

"Not the box, the seal-tab used to bind the duraplast strips." Corran pointed to the round tab that connected the crisscrossing straps. "See how the hologram imbedded in it doesn't fully line up. Look at it from the angle here. The corona on the suns here don't match up."

"I found another one," Riij announced.

"Good, bring it over." Corran hooked the edge of the spanner under the lip of the seal. "When they don't set up right you can pop them apart with a little shove and a twist." He lifted up, then twisted his wrist.

The seal popped apart, freeing the strips that secured the box. "Get both parts and we can reseal this thing once we've peeked at what's inside."

Maranne bent to recover both halves of the seal while Corran attacked the other one. It came apart easily, then he reversed the spanner and used a flat-bladed attachment to pry the box's lid up. "By the Emperor's black heart!"

Even before the lid came up fully Corran caught the sharp sour scent of spice. The box held seven single-kilogram bricks that had been wrapped up in heavy cello-plast. They'd been dipped in a waxy coating to seal them, but the job had been done hastily. One of the packets had split open and spilled a low-grade spice compound inside the box.

"What is that?"

Corran looked at Maranne. "You're joking, right?"

"Like I said, I'm a trader, not a smuggler."

"This is spice. It's a really lousy grade of glitterstim—the real stuff is crystalline, long fine fibers, not a powder like this. Dose up with this and you get really happy, at least really happy until you need more and the craving flows through your veins like plasma. Not a pretty thing."

Riij curled a lip distastefully. "You know from experience?"

"Just hearsay, and watching a guy try to sell a lung to get more glit."

"Sell a lung?" Maranne shivered.

Corran shrugged. "Wasn't his. Belonged to some passerby. Like I said, not good stuff."

Riij pried the lid off the second *sleight* box. "Sith-spawn!" He reached a hand in and withdrew a crystal spike the thickness of his thumb and a good hand-span in length. Purple filled the stone's core, running from light at either end to dark in the middle. As Riij held the stone up the light it trapped filled it with orange, yellow and red lightning bolts. All three of them fell silent in response to the brilliant display.

Corran stared at the stone, then shook his head. "Is that a Durindfire gem?"

"I think so." Riij's voice-box bounced up and down as he swallowed hard. "My father bought a ring with a Durindfire for my mother on their twenty-fifth wedding anniversary. Wasn't until the thirtieth that he had the debt paid off, and that was just a *little* stone."

"Not too many of those stones make it off Tatooine, and very seldom unworked like that finger there." Maranne took it from Riij and weighed it in her hands. "This would be enough to buy us a new ship."

Riij turned. "Let's find out what else is in these other boxes."

"No, stop." Corran held his hands up. "We don't have time enough to check them out. Put the stone back, we'll reseal these two boxes and set them in the landspeeder's front seat."

Maranne reluctantly returned the stone to its box. "What do you have in mind?"

"Look, we're going to need some insurance here if we're going to get off Corellia in one piece. We can reseal these boxes and no one will ever know they've been tampered with. You'll take those two boxes to Crisk and let him know you have, what, 198 more for him. He won't make a move against you until he has them."

Riij frowned. "He can come here and take them from us."

"Yeah, but they won't be here. We load the rest onto the speeder and take them to a storage facility." Corran frowned as if thinking hard about something. "Okay, I have it. There's a Dewback Storage Warehouse on the main road back into the center of Coronet City. You can rent a storage shed there and dump the other boxes. You go to your meeting and let Crisk know you'll give him the location of the other boxes when you're certain your friends are safe. Kast and I will go off to see Thyne and if we're not back in due time, you use Crisk to try to effect a rescue."

Maranne slowly shook her head. "I don't like the sound of this."

"Look, we've got a veritable fortune in those boxes. If Crisk doesn't want to help you, set up a meeting with Thyne and ransom us."

"How do we get in touch with Thyne?"

Corran smiled. "You did that back at your first stop on Treasure Ship Row, remember?"

"Right."

"Okay, let's get loading." Corran resealed the first box and then the second. "I know you don't like the way this is going, Maranne, but you're the one who said she's a trader. If things go badly, you're going to have to trade for our freedom and, speaking for myself, I hope you strike a super bargain in the process."

Colonel Maximillian Veers glanced down at the chair offered to him, but refrained from sitting. "Thank you for your kindness, Agent Loor, but I do not anticipate being here very long. You have looked at the message I had sent over to you."

The long, slender man sat forward in his chair, a motion that nearly tossed him sprawling up over the top of his desk. Loor caught himself with his hands, then brushed the lank of dark hair that had fallen over his face back into place. Veers felt certain the man wore his hair the way he did to accentuate his resemblance to the late Grand Moff Tarkin. *I served under Tarkin. Anyone who would think this Loor is at all similar to Tarkin should realize the similarity goes no deeper than the skin.*

"Something wrong with the springs on your chair, Agent Loor?"

The liaison officer snarled. "I have saboteurs who delight in finding ways to annoy me, and adjusting the chair is their latest form of expression.''

He reached over and hit a button on his desktop datapad. "And yes, Colonel Veers, I studied the message you sent over, as requested. I can't comment on its accuracy beyond saying it is true that Zekka Thyne maintains a little fortress east of Coronet City.''

"I already know that, Loor.''

Loor's head came up. "You do? I wasn't aware that Thyne's headquarters would have been something you studied, Colonel Veers. I was unaware the Imperial Armed Forces had been given cause to consider Black Sun facilities potential targets.''

Veers' nostrils flared. The only thing he hated more than having to deal with arrogant intelligence agents was turning a blind eye to the activities of the Black Sun. He assumed the Emperor's tolerance for the criminal cartel was based on reason, but Veers thought that tolerance was truly a detriment to the Empire. Allowing *any* outlaws undermined the rule of authority. If people could see Black Sun as somehow more malevolent than the Rebellion, then they could justify joining the Rebellion all that more easily.

"It is incumbent upon me, Agent Loor, to view any stronghold that is filled with armed individuals as a potential target. In this case I am told that Thyne is meeting with elements of the Rebel underground.''

"Yes, but I am uncomfortable with your source. Who is it?''

"You saw the verification code. It is valid.'' Veers frowned heavily. "There is no reason to distrust the information. It is accurate and I plan to act on it.''

"So you mean you don't know who your source is?''

"I don't need to know.''

With a superior smile slithering over his face, Loor eased himself back in his chair. Veers hoped it would overbalance and spill him to the floor. "If you believe in this intelligence source, why come to me?''

Veers restrained himself from reaching out and slapping Loor. "I came to you, Agent Loor, because you are the Imperial Liaison Officer and you liaise with the Corellian Security Force in this administrative sector. I want to know if they have any operatives working in or around Thyne."

"Are you looking to use their extraction as a pretense for your attack, or were you worried I would lodge a protest over collateral damage?"

Veers narrowed his eyes. "There is no reason for good people to die."

Loor shrugged lazily. "If they do die, they die heroes. If you get me Zekka Thyne, you can be a hero, too."

"I believe, Agent Loor, I can find my own way to be a hero." Veers spun on his heel and stalked from the office. *With Imperials like you, Loor, I often wonder why the Rebellion has not yet succeeded in overthrowing the Empire. If things are left in the hands of people like you, can the Empire possibly survive?*

Corran took one look at the SoroSuub X-34 Landspeeder Kast was piloting and sighed. "Buy or borrow?"

The bounty hunter looked up at him from behind the wheel. "Does it matter?"

"If I'm going to get arrested for traveling in a stolen landspeeder I'd kind of been hoping it would be something newer and sportier, like an XP-38."

"You can always walk, Corran."

"Good point." With his left hand on the windscreen, Corran hopped up and into the passenger seat. "Punch it."

Kast spun the landspeeder's wheel, fed power to the repulsorlift coils and eased the throttle forward. "How did the loading go?"

"Loading? It went fine." Corran shifted around in the cramped seat. "They should be ready to make their rendezvous."

"Good."

Corran heard the correct emphasis and inflection given to the word, but somehow he thought Kast was being something less than genuine in his response. Corran tried to put his finger on it but couldn't, and that bothered him. In the past he'd had an almost sixth sense about hardcases like Kast, but he didn't seem to be able to read the armored mercenary. *The fact that my father has been captured by a man who will fillet him is destroying my concentration.*

Kast piloted the landspeeder in toward the center of town. The bright lights and raucous sounds of Coronet City and Treasure Ship Row all started to press in on Corran. As a member of CorSec he saw Dirtdock—CorSec slang for Treasure Ship Row—as a dangerous place. While the fringes might not be that bad—and plenty of respectful folks dabbled in minor transgressions at some of the flashier places—there were locations there where even Darth Vader would fear to tread. Most of those establishments were controlled by Black Sun.

Corran's grandfather had lamented the changes in the criminal class since the rise of the Empire. Rostek Horn had been in CorSec back in the days of Moff Fliry Vorru, back when flouting the law had been an art. In those days, Corran had been told, criminals only made war on criminals. The abduction of Hal and Trell never would have been tolerated back then—civilians would have to get involved with criminal activities a lot more deeply before they were considered fair game.

Then Prince Xizor and his Black Sun organization had come to the fore. Xizor had betrayed Vorru to the Emperor, in one step eliminating Vorru and gaining favor with the Emperor. Xizor had used Corellia as training ground for some of his lieutenants. The most recent and most brutal of them was Zekka Thyne.

Corran glanced out of the landspeeder as the Dewback storage facility flashed past. As he turned to look back in the direction they were traveling, he caught Kast watching him. "Something the matter?"

"You seemed to find something interesting out there."

"Yeah, I did." *Think, Corran, think of something good.* "It was the street art on the walls."

"Art? You think the defacement of buildings is art?"

Corran shrugged. "It's not the work of Venthan Chassu but it beats peeling Star Destroyer-white for holding my interest."

Kast studied Corran for a second or two. "How does someone like you know the work of Venthan Chassu?"

"I could lie to you and tell you that my mother used to take me to museums, but you'd see through that." Corran forced himself to stare straight forward as he abandoned the truth and started fashioning a lie from a wild tale a thief he'd once collared had started spinning for him. "I knew a guy who said he had a client who would buy anything in the fine arts from Corellia. He said he'd already lifted and sold a handful of paintings, some sculpture and a couple of holographic dioramas. The client seemed impressed, but wanted more. He was spending credits like they were made of free-floating hydrogen atoms, so this guy said he wanted to plan a heist to hit the Coronet City Museum of Fine Art. He wanted me in on the crew, so I cased the place."

Kast nodded slowly. "Who was the client?"

"Don't know. My man talked to a broker, then he got tractored by CorSec and caught a shuttle to Akrit'tar. He died there."

"So what did you think of Chassu's work?"

Corran frowned. *Why would a bounty hunter care about art and care what I thought about art?* "It was interesting. The Selonian nude studies were what I liked the best—but not because they were nudes. Selonians have fur, so can they ever really be nude? And if it were nude Selonians I wanted," Corran held his hands up above the windscreen, "I could find plenty of them here in Treasure Ship Row."

"Why did you like them?"

"Chassu caught the two essential elements of Selonians: their sensual, sinewy forms and, because their faces were always obscured, their desire for privacy." Corran shrugged. "Some of his other work was fine."

"What did you think of *Palpatine Triumphant?*"

"The throne being built of bones gave me nightmares." Corran shivered, knowing the nightmares had not come from the skulls and shattered bones, but the homicidally gleeful expression of joy on the Emperor's face. "As a final masterpiece it does the job, but I would have liked to see him return to Selonian studies."

"His loss was a pity." Kast's helmet turned toward him. "There would appear to be more to you than meets the eye."

"Oh?"

"Indeed. The last time Chassu's Selonian nudes were on display at the Fine Arts museum was ten years ago."

Corran covered his surprise with a smile. "Not exactly. New Year's Day, two years ago, they were displayed for a private reception for Museum patrons. Four hours, ten thousand credits per person." Corran tapped Kast on the shoulder of his armor. "You would have loved it, but you'd have had to get a new paint job on the armor first."

"And you were there."

"I was." *So was Hal. My mother had volunteered with the museum for so long that when it came to hiring additional security for the reception, the administration brought us on board.* "I'll let you know when they throw another of those get-togethers, if you want."

"Please. I'll have to see if I can obtain an invitation to it."

Corran laughed. "If you can do *that,* perhaps you *can* get us an invitation to visit Zekka Thyne. How are you planning to get us in there?"

Kast's voice echoed from within his helmet. "I thought I would appeal to Thyne's sense of justice."

"You'd have an easier time finding the *Katana* fleet."

Corran shook his head. "Zekka Thyne is a human-alien mongrel with big blue blots all over his pink-white flesh. His eyes are blood red except for black diamond pupils that are outlined in gold. He's got sharp ears, sharper teeth and the sharpest sense of retribution you've ever run into this side of a Wookiee bearing a grudge. I heard he shot a spice courier because the courier told Thyne she'd borrowed credits from a payoff, but had already repaid the momentary loan, with interest."

"What would Thyne have done had the woman not told him?"

"Killed her more slowly. He's a real artist with a vibroblade." Corran frowned heavily. "What Patches lacks in brains he makes up for in feral viciousness. What would you charge to kill him?"

Kast's head came up just a centimeter or two. "Are you asking me to murder him?"

Corran hesitated for a second. "No, I guess I'm not. I was just wondering. I thought maybe if I did it I could consider the amount you'd get paid as some sort of charitable deduction on my taxes. If I paid any, that is."

"I would not be averse to seeing Thyne eliminated, but that is outside the purview of my immediate task." Kast looked over at him. "I believe, however, I can get us in to see him. I think the diplomatic approach would be best."

"I agree. I prefer diplomacy." Corran tapped the blaster holstered beneath his left armpit. "I'm also ready in case we have to be undiplomatic."

"Which means?"

"Which means I go low, you go high."

Kast nodded solemnly. "That shall be our backup plan, then."

The bounty hunter piloted the landspeeder with ease through the darkened hills outside Coronet City. Thyne's estate had once belonged to a shipping magnate who was arrested and sent to Kessel for smuggling spice. Thyne had obtained the deed at auction, after which rumors started through the Corellian underworld suggesting

Thyne had provided the evidence that got the magnate convicted. Corran always suspected that bit of subterfuge had actually been planned and executed by Prince Xizor, since Thyne had not since shown himself to be that clever.

As they crested the last hill and came down into the broad valley in which the estate had been built, Corran pointed at the main building. "It doesn't look like much, but those rolling hills serve as great revetments and channel an assault force in toward areas where he has mines in place. Up in the towers he's supposed to have E-webs capable of sweeping any soldiers off the grounds. Thyne is even supposed to have a bolthole ready to let him get safely away if trouble starts, which isn't likely. Double-thick walls, double-paned transparisteel windows, complete electronic sensoring systems and forty to fifty blaster-boys make this a pretty tough nut to crack. I've heard CorSec has an open warrant to search the place, but without the Imp garrison to back them up, no one is stupid enough to try to deliver it."

"You weren't joking about the sensors." Kast directed the landspeeder toward two men coming out of a side entrance, catching them in the glow of the ridelamps, then turned the speeder to the left and let it settle to the ground. "I'll go speak with them. You be ready in case things go badly."

"You'll give me a sign?" Corran watched the bounty hunter unfold himself from the driver seat and mentally catalogued the weapons he could see. "Dumb question. If they fall I'll come running."

He watched Kast approach the two men. The bounty hunter held his hands open and out away from his sides, but not up in any sign that could be taken as surrender. *He wants them to know he doesn't intend to kill them, but that he's capable of doing just that given sufficient provocation.* The trio met and Corran could hear the buzz of voices, but could make out no words. One of Thyne's men spoke into a comlink, then Kast raised his left hand and beckoned Corran forward with a casual flutter of fingers.

Corran left the landspeeder and approached the three men, aping Kast's open-handed posture while doing so. One of Thyne's men came toward him, clearly intent on taking his blaster, but Corran frowned at him. *What, you think I'm stupid enough to try to shoot my way in and out of here?*

The blaster-boy hesitated, then sunk his hands into his pockets.

The other Black Sun hireling pointed at Corran. "Go ahead, take his blaster."

"You think he's stupid enough to try to shoot his way in and out of here?" The first gunman shook his head. "Let's take them to the boss. We don't want to keep him waiting."

"True. Follow us."

Their guides conducted them to the main entrance and into a foyer that Corran thought might have once rivaled that of the Coronet City Museum of Fine Art for splendor. Rose granite and black marble had been inset into the floor in a complex and chaotic pattern. A stone staircase spiraled up to the second and third floors, and drew the eyes upward to the holographic representation of the night sky above them. Small alcoves in the walls housed statuary and huge goldenrod wall panels provided ample space for the display of a vast array of paintings and original holographic works of art.

It's amazing how something that could have been so beautiful can so easily be made so . . . vulgar. It seemed as if Thyne's definition of art was intimately wrapped up with the concepts of nudity, excess and a color scheme that relied heavily on pinks, purples and an irritatingly vibrant shade of green. Some of the statuary—what little of it actually could have found a home in the Museum of Fine Arts— had been garishly *corrected* by application of this color scheme, with excess paint having spilled down the walls. The paintings showed Corran a view of models he thought more appropriate for xenobiological textbooks and the holographs seemed the visual equivalent of a high-pitched scream.

"How much were you going to offer me to kill him?" Kast whispered.

"Not enough."

They followed their guides through the foyer and a huge set of double doors into Thyne's office. Here the clash of artworks had a new element added to it: a war between style of furnishings. Thyne's desk had been carved from deep brown *vweliu* tree wood and was in itself a work of art. Surrounding it were other pressed-form duraplast and fiberplast chairs and tables—the sort of things that could be left out in a glen because weather would not hurt them. A few stainless steel tables topped with transparisteel sheets completed the decor and a riot of lamps—no two matching—provided illumination for it all.

Corran looked over at Hal and caught a brave nod from him despite the twin lines of blood dripping down from his nose. Haber Trell looked in worse shape, with a rapidly swelling eye and an inert vibroblade stuck into the seat of his chair between his thighs. The Tunroth's yellow flesh had greyed up a bit, and a dollop of bluish blood trickled from one nostril, but Rathe otherwise looked alert.

Zekka Thyne smiled at Kast and Corran found the expression nothing short of obscene. "Ah, Jodo Kast, finally we meet. Normally I do not retain an individual I have not met, but your reputation precedes you. I decided the credits were well spent." Thyne's scarlet gaze sharpened. "Don't disappoint me."

"I have no intention of doing so." With a swift, smooth motion, Kast drew a blaster in his right hand and jammed the muzzle against Corran's left temple. "Haber Trell and the Tunroth are assassins who were hired by Borbor Crisk to eliminate you. Their partners are even now arranging for Crisk to fill a couple hundred *sleight* boxes with the price for your head."

"That's not true!" Haber Trell snarled angrily. "He's lying."

Thyne silenced him with a backhanded slap. "So who are these other two?"

Kast grunted what almost seemed to be a laugh. "They hired these two locals to help them get around and as camouflage. With these two in tow, who would think they are galaxy-class assassins?"

Corran started to raise a hand to massage his head, but Kast kept the gun pressed hard against his skull. Corran wasn't certain which hurt more: his head or his pride at having been fooled by Kast. *He played me very well, just like he played the rest of us. Better I was in my father's place because Kast never would have fooled him.*

Corran glanced sidelong at Kast, then nodded toward Thyne. "You know, you really can't trust the word of a bounty hunter."

"True, but I am more willing to trust him than some assassin's local fetch-and-carry."

Kast reached over and relieved Corran of his blaster, then lowered his own gun. "My story is fairly easy to check out. You should dispatch some of your people to the Mynock's Haven. It is the cantina where Trell's partners are meeting within the hour with Crisk to finalize the payoff details. You'll find the *sleight* boxes at the Dewback storage yard near the spaceport. You can send other of your people there and wait for Crisk and his men to come and fill the boxes."

Corran rubbed at his temple. "You figured that out from my look at the place? You're good."

"That's why people retain me." Kast looked over at Thyne. "I take it you have detention cells here?"

"Wine cellar is empty. You can put them in alcoves down there."

"Good. I shall do that while you prepare the ambush

for Crisk." Kast motioned with his blaster for Corran to head toward the door. "Once your people report back, you'll know who you can trust."

"Yes." Thyne hissed the word. "And those who are lying will pay the ultimate price for daring to deceive me."

Side Trip Part Three
by Michael A. Stackpole

Propelled by a poke in the kidneys with a blaster carbine, Corran Horn stumbled into the makeshift cell.
He got control of himself fast enough to avoid bumping
into his father and turned back quickly, but Jodo Kast
swung the wrought-iron gate shut. That effectively sealed
the two Horns in a small, dusty grotto that had once been
home to a fine collection of wines from throughout the
Empire. *At least that's the impression I get from all the broken
bottle bits on the floor.*

Corran skewered Kast with the nastiest stare he could muster. "This isn't over between us, Kast."

The bounty hunter regarded Corran placidly, but the trio of Zekka Thyne's henchmen forcing the other man and the Tunroth into a second grotto across the cellar laughed out loud. Their leader, the beefy, red-haired man who had given Corran the shove, sneered at the undercover Corellian Security Force officer. "You're strictly small time, pal. The boss isn't going to give you a crack at this guy. I'll be the one to take care of you."

"Oh?" Corran gave the man a feral grin. "I didn't realize Thyne was into doing favors for the hired help. You're welcome to try me any time."

"He won't get the chance." Kast's voice came low and cold. "I've put up with your prattling and bragging and threats, Corran, and I am not of a mind to let someone else eliminate annoyances from my life." The armored mercenary pointed a finger at the redheaded man. "Touch him and I will consider it a matter of honor to turn you inside out."

The redhead paled. "Yes, sir."

Another of Thyne's Black Sun underlings closed the other gate and secured it. "They're in. Wanna threaten any of *them*, Nidder?"

The redhead frowned. "Suck vacuum, Somms. You think you're so funny, you can think up jokes while you stand guard on these clowns."

Somms' blond brows arrowed down toward his nose. "They're in here secure, they don't need guarding."

Kast shook his head. "No, not in here, of course not, but outside the room, on the first stair landing. There you can hear commotion from in here or the main floor and be able to respond."

Nidder shoved his blaster carbine into Somms' hands. "You heard him."

Corran smiled. "Just what I expected, Kast. You want someone stationed between you and me."

Kast grabbed the grate's iron bars and shook it once,

hard. The metal rattled loudly and, startled, Corran involuntarily took a step back. Nidder, Somms and the third Black Sunner started laughing, but their mirth didn't stop Corran from hearing Kast's reply to his remark.

"I've no fear of you, Corran. I look forward to you getting out of here because with Thyne sending his blaster-boys off to ambush Maranne and Riij, I'm pretty much assured that I'm all that stands between you and your freedom. You may be good—you may even be better than I give you credit for being—but I'm still better."

Corran's left temple throbbed from where Kast had jammed his blaster pistol against it. "Keep thinking that, Kast, and don't be surprised when I prove you wrong."

"Come see me, Corran, when your boasts are not idle." Kast turned and herded the rest of the men from the small room. An old wooden door closed behind him and clicked shut.

Corran stared after him for a moment, then spun on his heel and swore. "Sithspawn! That son of a rancor played me for an idiot." He looked up at his father. "I'm sorry, Dad. I really made a mess of things."

The elder Horn's hazel eyes narrowed. "How do you plot our predicament being your fault?"

"I should have known there was something wrong." Corran scrubbed his hands over his face. "Their ship, the *Hopskip*, is a piece of trash that Crisk wouldn't use to haul dead bodies, much less valuable merchandise. The others had no idea what was in their cargo hold and it turned out to be full of *sleight* boxes."

Hal frowned. "*Sleight* boxes are hardly state of the art for smugglers these days. It's almost as if they wanted to be caught."

"Right, exactly." Corran leaned against a fiberplast wine rack built into the grotto's wall. "Kast told Thyne the boxes are empty, but I found some with junked holoseals and popped them. One box had spice—strictly joy-dust grade, but spice nonetheless—and the other had a fortune in uncut Durindfire gems. Even if we figure that one box of gems is it and the other 199 are spice, Crisk can use the gems to buy an army and use the spice to flood the market and kill Black Sun's profits."

Hal Horn turned a wooden wine-box over and sat. "So what you're telling me is that we have non-smugglers bringing in two hundred *sleight* boxes and they have no idea what's in them. You find gems and spice in two and the shipment is headed for Crisk. Crisk himself can't put together that sort of shipment, so he has a backer. Who?"

Corran frowned. "The gems come from Tatooine. Isn't there a Hutt out there working the spice trade?"

"Jappa or Jadda or something like that, yes. He's powerful there, but expanding into Corellia? That's too bold a move." Hal's mouth opened, then he shook his head. He motioned his son aside and looked past Corran toward the other cell. "Haber Trell, how long have you known Jodo Kast?"

The *Hopskip*'s pilot stood and grasped the bars of his prison. "I don't know him. He's along for the ride."

"Yes." Hal leaned back against the wall and laughed lightly. "That's it."

Corran shook his head. "You're saying Kast is behind the shipment going to Crisk? But that makes no sense since he's told Thyne's people where to find the boxes with the spice and gems."

"No, Corran, Kast isn't the mastermind, *he's* what's being smuggled into Corellia."

Corran's jaw shot open. "It doesn't make any sense."

"No?" Hal gave Corran an appraising glance—of the sort that in the past had warned Corran that his father thought he was being lazy in his thinking. "What do you make of Kast's last remark?"

Corran thought back. "He was taunting me."

"Agreed, but what did he tell us by taunting you?"

The sigh came up all the way from Corran's toes. "He told us that he was all that stood between us and freedom—that Thyne's guys are all gone. He told me to come find him when we got free." Corran slapped his forehead with the heel of his hand. "I should have seen that."

"You did."

"Yeah, but it took you to point it out to me." Corran shook his head and toed the neck of a broken bottle. "There are times when my brain just doesn't work."

"No, Corran, your brain works fine." Hal kept his tone even, but pointed a finger at his son. "You just need to focus your thinking. You're angry because of how Kast tricked you, and I think you were a bit afraid for how I was doing."

"Right on both counts."

"It's understandable, son, and appreciated in the case of your concern for me, but you can't let your emotions and incidental things deflect you."

"I know that, Dad. I really do." He smiled at his father. "I try to follow your example, but you're better at it than I am."

"I have a few years on you, Corran."

"It's more than just the years, Dad." Corran winced. "I never would have read Kast's message right the way you did."

The elder Horn's eyes twinkled. "I have to admit to you, Corran, I cheated this time out."

"What?"

Hal pointed past him. "Up there, on the bars Kast shook, see what that little thing is, will you?"

Corran turned and looked closely at the bars. Where Kast had grasped one in his right hand, Corran saw a small black cylinder about a hand-span in length and about the diameter of a blaster-bolt. He freed it from the bar with a tug, leaving an adhesive residue on the wrought-iron, and felt a small button beneath his thumb, near the cylinder's tip.

"Be careful with that, Corran."

The younger man nodded and hit the button. All but invisible in the half-light, a delicate monomolecular blade slid from the cylinder. "I know what it is, and I remember what happened to Lefty Dindo." Corran cut carefully down with the blade and through the lock's bolt. He retracted the stiletto's fragile blade and swung the door open. "Freeing us from this cell is a bit easier than Lefty trying to use one of these to free himself from binders."

Hal Horn paused in the door cell's doorway. "You might want to cut us a couple of the bars to use as weapons. Somms might not be the brightest of Black Sunners, but I think he's going to take some convincing before he lets us out of here."

"Agreed." Extending the blade again, Corran cut a pair of 50-centimeter-long bars from the bottom of the grate and handed one to his father.

Hal swung the club against his left hand with a meaty thwack. "This will work. Now how do we lure Somms in?"

Corran squinted at the room's closed door. "You figure Somms as someone who will raise an alarm immediately, or will wait to report success?"

"After Nidder's giving him the duty? He'll act, then report."

"That's my read, too. The landing was ten steps up and we're far enough away from the office that if we make some noise, no one will notice, I think." Corran smiled. "I'll do the hard work if you want to do the yelling."

"Yelling works for me." Hal Horn smiled. "Be careful."

"Right." Corran walked over to the wooden door and set the length of the blade to a half-centimeter shy of the door's depth, then cut very cautiously. He scored a circle in the center of it. Once he had the circle taken care of, he cut lines heading out from it as if a child drawing a sunburst. Lastly he carved little semicircles around the hinges and the lock.

He closed the blade and handed it to his father in exchange for one of the clubs. "Okay, here goes nothing."

"Wait!"

Corran looked over at Haber Trell. "What do you want?"

"Don't leave us in here. If you're busting out, we want to go, too."

"I don't think so, Trell." The flesh tightened around Corran's eyes. "Even if you're twice the fighter that you are a smuggler, you'll still be in the way."

Hal nodded in agreement, but tossed them the molecular stiletto anyway. "Corran's right, you won't want to come with us. We'll head out and deal with Thyne. Give us a couple of minutes, then go fast. Steal one of Thyne's airspeeders and fly. Head back to your ship and get out of the system."

Trell nodded. "Thanks."

Corran frowned at his father, then pointed at Trell. "And, listen, don't put that cargo back on your ship. You don't want to be shipping spice around."

Trell shivered and Corran took that to be an eloquent answer to his caution.

"Ready, Dad?"

"All set."

Corran smiled and ran backward at the door. He leaped up and hit it smack in the middle with his back. The door exploded into fragments around him, spraying large chunks of wood into the narrow corridor outside the makeshift prison. Corran crashed down amid it all, yelping involuntarily instead of letting forth with a great *oof* as he had planned. *No jagged edges, but the debris sure is lumpy.*

Hal's voice flooded through the dying echoes of the door's crisp crack. "Keep that Tunroth away from me!"

With his eyes nearly shut, Corran saw Somms come flying down the stairs to the landing. The man kept his back to the stone wall as he crept toward the cell, then he brandished the blaster carbine and prepared to rush into the cell. To do that he prepared to pivot on his right foot, fill the doorway, then go in.

As Somms' left foot came around in the pivot move, Corran caught it in his left hand. Letting Somms' momentum pull him up into a sitting position, Corran brought his metal truncheon down on the top of the man's pelvis. Somms started to cry out, more in surprise than pain it seemed, when Hal appeared in the doorway and clipped him with a fist in the head.

Somms collapsed to the floor and did not move.

Corran frowned at his father. "Why cut the club if you aren't going to use it?"

"Didn't need it." Hal snaked the blaster carbine from beneath Somms, flicked the selector lever over to stun, and pumped a blue bolt into him. The Black Sunner twitched once, then lay gently still. "I expect he'll still feel the blow you dealt him when he wakes up."

"We can but hope." Corran rolled him over and unfastened his blaster belt. Donning it himself, Corran pulled the blaster from it and checked the power pack. He glanced up at his father. "You going to leave that set on stun?"

"I haven't noticed that killshots fly any more true than stunbolts."

"True, but there's just so many more forms to fill out when we bring them back alive."

"Don't even joke about that, Corran." His father gave him a reproving glance that made Corran feel about as big as a hologame piece. "Set it on stun and you won't regret accidentally hitting a friend."

"Yes, sir." Corran flicked the pistol's selector lever to stun and stood up. He waved his father toward the door. "Time to get Thyne. Age before beauty."

"Brains before impudence." Hal tossed a quick salute to Haber Trell and Rathe. "Luck to you, but keep your heads down and get out of here fast. If Thyne doesn't react well to our refusing his hospitality, you don't want to be in the blast radius."

Arl Nidder matched Jodo Kast's long-legged stride as best he could. The bounty hunter impressed him, but the armor impressed him more. *Now if I had a suit of that Mandalorian armor I'd be pretty tough. I'd be able to get a lot of light-years between me and the rest of the Bromstaad boys. Maybe*

I'd hire out to do wetwork for some Moff, or maybe even Prince Xizor.

His ruminations ended abruptly as they reentered Thyne's office. Nidder liked the office because it seemed like a museum to him. He'd never been in a real museum, but he knew they were places where old and valued things were collected. He took it as a mark of pride that Thyne kept him close enough to protect the crime lord's prized possessions.

Surrounded by beauty though he was, Thyne did not look happy. The holoprojector plate built into his desk showed a view of Thyne's fortress and the surrounding valley in translucent green detail. Moving around the area were small orange icons that Nidder had seen in security simulations, but only when they were running worst case scenarios to scare the wits out of new recruits.

Nidder's jaw dropped. "Are those really storm-troopers?"

Thyne nodded, then snapped a comlink on. "All personnel report to battle stations. This is not a drill. We have hostile deployment to the north and east. Move it, I want all defenses reported as operational in thirty seconds."

Nidder and Deif started toward the room's partially ajar doors, but Thyne stopped them with a snarl. "Not you two. Not that I don't trust you, Kast."

Kast raised his hands. "But you don't trust me. I'll remind you of this next time we negotiate a price for my services." The long, tall bounty hunter pulled a chair around where he could watch Thyne on the right and the doors at the left, but did so in such a casual way that it took Nidder a moment or two to recognize exactly what he was doing. Kast looked directly at Nidder, then calmly crossed his right leg over his left.

Nidder shifted uncomfortably and got the distinct impression that the only way he'd get a suit of that armor was to be lucky enough to be around when someone else killed Kast and peeled him out of it. Of course, the thought didn't form itself exactly that way in Nidder's brain. He just knew he didn't want *that* suit of armor, just one like it.

His momentary feeling of inferiority vanished as he realized Kast wasn't as smart as he thought himself to be. If the mercenary had turned his chair around he still could have watched the desk and doors, but also could see the painting of frolicking nudes on the wall. As it was, Nidder could fully appreciate it—though he was at a loss to explain why the artist had included gardening implements in the painting—and smiled to let Kast know what he was missing.

The hologram shifted to a schematic of the house, with the corridor outside the door rendered in yellow light that blinked on and off. Thyne hissed furiously. "Someone is in the hall. The Imps have already infiltrated the building." He pointed Nidder and Deif toward the door.

Kast started speaking in a loud voice. "Of course, handling things in a diplomatic manner works best." The bounty hunter pointed toward two spots along the wall where the Bromstaad mercenaries could cover the doorway with a murderous cross fire. "Then again, there are times when one has to be *undiplomatic.*"

Nidder marveled at how Kast's voice covered the sound of his approach to the door. He stopped exactly where Kast wanted him to and drew his blaster pistol. He set it to kill and waited, but shot Kast a wink and a nod. When the nod was returned, Nidder even began to imagine that Kast might take him on as an apprentice, or even a partner. *He's seen how good I am. He knows what he'll be getting when we work together.*

The exploding of the lower half of one door interrupted Nidder's fantasy. Through the smoke and spray of fiery debris came the smallest of the prisoners they'd left below. Coming up into a crouch from the somersault that carried him through the hole, the brown-haired man raised a blaster pistol and triggered two shots. The first blue bolt missed, but the second caught Deif in the stomach, wreathing him in azure energy.

Nidder brought his pistol in line with the little man. *He doesn't see me. He doesn't know I'm here. His mistake.* Nidder started to tighten his finger on the trigger when he felt himself moving backward. He felt his shoulders hit the wall, then his head rebounded from it. Through the exploding stars he saw a second bolt flash out from the blaster built into the thigh of the Mandalorian armor.

In the nanosecond it took for the scarlet bolt to sizzle through his chest, Nidder realized Kast had positioned him so carefully and precisely because the bounty hunter wanted to kill him. Nidder did not feel outrage at having been so easily betrayed and slaughtered, nor did he, in his dying moment, grant Kast a modicum of respect for having worked so coolly to slay him. No, for Arl Nidder, dying as he slid to the floor, there was only one final thought. *Now if I had a set of that armor. . . .*

Corran saw the red bolts burn by on his left and swung around in that direction as his target flopped to the ground. At the back of the room, Corran saw Thyne running for where a wall panel slid back to reveal a black recess. He started to track the fleeing crime lord, but pulled his pistol back as Kast's head and shoulders eclipsed Thyne. *He's getting away.*

Corran glanced back at the door. "All clear."

Hal stepped through, looked at Nidder's body, then at Kast. "That's another round of drinks on me by way of thanks."

The bounty hunter uncrossed his legs and stood. "Pest control."

Corran pointed at the dark opening in the wall. "Thyne went out through there."

Hal approached it cautiously. "Looks clear."

Corran appropriated the blaster carbine the man he'd shot had been carrying and set it for stun. "Let's go find him."

He turned to Kast. "Come along. We could use your

help. There's a bounty on Thyne. We're going to get him, but the bounty can be yours." Corran looked around the room at the garish decorations and horrific art. "It might even be sufficient to buy some real art and offset memories of this place."

"You tempt me very much." Kast shrugged. "However, someone with such inferior taste in art should not be hard to catch. I would join you, but I'm a simple bounty hunter and I still have a job to do."

Despite having no read on Kast, Corran knew he was lying. He raised an eyebrow. "I don't believe you're a simple bounty hunter."

"Nor do I believe you and your father are simple hoodlums looking for underworld employment." Kast crossed to the desk and punched a button on the holographic display unit's control panel. A view of the surrounding area came up and Corran saw small orange icons moving in swarms over the terrain. "These are Imperial stormtroopers. They're likely to make things uncomfortable if you don't get going. You don't want to be caught here."

"Neither do you."

"I won't be."

Corran nodded. "Another time, then."

"Perhaps." The finality in Kast's voice told Corran there never would be a next time, and somehow he didn't find that prospect cause for anything but relief.

Corran rejoined his father just inside the entrance to Thyne's escape passage. The narrow corridor had been melted through the native stone with a gentle slope downward. Every fifteen meters or so it cut back on itself, forcing the Horns to advance carefully. The brevity of the passages meant any firefight would be at close quarters and extremely deadly.

Corran clutched his blaster carbine in both hands and snuggled it against his right flank. It had been modified slightly after its arrival from the factory by the inclusion of a pinpoint glow rod attached to the left side of the barrel, and more work had been done on it to make it what was known in street parlance as a *hotshot*. The trigger guard had been cut away, leaving the trigger free and the weapon liable to be fired when the trigger caught on clothing or was otherwise jarred. Using a *hotshot* was supposed to indicate how tough a person was, but it only took one view of the results of an unsafed *hotshot* pistol being tucked into a waistband to convince most folks it was a foolhardy modification.

Of course, no one is going to tuck a carbine into his pants. Corran smiled slightly, then nodded as his father signaled him to come forward. Remaining low, Corran came around the corner of the corridor, then dropped to the ground as a red blaster bolt sizzled through the air above him.

He shot back twice, but neither blue bolt hit anything but stone. "Corridor widens out into a natural cave. We're probably at the rear of the property."

"Okay, take it slow. Lose the light."

Corran flicked off the pinpoint glow rod and closed his eyes. He waited for a count of ten for his eyes to get adjusted to the darkness, then opened them. Bioluminescent lifeforms—lichen and the things that ate it—gave off a purplish glow that allowed Corran to make out shadowed shapes. Some were regular and appeared to be duraplast boxes of varying sizes, while the larger, more menacing ones were curiously hunched and gnarled stone formations. There seemed to be little physical modification of the cave; the floor remained uneven and boxes had been wedged in various places where space allowed. Corran assumed the previous owner had kept the cave in its natural state and Thyne had stored in it precious or vital cargoes that he did not trust to have any place else.

Corran crept forward, remaining low. He reached the first box and in the faint glow made out the stenciled Imperial legend proclaiming it to be full of blaster carbines. He would have opened it, but the scent of spice lingered strongly enough in the immediate area that he knew what it really contained. *Either Thyne is just storing spice in this, or Black Sun has some backdoor Imperial connections that are allowing them to ship this stuff in past Customs. I'll have to ask Loor about that.*

Corran whistled short and sharp, then heard his father close the gap between them. For an older man, and one as big as he was, Hal moved pretty quietly. *I felt his presence before I picked up that slight scuff of his sole against the stone. Oh, Thyne, you don't know who you're messing with.*

A return whistle sent Corran forward. He moved slowly and carefully, wending his way from one dark rock to another. He did his best to avoid those that were glowing because he didn't want to silhouette himself against one. He took great care to make as little noise as possible, and smiled as he hunkered down behind a large black rock.

Corran looked back toward his father and was set to whistle when he heard the scrape of metal on a rock. He glanced up and triggered one shot from the blaster carbine. The azure bolt streaked past Thyne as he leaped down from a large dolmen, then Thyne's right heel caught Corran in the shoulder and spun him to the ground. His blaster carbine bounced away, firing off two random shots. He felt Thyne's left arm tighten around his neck and then he was hauled to his feet as the alien straightened up, his body shielding Thyne from fire.

The muzzle of a blaster pistol ground in under the right corner of Corran's jaw. A glow rod lit up, bathing the right side of Corran's face with light. The muscles on the arm around his neck bulged, constricting his breathing and killing any thoughts of struggling.

Thyne growled loudly, sending angry echoes of his voice throughout the cavern. "Your partner is dead if you don't show yourself in five seconds."

Those five seconds took an eternity to pass for Corran, and he filled it with an unending series of *if-onlies*. *If only I had tucked the blaster pistol into my waistband when I took the carbine. If only I had the stiletto. If only I'd been more quiet in my advance.* . . . Self-recriminations clogged his mind and fed the despair slowly creeping into his head.

Then his father stood up and the glow rod on his carbine burned to life. Illuminated by its backlight, Hal Horn stood twenty meters away, the carbine held steady in his right hand. He presented Thyne with a profile—offering him a target other than Corran. The expression on his father's face bore a gravity Corran had not seen since his mother's funeral. Hal's eyes seemed purged of anger and fear, but full of intent.

"It is my duty to inform you, Zekka Thyne, that I am inspector Hal Horn of the Corellian Security Force and you are under arrest. I have a valid warrant for your apprehension for violations of smuggling laws. Let your hostage go and stop making things more difficult for yourself."

Thyne's chuckle came low and ringing with contempt. "No, this is the way it's going to go. You're going to remove your finger from the trigger and lower your blaster."

"I can't do that."

"You *will* do that." Thyne tightened his hold on Corran's neck. "My eyesight is good enough even in full darkness here that I can tell if your finger so much as twitches toward pulling the trigger. And my reflexes are good enough that I'll pump three shots through your partner's head before you complete that move. You may get me, but your partner will be dead. Do it, *now*!"

Hal frowned. "Okay, don't do anything rash."

"Don't, Hal! Shoot him. . . ."

Thyne jammed the gun harder into Corran's jaw. "You were stupid enough to join CorSec, let's not be stupid enough to die for it."

Hal's left hand came up. "Okay, I'm doing what you said. I'm pulling my finger off the trigger."

Corran tried to shake his head to tell his father not to comply with Thyne's order. *He has to know that the second he disarms himself Thyne will shoot me and then shoot him. I may already be dead, but no reason for him to die, too.*

Hal Horn's right index finger slowly unhooked itself from the blaster carbine's trigger. As it did so the glow rod's backlight washed all color from the digits. The finger straightened and Corran saw bones pointing at him. *It's over. We'll both be skeletons left here to molder forever.*

Then the blue bolt shot from the carbine's muzzle. The air crackled and Corran's hair stood on end as the bolt sizzled past him and hit Thyne. The blue nimbus resulting from the shot sent a tingle through Corran's body and weakened him enough that he fell to his hands and knees. Behind him Thyne's body hit the ground with a heavy thump accompanied by the light clatter of the blaster pistol dancing off into the darkness.

Hal dropped to one knee beside his son, then pumped another stun round into Thyne. "Are you okay, son?"

Corran sat back on his heels. "I will be." He rubbed at the side of his neck with his right hand. "He gave me a bruise to balance the one Kast gave me. Having blaster bruises on my head and neck is an experience I could have done without."

"Beats having the bolts hit home, as our friend here discovered."

Corran looked at Thyne in the light from Hal's carbine. The area around Thyne's right eye had begun to swell indicating where the bolt had hit him. "How did you . . . ?"

Hal smiled. "The little gold diamond in his eye gave me a great target. I just focused on it—setting aside my concerns for you so I could—and hit him."

He frowned at his father. "No, not that. You had your finger clear of the trigger and the gun fired anyway. How did you do that? The spice vapor back there give you some sort of telekinetic power or something?"

"Me, move something with the power of my mind?" Hal shook his head and brandished the carbine. "This is a *hotshot*. At the same time I pulled my index finger off the trigger, I was able to bring my middle finger up and stroke the trigger. Nothing special or unusual, just sneaky.''

Despite the smile on his father's face, and the cold logic of his answer, Corran couldn't shake the feeling that his father wasn't telling the entire truth. *He probably doesn't want me to know how chancy his move was, but at least he had the guts to make it. I wouldn't have wanted to be in his boots for all the spice in the galaxy.*

Hal handed Corran Thyne's blaster pistol, then hauled Thyne to his feet and tossed him over his shoulder. "I can feel a breeze from ahead. We're almost clear.''

Corran retrieved his own blaster carbine and carried it by the pistol-grip in his left hand while using the blaster pistol in his right hand and its glow rod to light their way out. "I see something up ahead. Stars and Selonia out there.''

The two CorSec agents got clear of the cavern fairly easily. The mouth of it had been blocked with a lattice of iron bars with a door in it similar to those of the prison they'd escaped earlier. Corran shot the lock open then led the way out into a small grassy clearing.

Hal laid Thyne out on the ground and brought his blaster carbine to hand again. "Check him for a comlink. We can call for transport to come get us.''

Corran knelt over the body and began to search it when a vaguely mechanical sounding voice snapped an order at him.

"Drop the weapons, hands in the air.'' The first of eight stormtroopers emerged like ghosts from the trees surrounding the clearing. Their armor bone-white in the reflected moonlight, they made themselves very easy targets. The fact that each of them brandished a blaster carbine prompted Corran to raise his hands. *I can't imagine any of them has a weapon set on stun.*

Hal lowered his carbine to the ground carefully. "I'm Inspector Hal Horn and this is my partner, Corran Horn.

We're with CorSec. We've just apprehended Zekka Thyne."

The leader of the stormtroopers approached Hal. "Looks as if you are trying to help Thyne escape and are lying to me."

Corran frowned. "What a stupid conclusion to draw. I don't know why you've got that big helmet to protect your head because there clearly isn't anything you're putting to good use under it."

The stormtrooper swung his gun to cover Corran. "On your feet, Black Scummer."

Corran glanced at his father as he stood. "I guess we're their prisoners."

The stormtrooper shook his head. "Who said anything about taking prisoners?"

Hal's voice came low and calm, but full of intensity and power. "I think I would want a specific order from a superior about shooting us. I think to operate otherwise would seriously jeopardize your career, and possibly your life."

The stormtrooper reoriented himself toward Hal and Corran thought for a moment he'd have to jump the man to prevent him from shooting Hal. Corran would have gone for him, too, because he'd seen countless bodies that had ended up dead for making remarks that were no where near as confrontational. What held him back was the way the man's movements slowed as he watched Hal. The stormtrooper wasn't reacting to the tone or challenge in the words, he was clearly considering their full import.

Will wonders never cease?

A comlink clicked inside the man's helmet and the murmurs of conversation hummed into the night. Corran smiled and shrugged at his father. Hal winked back and allowed himself the start of a grin.

The stormtrooper's head came up. "It'll be a minute or two wait."

Hal nodded, then jerked a thumb back toward the cave mouth. "You'll want to have your squad secure that cav-

ern. It leads back into Thyne's office. Your people can get
inside and hit the towers from below because if shooting
starts, your people are going to die taking that place."

The stormtrooper thought for a moment, then sent
half his squad forward. The remaining trio set themselves
up to watch the clearing perimeter while the leader kept
his blaster on Corran and his father. The night air had
become a bit chilled and the fact that he'd been sweating
earlier became readily apparent to Corran.

"Mind if I lower my arms? I'm getting cold."

The stormtrooper shook his head. "You can get
colder."

"Nice night, isn't it?" Corran gave the man a toothy
grin and hiked his arms up higher.

A soldier in the olive drab uniform of the Imperial
Army broke through the brush, flanked by two more
stormtroopers. The eight bar box with rank cylinders on
each side worn on his chest proclaimed him to be a Colonel. His dark-eyed gaze flicked between father and son,
then lingered on Thyne's body. "Zekka Thyne. You may
put your hands down. I take it you must be the CorSec
agents."

Hal nodded. "Hal Horn. This is my son, Corran. I have
a disc that identifies me in my shoe. It also contains the
open warrant CorSec has for searching this place and ar-
resting Thyne. I can dig it out for you, if you wish, to
prove who we are."

"I'm Colonel Veers and I believe you are who you say
you are. My source indicated you would be coming out
somewhere in this vicinity and even suggested we might
want to backtrack you." He glanced at the stormtrooper
who had threatened to kill them. "Apparently my reasons
for dispatching this squad around here were not fully understood."

Hal shrugged. "No one got lit up, so no problem."

Corran pointed to Thyne. "We've gotten the nastiest of
them out of there. There aren't many people left in there
and, by now, they should all be Thyne's people."

Hal nodded. "You can safely consider it a free-fire zone."

"I'll remember that if they give us a reason to go in." Veers smiled. "You didn't happen to notice any signs of Rebel agents or Rebellion supplies in there by any chance?"

"No, but as a CorSec Inspector, I do believe it is within my discretion to ask for assistance in serving a warrant and apprehending suspects." Hal looked at the hillsides on either side of the valley. "I *should* check with my liaison officer, but calling back to Crescent City from here would be impossible, so I guess I'm on my own."

Veers shook his head. "Pity."

"Indeed." Hal waved a hand toward the cavern. "Colonel, if you and your squad would care to assist me, I would be most appreciative."

"We always like working closely with local officials." Veers gave Hal a nod and pointed his stormtroopers at the black hole. "You heard him. No waiting for them to shoot first, we're clear to go."

The stormtroopers jogged forward in a clatter of armor. Veers handed Hal a comlink. "Your transit code word is 'masterpiece.' At our perimeter just commandeer one of our landspeeders to get your prisoner out of here."

"Thanks." Hal, looking back toward the cave, pointed at a stream of green laser bolts coming from one of the mansion's towers toward the ground. "Looks like your war has started."

"Then we'll get in quickly and end it." Veers gave them a brief salute and ran off with his men.

Corran looked after the Imperial officer. "I thought Imps believed in leading from the rear."

"Not all of them, it seems." Hal grabbed Thyne's hands and hauled the man up onto his back. "Get the ankles there, will you?"

"Sure." Corran grabbed Thyne's ankles and trailed behind his father. "So, is this the end of Black Sun on Corellia?"

"I doubt it. Two CorSec agents, a handful of smugglers and a bounty hunter who isn't a bounty hunter aren't going to be enough to bring Black Sun down. Even if the Colonel and his people level that place, Prince Xizor still has enough power and the resources to restore it to what it was before, and you have to know there are countless individuals willing to take Thyne's place."

Corran shivered. "Yeah, I'm afraid you're right. How depressing."

"Depressing?" Hal turned and looked back at his son. "It's not depressing. As long as there are Horns to catch criminals, Prince Xizor is welcome to send all he cares to in our direction."

"And you don't find that prospect depressing?" Corran frowned at him. "If it isn't depressing, what is it?"

"I think it's obvious, son." Hal's hearty laugh blotted out the whines of blasters being fired back and forth. "It's job security. It may not be easy work, and it's dangerous quite a bit of the time, but it's work that holds evil at bay and there's nothing better you can devote your life to doing."

Corran nodded and recalled a bit of conversation he'd had with Riij Winward. "And what will we do when the only evil left in the galaxy is the Empire?"

"That's a good question, Corran, a very good question." Weariness seemed to creep into his father's voice. "It's one that each person must answer for himself. I just hope, when the time comes for me to answer it, I'll have the wisdom to choose the right answer and the strength to act upon it."

"Me, too."

"You will, Corran, no doubt about that." Hal gave him a wink and a nod. "When the time comes, you'll see the light and those wallowing in darkness who move to oppose you will regret that decision throughout what little remains of their lives."

Side Trip Part 4
by Timothy Zahn

Zekka Thyne's airspeeders were stored on the low end of a split-level section of the fortress roof, inside a bunker-like structure with a single entrance from the stronghold proper and a single hangar bay-style exit. Two guards were on duty, but their attention was turned outward, toward the distant blaster fire coming from the woods around the fortress, and neither noticed the shadowy bulk of Rathe Palror moving quietly up behind them. A pair of deceptively gentle-looking hand movements from the Tunroth, and both guards temporarily lost the ability to notice anything.

"I'll have to get you to teach me that trick," Trell commented, ducking down to peer through the window of a likely looking airspeeder. The vehicle looked ordinary enough, but in the dim light he could see the add-on weapons control board tucked coyly away under the main panel on the passenger side. Perfect. "We'll take this one. You still have that molecular stiletto?"

"Here," the Tunroth rumbled, pausing in his task of stripping the guards' weapons to dig the slender cylinder from his belt. "Should we not take one of the armored vehicles instead?" he added, pointing his chin horns toward one of the three KAAC Freerunners parked near the wide exit opening as he lobbed the weapon in Trell's direction.

"They're a little obvious for in-town driving," Trell told him as he caught the stiletto. Extending the almost invisible blade, he began carefully cutting around the airspeeder's lock mechanism. "This one's got some hidden firepower—means it's probably got some hidden armor, too."

By the time Palror joined him, he had the door open and was sitting in the driver's seat. "Yeah, this'll do just fine," he said, pulling the weapons board out for a closer look. "Are you hunters any good with non-traditional stuff like light laser cannon and concussion grenade launchers?"

"A *shturlan* can work with all weapons," Palror said, dropping his appropriated blaster rifles onto the rear seat and peering in over Trell's shoulder.

"Good—you're hired," Trell said, starting to strap himself in. "I'll drive."

Trell wasn't sure what exactly was happening out in the woods surrounding Thyne's fortress. But whatever it was, it definitely seemed to be getting worse. The forest was alive with the muted flickers of multiple blaster fire, the light peeking coyly out through gaps in the leaf canopy on at least two sides of the stronghold. "I sure hope they're too busy out there to bother with us," he muttered as he eased the airspeeder through the opening and onto the landing pad just outside the bunker. "Corran and Hal are going to have their hands full getting through all that."

"But less trouble than it could be," Palror said. "Do you not remember? Thyne has dispersed many of his people on errands."

Trell grimaced. "Yeah, I remember. One group to go grab our cargo, the other to snatch Maranne and Riij."

"But at Jodo Kast's recommendation," Palror reminded him. "If Kast is truly here to oppose Thyne, then he will not allow harm to come to our companions."

"I don't buy that," Trell growled. "Even if Corran and Hal were right about that, it doesn't mean he cares slork droppings about the rest of us. *And* that assumes they were right, which we don't have any proof of. Personally, I'd say there's an even chance that Thyne and Kast cooked up the whole thing together to expose a couple of undercover CorSec agents and lure 'em into a trap. In which case, they're probably already dead."

"If so, then we should be likewise," Palror pointed out. "Who are we that Kast would allow us to escape."

"Yeah, well, we haven't exactly escaped yet," Trell reminded him tartly, eying the open air off the edge of the landing pad with stomach-churning apprehension. But procrastination wouldn't gain them anything except increased odds that someone inside the fortress would notice they were missing and raise the alarm.

And besides—thanks to Kast—Maranne and Riij were walking into a trap out there at the Mynock's Haven cantina. Had possibly already walked into it. Riij he wasn't so much worried about—the guy was a Rebel agent and not his responsibility. But Maranne was his partner, and he was shragged if he'd abandon her to Thyne's thugs.

"We waste time," Palror rumbled at his side. "I will not leave Riij in danger."

"Likewise," Trell said, keying in the repulsorlifts and throwing power to the drive. He wouldn't leave Maranne, and Palror wouldn't leave Riij; and as the fortress roof dropped away beneath them he realized with hindsight's usual clarity that Kast had probably set up the various groupings with precisely those different loyalties in mind.

Though to what end, he still didn't know. And wasn't sure he wanted to.

He was still mulling over the question thirty seconds later when the two TIE bombers dropped neatly into formation beside him.

They'd been sitting in the Mynock's Haven for nearly half an hour; and in Riij Winward's opinion, it was yet another bust. "They're not coming," he said quietly to the woman on the other side of the small table. "Whoever we were supposed to meet here, they aren't coming."

"I think you're right," Maranne Darmic growled back, scratching viciously at the nape of her neck. "Score another big fat zero for the great and marvelous Jodo Kast."

"The greatly incompetent, you mean," Riij said, looking with distaste at the yellow and red jebwa flower in the center of their table. Kast's datacard had specified the flower as their identification marker, but so far none of the cantina's other patrons had given it a second glance. Considering the clientele, most of their first glances had been humiliating enough.

"Yeah," Maranne agreed. "It makes you seriously wonder about his chances of getting Trell and Palror and the others out of Zekka Thyne's place."

"It makes *me* wonder if he even wants to get them out," Riij countered darkly.

Maranne eyed him closely. "You think this whole thing was a setup?"

"It's looking more and more that way," Riij said, scowling as he glanced around the cantina. "Look at the series of events. First he sends Trell to the wrong booth in Treasure Ship Row, which apparently tips off Thyne and his people that we're looking for Borbor Crisk. Then he sends Trell, Palror, and Hal back and lets them get snatched. Finally, he goes there himself with Corran and sends us off on this idiot's errand. Someone in Kast's business can't possibly be that incompetent and have survived this long."

"You think it's someone else posing as Kast?" Maranne suggested. "I mean, all we've ever seen is his armor."

"Possibly," Riij said. "But now remember where this whole mess actually started: aboard an Imperial Star Destroyer."

"With us squeezed into running an Imperial captain's errand." Maranne swore gently. "You're right. How stupid can one group of people be, anyway?"

"We're in line for some prizes, all right," Riij agreed. "The only question is what exactly the game is that the Imperials are playing."

"I vote for them trying to stir up trouble between Thyne and Crisk," Maranne said. "Maybe looking for an excuse to come down hard on both sides."

"Using the spice and gems as bait," Riij said. "Still, whatever Kast's going for, there's one thing he doesn't know."

Maranne smiled tightly. "That the cargo isn't aboard the *Hopskip* anymore."

"Exactly." Riij dropped a couple of coins on the table and stood up. "Come on, let's get out of here. Crisk's people aren't going to show."

"So what's our next move?" Maranne asked, standing up beside him.

"Kast's Plan B, I guess," Riij said, turning toward the door and elbowing them a path through a pack of loiterers. "We take our sample boxes to Thyne's fortress and see if we can make a deal to buy Trell and Palror out."

Maranne caught up to his side. "You're going to follow *Kast's* plan?" she asked incredulously. "What are you, crazy?"

"No, just desperate," Riij conceded grimly. "Aside

from the two of us storming the place, I don't see any other options."

"What about your—" Maranne threw a quick glance around and lowered her voice. "What about your friends?"

Riij grimaced. His friends: the Rebel Alliance. A reasonable enough request, he supposed, especially since the only reason he and Palror had been aboard the *Hopskip* in the first place was to baby-sit the load of blasters Trell and Maranne had agreed to smuggle to the Rebels on Derra IV. Unfortunately—"They can't help us," he told her regretfully. "Even if the leaders agreed, it would take too long to gather together enough of a force to take on Thyne, Corellian Security, *and* the local Imperial garrison."

"You sure they just don't want Prince Xizor and Black Sun mad at them?" Maranne asked nastily.

"You have to pick your fights carefully, Maranne," Riij sighed. "Personally, I think we've already bit off more than we can swallow."

"I suppose you're right," Maranne muttered. "Fine. Let's give Plan B a try."

They had reached the door now, sliding their way through the middle of an incoming group of Duros and heading out into the muggy night air. The *Hopskip*'s dilapidated landspeeder was parked in the small lot to the left—

"Excuse me?" a hesitant voice called.

Riij turned, his hand dropping automatically to the butt of his blaster. A heavyset man had emerged from the cantina a handful of steps behind them, their jebwa flower clutched in a meaty hand. "Yes?"

"You forgot your flower," the man said, lobbing it through the air toward him. Automatically, Riij reached up to catch it—

And suddenly there was a small blaster in the heavy man's fist. "Nice and easy," the man said. "Selty?"

"I'm on it," a voice said from somewhere behind Riij.

There was a quick set of approaching footsteps, and Riij felt his blaster being lifted from its holster. Another moment, and Maranne had been disarmed as well. "Got 'em."

"Now just keep moving," the first gunman said, gesturing Riij and Maranne in the direction they'd been going. "Let's go take a look at your landspeeder."

The parking lot was dark and deserted. But it wasn't going to stay deserted for long. Even as Riij led the way toward the landspeeder he could see shadowy forms drifting in from all directions. Whoever had gotten the drop on them didn't seem interested in taking any chances. "You want to tell us which one's yours?" the heavyset man asked.

"You want to tell us whose side you're on?" Riij countered.

The other's eyes flashed. "Don't push it, scum," he warned harshly. "You're in enough trouble with us as it is."

"Must be with Zekka Thyne," Maranne said ruefully.

"Must be," Riij agreed, his heart pounding a little harder. So it was definitely to Plan B now. "It's that dirt-brown one over there."

Two of the approaching thugs veered toward the landspeeder, the rest forming a loose but competent enough guard circle around the prisoners and their two escorts.

A double-sided circle, Riij noted with interest, with as many of their members facing outward as inward. Expecting trouble, maybe?

The thugs had the storage compartment open now and with grunts of satisfaction hauled out the two *sleight* boxes. "Got 'em, Grobber," one of them said. "Couple of *sleight* boxes, just like the man said."

"All set to fill up, huh?" the heavyset man said, throwing a dark look at Riij. "I guess Kast wasn't blowing smoke rings after all."

Riij threw a glance at Maranne, got the same look in return from her. They'd been right; Kast was definitely

playing some crazy double- or triple-edged game here.
"Kast told you about this?" he asked.

"Sure did," Grobber assured him. "So what were these
for, the first payment?"

Riij shook his head. "Sorry, but I can't help you. We
were hired to deliver the boxes and that was it."

"Sure," Grobber growled. "Just deliver the boxes. And
if Crisk just happened to fill them up while your back was
turned—well, hey, that's none of your business, right?
Promk, what the frink are you doing?"

"What does it look like?" one of the men at the landspeeder retorted. He had carried one of the boxes
around to the hood and was in the process of popping
the seal with a knife. "A couple of wise guys, a couple of
empty boxes; I figured it might be fun to send 'em on to
Crisk with their heads inside."

Riij was suddenly aware of his collar pressing against his
throat. "I don't think that would be a good idea," he
said, striving to keep his voice even. "You don't know
where the rest of the boxes are."

"We don't, huh?" Grobber sneered, digging out a comlink and thumbing it on. "Skinkner? Hey, Skinkner, look
alive."

"Funny, Grobber, funny," a twisted voice came back.
"What d'ya want?"

"You at the Dewback Storage Warehouse yet?"

"Yeah, 'course we are. If you were hoping to report us
to Thyne for slogging off, you're out of luck."

"Wouldn't think of it," Grobber said, sending another
sneer toward Riij. "Still think we don't know where the
rest of the boxes are, hotshot?"

Riij felt his stomach tighten. So much for Plan B. So
much, too, for any leverage they might have had against
Thyne and his mob. Any chance of rescuing Palror and
Trell was now squarely in his and Maranne's laps.

Assuming they were able to find a way out of this, their
own private mess. Carefully, keeping his movements ca-

sual, Riij looked around the ring of thugs, trying to formulate some kind of reasonable plan—

"Mother of smoke!"

Riij jerked his head back around. Standing beside the landspeeder, Promk had finally gotten the *sleight* box open . . . and even in the faint light Riij could see the stunned look on his face. "Grobber—you gotta—what the frinking—?"

"Have you gone dust-happy?" Grobber demanded, striding toward him. He got two steps, and then suddenly his face changed, too. "What the—?" he gasped, all but leaping the rest of the distance to Promk's side.

Riij sniffed the night breeze carefully, caught the faint odor of spice. "You were saying something about empty boxes?" he asked.

Grobber ignored him. "Get the other one open," he ordered, pulling out a knife of his own and probing delicately into the spice. "Selty, get over here. The rest of you, watch for trouble."

Selty joined his boss as Promk brought around the second box and set to work, and for a moment the two thugs conversed in low voices over the spice box. The debate was interrupted by the crack of breaking duraplast, and the two joined Promk by the second box.

Someone whistled in awe. "Grobber—are those—?"

"Durindfire gems," Grobber said, lifting his eyes like twin turbolasers to Riij's face. "Let's have it, pal, and let's have it straight and fast. What the frink kind of game are you playing, anyway?"

"I told you before: we're not playing any games," Riij told him. "We were sent to deliver the cargo, and that's it. If there's a game going on, someone else is running it."

"Kast," one of the other thugs snarled.

"Or Kast and Crisk," Grobber snarled back, yanking out his comlink again. "Skinkner? Wake up, Skinkner."

"What d'ya want?" the other's voice demanded. "Frink it all, Grobber—"

"Shut up and listen," Grobber bit out. "You looked in any of those boxes yet?"

" 'Course not. Thyne said to just watch them until Crisk's blaster-boys came to fill them with—"

"You idiot—they're already full," Grobber snapped. "Which means the contract's already been filled."

The voice on the comlink swore. "Kast."

"That's my bet," Grobber said. "Start getting your boys together—I'm going to raise Control." He keyed the comlink again. "Control? This is Grobber. Control?"

"Grobber!" a new voice half barked, half gasped. "We've been trying to raise you for half an hour—where the frink are you?"

"At the Mynock's Haven," Grobber said. "Listen—"

"No, *you* listen," the other cut him off. "We're under attack here, skrag it—you've got to get back right away."

"Wait a minute, wait a minute," Grobber said. "What attack? Who's attacking?"

"Who do you think? The frinking Imperials, that's who."

Grobber threw a startled glance at Selty. "The *Imperials*?"

"Started out as some anti-Rebel operation," Control said. "At least, that's what they told us. Then someone took a shot at them, and suddenly here they are, burning their way through the east wall."

"Skrag! Where's Thyne?"

"I don't know—we can't find him."

"Must have gotten out," Selty muttered.

"Or ducked into some private bunker," Grobber said. "All right, Control, we're on our way. Skinkner?"

"We're packing up, too," Skinkner's voice confirmed. "You want us to do anything with these other *sleight* boxes?"

"To blazes with the boxes," Control snapped. "We need you *here*."

"No, pack 'em up and bring 'em along," Grobber said.

"Grobber—"

"They're worth a fortune," Grobber growled. "Thyne'll have our heads if we leave 'em behind. Come on, how much trouble can a few Imperials be?"

Faintly over the comlink came the sound of a distant explosion. "That answer your question?" Control snarled. "Get the frink back here."

And with a sudden hiss, the comlink went dead. "They're jamming it," Grobber growled, shoving the cylinder back into his belt. "Selty, you take Promk and Bullkey and get these two and their landspeeder back to the fortress. Everyone else, back to the airspeeders. *Move* it!"

The others scattered. "Don't get any ideas," Grobber warned softly, glaring from under creased eyebrows at Riij and Maranne. "We're a long ways from being done with you two yet."

With that he stomped off after the rest of his mob, disappearing just as they had appeared back into the shadows again. "Get over here," Selty snapped, waving Riij and Maranne forward. Somewhere in the distance an avian or insect whistled, sounding strangely out of place in the urban setting. "Bullkey?"

"I'm on 'em," a deep voice came from behind Riij, the confidence backed up by a blaster nudge in the back. "Come on, move it."

Riij started forward; and as he did so, Maranne veered slightly toward him and nudged him with her elbow. "Get ready," she murmured, just loud enough for him to hear. At the landspeeder Promk, under Selty's direction, had picked up the box containing the Durindfire gems and was carrying it back toward the storage compartment. The strange avian whistled again; and suddenly, inexplicably, one of the bottom edges of the box split open, spilling the gems out onto the ground.

"Promk!" Selty squeaked, aghast. "You stupid idiot." He jumped forward, grabbing at the box as Promk tried to turn it upside down. For a moment they both fumbled with it, the prisoners temporarily forgotten—

And from behind Riij came a short gurgle and a muffled thump.

Beside him, he sensed Maranne preparing to charge. "Not yet," he muttered, touching her warningly as he lengthened his stride. Preoccupied with the spilled gems, Selty and Promk hadn't yet noticed what had happened over here. Another four paces . . . three . . . if they'd just fight with the box another few seconds . . . one. . . .

"Now," he murmured; and jumping forward, he put his left palm down on the landspeeder's hood and leaped over the vehicle to slam both feet hard against Promk's chest.

The thug didn't even have a chance to gurgle as he hit the ground, the *sleight* box spinning out of his hands into the darkness. Selty did have time for a startled curse and a grab for his holstered blaster before he went down with Maranne on top of him. A savage jab with her knee, and he went limp.

"Are you injured?" Palror rumbled from behind them.

"No, we're fine," Riij assured him, regaining his balance and turning around. Behind the Tunroth, the third thug was lying in an unnaturally crumpled heap. "Nice job with Bullkey," he added.

"Not to mention the box," Maranne added, retrieving their appropriated blasters from Selty's belt and tossing Riij's back to him. "How'd you manage that one?"

"That was mine," Trell said, stepping out from behind one of the other parked landspeeders and crossing to them. "Just an exquisitely well-thrown molecular stiletto."

"A whistle code and a molecular stiletto," Riij said, shaking his head wonderingly. "You two are just full of tricks, aren't you?"

"The stiletto was a gift," Trell said, crouching down beside the *sleight* box. "Blast—the blade's broken."

"Never mind the blade," Maranne said, crouching down beside him. "Get the gems."

"Forget the gems," Riij told her, peering off in the

direction Grobber and the others had gone. The rescue had been remarkably quiet; but if Grobber took it into his head to fly over this spot on the way back to Thyne's fortress, the four of them could still end up fertilizing a patch of razor grass. "Let's just get out of here."

"But—"

"No, he's right," Trell said through clearly clenched teeth. "If whatever's going on back at Thyne's place dies down fast enough we could still find Grobber's buddies camping out in the *Hopskip*'s cargo bay. Just grab the box and whatever's still left inside."

Maranne hissed something vile sounding, but she nevertheless stood up, the now half-empty box in her hands. "Fine," she said bitterly. "What about the spice?"

"Leave it here," Trell told her. "Corran said we wouldn't want to get caught shipping spice, and I'm rather inclined to agree with him."

"We can call CorSec on the way and tell them where to pick it up," Riij added. "Now let's *go*."

They all piled into the landspeeder. "Speaking of Corran and CorSec," Trell commented as he spun the vehicle around and kicked power to the engines. "Turns out they're one and the same."

"Corran's with Corellian Security?" Maranne asked, frowning at him. "You're joking."

"That's how he and Hal were talking, anyway," Trell said. "Last we saw, they were heading off after Thyne."

Riij winced. "In the middle of Thyne's fortress? They haven't got a chance."

"That was also our estimation," Palror agreed. "But counting the number of Thyne's warriors here and those fighting the Imperials outside his stronghold, it seems likely the core areas within may have been nearly deserted."

"'Nearly' might not have been good enough," Maranne said. "And what about Kast? He was still there, wasn't he?"

"I've given up trying to guess what kind of game Kast is

playing," Trell said, twisting the landspeeder hard to get around a Herglic-parked speeder truck. "All I know is that he's the one who gave Corran the molecular stiletto that got us out of there."

"And we do not believe it was merely a trap," Palror added. "We were challenged by Imperial TIE bombers as we left the stronghold; yet upon identification, we were permitted to pass."

"That had to be Corran and Hal's doing," Trell said. "CorSec's supposed to be working pretty closely with the Imperials these days."

"Yes," Riij murmured, thinking back to the brief argument he'd had with Corran about the Rebellion. And now to find out Corran was actually CorSec. Could he have guessed Riij's true loyalties from that conversation?

"We were both permitted to pass," Palror reminded him softly.

"I understand," Riij told him. "I also understand that the way everything else here's been going, that doesn't mean a whole lot. If we get to the *Hopskip* without running into an ambush—from any of the sides of this crazy powerplay—then maybe I'll believe we've gotten away with it."

"Gotten away with what?" Maranne asked.

Riij spread his hands. "With whatever in blazes we did here."

There was indeed no ambush poised outside the *Hopskip*. Nor were any of their former companions—Corran, Hal, or Kast—waiting there.

What *was* there was a single datacard.

"Looks like the same stuff that Kast used to stick the molecular stiletto to Corran's cell bars," Trell commented, poking experimentally at the bits of adhesive residue that had been left on the datacard. "Should we read it here, or inside?"

"Inside," Riij said firmly, taking the datacard from him and glancing around. "And not until we're out of here.

You and Maranne get the pre-flight started; Palror and I'll check to make sure no one left us any surprises."

Trell had the engines nursed and sputtering to life, and Maranne had the nav computer working on their course, when Riij and Palror returned from their tour of the ship. "Looks clean," Riij told the others as the two of them took their seats. "Or at least, there's nothing obvious. You talked to the tower yet?"

"We're third in line to leave," Maranne told him. "You want to read us a sleepy-time story now?"

"Sure," Riij said. From behind Trell came a faint rubbing sound—Riij getting the last bits of adhesive off the datacard, probably—and then the brief scraping as he slid it into his datapad. "It's from Kast," Riij said. " 'To the crew and passengers of the *Hopskip:* well done.' "

"Well *done?*" Maranne growled. "What in blazes—?"

"Shh," Trell cut her off. "Go on."

" 'You have adequately completed the mission that was assigned you,' " Riij continued. " 'You may return now to the *Admonitor* and retrieve your cargo. This datacard will serve as proof to Captain Niriz that you have fulfilled your side of the bargain and may have your cargo returned to you.' Then it's signed with his name and what looks like some kind of ID mark."

"So he's not going back, huh?" Trell said, an odd feeling stirring in the pit of his stomach. "I'm not sure I like that."

"He must have arranged his payment to be delivered somewhere else," Maranne said. "It didn't look like he and Niriz got along very well."

"Perhaps his payment is in the remainder of the *sleight* boxes," Palror said.

"I wouldn't count on it," Riij said. "There's a postscript: 'Do not return to the Dewback Storage Warehouse for the other *sleight* boxes. They are empty.' "

"What?" Trell growled, half turning to glare back at Riij over his shoulder. "Come on, now, that's just crazy. You're telling me the two boxes you happened to take to the Mynock's Haven were the only ones with anything in them? What are the odds of that happening?"

"Not too bad, really," Maranne said grimly. "Not when you consider that they were the only two we knew we could open and then reseal again. They were leading us around by the nose the whole way, weren't they?"

"The whole way," Riij agreed. " 'And don't bother with either the Durindfire gems or the spice. Both are counterfeit.' "

Trell looked across the cockpit, to find Maranne looking back at him. There didn't seem to be anything to say.

There was another faint scraping behind him as Riij pulled the datacard from the datapad. "Look, we got in and out again alive," he reminded them, reaching over Trell's shoulder to hand him the datacard. "My instructors used to say that no mission you walked away from was a complete failure. Maybe we'll meet Corran and Hal someday and find out what this whole thing was all about."

Trell turned the datacard over in his hand. "I doubt it," he said. "I'd say chances are good that neither of them knew what was going on, either."

He slid the datacard into a storage slot on his board. "Come on, Maranne. Let's get out of here."

"I know this sort of thing embarrasses you," Captain Niriz said as he poured his guest a glass of aged R'alla mineral water, "so I'll only say it once. When I heard the reports of military action on Corellia, I was concerned for your safety. I'm glad to find out my fears were unfounded."

"Thank you, Captain," Grand Admiral Thrawn said, accepting the proffered glass and taking a sip. He was still wearing his Jodo Kast armor, though without the helmet and gauntlets. "You're wrong, though, about expressions of concern and support being an embarrassment. On the contrary, loyalty is one of the two qualities I value most in my subordinates and colleagues."

"And the other?" Niriz asked, pouring a glass of R'alla water for himself.

"Competence," Thrawn said. "Has the *Hopskip*'s cargo been reloaded aboard yet?"

"It's being done, sir," Niriz said. With most people, he thought distantly, the addition of Mandalorian armor would instantly create a powerful air of strength and mystery. With Thrawn, in contrast, it almost seemed to detract from the sense of authority that was already there. "The bridge has orders to let me know when they leave." He cocked an eyebrow. "Which reminds me: you promised to let me know what all this was about when you returned."

"And I intend to do so," Thrawn assured him. "I'm waiting for one other person to join us here first."

Behind Niriz, the door slid open. Niriz turned, opening his mouth to reprimand whoever this officer or crewer was who would dare enter the captain's private office without permission—

And an instant later was scrambling to his feet, the harsh words dying in his throat as if they'd been choked to death. The armored figure striding with casual arrogance through the door—

"Ah; Lord Vader," Thrawn said, rising more easily to his feet. "Welcome aboard the *Admonitor*. We're honored by your presence."

"As we are with yours, Admiral Thrawn," Lord Darth Vader said, a distinct edge of challenge in his deep voice. "You're nearly six hours late."

"I know, my Lord, and I apologize for keeping you waiting," Thrawn said, nodding his head deferentially. "As it turned out, I was forced to significantly modify the plan I originally outlined to you."

"But the objective *was* achieved?" Vader demanded.

"It was indeed," Thrawn said. "Zekka Thyne and the Corellian branch of Prince Xizor's Black Sun have been effectively eliminated."

Niriz looked at Thrawn in surprise. "Zekka Thyne? But I thought—"

"You thought the Emperor had an arrangement with Xizor?" Vader demanded, turning that grisly mask toward him.

Niriz swallowed. Vader's reputation concerning flag officers who had displeased him . . . but on the other hand, Thrawn demanded absolute honesty from his subordinates. "Yes, my Lord," he said. "I did."

Vader's stiff posture seemed to ease slightly. "For the moment, perhaps, that is true. But such arrangements are made to be altered." He turned back to Thrawn. "Yet I understood there was Imperial action against Thyne's stronghold."

"A small battle only," Thrawn assured him. "And the battle was instigated from Thyne's side, as both sides' recorders will bear out. The record will also show the Imperials were in the area solely because of information their commander received suggesting a Rebel force was gathering in the forest there."

"Information which you supplied, of course?" Vader asked.

"Of course," Thrawn nodded. "And since there can be no possible link between the verification code I used and any of your forces or contacts, Prince Xizor will be unable to create any connection between you and the mysterious informant."

"Yet Imperial troops *were* involved," Vader persisted. "His first thought will certainly be of me."

Thrawn shook his head. "In fact, my Lord, the marginal Imperial involvement will actually tend to exonerate you in his eyes. He would expect you to launch either a full-fledged Imperial attack—which he could easily trace back to you—or else to scrupulously avoid Imperial forces entirely, relying perhaps on your quiet bounty hunter or mercenary contacts. The ambiguity of the actual event will leave him confused and uncertain. Which, I believe, was one of your key objectives."

"It was," Vader said, sounding a little uncertain. "But as you say, Xizor knows of my bounty hunter connections. Even though Jodo Kast is not among them, your assassination of Thyne while disguised as Kast will again lead his attention to me."

Thrawn smiled. "Yes, but I *didn't* assassinate Thyne. I was able to leave his fate in the hands of a pair of undercover CorSec agents."

Vader cocked his head slightly to the side. "I don't recall Corellian Security ever being mentioned in our discussions, Admiral."

"The two agents attached themselves to my group," Thrawn said. "And it was obvious right from the start that they were in Coronet City for the specific purpose of getting to Thyne. It presented such a perfect opportunity that I decided to modify the original plan so that they would be the ones to deal with him."

"Then Thyne isn't dead?"

Thrawn shrugged. "At the very least he's out of power," he said. "Actually, having him in CorSec custody would actually serve your purposes better than a quick death. It would leave Prince Xizor wondering if the Corellians were digging any dangerous secrets out of him. A major distraction; and distraction, I believe, was another of your key objectives."

There was a tone from the comm. Stepping to the console, Niriz keyed it on. "Niriz," he said.

"Hangar Bay Control, sir," a voice said. "Reporting as per orders that the *Hopskip* has just left."

"Thank you," Niriz said. "Signal the bridge to watch its vector when it jumps to lightspeed."

"Yes, sir."

Niriz keyed the comm off. "I gather the smugglers and their Rebel friends performed their part adequately?" Vader asked.

"Quite adequately," Thrawn assured him. "They provided the necessary excuse for me to move Thyne's men out and clear the way for the CorSec agents."

The unseen eyes behind the black mask seemed to bore into Thrawn's face. "And the other part of your plan?"

Thrawn cocked a blue-black eyebrow at Niriz. "Captain?"

"Yes, sir," Niriz said. "A homing device has been installed inside each of the hidden blasters they were smuggling."

"And the boxes repacked exactly as they were?"

"To the millimeter," Niriz confirmed. "They'll have no way of knowing the boxes were even opened, let alone tampered with."

The Dark Lord nodded. "Excellent," he said.

The comm pinged again. "Captain, this is the bridge. The *Hopskip* just jumped to lightspeed. Their vector's confirmed for the Shibric system."

"Thank you." Niriz looked at Thrawn, lifted his eyebrows.

The Grand Admiral nodded. "Have them prepare a course back to the Unknown Regions," he instructed. "Our task here is finished."

"Yes, sir." Niriz gave the order and keyed off the comm.

"Unless," Thrawn added, looking at Vader, "you'd like me to deal with Prince Xizor directly for you."

"It is indeed a tempting thought," Vader said, his voice dark with veiled menace. "One alien against another? But no. Xizor is mine."

"As you wish," Thrawn said. "Incidentally, I doubt that Shibric is the final destination for those Rebel blasters. From their vector, and other bits and pieces I gleaned along the trip, my guess is that their ultimate collection point will be somewhere in the Derra system."

"The homing devices will show us for certain," Vader said. "But the Derra system is rumored to have a strong Rebel presence. I'll make sure to have some forces waiting there."

"Very good," Thrawn said. "One final suggestion, and then I suspect we must both be on our separate ways. I

understand the general in command of the *Executor*'s
ground forces resigned suddenly a month ago. I was able
to watch the battle outside Thyne's stronghold for a while
as I waited to make sure the smugglers escaped; and in my
opinion the Imperial officer in command is being wasted
in a garrison assignment."

"Your opinion carries considerable weight," Vader
said. "As I'm sure you know. The officer's name?"

"Colonel Veers," Thrawn said. "From the level of his
tactical skill, I'd also say he's long overdue for a promotion. Perhaps his political connections within the command structure leave something to be desired."

"Political connections do not concern me," Vader
rumbled, stepping to the door. "I will see what I can do
with this Colonel Veers. Thank you, Admiral."

"My pleasure, Lord Vader," Thrawn said with a respectful tilt of his head. "One favor for another. Perhaps we'll
have the chance to work again together."

Once again, the hidden eyes seemed to probe the
Grand Admiral's face. "Perhaps," he said. "Farewell, Admiral."

And with a swirl of his long cloak he was gone. "An
interesting exercise," Thrawn commented, crossing to
the R'alla bottle and refilling his and Niriz's glasses. "I
don't know though. I sense that this Rebellion is more
powerful and better organized than perhaps Lord Vader
realizes. I hope our activities here will allow him to deliver
a crushing blow against it."

His glowing red eyes glittered as he took a sip from his
glass. "But that's not our concern, at least for now. Our
concern is the Unknown Regions; and it's time we were
getting back."

"Yes, sir." Niriz hesitated. "If I may be so bold, Admiral . . . your last comment implied that you received
something in return for helping Vader against Thyne and
Black Sun. May I ask what that favor was?"

"A very personal gift, Captain," Thrawn said. "Which
was why I felt the need to personally orchestrate Thyne's

destruction. Lord Vader has turned over to me command of a group of alien commandos who have proven themselves highly valuable to him over the years. While I won't have much use for them in the Unknown Regions, I have no doubt I'll eventually be returning to the Empire proper. At that time—well, we shall see what they can do."

"I never heard of Vader employing aliens," Niriz said doubtfully. "Are you sure he's telling—well—"

"The truth?" Thrawn smiled. "Indeed he is. Mark their name well, Captain: the Noghri. I guarantee you'll be hearing more of them."

He drained his glass and set it down. "But now to the bridge. The Unknown Regions are calling; and we have a great deal of work yet to do."

About the Authors

After nearly ten years as a newspaper reporter and editor, **Laurie Burns** combined hobby with profession to start a West Coast horse magazine, now in its seventh year of publication. Branching out into writing fiction, she's had several short stories published in the *Official Star Wars Adventure Journal* and is currently at work on her first novel. In her spare time, Laurie likes to ride horses, climb rocks, and belly dance—though not all at the same time. Usually.

Erin Endom practices and teaches pediatric emergency medicine at a major Southwestern medical school. Most of her previous writing has been for medical journals. She took a break from writing about the infectious complications of animal bites and how to recognize child abuse to create "Do No Harm," her first story for the *Official Star Wars Adventure Journal*.

Patricia A. Jackson is an administrative assistant at Jackson (Really!) Elementary School in York, Pennsylvania. A veteran freelancer with nine published credits in the *Official Star Wars Adventure Journal*, she has learned much in the pursuit of the dark side. In the grip of a particular love/hate relationship with Jedi Knights—particularly dark Jedi—she enjoys exploring the sinister, less traveled roads of the Force with individuals who are no less heroic than their light-side counterparts. When not furthering the cause of the Empire, she rides and trains show horses. With a master's degree in English, she enjoys the complexities of language and has invented Old Corellian, a rare dialect used among smugglers and Socorran pirates. Her first game sourcebook, *The Black Sands of Socorro*, was published by West End Games in June.

Charlene Newcomb grew up in South Carolina, then joined the navy to "see the world." Working as a communications technician/interpreter, her "world" turned out to be Orlando, Monterey, San Angelo, and Fort Meade—her last assignment: working at the National Security Agency. After a five-year stint in the navy, and one year as a civil servant, Char moved to North Carolina, where her linguistic abilities were clearly not in demand. But the move led her to her second profession: as a librarian. Many years of procrastination (and three children and a move to Florida) later, she finally enrolled in graduate school. In 1996 she completed her master's degree at the University of South Florida in Tampa, and now works as a serials cataloger in Kansas. She began her freelance writing career while in grad school. Her first short story, "A Glimmer of Hope," appeared in the premiere issue of the *Official Star Wars Adventure Journal*. Since then she's written or cowritten ten stories for the *Journal*. The world she created for "Glimmer"—Garos IV—will be featured in *The Essential Guide to Planets and Moons*, forthcoming from Del Rey in 1998.

Angela Phillips works as a substitute teacher in her hometown of Hampton, Virginia, but hopes eventually to make a living as a novelist. She began studying writing at Duke University in the summer of 1982 at the age of thirteen. "Slaying Dragons" was her first short story for the *Official Star Wars Adventure Journal*. Her subsequent story in *Journal #9*, "The Most Dangerous Foe," told the tale of Vici of Alderaan and her final test before becoming a Jedi Knight.

As a high-school student, **Anthony Russo** was writing *Star Wars* stories long before it was considered cool (or profitable enough to be claimed on IRS Form 1040). He was heading down the dark path as your typical computer consultant when he published his first short story in *Aboriginal Science Fiction* magazine. Looking for alternative markets to break into, a friend directed him to the *Official Star Wars Adventure Journal*. He has since appeared in the credits of a number of West End Game products, including the *Star Wars Live Action Roleplaying System,* where you can play Imperials or Dark Lords and still wake up in the morning not hating yourself. He is currently pounding away on his first full-length novel and trying really hard not to give in to his son's pleas for a full-sized *Millennium Falcon* for Christmas.

Michael A. Stackpole is *The New York Times* best-selling author of the first four (and eighth) *Star Wars X-Wing* novels in which he chronicled some of the later adventures of Corran Horn. "Missed Chance" embodied three firsts: the first story about Corran, the first *published* story about Corran, and the first of Mike's efforts sharing characters with Timothy Zahn. In addition to *Star Wars* novels, Mike has worked on and has been scripting the Dark Horse *Star Wars X-Wing Rogue Squadron* comic series. In his spare time he writes BattleTech novels, fantasy novels, such as *Once a Hero, Talion: Revenant,* and *A Hero Reborn,* plays soccer, and still forces himself to ride his bicycle for exercise.

Kathy Tyers has contributed six short stories to the *Star Wars* universe, in addition to the novel *Star Wars: The Truce at Bakura* (Bantam Books, 1994), and several vignettes in *The Truce at Bakura Sourcebook* (West End Games, 1996). Three stories follow Tinian and Daye after "Tinian on Trial," including "To Fight Another Day" and "Only Droids Serve the Maker" from the *Official Star Wars Adventure Journal* (May 1995 and May 1996), and "The Prize Pelt" in *Star Wars: Tales of the Bounty Hunters* (Bantam Books, 1996). In *Tales from the Mos Eisley Cantina* and *Tales from Jabba's Palace,* she published "We Don't Do Weddings, the Band's Tale" and "A Time to Dance, a Time to Mourn, Oola's Tale." Kathy's other Bantam Spectra novels include *Firebird* and her 1996 release, *One Mind's Eye.* Kathy lives with her husband and son in Southwestern Montana, where she juggles science-fiction writing, vegetable gardening and orchard tending, Bible study, performing folk music with her husband, an occasional pit-orchestra gig, and developing a contemporary novel for the Christian Booksellers Association market. Someday she'll get organized.

Timothy Zahn is the author of *Heir to the Empire, Dark Force Rising*, and *The Last Command*, all *New York Times* bestselling *Star Wars* novels. The first book of his two-part *Star Wars* saga, *Specter of the Past*, is currently available; the second part, *Vision of the Future*, will be published this year by Bantam. Tim has been an avid supporter of the *Journal* and West End Games—his contributions to *The Official Star Wars Adventure Journal* include "First Contact" in issue No. 1 and "Mist Encounter" in issue No. 7. He also helped design and lend support to the *DarkStryder* game campaign.

The World of
STAR WARS Novels

In May 1991, *Star Wars* caused a sensation in the publishing industry with the Bantam release of Timothy Zahn's novel Heir to the Empire. For the first time, Lucasfilm Ltd. had authorized new novels that *continued* the famous story told in George Lucas's three blockbuster motion pictures: *Star Wars*, *The Empire Strikes Back*, and *Return of the Jedi*. Reader reaction was immediate and tumultuous: *Heir* reached No. 1 on the *New York Times* bestseller list and demonstrated that *Star Wars* lovers were eager for exciting new stories set in this universe, written by leading science fiction authors who shared their passion. Since then, each Bantam *Star Wars* novel has been an instant national bestseller.

Lucasfilm and Bantam decided that future novels in the series would be interconnected: that is, events in one novel would have consequences in the others. You might say that each Bantam *Star Wars* novel, enjoyable on its own, is also part of a much larger tale.

Here is a special look at Bantam's *Star Wars* books, along with excerpts from the more recent novels. Each one is available now wherever Bantam Books are sold.

The Han Solo Trilogy:
THE PARADISE SNARE
THE HUTT GAMBIT
and coming soon,
REBEL DAWN
by A. C. Crispin
Setting: Before *Star Wars*: A New Hope

What was Han Solo like before we met him in the first STAR WARS movie? This trilogy answers that tantalizing question, filling in lots of historical lore about our favorite swashbuckling hero and thrilling us with adventures of the brash young pilot that we never knew he'd experienced. As the trilogy begins, the young Han makes a life-changing decision: to escape from the clutches of Garris Shrike, head of the trading "clan" who has brutalized Han while taking advantage of his piloting abilities. Here's a tense early scene from The Paradise Snare *featuring Han, Shrike, and*

Dewlanna, a Wookiee who is Han's only friend in this horrible situation:

"I've had it with you, Solo. I've been lenient with you so far, because you're a blasted good swoop pilot and all that prize money came in handy, but my patience is ended." Shrike ceremoniously pushed up the sleeves of his bedizened uniform, then balled his hands into fists. The galley's artificial lighting made the blood-jewel ring glitter dull silver. "Let's see what a few days of fighting off Devaronian blood-poisoning does for your attitude— along with maybe a few broken bones. I'm doing this for your own good, boy. Someday you'll thank me."

Han gulped with terror as Shrike started toward him. He'd lashed out at the trader captain once before, two years ago, when he'd been feeling cocky after winning the gladiatorial Free-For-All on Jubilar—and had been instantly sorry. The speed and strength of Garris's returning blow had snapped his head back and split both lips so thoroughly that Dewlanna had had to feed him mush for a week until they healed.

With a snarl, Dewlanna stepped forward. Shrike's hand dropped to his blaster. "You stay out of this, old Wookiee," he snapped in a voice nearly as harsh as Dewlanna's. "Your cooking isn't *that* good."

Han had already grabbed his friend's furry arm and was forcibly holding her back. "Dewlanna, no!"

She shook off his hold as easily as she would have waved off an annoying insect and roared at Shrike. The captain drew his blaster, and chaos erupted.

"Noooo!" Han screamed, and leaped forward, his foot lashing out in an old street-fighting technique. His instep impacted solidly with Shrike's breastbone. The captain's breath went out in a great *houf!* and he went over backward. Han hit the deck and rolled. A tingler bolt sizzled past his ear.

"Larrad!" wheezed the captain as Dewlanna started toward him.

Shrike's brother drew his blaster and pointed it at the Wookiee. "Stop, Dewlanna!"

His words had no more effect than Han's. Dewlanna's blood was up—she was in full Wookiee battle rage. With a roar that deafened the combatants, she grabbed Larrad's wrist and yanked, spinning him around and snapping him in a terrible parody of a child's "snap the whip" game. Han heard a *crunch,* mixed with several *pops* as tendons and ligaments gave way. Larrad Shrike shrieked, a high, shrill noise that carried such pain that the Corellian youth's arm ached in sympathy.

Grabbing the blaster from his belt, Han snapped off a shot at the Elomin who was leaping forward, tingler ready and aimed at Dewlanna's midsection. Brafid howled, dropping his weapon. Han was amazed that he'd managed to hit him, but he didn't have long to wonder about the accuracy of his aim.

Shrike was staggering to his feet, blaster in hand, aimed squarely at Han's head. "Larrad?" he yelled at the writhing heap of agony that was his brother. Larrad did not reply.

Shrike cocked the blaster and stepped even closer to Han. "Stop it, Dewlanna!" the captain snarled at the Wookiee. "Or your buddy Solo dies!"

Han dropped his blaster and put his hands up in a gesture of surrender.

Dewlanna stopped in her tracks, growling softly.

Shrike leveled the blaster, and his finger tightened on the trigger. Pure malevolent hatred was etched upon his features, and then he smiled, pale blue eyes glittering with ruthless joy. "For insubordination and striking your captain," he announced, "I sentence you to death, Solo. May you rot in all the hells there ever were."

SHADOWS OF THE EMPIRE
by Steve Perry
Setting: Between *The Empire Strikes Back* and *Return of the Jedi*

Here is a very special STAR WARS story dealing with Black Sun, a galaxy-spanning criminal organization that is masterminded by one of the most interesting villains in the STAR WARS universe: Xizor, dark prince of the Falleen. Xizor's chief rival for the favor of Emperor Palpatine is none other than Darth Vader himself— alive and well, and a major character in this story, since it is set during the events of the STAR WARS film trilogy.

In the opening prologue, we revisit a familiar scene from The Empire Strikes Back, *and are introduced to our marvelous new bad guy:*

He looks like a walking corpse, Xizor thought. *Like a mummified body dead a thousand years. Amazing he is still alive, much less the most powerful man in the galaxy. He isn't even that old; it is more as if something is slowly eating him.*

Xizor stood four meters away from the Emperor, watching as

the man who had long ago been Senator Palpatine moved to stand in the holocam field. He imagined he could smell the decay in the Emperor's worn body. Likely that was just some trick of the recycled air, run through dozens of filters to ensure that there was no chance of any poison gas being introduced into it. Filtered the life out of it, perhaps, giving it that dead smell.

The viewer on the other end of the holo-link would see a close-up of the Emperor's head and shoulders, of an age-ravaged face shrouded in the cowl of his dark zeyd-cloth robe. The man on the other end of the transmission, light-years away, would not see Xizor, though Xizor would be able to see him. It was a measure of the Emperor's trust that Xizor was allowed to be here while the conversation took place.

The man on the other end of the transmission—if he could still be called that—

The air swirled inside the Imperial chamber in front of the Emperor, coalesced, and blossomed into the image of a figure down on one knee. A caped humanoid biped dressed in jet black, face hidden under a full helmet and breathing mask:

Darth Vader.

Vader spoke: "What is thy bidding, my master?"

If Xizor could have hurled a power bolt through time and space to strike Vader dead, he would have done it without blinking. Wishful thinking: Vader was too powerful to attack directly.

"There is a great disturbance in the Force," the Emperor said.

"I have felt it," Vader said.

"We have a new enemy. Luke Skywalker."

Skywalker? That had been Vader's name, a long time ago. Who was this person with the same name, someone so powerful as to be worth a conversation between the Emperor and his most loathsome creation? More importantly, why had Xizor's agents not uncovered this before now? Xizor's ire was instant—but cold. No sign of his surprise or anger would show on his imperturbable features. The Falleen did not allow their emotions to burst forth as did many of the inferior species; no, the Falleen ancestry was not fur but scales, not mammalian but reptilian. Not wild but coolly calculating. Such was much better. Much safer.

"Yes, my master," Vader continued.

"He could destroy us," the Emperor said.

Xizor's attention was riveted upon the Emperor and the holographic image of Vader kneeling on the deck of a ship far away. Here was interesting news indeed. Something the Emperor perceived as a danger to himself? Something the Emperor feared?

"He's just a boy," Vader said. "Obi-Wan can no longer help him."

Obi-Wan. That name Xizor knew. He was among the last of the Jedi Knights, a general. But he'd been dead for decades, hadn't he?

Apparently Xizor's information was wrong if Obi-Wan had been helping someone who was still a boy. His agents were going to be sorry.

Even as Xizor took in the distant image of Vader and the nearness of the Emperor, even as he was aware of the luxury of the Emperor's private and protected chamber at the core of the giant pyramidal palace, he was also able to make a mental note to himself: Somebody's head would roll for the failure to make him aware of all this. Knowledge was power; lack of knowledge was weakness. This was something he could not permit.

The Emperor continued. "The Force is strong with him. The son of Skywalker must not become a Jedi."

Son of Skywalker?

Vader's son! Amazing!

"If he could be turned he would become a powerful ally," Vader said.

There was something in Vader's voice when he said this, something Xizor could not quite put his finger on. Longing? Worry? Hope?

"Yes . . . yes. He would be a great asset," the Emperor said. "Can it be done?"

There was the briefest of pauses. "He will join us or die, master."

Xizor felt the smile, though he did not allow it to show any more than he had allowed his anger play. Ah. Vader wanted Skywalker alive, *that* was what had been in his tone. Yes, he had said that the boy would join them or die, but this latter part was obviously meant only to placate the Emperor. Vader had no intention of killing Skywalker, his own son; that was obvious to one as skilled in reading voices as was Xizor. He had not gotten to be the Dark Prince, Underlord of Black Sun, the largest criminal organization in the galaxy, merely on his formidable good looks. Xizor didn't truly understand the Force that sustained the Emperor and made him and Vader so powerful, save to know that it certainly worked somehow. But he did know that it was something the extinct Jedi had supposedly mastered. And now, apparently, this new player had tapped into it. Vader wanted Skywalker alive, had practically promised the Emperor that he would deliver him alive—and converted.

This was most interesting.

Most interesting indeed.

The Emperor finished his communication and turned back to face him. ''Now, where were we, Prince Xizor?''

The Dark Prince smiled. He would attend to the business at hand, but he would not forget the name of Luke Skywalker.

THE TRUCE AT BAKURA by Kathy Tyers
Setting: Immediately after *Return of the Jedi*

The day after his climactic battle with Emperor Palpatine and the sacrifice of his father, Darth Vader, who died saving his life, Luke Skywalker helps recover an Imperial drone ship bearing a startling message intended for the Emperor. It is a distress signal from the far-off Imperial outpost of Bakura, which is under attack by an alien invasion force, the Ssi-ruuk. Leia sees a rescue mission as an opportunity to achieve a diplomatic victory for the Rebel Alliance, even if it means fighting alongside former Imperials. But Luke receives a vision from Obi-Wan Kenobi revealing that the stakes are even higher: the invasion at Bakura threatens everything the Rebels have won at such great cost.

STAR WARS: X-WING
by Michael A. Stackpole
ROGUE SQUADRON
WEDGE'S GAMBLE
THE KRYTOS TRAP
THE BACTA WAR
Setting: Three years after *Return of the Jedi*

Inspired by X-wing, the bestselling computer game from LucasArts Entertainment Co., this exciting series chronicles the further adventures of the most feared and fearless fighting force in the galaxy. A new generation of X-wing pilots, led by Commander Wedge Antilles, is combating the remnants of the Empire still left after the events of the STAR WARS movies. Here are novels full of explosive space action, nonstop adventure, and the special brand of wonder known as STAR WARS.

In this very early scene, young Corellian pilot Corran Horn faces a tough challenge fast enough to get his heart pounding—

and this is only a simulation! [P.S.: "Whistler" is Corran's R2 astromech droid]:

The Corellian brought his proton torpedo targeting program up and locked on to the TIE. It tried to break the lock, but turbolaser fire from the *Korolev* boxed it in. Corran's heads-up display went red and he triggered the torpedo. "Scratch one eyeball."

The missile shot straight in at the fighter, but the pilot broke hard to port and away, causing the missile to overshoot the target. *Nice flying!* Corran brought his X-wing over and started down to loop in behind the TIE, but as he did so, the TIE vanished from his forward screen and reappeared in his aft arc. Yanking the stick hard to the right and pulling it back, Corran wrestled the X-wing up and to starboard, then inverted and rolled out to the left.

A laser shot jolted a tremor through the simulator's couch. *Lucky thing I had all shields aft!* Corran reinforced them with energy from his lasers, then evened them out fore and aft. Jinking the fighter right and left, he avoided laser shots coming in from behind, but they all came in far closer than he liked.

He knew Jace had been in the bomber, and Jace was the only pilot in the unit who could have stayed with him. *Except for our leader.* Corran smiled broadly. *Coming to see how good I really am, Commander Antilles? Let me give you a clinic.* "Make sure you're in there solid, Whistler, because we're going for a little ride."

Corran refused to let the R2's moan slow him down. A snap-roll brought the X-wing up on its port wing. Pulling back on the stick yanked the fighter's nose up away from the original line of flight. The TIE stayed with him, then tightened up on the arc to close distance. Corran then rolled another ninety degrees and continued the turn into a dive. Throttling back, Corran hung in the dive for three seconds, then hauled back hard on the stick and cruised up into the TIE fighter's aft.

The X-wing's laser fire missed wide to the right as the TIE cut to the left. Corran kicked his speed up to full and broke with the TIE. He let the X-wing rise above the plane of the break, then put the fighter through a twisting roll that ate up enough time to bring him again into the TIE's rear. The TIE snapped to the right and Corran looped out left.

He watched the tracking display as the distance between them grew to be a kilometer and a half, then slowed. *Fine, you want to go nose to nose? I've got shields and you don't.* If Commander Antilles wanted to commit virtual suicide, Corran was happy to oblige him. He tugged the stick back to his sternum and rolled out in an inversion loop. *Coming at you!*

The two starfighters closed swiftly. Corran centered his foe in the crosshairs and waited for a dead shot. Without shields the TIE fighter would die with one burst, and Corran wanted the kill to be clean. His HUD flicked green as the TIE juked in and out of the center, then locked green as they closed.

The TIE started firing at maximum range and scored hits. At that distance the lasers did no real damage against the shields, prompting Corran to wonder why Wedge was wasting the energy. Then, as the HUD's green color started to flicker, realization dawned. *The bright bursts on the shields are a distraction to my targeting! I better kill him* now!

Corran tightened down on the trigger button, sending red laser needles stabbing out at the closing TIE fighter. He couldn't tell if he had hit anything. Lights flashed in the cockpit and Whistler started screeching furiously. Corran's main monitor went black, his shields were down, and his weapons controls were dead.

The pilot looked left and right. "Where is he, Whistler?"

The monitor in front of him flickered to life and a diagnostic report began to scroll by. Bloodred bordered the damage reports. "Scanners, out; lasers, out; shields, out; engine, out! I'm a wallowing Hutt just hanging here in space."

THE COURTSHIP OF PRINCESS LEIA
by Dave Wolverton
Setting: Four years after *Return of the Jedi*

One of the most interesting developments in Bantam's STAR WARS novels is that in their storyline, Han Solo and Princess Leia start a family. This tale reveals how the couple originally got together. Wishing to strengthen the fledgling New Republic by bringing in powerful allies, Leia opens talks with the Hapes consortium of more than sixty worlds. But the consortium is ruled by the Queen Mother, who, to Han's dismay, wants Leia to marry her son, Prince Isolder. Before this action-packed story is over, Luke will join forces with Isolder against a group of Force-trained "witches" and face a deadly foe.

HEIR TO THE EMPIRE
DARK FORCE RISING
THE LAST COMMAND
by Timothy Zahn
Setting: Five years after *Return of the Jedi*

This No. 1 bestselling trilogy introduces two legendary forces of evil into the STAR WARS literary pantheon. Grand Admiral Thrawn has taken control of the Imperial fleet in the years since the destruction of the Death Star, and the mysterious Joruus C'baoth is a fearsome Jedi Master who has been seduced by the dark side. Han and Leia have now been married for about a year, and as the story begins, she is pregnant with twins. Thrawn's plan is to crush the Rebellion and resurrect the Empire's New Order with C'baoth's help—and in return, the Dark Master will get Han and Leia's Jedi children to mold as he wishes. For as readers of this magnificent trilogy will see, Luke Skywalker is not the last of the old Jedi. He is the first of the new.

The Jedi Academy Trilogy:
JEDI SEARCH
DARK APPRENTICE
CHAMPIONS OF THE FORCE
by Kevin J. Anderson
Setting: Seven years after *Return of the Jedi*

In order to assure the continuation of the Jedi Knights, Luke Skywalker has decided to start a training facility: a Jedi Academy. He will gather Force-sensitive students who show potential as prospective Jedi and serve as their mentor, as Jedi Masters Obi-Wan Kenobi and Yoda did for him. Han and Leia's twins are now toddlers, and there is a third Jedi child: the infant Anakin, named after Luke and Leia's father. In this trilogy, we discover the existence of a powerful Imperial doomsday weapon, the horrifying Sun Crusher—which will soon become the centerpiece of a titanic struggle between Luke Skywalker and his most brilliant Jedi Academy student, who is delving dangerously into the dark side.

CHILDREN OF THE JEDI
by Barbara Hambly
Setting: Eight years after *Return of the Jedi*

The STAR WARS characters face a menace from the glory days of the Empire when a thirty-year-old automated Imperial Dreadnaught comes to life and begins its grim mission: to gather forces and annihilate a long-forgotten stronghold of Jedi children. When Luke is whisked onboard, he begins to communicate with the brave Jedi Knight who paralyzed the ship decades ago, and gave her life in the process. Now she is part of the vessel, existing in its artificial intelligence core, and guiding Luke through one of the most unusual adventures he has ever had.

DARKSABER by Kevin J. Anderson
Setting: Immediately thereafter

Not long after Children of the Jedi, *Luke and Han learn that evil Hutts are building a reconstruction of the original Death Star—and that the Empire is still alive, in the form of Daala, who has joined forces with Pellaeon, former second in command to the feared Grand Admiral Thrawn. In this early scene, Luke has returned to the home of Obi-Wan Kenobi on Tatooine to try and consult a long-gone mentor:*

He stood anxious and alone, feeling like a prodigal son outside the ramshackle, collapsed hut that had once been the home of Obi-Wan Kenobi.

Luke swallowed and stepped forward, his footsteps crunching in the silence. He had not been here in many years. The door had fallen off its hinges; part of the clay front wall had fallen in. Boulders and crumbled adobe jammed the entrance. A pair of small, screeching desert rodents snapped at him and fled for cover; Luke ignored them.

Gingerly, he ducked low and stepped into the home of his first mentor.

Luke stood in the middle of the room breathing deeply, turning around, trying to sense the presence he desperately needed to see. This was the place where Obi-Wan Kenobi had told Luke of the Force. Here, the old man had first given Luke his lightsaber and hinted at the truth about his father, "from a certain point of view," dispelling the diversionary story that Uncle Owen had told, at the same time planting seeds of his own deceptions.

"Ben," he said and closed his eyes, calling out with his mind as well as his voice. He tried to penetrate the invisible walls of the Force and reach to the luminous being of Obi-Wan Kenobi who had visited him numerous times, before saying he could never speak with Luke again.

"Ben, I need you," Luke said. Circumstances had changed. He could think of no other way past the obstacles he faced. Obi-Wan had to answer. It wouldn't take long, but it could give him the key he needed with all his heart.

Luke paused and listened and sensed—

But felt nothing. If he could not summon Obi-Wan's spirit here in the empty dwelling where the old man had lived in exile for so many years, Luke didn't believe he could find his former teacher ever again.

He echoed the words Leia had used more than a decade earlier, beseeching him, "Help me, Obi-Wan Kenobi," Luke whispered, "you're my only hope."

PLANET OF TWILIGHT
by Barbara Hambly
Setting: Nine years after *Return of the Jedi*

Concluding the epic tale begun in her own novel Children of the Jedi *and continued by Kevin Anderson in* Darksaber, *Barbara Hambly tells the story of a ruthless enemy of the New Republic operating out of a backwater world with vast mineral deposits. The first step in his campaign is to kidnap Princess Leia. Meanwhile, as Luke Skywalker searches the planet for his long-lost love Callista, the planet begins to reveal its unspeakable secret—a secret that threatens the New Republic, the Empire, and the entire galaxy.*

The first to die was a midshipman named Koth Barak. One of his fellow crewmembers on the New Republic escort cruiser *Adamantine* found him slumped across the table in the deck-nine break room where he'd repaired half an hour previously for a cup of coffeine. Twenty minutes after Barak should have been back to post, Gunnery Sergeant Gallie Wover went looking for him.

When she entered the deck-nine break room, Sergeant Wover's first sight was of the palely flickering blue on blue of the infolog screen. "Blast it, Koth, I told you . . ."

Then she saw the young man stretched unmoving on the far side of the screen, head on the break table, eyes shut. Even at a distance of three meters Wover didn't like the way he was breathing.

"Koth!" She rounded the table in two strides, sending the other chairs clattering into a corner. She thought his eyelids moved a little when she yelled his name. "Koth!"

Wover hit the emergency call almost without conscious decision. In the few minutes before the med droids arrived she sniffed the coffeine in the gray plastene cup a few minutes from his limp fingers. It wasn't even cold.

Behind her the break room door *swoshed* open. She glanced over her shoulder to see a couple of Two-Onebees enter with a table, which was already unfurling scanners and life-support lines like a monster in a bad holovid. They shifted Barak onto the table and hooked him up. Every line of the readouts plunged, and soft, tinny alarms began to sound.

Barak's face had gone a waxen gray. The table was already pumping stimulants and antishock into the boy's veins. Wover could see the initial diagnostic lines on the screen that ringed the antigrav personnel transport unit's sides.

No virus. No bacteria. No Poison.

No foreign material in Koth Barak's body at all.

The lines dipped steadily towards zero, then went flat.

THE CRYSTAL STAR
by Vonda N. McIntyre
Setting: Ten years after *Return of the Jedi*

Leia's three children have been kidnapped. That horrible fact is made worse by Leia's realization that she can no longer sense her children through the Force! While she, Artoo-Detoo, and Chewbacca trail the kidnappers, Luke and Han discover a planet that is suffering strange quantum effects from a nearby star. Slowly freezing into a perfect crystal and disrupting the Force, the star is blunting Luke's power and crippling the Millennium Falcon. These strands converge in an apocalyptic threat not only to the fate of the New Republic, but to the universe itself.

The Black Fleet Crisis
BEFORE THE STORM
SHIELD OF LIES
TYRANT'S TEST
by Michael P. Kube-McDowell
Setting: Twelve years after *Return of the Jedi*

Long after setting up the hard-won New Republic, yesterday's Rebels have become today's administrators and diplomats. But the peace is not to last for long. A restless Luke must journey to his mother's homeworld in a desperate quest to find her people; Lando seizes a mysterious spacecraft with unimaginable weapons of destruction; and waiting in the wings is a horrific battle fleet under the control of a ruthless leader bent on a genocidal war.

Here is an opening scene from Before the Storm:

In the pristine silence of space, the Fifth Battle Group of the New Republic Defense Fleet blossomed over the planet Bessimir like a beautiful, deadly flower.

The formation of capital ships sprang into view with startling suddenness, trailing fire-white wakes of twisted space and bristling with weapons. Angular Star Destroyers guarded fat-hulled fleet carriers, while the assault cruisers, their mirror finishes gleaming, took the point.

A halo of smaller ships appeared at the same time. The fighters among them quickly deployed in a spherical defensive screen. As the Star Destroyers firmed up their formation, their flight decks quickly spawned scores of additional fighters.

At the same time, the carriers and cruisers began to disgorge the bombers, transports, and gunboats they had ferried to the battle. There was no reason to risk the loss of one fully loaded—a lesson the Republic had learned in pain. At Orinda, the commander of the fleet carrier *Endurance* had kept his pilots waiting in the launch bays, to protect the smaller craft from Imperial fire as long as possible. They were still there when *Endurance* took the brunt of a Super Star Destroyer attack and vanished in a ball of metal fire.

Before long more than two hundred warships, large and small, were bearing down on Bessimir and its twin moons. But the terrible, restless power of the armada could be heard and felt only by the ships' crews. The silence of the approach was broken only on the fleet comm channels, which had crackled to life in the first moments with encoded bursts of noise and cryptic ship-to-ship chatter.

At the center of the formation of great vessels was the flagship of the Fifth Battle Group, the fleet carrier *Intrepid*. She was so new from the yards at Hakassi that her corridors still reeked of sealing compound and cleaning solvent. Her huge realspace thruster engines still sang with the high-pitched squeal that the engine crews called "the baby's cry."

It would take more than a year for the mingled scents of the crew to displace the chemical smells from the first impressions of visitors. But after a hundred more hours under way, her engines' vibrations would drop two octaves, to the reassuring thrum of a seasoned thruster bank.

On *Intrepid*'s bridge, a tall Dornean in general's uniform paced along an arc of command stations equipped with large monitors. His eye-folds were swollen and fanned by an unconscious Dornean defensive reflex, and his leathery face was flushed purple by concern. Before the deployment was even a minute old, Etahn A'baht's first command had been bloodied.

The fleet tender *Ahazi* had overshot its jump, coming out of hyperspace too close to Bessimir and too late for its crew to recover from the error. Etahn A'baht watched the bright flare of light in the upper atmosphere from *Intrepid*'s forward viewstation, knowing that it meant six young men were dead.

THE NEW REBELLION
by Kristine Kathryn Rusch
Setting: Thirteen years after *Return of the Jedi*

Victorious though the New Republic may be, there is still no end to the threats to its continuing existence—this novel explores the price of keeping the peace. First, somewhere in the galaxy, millions suddenly perish in a blinding instant of pain. Then, as Leia prepares to address the Senate on Coruscant, a horrifying event changes the governmental equation in a flash.

Here is that latter calamity, in an early scene from The New Rebellion:

An explosion rocked the Chamber, flinging Leia into the air. She flew backward and slammed onto a desk, her entire body shuddering with the power of her hit. Blood and shrapnel rained around her. Smoke and dust rose, filling the room with a grainy darkness. She could hear nothing. With a shaking hand, she touched the side of her face. Warmth stained her cheeks and her earlobes. The ringing would start soon. The explosion was loud enough to affect her eardrums.

Emergency glow panels seared the gloom. She could feel rather than hear pieces of the crystal ceiling fall to the ground. A guard had landed beside her, his head tilted at an unnatural angle. She grabbed his blaster. She had to get out. She wasn't certain if the attack had come from within or from without. Wherever it had come from, she had to make certain no other bombs would go off.

The force of the explosion had affected her balance. She crawled over bodies, some still moving, as she made her way to the stairs. The slightest movement made her dizzy and nauseous, but she ignored the feelings. She had to.

A face loomed before hers. Streaked with dirt and blood, helmet askew, she recognized him as one of the guards who had been with her since Alderaan. *Your Highness*, he mouthed, and she couldn't read the rest. She shook her head at him, gasping at the increased dizziness, and kept going.

Finally she reached the stairs. She used the remains of a desk to get to her feet. Her gown was soaked in blood, sticky, and clinging to her legs. She held the blaster in front of her, wishing that she could hear. If she could hear, she could defend herself.

A hand reached out of the rubble beside her. She whirled, faced it, watched as Meido pulled himself out. His slender features were covered with dirt, but he appeared unharmed. He saw her blaster and cringed. She nodded once to acknowledge him, and kept moving. The guard was flanking her.

More rubble dropped from the ceiling. She crouched, hands over her head to protect herself. Small pebbles pelted her, and the floor shivered as large chunks of tile fell. Dust rose, choking her. She coughed, feeling it, but not able to hear it. Within an instant, the Hall had gone from a place of ceremonial comfort to a place of death.

The image of the death's-head mask rose in front of her again, this time from memory. She had known this was going to happen. Somewhere, from some part of her Force-sensitive brain, she had seen this. Luke said that Jedi were sometimes able to see the future. But she had never completed her training. She wasn't a Jedi.

But she was close enough.

The Corellian Trilogy:
AMBUSH AT CORELLIA
ASSAULT AT SELONIA
SHOWDOWN AT CENTERPOINT
by Roger MacBride Allen
Setting: Fourteen years after *Return of the Jedi*

This trilogy takes us to Corellia, Han Solo's homeworld, which Han has not visited in quite some time. A trade summit brings Han, Leia, and the children—now developing their own clear personalities and instinctively learning more about their innate skills in the Force—into the middle of a situation that most closely resembles a burning fuse. The Corellian system is on the brink of civil war, there are New Republic intelligence agents on a mysterious mission which even Han does not understand, and worst of all, a fanatical rebel leader has his hands on a superweapon of unimaginable power—and just wait until you find out who that leader is!

THE ILLUSTRATED STAR WARS® UNIVERSE
Art by Ralph McQuarrie
Text by Kevin J. Anderson

Experience the *Star Wars* universe as never before in this stunning visual journey that carries you to the farthest reaches – and into the deepest mysteries – of George Lucas's cinematic masterpiece. Ralph McQuarrie, the legendary main concept artist for all three *Star Wars* films, and Kevin J. Anderson, the *New York Times* bestselling *Star Wars* author, present the ultimate voyage: a vivid and close-up look at the exotic worlds and remarkable inhabitants of the *Star Wars* universe.

The breathtaking artwork of McQuarrie and Anderson's delightful text are your guide to the eight different *Star Wars* locales. Here, detailed as never before, are the worlds of *Tatooine*, the stark desert home planet of Luke Skywalker; *Coruscant*, the glorious center of the Empire; *Dagobah*, the swampy world of Yoda; *Bespin*, site of the famed floating metropolis of Cloud City; *Endor*, the forest moon sheltering the Ewoks; *Hoth*, the frozen wasteland and site of a secret Rebel base; *Yavin 4*, the jungle moon, nearly destroyed by the first Death Star; and *Alderaan*, Princess Leia's homeland, cruelly annihilated by the same Death Star. Each world is lavishly illustrated and described by a qualified expert, including scientists, scouts, soldiers, poets, and even Imperial agents. *The Illustrated Star Wars Universe* is an epic achievement, a visionary treat no *Star Wars* fan will want to miss – and a true collector's item you'll enjoy for years to come.

A Bantam Paperback
0 553 50665 X

A SELECTION OF STAR WARS TITLES
AVAILABLE FROM BANTAM BOOKS

THE PRICES SHOWN BELOW WERE CORRECT AT THE TIME OF GOING TO PRESS. HOWEVER TRANSWORLD PUBLISHERS RESERVE THE RIGHT TO SHOW NEW RETAIL PRICES ON COVERS WHICH MAY DIFFER FROM THOSE PREVIOUSLY ADVERTISED IN THE TEXT OR ELSEWHERE.

☐	40808 9	STAR WARS: Jedi Search	Kevin J. Anderson	£5.99
☐	40809 7	STAR WARS: Dark Apprentice	Kevin J. Anderson	£5.99
☐	40810 0	STAR WARS: Champions of the Force	Kevin J. Anderson	£5.99
☐	40971 9	STAR WARS: Tales from the Mos Eisley Cantina	Kevin J. Anderson (ed.)	£5.99
☐	50413 4	STAR WARS: Tales from Jabba's Palace	Kevin J. Anderson (ed.)	£5.99
☐	50471 1	STAR WARS: Tales of the Bounty Hunters	Kevin J. Anderson (ed.)	£5.99
☐	40880 1	STAR WARS: Darksaber	Kevin J. Anderson	£5.99
☐	50546 7	STAR WARS: The Paradise Snare	A. C. Crispin	£5.99
☐	50547 5	STAR WARS: The Hutt Gambit	A. C. Crispin	£5.99
☐	50548 3	STAR WARS: Rebel Dawn	A. C. Crispin	£5.99
☐	40879 8	STAR WARS: Children of the Jedi	Barbara Hambly	£5.99
☐	40926 3	STAR WARS X-Wing 1: Rogue Squadron	Michael A. Stackpole	£5.99
☐	40923 9	STAR WARS X-Wing 2: Wedge's Gamble	Michael A. Stackpole	£5.99
☐	40925 5	STAR WARS X-Wing 3: The Krytos Trap	Michael A. Stackpole	£5.99
☐	40924 7	STAR WARS X-Wing 4: The Bacta War	Michael A. Stackpole	£5.99
☐	50599 8	STAR WARS X-Wing 5: Wraith Squadron	Aaron Allston	£5.99
☐	50600 5	STAR WARS X-Wing 6: Iron Fist	Aaron Allston	£5.99
☐	50605 6	STAR WARS X-Wing 7: Solo Command	Aaron Allston	£5.99
☐	50688 9	STAR WARS X-Wing 8: Isard's Revenge	Aaron Allston	£5.99
☐	50431 2	STAR WARS: Before the Storm	Michael P. Kube-McDowell	£5.99
☐	50479 7	STAR WARS: Shield of Lies	Michael P. Kube-McDowell	£5.99
☐	50480 0	STAR WARS: Tyrant's Test	Michael P. Kube-McDowell	£5.99
☐	40881 X	STAR WARS: Ambush at Corellia	Roger MacBride Allen	£5.99
☐	40882 8	STAR WARS: Assault at Selonia	Roger MacBride Allen	£5.99
☐	40883 6	STAR WARS: Showdown at Centerpoint	Roger MacBride Allen	£5.99
☐	40878 X	STAR WARS: The Crystal Star	Vonda McIntyre	£5.99
☐	50472 X	STAR WARS: Shadows of the Empire	Steve Perry	£5.99
☐	50497 5	STAR WARS: The New Rebellion	Kristine K. Rusch	£5.99
☐	40758 9	STAR WARS: The Truce at Bakura	Kathy Tyers	£4.99
☐	40807 0	STAR WARS: The Courtship of Princess Leia	Dave Wolverton	£4.99
☐	40471 7	STAR WARS: Heir to the Empire	Timothy Zahn	£5.99
☐	40442 3	STAR WARS: Dark Force Rising	Timothy Zahn	£5.99
☐	40443 1	STAR WARS: The Last Command	Timothy Zahn	£5.99
☐	40879 8	STAR WARS: Children of the Jedi	Barbara Hambly	£5.99
☐	50529 7	STAR WARS: Planet of Twilight	Barbara Hambly	£5.99
☐	50417 7	STAR WARS: Specter of the Past	Timothy Zahn	£5.99
☐	50686 2	STAR WARS: Tales from the Empire	Peter Schweighofer (ed.)	£5.99
☐	50601 3	STAR WARS: The Mandalorian Armor	K. W. Jeter	£5.99
☐	50603 X	STAR WARS: Slaveship	K. W. Jeter	£5.99
☐	50687 0	STAR WARS: Hard Merchandise	K. W. Jeter	£5.99
☐	50665 X	STAR WARS: The Illustrated Star Wars Universe	Kevin J. Anderson	£12.99
☐	50705 2	STAR WARS: The Magic of Myth	Mary Henderson	£14.99

All Transworld titles are available by post from:

Book Service by Post, PO Box 29, Douglas, Isle of Man IM99 1BQ

Credit cards accepted. Please telephone 01624 675137, fax 01624 670923 or Internet http://www.bookpost.co.uk or e-mail: bookshop@enterprise.net for details.

Free postage and packing in the UK. Overseas customers allow £1 per book (paperbacks) and £3 per book (hardbacks).